MADELEINE

Mademoiselle de Larminat noticed Madeleine's absorption and wondered if the tall maid of honour intended to work up one of the imitations which made the Empress laugh hysterically and the Emperor grin behind his heavy waxed moustache when they played charades at Compiègne. But Madeleine was not disposed to find James Bruce funny, neither when, asked if he ever visited Paris, he gravely told the Empress that he was often there "in transit," a phrase which normally would have struck her as ludicrous; nor when Eugénie, seeking some especially graceful way of bringing the audience to a close, herself offered him a crystal goblet of champagne from the table prepared for her alfresco luncheon. It was a gesture taken straight from Sir Walter Scott, the sort of thing which her enemies criticized as meretricious and left the unsophisticated at a loss. James was equal to the occasion. He bowed low to her and, murmuring, "Madame, your humble servant," he touched his lips to the wine when she asked him to drink to the future of the Suez Canal. But he looked across her shoulder as he raised his glass, into the eyes of Madeleine.

Madeleine

Catherine Gavin

CORONET BOOKS
Hodder Paperbacks Ltd., London

Copyright © 1957 by Catherine Gavin
First printed by Hodder and Stoughton Ltd 1957
Entirely revised for Hodder Paperbacks by the Author
Coronet edition 1970
Second impression 1973

_____

Printed and bound in Great Britain for
Coronet Books,
Hodder Paperbacks Ltd,
St. Paul's House, Warwick Lane,
London, EC4P 4AH
by Hazell Watson & Viney Ltd,
Aylesbury, Bucks

ISBN 0 340 12611 6

ONE

A Light Woman: Egypt 1869

I

The ball at Kasr-el-Nil was still going on at sunrise, when the muezzin called the faithful to their prayers.

Eugénie, Empress of the French, had left the ballroom long before midnight. The viceroy of Egypt, the Khedive Ismail, himself led her down a lane of flaming torches to the great gates where her Bodyguard waited to escort her to the villa which he had built especially for her stay in Cairo. Then the Khedive disappeared into the rat-infested recesses of his palace, and the pashas took their departure with the envoys of his overlord the Sultan of Turkey. The diplomatic corps, worn out by the festivities which had occupied most of the month of November, 1869, left Kasr-el-Nil as soon as protocol permitted. Only the Khedive's French guests remained to keep the ball going until morning, tirelessly enjoying the last gala before the opening of the Suez Canal.

After the official carriages drove off about two o'clock an uneasy silence fell on the environs of the palace on the Nile. From the hills around the city the wild dogs bayed at the setting moon. From inside Kasr-el-Nil came the faint echoes of waltzes by Offenbach and Strauss; the sound of laughter floated out too, and occasional applause. Otherwise nothing disturbed the sleep of the beggars lying on the bare earth in front of the palace with their ragged robes huddled about their heads. The Khedive's horseboys slept in the stable straw, and his slovenly sentries leaned against the gates and dozed until the muezzin's chant rang from Mehe-

7

met Ali's mosque. Then, every man was roused, and turning towards Mecca bowed himself down in prayer.

While the brocade curtains remained drawn across the long windows of Kasr-el-Nil, and only a movement of carriages into the courtyard indicated that the ball might at last be coming to an end, the great doors were flung violently open. The groom of the chambers had hardly time to take up his position with his wand of office, his underlings form a line on the terrace in the prescribed attitude of salute, before the Khedive's son rushed frantically over the threshold of his father's palace.

Prince Tewfik, that one among his twenty acknowledged children whom Ismail had designated as his heir, was eighteen years of age, and as yet free of the excesses which had made his father, at forty, a gross and sodden voluptuary. Like a slim dark bird he stood preening himself in the morning light, a diamond-hilted scimitar belted round his black dress coat and a diamond aigrette flashing in his crimson fez. The star of some Order was glittering on his breast. For three weeks he had been trying to impress the foreigners, prancing and parading with his Zouaves and ogling the fascinating ladies from Paris and within a few days he expected to welcome them all to Port Tewfik, at the south end of the Suez Canal, the new town which had been given his name. The contradictory orders he was shouting at the soldiers and servants who came running to the terrace showed how completely the whole thing had gone to Tewfik's never very steady head.

"Your Highness, I ask you to reconsider—"

"Prince Tewfik, this is really most imprudent—"

Hands on narrow hips, the boy swung round with an insolent look for the Murat princes, who had hurried from the supper room to remonstrate with him. Behind them was a growing crowd of Frenchmen in the blue and silver of the Imperial Guard and beautiful women with gilt powder in their hair, their lip rouge smeared and their eyelids swollen with fatigue. To the excited young Egyptian it seemed they had eyes for no one but himself.

"Clear the streets! Get those brats off the esplanade! Make sure the way is clear right up to the Citadel!"

Tewfik barked out his orders to a lieutenant of Egyptian Zouaves who had succeeded in getting his men to horse. That would show Prince Joachim Murat and his dandy brother Achille who was master at Kasr-el-Nil! To defy the Emperor's cousins in public, with his own friends admiring him, was one more mark of prestige for the Khedive's son.

"You heard what the lady said!" he blustered. "She accepted my challenge and the stake I offered! Do *you* want to call off your bargain, Mademoiselle d'Arbonne?"

"No indeed, Your Highness. I'm ready to race against you to the Citadel!"

The girl who answered came forward with the grace of a court lady, one gloved hand looping up the train of a dress which the deepening sunlight dyed to the same gold as her parure of topaz and diamonds, but there was none of the French court's artificiality in the bold proud look she gave the young Egyptian. She was a fair girl, with bright Norman colouring and confident blue eyes, whose hair had escaped from two pomaded curls to spring in loose waving strands across her bare shoulder. Only the taut line of her jaw and her quickened breathing betrayed that Mademoiselle d'Arbonne was nervous. Her old friend Comte Clary, wiser and more perceptive than the rest of the Murat set, saw her press her lips together as the new rigs came round from the stables with the Khedive's matched and matchless Arabs plunging and curvetting between the shafts.

"Madeleine!" he said, thrusting himself between the Murat brothers. "Those brutes will be too much for you! You never drove anything like them at Longchamps, let alone through the streets of Cairo!"

"They're fresh, that's all," she said. "The troopers will clear the way for us."

"Never mind that! Do you realize you're not going to drive a park drag? This is one of those two-wheeled gimcrack American rigs, meant for trotters instead of blood Arabs. Tewfik or you, or both of you may break your necks! What will the Empress say to that—or the Khedive Ismail? You, sir—Fuad Pasha—or you, Prince Ali—why don't you send to the viceroy immediately?"

Tewfik's friends fidgeted and giggled and made no reply. At that hour, in that palace, none of his subjects might invade the Khedive's privacy.

"Good God!" cried Clary, "then where's her brother? Has nobody seen Victor d'Arbonne since he came back from the Villa? Wait, for heaven's sake, my dear, until I fetch your brother!"

Madeleine laughed a little. The high-wheeled rigs were already in position at the foot of the terrace steps, and Prince Tewfik was bowing low to her and offering his hand. Comte Clary turned and began to shoulder his way through the buzzing crowd.

"Madeleine!"

Antoine de Noailles, the husband of Princess Anna Murat, caught up with her as Tewfik led her down the steps. He had been drinking heavily and was still struggling to fasten the collar of his pale blue tunic, which he had unhooked in the stifling supper room, but his head was clearing in the fresh air, and he knew exactly what he wanted to say.

"Let me help you up into that damned thing—"

She gave him a sidelong glance of mischief, sketched a little curtsy to Tewfik Pasha and said, "Your team is waiting for you, Sir! We'll meet again outside the Citadel!" And then, in a whisper to Noailles, "Bless you, Antoine, this dress wasn't meant for driving! Wait a minute!"

She drew up the Chantilly lace stole lying loosely on her shoulders, knotted it round her throat and secured the ends to her bodice with the brooch, bearing an interlaced E and I in diamonds, which was her badge of office as a maid of honour to the Empress of the French.

"I don't want this scarf blowing up across my face," she said.

"Will you listen to me, Madeleine? Whatever you do, *don't use the whip!* The brutes are too frisky for it; they'll bolt at a touch. Just hold on to them, and you'll be all right! Here, I'll lift you up."

Antoine de Noailles put his arm round her waist, perfectly aware that his wife, like all the crowd lining the terrace balustrade, was staring at them both. He didn't care; he was furious with Anna, and with those jackanapes her brothers, who had permitted this idiotic race to come about—and he had once been the lover of Madeleine d'Arbonne.

She was a tall girl, but so slim that he lifted her easily into the driver's seat. She smiled her thanks, flashed a quick glance of amusement at his wife, and then gave all her attention to her opponent. The way he took up his reins told her a good deal.

Madeleine d'Arbonne drew two or three long breaths. The crystal air of the November morning blew away the last fumes of champagne as she looked out across the course they were to run. Not much like the Longchamps track, indeed—none of the velvet greensward, edged with flowering acacia, down which she had driven a drag to victory in the Ladies' Race last June! They were eight days from Paris here instead of twenty minutes, and the first lap would be up a palm-fringed boulevard, one of the ambitious projects Ismail had started since his visit to Paris with the Sultan. "I must pass Tewfik in the boulevard," she told herself. "The first into the Old Town wins the race!"

Between the palace and the boulevard a half-levelled esplanade was being beaten into something like the parade ground which had taken Ismail's fancy at Versailles. Turkish slavemasters were swinging their knotted whips round the legs of child labourers carrying baskets of dirt on their little heads, who sank down thankful for even such a respite as the Khedive's servants beat the adult beggars further back. In the distance, over the crowded flat roofs of the Old Town, Madeleine could see the spurs of the Mokattam hills shimmering in the rising heat. The beautiful minaret of the new mosque cut the line of the brown hills, below which was their goal, the Citadel, where the Albanian bandit who was Tewfik's ancestor had seized power in Egypt after a bloody massacre of his opponents. Tewfik's advance on the Citadel was to be more peaceful. She saw that he had unbelted his absurd scimitar and handed it to one of his entourage.

"You all right, ma'am? Here you are!"

The head groom put the reins into her hands. He was an Irishman, whose long upper lip was drawn down in disapproval of a caprice which might mean broken knees for his precious horses. He stood back, and the grooms holding the leaders stood away, and suddenly Madeleine saw nothing but the Arabs' noble heads, the silken manes plaited with turquoises for good luck, the shining rumps ready to move in perfect rhythm; felt nothing but four mouths made of steel and velvet, as her fingers closed between the reins. A starting pistol was fired from the terrace, and to a roar of applause both teams went neck and neck out of the gates of Kasr-el-Nil.

In the first moment Madeleine was almost lifted from the driver's seat. She had driven the Emperor's American trotters, and all the horses, two-in-hand and four-in-hand, that her uncle kept in his magnificent stables at Arbonne, but she had never felt anything like the thunderbolt of power released by the four Arabs as they raced across the esplanade and into the boulevard. The American rig, too, was so much lighter than the French vehicles she knew that she felt herself perched insecurely on a collection of flimsy rails. But for all her slimness she had strong arms and shoulders; she flung her weight back, and pulled, and felt the rasp of the reins through her gloved fingers as the Arabs steadied from their near runaway. She heard a shout, and, risking a glance sideways, saw Tewfik's four run out too far to the right toward the palm trees as his leaders and wheelers fumbled their matched gait. "The whip now, if this were Longchamps!" she thought. "But Antoine was right—I daren't risk it here!"

The whip stayed in its silver socket, and the Arabs, feeling the pressure of the steady hands behind them, responded nobly without the lash. They ran straight and true for the archway where the new boulevard lost itself in the souks of the Old Town, and shot ahead of Tewfik's rig with four yards to spare. The real test came as Madeleine slowed for the turns and twists of a road irregularly posted by the Zouaves who had herded beggars and beasts indiscriminately into the alleys to let the great lord Tewfik pass. The two rigs went through the Old Town almost as a single unit. Then the rough road up to the Citadel opened before them, and from somewhere among the boulders a pariah dog came barking out, and ran snapping alongside the leading team.

The rig rocked dangerously, and Madeleine became stunningly aware of the nearness of death. One more leap of the dog, one swerve of her team, and the light vehicle might overturn and fling her beneath Prince Tewfik's wheels. Recklessly she gathered the reins into her strong left hand, felt the glove split, snatched the whip with her right and with a single adroit movement flicked it out and across the horses' backs to catch their tormentor under the jaw and drive him howling back. It was done as skilfully as a fisherman casts a fly. The Arabs felt nothing but a disturbance of the air above their harness, and Madeleine, with the whip still in her hand and the reins taut, pulled them to a standstill before the lowered drawbridge of the Citadel two lengths ahead of Tewfik's team.

II

At half-past six a trainload of travellers from the Orient and Suez arrived in Cairo, and the rough open space in front of Shepheard's Hotel was filled with their cabs and luggage.

Among the tired and dusty passengers who had come by the night train across the desert, one group was distinguished by its style and general air of opulence. It revolved around a tall, burly man with a grizzled blond moustache and imperial, whom the deferential hotel clerks addressed as "Monsieur Bertaux," and a lady, dressed in the extreme of fashion, who was his sister, the Comtesse d'Arbonne. Madeleine's mother looked pale and weary, but both she and her youngest daughter, Louise, contrived to appear both cool and elegant in the hubbub at the foot of Shepheard's steps. Two gentlemen, green-veiled topis in hand, were taking leave of these ladies, with whom they had travelled from Suez; two maids and a courier were directing the hotel Sudanese in their selection of dress hampers and portmanteaux. On the edge of the group, jostled by *farrashes* and cabdrivers, stood Captain Victor d'Arbonne, shaken by the muttered storm of his uncle's anger.

The Norman beauty which Michel Bertaux' sister had brought to the d'Arbonne family had made of her only son an exceptionally good-looking young man, and an ornament to the Imperial Guard. He still wore the uniform in which he had escorted the Empress to her Villa several hours earlier, and his horsetailed helmet was heavy above his sulky eyes. He pulled savagely at his blond imperial as he listened to his uncle's rebuke. Victor was twenty-four, a year younger than Madeleine, and had been the object of his uncle's criticisms for the greater part of his life.

"You were playing cards—*of course*!" Bertaux's suppressed voice was savage. "You were too late to stop her—*of course*! You didn't get my message until it was nearly too late to meet your mother—*naturally*!"

14

"Madeleine won't come to any harm, uncle Michel. They were giving two to one on her when I left Kasr-el-Nil."

"*Two to one on Madeleine!*" Bertaux repeated in a vicious whisper. "You let your brother officers *bet* on her! And where's Adèle's husband, Roccanuova? Does *he* think he can behave disrespectfully to your mother? He should have come to the train to welcome her!"

"Michel, do stop scolding poor Vic," interposed Madame d'Arbonne. "How can you keep us standing here in this heat, when you know how I'm longing to see my darling Adèle? Give me your arm, and let us go indoors."

"We'll go to Adèle together, maman. I'm longing to see her too."

It was the young girl, Louise, who spoke, her voice as cool and refreshing as the picture she made in that brassy square.

She was a small girl, not much more than seventeen, with a neat little face like a kitten's, soft dark eyes and black curls escaping from under a wide Italian straw hat tied with a velvet ribbon. Louise was still dressed as a schoolgirl, with two inches of slim leg visible above her little silk boots; her white muslin dress, long-sleeved, was tied with a broad green sash. Her uncle's angry face softened as he looked at her.

"That's my little pet—"

He caught his breath. A barouche glittering with silver inlay and mother-of-pearl had swung into the square. It was escorted by a half-squadron of Egyptian troopers, green and purple pennants fluttering from dirty lances, and by a group of French officers on the mounts they had commandeered at Kasr-el-Nil. The Frenchmen were in tearing spirits, laughing and calling out to the occupants of the carriage. To Tewfik Pasha, silent and glum. To the Murat princes, sitting with their backs to the horses—

And to Madeleine d'Arbonne.

She never stopped to think, until after the coachman had been made to pull up and Prince Murat was giving her his arm across the rough ground in front of Shepheard's, of the sort of figure she cut alone in that crowd of men. She realized it by the silence

15

that fell on the remaining travellers and their Oriental servants, by the anger in her uncle's eyes, the hostility in her mother's— even by the amazed looks of the two strange men who had just taken leave of her family, and now stood watching her from the top of Shepheard's steps. She became aware that her dress was stained with the blown froth from the Arabs' mouths, her gloves torn, the hem of her dress ripped, her bosom scarcely covered by the knotted stole. It was typical of Madeleine that she then took her hand from Prince Murat's arm, dismissed him with a graceful word of thanks and went up to Madame d'Arbonne with her head held high.

"Mother, dear! We didn't expect you until tomorrow!"

The comtesse suffered her kiss, held her at arm's length and said in a choked voice:

"How dare you make us all conspicuous?"

"What infernal folly is this, Madeleine?" A nervous tic, which twitched the muscles of his cheeks, convulsed Michel Bertaux' angry face. "Racing four-in-hand with the Khedive's son, indeed! Your mother has been worried to death about you."

But Madeleine had turned away to take her little sister in her arms.

"How are you, Louise, my darling? You're so pretty, and I declare you've grown!"

Madame d'Arbonne studied the tableau with a curling lip.

"Come indoors at once, Madeleine," she said. "You look perfectly ridiculous. I'll talk to you later—after I've seen Adèle. I won't be kept any longer from my precious girl!"

All the bright gaiety faded from Madeleine's face.

"Your concern for me is overpowering, mother," she said. "I must beg to be excused from the family reunion. The Empress will be expecting me on duty very soon."

"Then you can march straight back to the Villa," said Bertaux sharply. "Josef, get me a cab. Victor, take your mother to the Roccanuovas' rooms. Now get in, Madeleine; people are looking at you."

He took her wrist as he spoke, in a grasp that made her wince, and pushed rather than assisted her into the closed cab. The Swiss courier shut the door firmly on the uncle and the niece.

Bertaux removed his topi and mopped his brow with a fine silk handkerchief. He was annoyed with himself for having lost his temper, jarred by the clash between his beloved sister and Madeleine, for he knew too well that displays of anger had no effect on the girl. Her will only rose the more stubbornly to match his own, causing sometimes a terrible excitement to twitch the betraying muscles of Michel Bertaux' face.

"I spoke too harshly, Madeleine," he said at last. "I'm tired and nervous, I admit. We had a wretched passage up the Red Sea, and it was a shock to find none of you expecting us."

"I suppose mother is tired and nervous too, after a three-month voyage for her health?"

"Yes, she is. She found the planter society of La Réunion provincial and wearisome. Lately she's been very anxious about Adèle."

"Adèle's all right as far as health goes, and the baby isn't due until June. Don't I deserve a kind word too?"

"You didn't wait to hear one. You had to hurry, as usual, back to Madame Eugénie."

Madeleine did not take up the challenge. Instead she drew a cobweb of lace handkerchief from the bosom of her dress, and began to unfold it.

"Michou!" It was her own pet name for him, and against his will it made him smile. "Will you do something for me? Will you see that this is returned to Prince Tewfik?"

In her palm lay the jewelled Order that had glittered on the black coat of the Khedive's son.

"My God, Madeleine! The Star of Egypt! How did you come by that?"

"That's what Tewfik wagered on the race!" she said with a light laugh. "I never meant to keep it, Michou dear. I have the diamonds you gave me, haven't I? Tewfik's father would kill him if he lost it—the thing was a present to celebrate the opening of the Suez Canal."

"Your friend de Lesseps would call it an evil omen—for the

Khedive," said Bertaux with a grin. He turned the Star of Egypt in his hard hands, not covetously but appraisingly. "Now tell me the whole story, Madeleine. He staked the Star, and challenged— whom? Not you personally, I hope?"

"N—no," she said reluctantly. "Any of us—all of us at the supper table. Then Princess Anna Murat called out, 'Will no one drive against Prince Tewfik, for the honour of France?' I said I would."

"So that was it," said Bertaux, his mouth set. "But Anna Murat's flowery phrase didn't inspire any of the *men* to volunteer? Not de Noailles? Not Robert de Voguë, one of the finest whips in Europe? Of course not. Only Madeleine d'Arbonne was simpleton enough to take it seriously—"

"I can't think of anything I take *more* seriously than—what she said."

"You read too many romances with the Empress." Bertaux thrust the diamond Order in his pocket and studied his niece's face. She was lying back against the greasy cushions with her eyes shut, as if with her last words she had brought her long night to a close. The gold-brown lashes swept cheeks still glowing with colour; the mouth, with its full lower lip, was as fresh as a child's. It cost him an effort not to slip his arm round her and let his hand cup the smooth warmth of her naked shoulder.

"Michou, who were those men?"

Accustomed as he was to her caprice, the change of topic took him by surprise. Searching her face, with its closed eyes, he asked what men she meant.

"The men talking to mother and Louise when we drove into the square. They were staring at me."

"Trust you to notice them! The older man is a pet of de Lesseps', Bruce by name—a Scots engineer with the Peninsular and Oriental. I used to know his brother out in China, and they both happened to be in Suez when we landed. The young fellow was in their company, and he went to no end of trouble to get ice and fruit for your mother and Louise. His name is Hartzell—an American."

Madeleine opened her blue eyes and surveyed, first her uncle

18

and then the Nile bank along which they were driving to reach the Villa.

"Are you going to go in for Americans now, like Their Majesties?"

"To better purpose, I should hope. The way they're handling *their* affairs, it might be prudent to have reliable associates in the United States! This boy is one of the Hartzells of Philadelphia— teas and spices—food importers on a very large scale. If the Prussians mean business, a dollar account with Hartzell Brothers might be very useful to me."

"You're not still harping on a war with Prussia?"

"I don't think Bismarck has had a change of heart, even though he allowed the Crown Prince Fritz to come and drink our health on the Suez Canal. That Empress of yours is such a vain conceited fool, Madeleine! She swallows every flattery, and this whole trip has done nothing but feed her vanity! The Sultan—the Khedive— the princes bowing and smirking; Cousin de Lesseps vowing that she and she alone shall lead the first procession down his Canal— the whole thing presents her as a stateswoman, which she will never be! As a ruler, not a consort! As a Regent, when the Emperor dies! As a madwoman who will plunge France into war, to set her only son more securely on the throne!"

He had raised his voice as he spoke. Instinctively she laid her hand, in its tattered glove, across his lips, with a warning glance at what they could see of the Egyptian driver's robe. They were hundreds of miles from the palace of the Tuileries, but both thought in that instant of the secret agents of the Emperor Napoleon III.

"Here we are at the Villa," said Madeleine, with an attempt at her natural voice. "Tell him to stop at the side gate. With any luck I can slip in through the rose garden and dodge the Princesse d'Essling."

"With any luck you'll get some sleep, I hope."

"You forget it's Her Majesty's name day—*la Sainte Eugénie*. That means chapel, and compliments, and exclaiming over the telegrams from the Emperor and Loulou. Then we rest until tomorrow, and start for Alexandria and Port Said."

Bertaux helped his niece to the ground and held her, with a caressing gesture, by the smooth bare flesh of her upper arm.

"Try to come to your mother later in the day," he urged. "She'll forget this morning's escapade after she's seen Adèle, and rested."

"If the Comtesse de Pierrefonds will excuse me."

"The Comtesse—?"

"Her Majesty wishes to be known by that name until the *Aigle* enters the harbour at Port Said."

Bertaux laughed grimly.

"Incognito! Another romance! Good-bye, my dear!"

III

Not long after Madeleine returned to the Villa, the two men who had watched her from the steps of Shepheard's found places in the crowded dining room of the hotel and sat down to order breakfast.

"It was uncommonly kind of you, Mr. Hartzell," said the elder man, "to let me shave and change in your bedroom. I've never known Shepheard's to be booked out before. If all those people are bound for the Canal festivities, they'll have to take their own tents with them."

"Glad to help!" said the young American. "But what are you going to do about a bed for the night?"

"Nothing. I'll take the overnight train to Alexandria and get a few hours' sleep in *Delta* before she leaves for Port Said. Two of my Directors came out for the Canal opening; they'll want my Suez report as soon as possible."

"You don't give yourself much rest, Mr. Bruce."

"It's routine—or rather," said James Bruce, shaking out his napkin, "it was routine. Odd to think that this is the last time anyone will travel Overland from Suez to Cairo and the Mediterranean. When I was a young fellow we crossed the desert in carriages. Then the Peninsular and Oriental built the railroad. After next week, if I get back to Suez at all, it'll be by way of the Canal. It's the end of an era for P. and O. men like me."

"You don't expect to come East again?"

"Well—my inspection trips are bound to be curtailed when our boats come straight through to Southampton for refitting. That's only one of the changes we can expect from the Suez Canal. Ah! here comes breakfast."

It was a resolutely British meal, copied by old Sam Shepheard from the P. and O. menus he had supervised as a purser on the steamship line. Tiny local eggs sizzled in goat's milk, butter with thick rashers of bacon, mounds of soggy toast were offered with Dundee marmalade, and the tea was black and strong, but Frank

21

Hartzell fell upon the food with appetite. He was a tall, broad-shouldered young man with light chestnut hair and clear grey eyes. His face was rather pale and thin from the effects of China fever.

"This means you won't see your brothers quite so often," he said when the first edge was off his hunger.

"No, but they're both due for home leave early in '71. Then we'll all have a family reunion at Sauchentree."

"That's the name of your father's estate in Scotland, where he has his ironfoundry?"

"Estate? My dear Hartzell, it's a farm, and a small farm at that, in a particularly bleak part of Aberdeenshire."

"Your brother George said the ironfoundry was in Buchan."

"Buchan lies in the north-east corner of Aberdeenshire, on the sea coast, and the ironfoundry's a very small concern, I'm afraid. You mustn't be misled by poor George's family pride!"

"I liked George," said Frank defensively. "I enjoyed meeting him when the *Deccan* put in to Canton."

"George is a good fellow, and my especial pride. I tutored both Robert and him before they followed me into the P. and O. You don't know Robert quite so well?"

"George introduced us the other day at Suez, just a few hours before I met you."

"Yes, of course. It's very seldom we're all in the same port together."

"And you've another brother in Scotland, a minister, I believe?"

"William, yes; and three married sisters. And my father, worth all the rest of us put together."

He smiled; and Frank saw how attractive James Bruce was when his Scots reserve relaxed and his formal manner was warmed by any reference to his younger brothers. After the ready friendliness of Robert and George Bruce he had been rather chilled by "Mister James," as their eldest brother seemed to be known to all the engineering fraternity at Suez; but he had to admit that the man was impressive. Bruce's face was remarkable even in repose, with a beautiful proportion of broad brow, jutting nose and strong clean-shaven mouth and chin. His dark hair, which he wore curled behind his ears in the fashion of several years earlier, had not a thread of grey in it. But it was the eyes which gave eloquence and animation to what might have been merely austere good looks. They were large, and very dark brown—a poet's eyes, set in the head of a practical man. Frank Hartzell, who had quick perceptions, thought that for all its disciplined calm James Bruce's was the face of a man with a capacity for strong emotion.

"Well—I envy you!" Frank said abruptly. "I haven't a relative in the world except my dear cousins in Philadelphia, who recalled me from Canton with a year's leave of absence—off the payroll!—after I came down with a second go of fever."

"Leave of absence!" said James. "What might that mean?"

"In the States it means you're fired," said Frank simply. "I don't know: my cousin August Hartzell would probably take me back, if I want to be taken; but I think I'll look for a job in Europe, for the time being at any rate. I'm damned if I'm going to cool my heels in Philadelphia for the next ten months."

"Don't overtax your strength, then. China fever can recur, you know."

"Prison fever too."

In the train crossing the desert, James had heard something of Frank's three years as a Union Army prisoner, and also more than enough of General Cluseret, the French adventurer whom Hartzell blamed for his wound and capture at Cross Keys. He looked at the American now with sympathy slightly tinged with irritation. The returned soldier was a familiar figure in England, where young men had come back from the Crimean War in much the same state of mind and body as Frank Hartzell had limped out of Libby prison. The P. and O. had employed some of them—the misfit veterans, living over the Charge of the Light Brigade or the taking of Sevastopol in the beershops and gin palaces of the City every night after office hours until they found themselves in the gutter, ticketed "unemployable." James, who always came down heavily on the side of authority, thought that possibly the brothers Hartzell had had their own troubles with their cousin Frank. But then he was such a likeable beggar, with an honest sincere manner and a gay, ready smile—George seemed to have struck up quite a friendship with him, and George was a good judge of a man. Wounded and a prisoner of war—none of the Sauchentree boys had had *that* start to their careers!

"I wish I could give you some practical help, Mr. Hartzell," he said, ruffling his dark hair in perplexity. "I don't know much about the food business, but I've some good mercantile contacts in European ports. If you thought of looking about you in Prussia, for instance, I could give you letters to Stettin. The Company lent me to the royal dockyards there some years ago, at the time of the expansion of the Prussian fleet."

"That's very good of you," said Frank. He pushed his chair back from the table and brushed a crumb from his tussore silk coat. "As a matter of fact I was rather thinking of France. That's why I was so grateful to your brother Robert for introducing me to Monsieur Bertaux. He's a big dealer in comestibles—you heard him say that before he left Réunion Island he had bought the entire tapioca and vanilla crops for the next five years. Last night in the resthouse we had a long talk about the possibility of a two-way import-export deal in his French wines and our Havana cigars. I was hoping he could find a place for me, say at Marseilles."

"So that's the way of it!" said James Bruce. The servants had cleared away the remains of their meal, and he now leaned both elbows on the table and rubbed his firm chin thoughtfully. "I see. I know the Marseilles warehouse, of course. You can see BERTAUX S.A. in letters a yard high from Estrine's, our agents, office windows in the rue Colbert. According to Albert Estrine the Pereire bankers are joint stockholders in the Société Anonyme Bertaux. They seem to have stuck to him, although the row he had with the Emperor's bastard brother over the Mexican War made Monsieur Bertaux *persona non grata* at court."

"Well, surely Bertaux was right in that and the Duc de Morny was wrong?" said Frank. "He was telling me only last night that he always knew the United States wouldn't stand for French intervention south of the border. Pretty farsighted of him, don't you think?"

"He's reported to be one of the smartest operators on the Paris Bourse," said James. "And everyone has heard the romantic story

24

of his start in life. A fisher boy from Trouville, wasn't he, who ran away to Paris with his sister, both of them barefoot and in rags, and made his first fortune before he was twenty-five? But I know nothing of the man personally, though Robert seems to know him well."

"But you think he's all right, don't you?" Frank bent forward in his turn and lowered his voice, although their nearest neighbours were only a distracted ayah and her three pallid, peevish little charges on their way Home from Bombay.

"He's got almost too many irons in the fire, it seems to me," said James. "Railroading in the early days, comestibles, now a controlling interest in two new hotels in Paris. Fellows like that have been known to come a cropper; I shouldn't be in too great a hurry to do business with him if I were you."

"He's asked me to go on to Ismailia with them," said Frank with a grin.

"Oh! You'll be glad to continue in Miss Louise's company, I imagine?"

"She's one of the sweetest girls I ever met," said the young man simply, and Bruce smiled.

"She's a pretty child. Waiter! My bill, if you please."

He paid for their meal and pocketed his change, and Frank watched him with a troubled face.

"What don't you like about the Bertaux idea?" he persisted.

"Well, as far as the man himself is concerned," said James deliberately, "I thought that was an extraordinary display of temper we saw outside here this morning."

It was the first reference either had made to the episode of Madeleine's arrival. Each knew that it had made a deep impression on the other.

"I guess he was mad when he saw his niece making such an exhibition of herself," said Frank. "I bet you she has a temper too! Gad! she did look stunning, coming across the square. That must be the girl at court, the one your brother was talking about in the bar at Suez the other night. What—"

He was going on to say "what was it he called her?" when some saving intuition told him to hold his tongue. Mr. Bruce had not moved. His large capable hands lay clasped on the tablecloth, but a well of feeling seemed to have poured into the dark eyes fixed on the American.

"What did you think of her?" Frank ended his phrase successfully.

"The most beautiful woman I ever saw in my life."

IV

Less than forty-eight hours later James Bruce sat on a low couch in the tent of Ferdinand de Lesseps, wondering how he could bring his conversation with the great Canal-builder round to the subject of Madeleine d'Arbonne.

All the way across the desert to Alexandria, all next day on the sea passage to Port Said, he had nursed the image of the golden girl. Fair hair, dark gold jewels, dishevelled yellow gown, creamy bare shoulders—every detail, in its troubling perfection, had risen before him again and again. And every time he pictured the proud face he saw behind it the smoke-laden bar at Suez, and heard his own brother, before a crowd of engineers, repeat the words his glance had silenced on the lips of Frank Hartzell.

"They say she's a wild lassie! Bonny, and full o' spirit! But like a' the rest o' the Tuileries *cocodettes*—a light woman!"

He had to know more about her. De Lesseps would be sure to know: he was proud of his relationship to the Empress and his entrée to the court. But it was not easy to open such a discussion —not for a man who made a habit of reticence; so James waited, soothed in spite of himself by the click of the amber prayer beads as de Lesseps mechanically numbered them off on his sturdy old wrist, and by the warm luxury of the tent on the Port Said dunes.

It was a scene familiar to him through many visits to de Lesseps while the Canal was in progress, as its builder pitched his tent up and down the Isthmus of Suez. The tent flaps were closed now, for the night was stormy, but through the silken fabric could be seen the glow of the fires round which de Lesseps' servants —fifteen grooms and twenty-four other attendants—waited at two o'clock in the morning to obey the commands of the great French lord. A cluster of lanterns slung on the centre pole lighted a rich carpet from Ispahan in shades of chrysanthemum and blue, and silk rugs in the same colours on the walls. A low table holding gilt cups of Turkish coffee, glasses of cognac and de Lesseps' water pipe was set between the two men. The host, seated on a couch a little higher than his guest's, had propped his back comfortably against a dromedary saddle covered with a red Sennaar rug. It had been his desert bedrest through nearly twenty years of labour on the Canal—the years which within a few hours were to be crowned with success.

Deep lines of fatigue were etched into the fine square face of Ferdinand de Lesseps. He was over sixty, and his thick hair was quite white, but his eyebrows and moustache had remained as dark as his bright kindly eyes, and his expression was sanguine and genial. To James he appeared, that night more than ever, a gentle, brilliant and patriarchal figure.

'It was good of you to drive back here with me after the banquet, Mr. Bruce," de Lesseps was saying. "I'm tired, you know. Too tired to stay in my rooms at the Canal Building; too tired to sleep. I keep remembering what a soothsayer told me once—that my greatest project was fated to end in ruin and disgrace."

James knew that the Frenchman was extremely superstitious, and allowed his desert home to be besieged by the fortunetellers and astrologers of half Asia.

"Everything will go well tomorrow," he said reassuringly. "You can't fail now—you never could!"

De Lesseps looked at him affectionately.

"You've always thought so, haven't you? You're one of the few British engineers to believe in me as completely as my own men," he said. "I remember when Brodie Willcox first brought you to visit me in the desert, how generous and how enthusiastic you were about my plans; and even when your government opposed them, *you* never wavered—did you?"

James shook his head slowly, and de Lesseps, looking at the compressed lips and the steady hands filling a pipe with tobacco, thought how unlikely it was that the Scotsman would ever waver from a course once it was set.

"Fourteen years ago!" James lit his pipe and watched the first puff of smoke curl up to the clustered lanterns. "When I think of all you've done in fourteen years compared with me, I feel very small tonight, Monsieur de Lesseps. . . . When I came to Egypt with Mr. Willcox in '55, I thought I was on my way to the top of the tree. And now I'm Chief Shore Engineer of the P. and O., with two or three new engine designs to my credit; and Willcox and Anderson are dead; and I seem to be as far away from a Managership as ever."

There were very few men to whom James would have admitted as much; certainly not to his own father. But something in the bright paternal look turned upon him made him go on, even more slowly and painfully.

"When I was a lad in Scotland, I had great plans for myself. The sea drew me away from Sauchentree, the farm and the smithy, to the new world opened up by steam and the iron ships. . . . I was to be a great man, nothing less than that would do. A great man, who would win the love of a great woman. Well, I went through the university, and through the shops, and I went to sea, and from there back to my desk, and I know now that to be a great man is not in me."

De Lesseps, in his wisdom, was silent for a time. Then he said gently, "I think you're a *lonely* man, my friend. You need a loving wife, and a settled home."

"I'm over forty, monsieur. Rather too old to start a courtship!"

De Lesseps' sun-tanned face crinkled with sudden laughter.

"Oh no, Mr. Bruce!" he said. "Oh no! Forty is no age at all!"

They both heard the stumbling hoofbeats at the same moment. They were at the tent door before the startled boys ran out of the horse lines, in time to see a tall Egyptian in a white uniform covered with grit and slaver slide from a foundered horse and stand swaying in the sand. He unwound an Arab djibbah from his mouth and nostrils and sketched a formal salutation to de Lesseps before he began to speak.

At his first words the Frenchman cried out, and collapsed against James Bruce's shoulder like a man felled by a stroke.

"For God's sake, tell me what he said to you. Speak, de Lesseps! Has anything happened to the Empress?"

With one arm round the thick old body, James felt de Lesseps' racing heart plunge and steady at the sound of that beloved name.

"No!" he cried. "Not her, thank God! But what will she say to me? The Canal is ruined!"

The man in the white uniform, who had drunk deeply from a goblet brought by one of the servants, began a torrent of explanations while the horseboys whimpered in dismay.

There had been an accident at El Kantara—de Lesseps brokenly translated. Night steaming was forbidden on the reaches of the Canal already in operation, but an Egyptian vessel, the *Latif*, had slipped away from Port Said and started an illegal run to Ismailia with a cargo of Greek wine and grain. She had run aground three miles north of El Kantara, fouling the Canal to all other traffic. Her engineer had been severely scalded, and carried to the town.

"What caused the trouble?" said James. "Ask him if he saw it happen."

No—the messenger had enough French to tell James directly, he had been on duty at El Kantara with a detachment of the Khedive's troops. His captain had ordered him to ride up the causeway to Port Said to spread the alarm.

"Alarm? That's what we must try to avoid," said James shortly. "Monsieur de Lesseps, I don't think the Canal is ruined; all we have to do is float the *Latif* and the show goes on. Couldn't the Khedive's heroes have organized something in the tug and tow-rope line at El Kantara before starting a hue and cry?"

"There are no tugs at El Kantara; we shall have to send a repair crew down from Port Said in the morning. The inauguration must be postponed until the channel is clear. The effect on my reputation, you can guess." And de Lesseps sank his white head in his hands, and groaned.

James had no need to guess; he knew. The accident would be quoted everywhere as proof of what had always been said against the Suez Canal: that its shallow depth made it unsafe for traffic. Not de Lesseps only would be affected, but the whole business world, beginning with a panic on the Paris Bourse when the gilt-edged Canal stocks began to fall.

"I'd better cut along," he said laconically. "The faster I get down there, the sooner I can start on the repairs. We've still a few hours in hand, you know."

30

De Lesseps raised his haggard face and stared at him. In the light of the campfires the Scotsman was a massive figure, with his feet firmly planted in the sand and his fists, in a characteristic gesture, thrust deep into his pockets. The firelight played on the broad expanse of his white dress shirt and lit up the dark, handsome face that was as keen and eager as a boy's.

"You, Mr. Bruce?" stammered de Lesseps. "How can you possibly get from here to El Kantara, and all alone?"

"What about that smart little yacht you pointed out to me in the boat basin below there, as we drove out from the town, with steam up, and her crew aboard? The Khedive's yacht, *Pride of the Nile?*"

De Lesseps looked at him incredulously.

"The *Pride* is waiting to join the procession with His Highness on the bridge," he said. "He won't consent to lend it to a foreigner."

"Then let's go and tell him we must *take* it," said James Bruce.

About fifteen minutes' drive away, in the Frenchman's little basket chaise, the Khedive's pavilion bloomed on the desert night like a gigantic rhododendron flower. Music throbbed inside the silken walls, lighted by rosy lamps half dimmed now by the indefinable luminosity, less light than the promise of light, which heralded the dawn. Nubian guards armed with scimitars, their naked chests glistening, were posted close enough together to form a living hedge around the viceroy's privacy.

The music throbbed, and to its rhythm a lash rose and fell. Somewhere a boy was sobbing in a broken alto that now and again rose to a scream. James and de Lesseps, waiting for an official to be brought, did not look at one another.

The man who came to them was Nubar Pasha, one of Ismail's ablest counsellors and also a violent opponent of the French Presence in Egypt. He listened with cold concern to the story of the wreck. He made them wait for twenty minutes in his own tent, drinking the ritual coffee, before conducting them to his master.

The pavilion which from the outside looked like a burning flower resembled, on the inside, a bullring in the closing stages of a corrida. The carpet of sand-coloured velvet which stretched

31

from wall to wall had been pawed and torn by churning feet and splashed with what was either wine or blood. The room smelled of women, but they had been hurried out, and the only entertainer remaining was the boy who had been heard crying. He lay in a stupor with a bloodstained rug thrown over him behind a ransacked supper table.

Ismail himself stood swaying in the middle of the room, where two bronze cressets burned. The Western prince had disappeared along with the dress clothes and jewelled Orders. The thick animal smell which filled the place seemed to be concentrated in his gross body, barely covered by a thin silk robe. The red fez which he still wore on his sweating head made his near nudity all the more revolting.

"What is the meaning of this intrusion?" he said.

"Your Highness"—de Lesseps bowed low—"I apologize sincerely for disturbing your privacy. The reason is of course imperative. A vessel is aground near El Kantara, and the Canal is barred to traffic at this point."

He had to repeat his words before the viceroy understood. Then, with a fierce shake of his head like an animal shaking blood from its eyes, Ismail articulated,

"Who did it?"

"Sir, I have very few details at present. We hear there has been an accident, we know the *Latif* has fouled the bank, but we are concerned with the facts, not the responsibility. In a few hours the Empress—"

The Khedive interrupted.

"Blow it up!"

"Your Highness?"

"I said—blow up the *Latif*. Crew aboard, or not. Get—out of the way before morning. Haste!"

De Lesseps looked helplessly round for James, who came forward from the place he had taken up beside the door.

"With respect, Your Highness, blowing up the *Latif* would be quite unsatisfactory. The wreckage would merely settle back into the Canal and block the passage completely until dredgers could be brought down from Port Said. The only hope is to get the engine going and move the vessel under her own steam."

"Who is this man?" the Khedive asked de Lesseps.

"Sir, this is Mr. James Bruce, an experienced engineer of the Peninsular and Oriental Company. He has offered to go down-Canal and see what can be done if Your Highness will lend him your own yacht to get to El Kantara."

The Khedive pointed a shaking hand at James.

"Sabotage! An English plot! Your people have done this to disgrace me in front of the princes of Europe—"

"You are absurd, Ismail Pasha." James Bruce's curt words froze them all to silence. "You will be disgraced before the world if your men use explosives at El Kantara, and wreck in five minutes what the French have done for your country in twenty years. Torture the *Latif's* skipper later, if that amuses you, but let me take the *Pride* down to Kantara now. If the *Latif* can be made to float—by God! I'll do it!"

*   *   *

When the sun rose James was standing on the deck of the Khedive's yacht, and the *Pride* was logging off her steady ten knots beneath his feet.

He was now in excellent spirits. The *Pride's* commander, a sloe-eyed, sway-hipped young man called Mahmoud, had accepted his suggestion to use sail as well as steam, and the gale which had blown in overnight from the Mediterranean was swelling her canvas as she ran down the cut across Lake Menzaleh. James had overhauled the yacht's repair equipment and changed from his black dress clothes into a clean cotton slop suit and a peaked cap with a neck veil; there was nothing more he could do until they reached the wreck. He was entitled to stand there idle, tunelessly humming a song his father sang in the smithy at Sauchentree:

> "Adown the firth and away we go
> With a sweet and pleasant gale!
> And fare you well to bonny Montrose
> And the girl I love so well!"

33

From time to time he took a gold watch from his pocket and checked the hour and the probable distance from the wreck. It was a favourite possession, presented to him by the King of Prussia in recognition of his work at Stettin; its chased gold hands, travelling round the solid black Roman numerals, had marked off the hours for him in many strange ports. Now minutes, not hours, counted as the yacht raced down the "Ditch." Over the tops of the dredging shovels still lying on the causeway he saw a company of Bedouins venturing shyly to the water's edge. If all went well, these nomads would soon see Empress and Khedive, Mufti and Christian priest go by, but in the meantime . . .

"By God!" said James, as the truth dawned upon him, "I'm leading the procession down the Suez Canal!"

The idea pleased him. It helped to dispel the vile remembrance of the scene in Ismail's pavilion.

James Bruce thought of himself as a man of the world, well enough accustomed to the rough life of the Mediterranean ports, but the perversions of Ismail were outside his experience and hateful to him. He felt a sour taste in his mouth at the very thought that the swollen dark face of the Khedive would soon be bent to kiss the white hand of the Empress of the French.

But the sexuality rank in Ismail's pavilion had insensibly aroused a passionate man whose virility had been shackled in his adolescence by the sanctions of Scottish Calvinism and sublimated into a compulsive need to hurry, an ambition to excel. Ismail's self-indulgence, following immediately on de Lesseps' advice to take a wife, turned Bruce's thoughts back to the path they had followed ever since in the dusty square outside Shepheard's he had seen the bold lovely laughing face of Madeleine d'Arbonne.

"There she is!" cried Mahmoud.

The *Pride* had arrived at the scene of the wreck.

The *Latif* had rammed the canal bank at an obtuse angle, and sat there with her paddle wheels half in and half out of the water like an ancient duck struggling out of a nest of sand and stone. James noted thankfully that not much damage had been done to the bank itself, and that the military commandant of El Kantara had apparently provided a supply of sandbags when his men removed the scalded engineer. The rest of the crew had made no attempt at any repair work. They were eating a meal of sorts on the causeway, waiting apathetically for someone to give them orders.

"Picnicking, hey?" James shouted, as the *Pride* came alongside. The dark faces stared blankly up at him. "Which is the skipper? You, mister? Made a proper hash of this, haven't you? Should teach you a useful lesson—no night steaming on the Canal! No, Nubar Pasha!"—as the Khedive's representative burst out in a torrent of accusation—"You can decide later, as I told your master, whom to torture for all this. I need this fellow now! Come on, let's get aboard."

The *Latif's* between decks were awash, and although the sky-light hatch on the deck was open, her little engine room was still heavy with escaping gas. The fires had been doused in the panic following the accident and in the process the engineer had received steam burns, but for the time being it was impossible to use a lamp. James made his inspection by the hatch light and by touch, crawling about over the gratings to emerge on deck black-faced and choking. The visor of his borrowed cap was broken and the wisp of veiling soaked with oil.

"Well, sir?" Nubar Pasha was with him immediately.

"Port side lever broken," said James laconically. "The forging was old and overstrained and this jaunt was the one trip too many. I'll have to splice the lever with iron plates, but I can't start work or even breathe inside there yet. Captain Mahmoud! Be good enough to order your royal rigged across the hatch. The breeze is stiff enough to give us a draught right through the engine room and clear the gas away, while I get out your drilling equipment. Tell your fellows to make everything available to me."

The peremptory orders were rapped out, and James waited only to see the *Pride's* great sail rigged as he had directed before turning back to the causeway, where the mukhtar of El Kantara and the leading villagers had arrived with provisions for the great lord Nubar and his guest. James set them to work at once, shoring up the bank with sandbags. He had no appetite for rice and greasy mutton as the heat of the desert increased under the sun of six

35

o'clock. The hands of his watch travelled to seven, and on to eight, the hour when the Empress was due to leave Port Said, before he could begin to fit the broken lever with the new iron plates.

The *Latif's* engine was a British model, with a lever placed below the crank, and James had been perfectly familiar with it in his days on the "black squad" of the P. and O. The drilling equipment was American, and in the desperate need for hurry he handled it with less assurance, longing for the help of a Clydeside riveter, and blaspheming at the go-slow tactics of the *Pride's* engineers, who plainly resented taking orders from an Englishman. Somehow, with every muscle of his back and shoulders aching from the fast hard work in that constricted space, he finished the bolting to his satisfaction and drove the stokers on to the relighting of the fires. With every available man at the shovels, James himself took charge of the engine when the spliced lever began to move and the piston rod to lift. He watched the hand of the primitive signal jerk round until, with a shudder and a slip, the *Latif's* bows slid down six feet of canal bank and her keel met the water squarely once again. He took her out with an excess of caution into mid-channel, the wooden paddle wheels beginning to churn the water and the smoke to belch from her little funnel, feeling the same exultation as when he took charge in a P. and O. engine room during the trials of one of the new three-thousand-tonners along the measured mile in the Firth of Clyde. He laughed aloud when on the bridge the *Latif's* skipper, now hysterically optimistic, moved his signal imperiously to Full Steam Ahead. Nothing doing! He was going to inch into El Kantara so slowly that a man walking on the causeway might outpace him, but so surely that he would be certain to clear the channel for the passage of the Empress of the French.

He completed the three miles with more than half an hour to spare. He berthed at El Kantara, where a jabbering crowd had gathered on the quay, fully forty minutes before the Imperial Standard appeared far up the channel, with two French ironclads flying the Tricolore close behind. He was watching from the deck, and swigging down a pint of Greek wine from the *Latif's* cargo, when he realized that his head and arms were black with oil and coal dust and his wet slop suit sticking to his back. "I can't be seen like this!" he said to himself. "I ought to go back to *Pride* and get my own clothes off that scented whoreship!" But fatigue had suddenly caught up with him. He went down to the hold, wadded his jacket between two sacks of grain for a pillow and fell asleep almost at once.

He was awakened by a hand in an immaculate white gauntlet pulling gingerly at his shoulder. He looked up unwillingly, turning his head in a puddle of sweat that ran in rivulets down his neck and back, and rubbed his swollen eyelids with his blackened fists.

A young man in the uniform of the Imperial Guard was bending over him. A blue-eyed young man, with a blond moustache and imperial, the forehead beneath his silver helmet beaded with the perspiration of a Kantara noon. A young man he had seen in Cairo, discountenanced and surly, standing at the elbow of Michel Bertaux.

"Mr. Bruce!" said Victor d'Arbonne urgently, as James sat up with a start, "I apologize for disturbing you! Her Imperial Majesty commands your presence now, aboard the *Aigle*!"

V

The Empress of the French was seated on the deck of the *Aigle*, under a crimson canopy which cast a warm glow on the long white gandoura she had thrown over her muslin dress. It had been her whim that morning to put on the simplest of all the two hundred and fifty toilettes which Worth had created for her visit to the East, and it contrasted strangely with the diamond coronet which sparkled in her bronze-gold hair. The ladies who sat around her chair of state were far more elaborately dressed in silks and laces, fans fluttering in their hands and court curls lax on their shoulders; their pale skirts swept the deck like gigantic bells of lily of the valley.

Time, wars and the shame of her husband's flagrant infidelities had hardly flawed the loveliness of Eugénie de Montijo, the Spanish lady of no fortune whom Louis Napoleon Bonaparte, the greatest adventurer of the age, had made his consort on the imperial throne of France. Her wonderful pale face owed nothing to cosmetics, except where a pencilled line of black enhanced the pure violet of her eyes. The Chinese slant of those deep eyes, the almond shape of those thick white lids, were what gave Eugénie's face its character, oddly at variance with her lovely heartbreaking smile.

Sonnets had been written to that cryptic smile, rich in the promise of compassion, by court poets who were in reality no more moved by it than by the expression on the face of the moon. For it was a remarkable fact that the most beautiful woman in Europe made no appeal to men. In all the years since her husband left her bed no lover had ever possessed her, and at the licentious court, in the most scandal-loving of all cities, her name had never been linked with any man's. Her marked preference for the company of young women—beautiful blondes for choice—was accompanied by a smiling determination to ignore everything unpleasant in the backstairs intrigues of the Tuileries. In the little court which surrounded her on board the *Aigle* there was more than one woman, now close to the Empress, who had been formerly the mistress of the Emperor.

El Kantara grilled in the heat of noon, and the *Aigle* swung at her moorings with a seasick motion. The Murat princesses were at no pains to conceal their boredom as the Empress held her levée. The two little Spanish duchesses, Eugénie's motherless nieces, yawned and pulled furtively at their tight bodices. Only the maids of honour, Madeleine d'Arbonne and Angèle de Larminat, were motionless in their prescribed postures of graceful attention at the back of Eugénie's chair.

The Crown Prince of Prussia, a giant with a blond beard and a tunic covered with war medals, came aboard to kiss the hand of the Empress and drink a congratulatory toast to France. The Emperor of Austria followed him, then the Dutch prince; de Lesseps came, and asked leave to present various Canal officials. The Empress began to twist the five plain gold rings she wore on her wedding finger, each representing some great event in her life, and more than once she touched the emerald brooch in the form of a four-leaf clover with diamonds for dewdrops which had been Napoleon III's first gift to his future wife. These were signs of fatigue which her ladies could interpret, but the perfection of Eugénie's manner never altered as one man after another made his bow.

Soon after her marriage she had been trained by Rachel, the greatest dramatic actress of the day, in deportment suited to all the contingencies of her new life. How To bow from a state coach or nod to members of the Imperial Hunt. How To grade the courtesies due to Prefects, prison governors, curators of provincial museums. Madame Rachel was dead long ago; she had never given a supplementary lesson on How To open the Suez Canal, but the pupil was now letter-perfect in her imperial part. She sat in her grave beauty in the heart of the Egyptian desert, and bestowed on all comers her enigmatic Tuileries smile.

"Is that the last presentation, Princesse?"

The Grand Mistress of the Household said reluctantly,

"Your Majesty was good enough to summon the Scots engineer,

Monsieur de Lesseps' friend. Captain d'Arbonne went to find him —some time ago."

Victor had been detained aboard the *Latif* by his own obstinacy. He had refused to hear of Bruce's going back to the P. and O. boat to change his clothing, and had thus been forced to wait while the engineer plunged his head and arms in a bucket of gritty canal water and used his torn shirt sleeve for a towel. The reflection James saw as he bent over the water pail, with a line of stubble round his mouth and jaw and his dark brown hair tousled behind his ears, caused him to groan inwardly. Not like this would he have wished to appear before an empress or have another chance of seeing Madeleine d'Arbonne!

Madeleine recognized him as soon as he appeared on the deck of the *Aigle*, walking in front of instead of behind Victor, with the young guardsman flushed and exasperated at his heels. So the Scotsman of de Lesseps' praises was the man who had stared at her so intently from the steps of Shepheard's Hotel! Well, now it was her turn to stare at him, with time to take him in thoroughly, from the stoker's cap with the broken visor, which he held as carelessly as her ballroom partners held a cotillion favour, to the wet and stained black patent-leather shoes. But then their eyes met—once—before he transferred his gaze to the face of the Empress, and respectfully kept it there. Madeleine let the white lace fan drop to her lap. Her hand felt suddenly limp and hot.

She found herself looking at what she seldom saw among the Jockey Club dandies and *petits crevés* of Imperial Paris, a completely masculine man. She saw the wonderful eyes burning in the exhausted face and the pectoral muscles lifting the sleazy jacket which refused to fasten over Bruce's broad chest. She looked at his hands, and saw that though stained and calloused they were a gentleman's hands, and she thought that no ambassador had ever stood before Eugénie with a prouder or more dignified bearing. She also saw, for her perceptions were sharp where the Empress was concerned, that Eugénie was having a little difficulty in placing him. De Lesseps had said that James Bruce was "*un brave bourgeois*," yet here he was dressed as "a man of the people" and at the same time answering her gracious questions in the

French of the *ancien régime*. The Empress wondered if she should give him her hand to kiss.

Mademoiselle de Larminat noticed Madeleine's absorption and wondered if the tall maid of honour intended to work up one of the imitations which made the Empress laugh hysterically and the Emperor grin behind his heavy waxed moustache when they played charades at Compiègne. But Madeleine was not disposed to find James Bruce funny, neither when, asked if he ever visited Paris, he gravely told the Empress that he was often there "in transit," a phrase which normally would have struck her as ludicrous; nor when Eugénie, seeking some especially graceful way of bringing the audience to a close, herself offered him a crystal goblet of champagne from the table prepared for her alfresco luncheon. It was a gesture taken straight from Sir Walter Scott, the sort of thing which her enemies criticized as meretricious and left the unsophisticated at a loss. James was equal to the occasion. He bowed low to her and, murmuring, "Madame, your humble servant," he touched his lips to the wine when she asked him to drink to the future of the Suez Canal. But he looked across her shoulder as he raised his glass, into the eyes of Madeleine.

Many hours later, well groomed again and dressed in tropical white, he stood up with de Lesseps' arm laid affectionately round his shoulders and listened to the applause of two hundred men ringing through the banquet hall of the Canal Building at Ismailia. Through the open doors a warm night wind brought the smell of ten thousand cooking pots from the desert where the tribesmen feasted with the Khedive Ismail. Out of the palm-fringed streets of the toy town on the shores of Lake Timsah, where hundreds of tourists were strolling up and down, drifted perfumes less barbaric: of the Provence roses growing in the new gardens, and the essences clinging to the hair and dresses of the beautiful women of the west.

"Gentlemen!" said Ferdinand de Lesseps, his happy face burning with generous praise, "You all know what Mr. Bruce did to make possible our arrival here, halfway on our journey from sea to sea. I know you want to give him the ovation he deserves. But

I happen to know him rather well, and I believe he would prefer us to toast instead the pioneers whom he represents in his own person. Gentlemen, I give you the leaders in steam navigation! The men who opened the modern route to the East before a spade was turned in the sand of the Sinai desert! Here's to our rivals, and our friends! To The Scots Engineers!"

". . . One moment, Mr. James." The company was dispersing, the sound of dance music rose from the gardens of Ismailia. At the door of the Canal Building Mr. Hadow, a Director of the P. and O., caught James by his white coat sleeve.

"That was a remarkable achievement. Ve-ery remarkable! They are going to be ve-ery pleased about it in Leadenhall Street! I don't mean your exploit aboard the *Latif*. That was standard, as you said yourself this afternoon. That was what the Company expects of any engineer of your ability. The gratifying thing was that public tribute from de Lesseps, who has no special cause to love the P. and O.—or the British Government. It may have important consequences for you and all of us."

"Consequences—what consequences?" said James, more abruptly than he usually allowed himself to speak to any member of the Court of Directors. "The *Latif's* skipper will get a flogging, personally administered by Ismail Pasha; de Lesseps has spoken generously of me, and there's an end of it."

"No, Mr. James," said Hadow, "there's a beginning!"

He drew the Scotsman away in the direction of the landing jetty. A dozen official banquets were winding up; guests and spectators were drifting to the lake to see the great fireworks display arranged by the Khedive.

"You're going back to Alex. tomorrow?" said Hadow. "Pity! Or—I don't know, there's no need to hang about with the imperial cortège. What I feel, and Mr. Bayley feels the same, is that you are just the man we need to keep in closer touch with de Lesseps. If the French go to war with Prussia in the near future, their shipping will be tied up for the duration. If we were sure of a real friend at court like de Lesseps we could lease them *our* carriers—for a consideration. It would balance some of the losses we're bound to take in the Ditch!"

James stared at him. In the clear bright desert moonlight, in the ruddy British face of Mr. Hadow, he could trace no shadow of a coming war.

"You aren't serious, sir?" he said. "After their recent losses in Mexico, would the French dare to enter on another war of aggression?"

"Perhaps not, but as long as the Spanish Question remains open, the danger's always there. Well, it's been a long day for you, Mr. James. Better come back to *Delta* and have a whisky peg before we turn in."

"Would you excuse me, sir? I have a card for the Canal Commissioner's evening party. In view of what you've said, mightn't it be politic to show up?"

"I never thought of you as a party man." But Hadow let him go at last, and James was off—walking as fast as he could through the crowds, in what direction he had no idea. His head was whirling. Not with drink, although he had taken more than usual at the banquet. Not with words, though the ideas Hadow had thrown out would normally have filled his practical mind. But with a heady mixture of success and praise and kindled desire, all foaming and frothing round the one figure, the girl he was determined to find that night.

He had no idea where she might be. He knew that the Empress had come ashore, but there were no ladies at de Lesseps' banquet, nor could he believe that Eugénie would have accepted the Khedive's hospitality in the desert. It was probable that she and her little court had dined with one of the foreign royalties, in which case there was a hope that the equerries and maids of honour, like himself, would end the evening at the Canal Commissioner's residence. One of the Canal Company's policemen directed him to the place just as the first rockets of the fireworks display broke in golden rain across the moonlit sky. The sound brought all the revellers quickly out of doors. James made his way through the trim gardens, past groups of women in bright shawls, leaning on the arms of men in all the uniforms of Europe. He saw Mr. Bayley of the P. and O., eating an ice and listening indulgently to a voluble man from the Messageries. He saw de Lesseps,

43

surrounded by an admiring group, and veered away. He saw Madame d'Arbonne, in her overblown and weary beauty, resting beneath a palm tree with her brother in devoted attendance, and the sight encouraged him to look further. It was just as the second burst of rockets coloured the night that he came upon Madeleine.

She was etched in moonlight and shadow, in a dress which melted like a snowdrift into the trampled grass. About her shoulders she had drawn a gandoura such as the Empress wore, the colour of the imperial violets. Her uplifted face, watching a rocket expire in a shower of stars, was as pale as her clasped hands.

James walked towards her across the Commissioner's lawn, dimly aware that those around her were staring at him as he came. He bowed to her as he had bowed to her Empress, and said,

"Mademoiselle d'Arbonne, forgive me, and allow myself to present myself; my name is Bruce."

An appalling silence crashed about his ears.

Then he heard her say wonderingly.

"You know my name? I know who you are. I saw you aboard the *Aigle* today."

"The Empress was very gracious to me, madam. Will you be more gracious still?"

"In what way, monsieur?"

"Will you walk a little way with me, down there where the band is playing?"

She looked at the astonished spectators. At her two sisters. At Frank Hartzell, and at the debauched face of her brother-in-law Federico di Roccanuova. With a little excited laugh she drew about her the long gandoura, colour of the night, and laid her fingers in the crook of the arm he offered. She let James Bruce lead her out into the throng of Europeans walking by the lake as the first of the firework set pieces, a Tricolore surrounded by stars, exploded in the sky above their heads,

"Are you in the British Navy, sir?"

"I, madam? No. I have been to sea, though. I used to be a ship's engineer in the merchant fleet. Why do you ask?"

"Because this must be what they call in the Navy 'a cutting-out expedition.' "

Her laugh was light, inconsequent, amused.

"Will you forgive my presumption, Mademoiselle d'Arbonne? I can claim a slight acquaintance with some members of your family. I met your brother, as you saw, this very morning. And every time I've seen you I've wished to speak to you. Today on the *Aigle*. Yesterday, when I saw you near the Empress as she came into harbour at Port Said—"

"And even when I drove into the square at Cairo with Tewfik Pasha? I saw you watching me."

James met her challenge calmly enough.

"You saw me *looking* at you," he said. "Do you wonder? I thought when I saw you in the barouche that *you* were the Empress."

Madeleine smiled. This escapade on the moonlit promenade had not, for her, the dramatic unconventionality it held for James. The summer balls at the Tuileries, above all the costume balls, were full of such episodes. A lady in a mask slipped away with an insistent partner, also masked, to stroll in the shadow of the chestnut trees and the stone statues, to exchange a few secret kisses, sometimes to make an even more secret assignation—there was no harm in it by Paris standards. The only disagreeable thing was the occasional case of mistaken identity—the mask snatched off, the angry confrontation—or the risk of being pawed by the Emperor. Madeleine, like every other girl at court, had quickly learned that no fancy dress or enveloping mask could help the Emperor to disguise his voice. The low, husky tones were unmistakable: Napoleon knew it too, and when he was on the prowl he kept absolutely silent until his prey was in his arms. "Never stroll in the gardens with a *silent* mask," was wholesome advice for young ladies who did not aspire to follow a long train of initiates to the alcove next the imperial study.

But this man was different. He had come boldly up to her before them all—she liked that. It was not possible, with those grave dark eyes upon her, to make the obvious impertinent rejoinder, in the tone of a Tuileries flirtation: Did you think the

Empress had had a morning rendezvous with Tewfik Pasha? She said instead.

"I'm a little like Her Majesty, in height and colouring at least. Most of the ladies at court are chosen just for that. The Empress prefers fair women to dark and likes to have them about her. Then when she looks at us she feels that she sees herself in a mirror; only of course her reality is far more lovely than our reflection."

It was a strange, narcissistic picture which her words created. James had seen the Empress looking serenely on the world from the lovely frame of her ladies: what thoughts could move behind those violet eyes when the slanting look, the hieratic smile were turned inward instead of out? Looking at herself in a mirror! This girl, he knew instinctively, would never be content to be merely the reflection of an imperial image. There was force and purpose, not passivity, in the face so near his own.

A string band, augmented by one or two brasses, was playing patriotic airs in a little conch-shaped bandstand at the far corner of the promenade.

"That's the *Egyptian Hymn*," said Madeleine. "They played it night and day beneath our windows on the Nile."

"I've no ear for music," said James, "but I'll know when they play *God Save the Queen*!"

They strolled as far as the bandstand, turned and walked in the direction of the Commissioner's house, while the band played the *Chant de Riégo*.

"Monsieur de Lesseps thinks the world of you, monsieur. He said some wonderful things about you to Her Majesty."

"I happen to think the world of him."

"You're going on to his wedding, I suppose?"

"To his *what*?"

James stopped dead. They had left the other strolling couples behind them and were standing in a little circular walk hedged with flowering oleanders.

"Didn't you know? The engagement is to be announced the day after tomorrow, before we leave the Bitter Lakes. Won't you come on with us to the Bitter Lakes and help us celebrate?"

"Celebrate!" repeated James. "Good heavens, madam, I'd no

46

idea he was planning to marry! Wait—I think now he might have been going to tell me about it last night—something I said might have prompted him; but then the *Latif* trouble started. He's been a widower for sixteen years, and—have you any idea how old he is?"

"Sixty-four in two days' time," said Madeleine demurely. "His astrologers foretold a large family if the betrothal took place on his birthday, and the marriage is to follow as soon as we reach Suez."

"A large *family*!" said James. "Pray is the lady ... Who is she? Do you know her?"

"Very well indeed, though she came to court long after I did. Her name is Hélène de Bragard, and she must be all of twenty-one years old."

The image of the night before, of the old patriarch in his desert tent, the figure so confused in his mind with that of his own father, shattered abruptly in James Bruce's head. He saw de Lesseps a lover—a man like other men.

"Good God!" he said. "He could be her grandfather!"

"Yes, he could. I wonder," said Madeleine dreamily, "what the astrologers had to say to *that*."

Suddenly they were both laughing, their hands meeting and clinging, while the shadows flung by the oleanders vanished in the violence of a silver and scarlet transparency painting the cipher F. & E. upon the sky.

"France and Egypt!" said Madeleine. "Mr. Bruce, I wouldn't give much for your chance of hearing *God Save the Queen* to-night!"

But Bruce was still laughing, with delight in her sharp tongue, with delight in her nearness; with the champagne and the *Latif* and the fireworks all whirling in his head together. And with that laughter on his lips he took her in his arms, white dress, cloak the colour of imperial violets and smooth bare arms, and began to kiss her: first the temples where the bright hair sprang away, then the closed eyes, and then in a sudden frenzy the burning lips that parted gently underneath his own.

If he drew his head back after that first wild kiss it was only

47

for a moment. It was only because the dead and gone generations of Scots Calvinists, his ancestors, leaped upon his living neck and warned him that carnal pleasure was a sin in the eyes of the Lord. But he never loosed his hold upon her, and then he felt her arms twine with surprising strength about his shoulders and her breasts push out against him.

And while they kissed and kissed again, and the noise of the rockets and the cheering seemed to come from a million miles away, they heard the band strike up, with the brasses beating out a measure that commanded them to listen—that ended after a dozen bars.

Madeleine, with her cheek against Bruce's, laughed softly in his ear.

"Bandmaster, change the tune!" she whispered. "I wonder who bribed them to start that!"

"What were they playing?"

"Don't you know? It's been banned in France for twenty years. But I thought—somewhere—you might have heard the *Marseillaise*!"

Another transparency, this time a cipher of the letters N & E in blue and silver, surmounted by an imperial crown in gold, sprang into light above their heads,

"Look, look! Napoleon and Eugénie!"

It was then, while the initials of France's rulers faded out of the sky, that Egyptian folly for the second time threatened the French achievement on the Suez Canal. An appalling crash from the warehouse where the Khedive's fireworks were stored was followed by a series of explosions blasting from one building to another. Then a column of fire sprang a hundred feet into the air and broke into a hundred cruel tongues of orange and vermillion that began to lick at the Canal Building, and the white villas, and the whole toy structure of Ismailia town.

Two

PARIS IN HER SPLENDOUR

January 1870

I

"Toss you for it!"

Madeleine d'Arbonne spun a coin with a stableboy's dexterity, and laughed at Mademoiselle de Larminat's disgusted face.

"Now *you* play blindman's buff at the children's party and I stay up here until four o'clock!" said Madeleine. Her colleague, with a groan, hurried into the adjoining bedroom and began to change her morning costume for the stiff silk of afternoon.

"The Prince Imperial is too old for a children's party—in another year he'll be pinching us, if he's anything like his father!" Madeleine heard her say in a muffled voice, as she pulled her close-fitting cashmere over her head. The maids of honour had no maids of their own. They tugged at each other's stay laces, brushed each other's hair and had learned after years in the palace of the Tuileries to get ready for their hours on duty with the speed of firemen answering an alarm bell.

The two girls shared a small chilly sitting room three floors above the grand entrance to the palace and one below the servants' quarters. On New Year's Day, 1870, it was more comfortable than usual, for the Grand Mistress had grudgingly doled out a few extra logs for their little blue porcelain stove. The round table and whatnot were covered with boxes of candied chestnuts, dragées from Gouaché the imperial confectioner, and the bouquets of violets—dark Russian and Parma mauve—which were the usual New Year tribute to the ladies of the court.

Madeleine dragged the small horsehair sofa as close to the stove as possible and brought a magnificent sheared beaver rug from her own bedroom to spread over it before settling down to rest. She had escaped the children's party, but there would be two hours of standing behind the Empress later in the afternoon when Her Majesty received her New Year's Day guests, and many more hours of standing beside the thrones at the court ball that night.

"How comfortable you look," said Angèle de Larminat resentfully, giving a last pat to her blonde curls as she came out of her room. "I really think we might have been excused the New Year service after all we went through in Egypt! D'Elbée and Marion have all the luck, coming on duty tomorrow morning after all the fuss is over!"

"But think of the week at home we're going to have," said Madeleine lazily. It was produced as a consolation to the other girl, who missed the luxury of her father's house near the Parc Monceau; Madeleine herself greatly preferred the Tuileries to the vast new mansion on the rue du Faubourg St. Honoré, where the Comte and Comtesse d'Arbonne and their family lived at the expense of Monsieur Bertaux, the master of the house, in an atmosphere of strain and tension for which no opulence could compensate. In the magnificent discomfort and disorder of the Tuileries there were tensions too, but these were caused by intrigues of perpetual interest to Madeleine and others like her who had grown up in the shadow of Napoleon III's Black Cabinet and his palace police.

Angèle's hand was on the knob when a knock fell on the sitting room door. She opened it to admit a footman who presented yet another florist's box on a silver salver.

"Not more violets!" said Madeleine, as she came across the room in her silk-stockinged feet to open it. "There won't be a flower left in Grasse to make perfume this spring!"

But what the box revealed was a tight bouquet of moss rosebuds in a frill of lace. It was set in the kind of filigree holder fashionable about the time Madeleine was in the schoolroom, when flowers were an essential part of a ball toilette and before the new interior decorators had banished them to épergnes and conservatories.

"Now who in the world can have sent you that?" marvelled Angèle.

"I wager I know," said Madeleine. The very look of the offering, so prim in its arrangement of clear bright pinks and greens, prepared her for the card engraved

Mr James Bruce

and inscribed in ink

> —*with his deepest respects*
> *begs the favour of a dance*
> *at the New Year Ball.*

"Not the Scotsman!" cried Angèle de Larminat, as Madeleine looked at the card in silence. "Why, I thought you never heard of him again after we left Ismailia?"

"Not a word."

"Then how did he get an invitation to the ball? Who would put *his* name on the imperial list? Come on now, confess—you arranged it yourself!"

"Not I!" said Madeleine with perfect truth. "It may have been the Empress, to please de Lesseps—or someone in the Bodyguard, for all I know. Anybody but my brother Victor!"

"Victor found you with him by the lake after the fire started, didn't he?"

"Victor came rushing at us like a tiger just outside the Commissioner's house, and dragged me off to join the rest of you. Will you ever forget the shrieking and sobbing before we got the Empress safely to the barge? Ridiculous—they had the fire under control in half an hour."

"Well, but did you ever think you would see the Scotsman again?"

"You're going to be terribly late for precious Loulou and the other brats, my dear!"

Madeleine put the roses in water and returned to her sofa after Angèle, with an agreeable shriek, had rustled away along the corridor. But the Goncourts' new novel and the latest copy of the *Gazette Rose*, which she had meant to glance at while she rested, slid off the beaver rug and lay unheeded on the floor while Madeleine faced the knowledge that James Bruce had come to Paris. She had thought of him often—always against the background of the Canal and the splintering rockets; how would he look, how would he act, in the artificial world of the Tuileries?

She went restlessly to the window, cooling her hot cheeks against the pane and looking down into the forecourt of the Place du Carrousel. Napoleon III had transformed it, within her own memory, from a flea market where the barrows of hucksters selling old clothes and sheet music were backed up against the first billboards ever seen in France, into the splendid square where his sentries paced on duty. Half an hour earlier, when she came upstairs with Angèle, the Carrousel had been full of the coaches of the diplomatic corps, coming to pay their respects to the Emperor, the first and most important on their list of New Year's Day calls. Now she saw to her surprise that the line of vehicles was forming again, the flunkeys hurrying to open the doors for the elderly gentlemen with gold-laced tricornes held flat beneath their arms. "Already!" she thought, consulting the enamelled watch pinned to her bodice. She was so completely attuned to the life of the Tuileries that the slightest departure from imperial precedent was a matter for uneasiness. "The levée over already, and the envoys going away? . . . I hope there's nothing the matter with His Majesty!"

In the Salle du Premier Consul, under the gigantic shadow of the great Napoleon, his nephew and successor—sometimes called Napoleon the Less—had been compelled to cut short the reading of a prepared speech announcing that 1870 would be a memorable year for France and one of great prosperity for the whole world. Before the concerned but calculating eyes of the entire diplomatic corps, the short obese man with the clay-coloured face had passed a handkerchief across his lips and left the room without waiting for the escort of Achille Bazaine, Marshal of France, and the four general officers in brilliant uniforms who stood behind him. It did not escape any of the watchful eyes that Dr. Conneau, the Emperor's chief physician and lifelong friend, hurried out of the room behind his master, and more than one envoy regretted that protocol prevented him from seeing what went on in the anteroom. But the Emperor, with his arm in Conneau's, mastered his pain sufficiently to walk quite steadily down the grand staircase between the impassive rows of his tall Cent-Gardes. There was no giving way until he was back in his own study, with a closed door between him and the world.

The doctor settled Napoleon in a huge easy chair beside the fire, with his feet propped on a hassock and his eyes shaded from the light, and hurried through the adjoining bedroom into the cabinet de toilette where an anxious valet was hovering, and where sedatives for the recurrent attacks of pain were always kept at hand. But the Emperor, when the medicine was brought, held up his hand in refusal.

"No, Conneau," he said hoarsely, "don't give me a sedative. It confuses me, and makes me drowsy, all day long. The pain's passing off now. I'll rest after I've seen Monsieur Ollivier, and wake refreshed for the ball tonight."

Conneau shook his head. "I wish you would allow the Empress to receive alone."

"And start the eternal rumours once again—of a rift in our marriage, of myself stretched on the surgeon's table? No, my friend. While I can appear by her side, I will."

Then, his voice growing a little stronger, he added.

"Though I think my big decision in 1870 will have to be—to summon up enough courage to undergo the knife."

"It's not a question of courage," said Conneau loyally. "It was the six years in prison, Sire, that undermined your ability to resist pain."

"Aye!" said the Emperor. "When you and I spent our first New Year's Day in Ham fortress—'41, was it?—with the water running down the walls, and the mist rising off the St. Quentin

53

canal, we didn't anticipate such snug quarters as these, eh, Conneau?"

The imperial suite was more than snug. It was positively oppressive, for the Emperor had inherited a love of warmth from his Creole mother, Hortense de Beauharnais, and his apartments, a series of small gilt boxes opening into one another, were always kept extremely hot. Even Eugénie, the Spaniard, protested at the heat when she visited her husband's study, which she did very seldom and only on invitation. There had been devastating scenes in their early estranged years when his wife, descending the private staircase unannounced, had found the Emperor entertaining some lightly clad lady who had been admitted through the little postern door in the palace wall. Now the pink and gold alcove, where the Emperor's lusts had been spent so many times, witnessed nothing but the pain of a broken man with whitening hair; and the study itself had always been irreproachable, a statesman's room. Over the fireplace hung a full-length painting in oils, by Ingres, of Julius Caesar. Marble pedestals supported busts of Napoleon I, the Emperor's uncle, and of his fledgling son, who, if he had lived and reigned, would have borne the title of Napoleon II.

"Shall I summon the Empress, Sire?" Conneau had been anxiously watching a light sweat gathering on his master's brow.

"I'll call her myself," said the Emperor. He hoisted himself out of the great chair with a painful effort, and moved slowly to the door opening on a short inner staircase which led to Eugénie's private rooms. Down the well of the stair, clear voices floated; even by the fireside, Conneau could hear Eugénie's merry laugh.

"Ugénie! Ugénie!"

The Emperor had an individual way of pronouncing his wife's beautiful first name. In their first happy years the courtiers had heard the call of "Ugénie!" a hundred times a day; few had ever heard her call him "Louis." "*Majesté*" or "*Sire*" when she remembered her stiff Spanish manners; "*vous*" for everyday; never in public, and never for years now in private the intimate and tender "*tu*."

"The Empress is busy with the children's party." A little stout

54

man, wearing spectacles, peered over the rail of a mezzanine floor halfway up the staircase. "Shall I strike the gong?"

"No, don't disturb her, Charles. Come down and join us instead. I forgot about the children's party," said the Emperor, turning back to Conneau, "but now I hear Loulou laughing and shouting. He's getting too old for romping; we must plan something more adult for next year."

Charles Thélin was permitted to address the Emperor in the same tone of affectionate intimacy as Dr. Conneau, although he had once been no more than Louis Napoleon's valet. Long ago, he had been promoted to Keeper of the Privy Purse, and the position of his little office on the mezzanine between their private suites had always been a thorn in the flesh of Eugénie. "He watches me! He spies on me! Send him away!" she had raged in the confidence of her young beauty, and the Emperor had laughed and patted her cheek and refused.

"I can't dismiss Charles, he knows far too much about me!" he said. In fact there was no secret of the Emperor's manhood unknown to Conneau and Thélin. They had gone to jail with him at Ham, when King Louis Philippe's judges sentenced him to life imprisonment for one of his comic opera attempts to seize the throne. They had helped him to escape from prison, shared his poverty in exile and followed him through the bloodstained coup d'état which made him Emperor and his Star shone at last above the Tuileries. Death had taken many of his friends and fellow plotters, but the Emperor, the younger Pietri and the faithful Thélin, still formed the Black Cabinet to whose conclaves no elected minister would ever be admitted. Conneau, who had gone with them all the way, had never been a politician; but Conneau, watching the Emperor's fluttering eyelids and painful breath that New Year's Day, realized that he was at last the most important of them all. He had to keep the sick man alive—if he could—until his thirteen-year-old son was old enough to reign without the Regency of Eugénie.

He signed to Thélin to say something—anything—to rivet the Emperor's attention.

"How did the speech go?" asked Thélin casually. "Were they all impressed by your plans for constitutional government?"

The ghost of a grin appeared beneath the Emperor's great moustache.

"Yes, I think they were, Charles," he said, making an effort to rouse himself. "Sit down, man, and give me a cigarette. What hour did they set for my audience with Ollivier?"

"Four o'clock. He's been hanging about the palace for an hour already, on tenterhooks in case you change your mind about the great announcement."

January 2, a Sunday, had been fixed as the day when Emile Ollivier and a Liberal ministry would take over the policies of France from the Emperor's dictatorship.

"Ollivier has nothing to fear," said the Emperor. "We adjusted our difficulties while the Empress was in Egypt, and all he and his friends have to do now is draft the Constitution of 1870. We must move with the times, eh Charles?"

He grinned again and his companions laughed. But Napoleon's smile turned to a grimace of pain, and involuntarily he clapped his left hand to his groin. Very gently, Conneau took the stub of his cigarette from between his fingers and pushed up the stiff cuff to feel for the pulse in that flaccid wrist. Then as the treasurer, obeying his nod, went on tiptoe to tell the valet to prepare the Emperor's bed, Dr. Conneau reached out for the medicine he had set down on the great desk, and held it to Napoleon's lips.

At about the same time as the ailing Emperor was being assisted to bed by his servants, James Bruce, in robust health, was getting out of a cab at the main entrance of the Bois.

The infectious sense of holiday sparkling in the Place Vendôme, where he bought the flowers for Madeleine, had sent him straight through the sunny streets, crowded with Parisians on their round of New Year calls, to the Bois de Boulogne. Since the days when business had taken him to the old cramped Paris of King Louis Philippe, half stifled in its ring of forts, he had watched the construction of the Faubourg St. Honoré, the Parc Monceau and the beautiful avenues west of the Arc de Triomphe

56

with an engineer's eye. Now, with a rising sense of pleasure and excitement, he strolled along the wooded allées laid out on what had been a wet marshy waste of shacks and truck gardens beside the Seine.

The winter sun was sinking behind the Bois, and the great procession of carriages round the two lakes began to thin out as the fashionable world ended its New Year's drive and started for home. The "Ladies of the Lake" pulled the fur cloaks closer round their throats, the fur rugs more snugly round their knees. Few of them supposed, as they drove serenely into the red sunset of the first day of 1870, that they were also driving into the sunset of an age which ever since the *Dame aux Camélias* expired in the bloody froth of consumption had glorified prostitution and set an inflated value on the embraces of the courtesan. The hours of the famous kept women were numbered. Less than three hundred days of 1870 would see the breaking of the spell which caused men to pour out fortunes in jewels, furs, horses and furniture to gratify the greed of mistresses who would end where they had been born—on straw—and to vie with one another for the fly-blown favours of light women in the same way as they competed on the Bourse for control of mines and railroads. But on New Year's Day the great show still went on. The matched greys, the piebald ponies, the black steppers drew the most expensive whores on earth round the ring. The pines grew black against the sky and a little fleet of moor hens with bright red beaks cruised tirelessly round and round the iris-coloured waters of the lake. For twenty minutes Bruce stood by the railings, looking on with the dandies of the town, although he knew too little about the demimonde of Paris to recognize many of the notables. He thought he saw Hortense Schneider, but he missed La Païva, sulking at her Prussian bully, Henckel von Donnersmarck, and he missed Madame Musard, who had risen from the kitchen of an Ohio tavern to become the mistress of the King of the Netherlands. Of them all he was only sure of Cora Pearl, whom he had seen on the stage as Cupidon, and who had recently started a fashion of being served up to her men friends at supper stark naked on an outsize silver dish. Once when two equipages drove too close in the double ring and there was a halt in the procession, he saw Michel Bertaux, upright and benevolent in a maroon-coloured brougham, and his heart stopped. But the financier's companion was a vivacious redhead, fondling two yapping white Pomeranians; and soon after they passed James left the Bois and walked with great strides back to the city by the avenue de l'Imperatrice.

At the Etoile, where the rays of the setting sun struck through the Arc de Triomphe, he saw Paris in her splendour, as the carriages of the rich drove home down the avenue du Roi de Rome, the avenue Joséphine, the avenue de la Reine Hortense and all the other spokes of a golden wheel eclipsed in brilliance only by the Champs Elysées, where the Parisians were enjoying the last daylight moments of the New Year. Behind him violet shadows were lengthening across the Bois, and the fortress of Mont Valérien, the strong point of the fortifications on the west of Paris, could be dimly seen as a huge dark bulk against the sky. Before him the long slope of the Champs Elysées seemed to shimmer with powdered gold all the way down to the Rond Point, where the man who hired out goat carriages beneath the bare chestnuts was leading his little flock of twelve goats away to their barn on the other side of the Seine. The lights of two double rows of red and white gas lamps came on all along the avenue, while at the foot, in the Place de la Concorde, the new electricity was employed to throw the national colours, blue, white and red, on the jets of water from the great fountains. It was the *Ville Lumière* of Napoleon III's creation, a city rippling with light, as James Bruce, with his long vision, looked over the glitter to where the Tuileries straddled across the entire space from the rue de Rivoli to the Seine. The standard hung motionless in the frosty air above the Clock Pavilion, and the rows and rows of windows reflected the light from the city, as if the palace were on fire.

James walked down the Champs Elysées like a man possessed. Somewhere inside that palace was Madeleine d'Arbonne.

"Hev' I the pleesure of addressin' Mr. James Bruce?"

The strong Scots accent roused James from the reverie into which he had fallen while a mutton chop congealed on the plate before him. There were only a few other guests at the early table d'hôte of the Hotel St. Honoré, a modest establishment run by an Englishman named Unthank, and the individual who had pulled up a chair on the opposite side of the dinner table was a stranger to him. He was a short, lean man with an inquisitive snout, a fringe of brindled whisker above a rusty black neckcloth and a high-buttoned frock coat of old-fashioned cut. A trumpet stethoscope was sticking out of his breast pocket.

"You have the advantage of me, sir," said James in his coolest manner, and the little man laughed.

"Aye, that's the auld Jeems Bruce," he said cheerfully. " 'Gentleman James,' that had more lang-nebbit words and white-iron English to his command than ony ither lad in the King's College o' Aberdeen. Don't you not mind on me? I'm Hector Munro, that stood thirtieth in Bajan mathematics when you were first prizeman—and that was the year '48, by my count!"

James, with his rare charming smile, stretched a hand across the table.

"Hector Munro—of course I remember you! You began to study medicine, when I went to serve my time at Hall's. Is it really twenty years since we were students at King's?"

"It's all that, but you've kept your age far better nor what I have. My head's as white as a badger's bottom, but I kent you the moment ye cam' stalkin' in! Ye see I was half expectin' you: I knew you was comin' to Paris, and this is a great howff for our folk. Waiter! Bring ben a bottle o' whisky, and a kettle o' b'ilin' water, fire-hot, and lemons, and sugar. We'll have a New Year toddy, Mr. Bruce, and drink to the year Eichteen hunder' and Saiventy."

"Suppose we change that order, Munro? A whisky punch means a fairly long session, and I'm going out this evening. Let me offer you a glass of brandy instead."

Munro laid one finger to his remarkably sharp and reddened nose.

"Gettin' in trim for the Tuileries, eh? The Emp'ror will gie ye a bottle o' champagne to yer own cheek at the supper table, and a pint o' good claret into the beat o' the bargain; but durin' the dancing they serve nothing but rum punch and sangwitches, so sit in about and taste the Mountain Dew while ye may."

"How the devil did you know that I was going to the palace?"

"Ah, weel, that's part o' the story o' ma life, Jeems man," said Hector Munro. "Ye see, I opened a surgery in Huntly—that's where I come from—and I warstled awa' there, year in year out, drawin' teeth here and giein' the midwives a hand there, and whiles even glad o' a consultation wi' the fairrier when the Duke o' Richmond had a pedigree mare in foal. At lang length it dawned upon me that the folk in Strathbogie were just naturally healthy and I would never mak' ma fortune there. So last year I sold ma practice and cam' to try ma luck in Paris. There's mony an honest half-guinea to be made among the British tourists, when they've eaten and drunken till they're laid low wi' the bellyache."

"Are you married, Munro?"

"Nae fears! If I had a wife, I would still be at hame in Huntly. Weel, it's uphill work in Paris, but it's aye divertin', and the porter at the British Embassy has been right nice aboot lettin' me see wha signs the book. Then I pay a call on the nobs at their hotels, and offer ma professional services. Sometimes I even get a keek at the imperial list, and that's the way I saw your name. I'm goin' to the Tuileries maself tonight—does that surprise ye? Oh, I'll just be one o' the crowd, ye ken—it's only swells like you that gets in under the Ambassador's wing; but what do you say we tak' a cab along together, and halver the expenses?"

James escaped from him after the second rummer of toddy, and went upstairs to dress. When he came quietly down again the little doctor was still punishing the Mountain Dew, and it was easy for James to dodge the proposed economy in cab fare, and make his way alone to the palace. He had no intention of making a comic entry at the Tuileries with a cheerful clown like his former classmate, and in the event nothing could have been more dignified than his appearance in the Galérie de la Paix. Walking up the grand staircase lined with motionless soldiers of the Cent-Gardes, the Emperor's crack parade troops, and leisurely putting on his white kid gloves, James Bruce was taller by half a head than most of the chattering Frenchmen and their ladies pressing up toward the ballroom in a wave of silk and scent and brilliant uniforms. He was not a vain man, but the mirrors in the gallery told him unmistakably that no costume had ever suited his dark good looks better than the court dress created at short notice by Poole. Black coat, satin knee breeches and silk stockings might have been designed to show off his broad shoulders and strong legs. "A sad expense," was his inward comment as a footman in green and gold bowed him into the Salle du Premier Consul, "but worth the money. If I join Management next year I may wear it at Windsor Castle yet! And tonight, at least, I won't appear before *her* dressed like an Arab stoker!"

"Good evening to you, Mr. Bruce," said the British Ambassador affably, as the engineer approached. "Delighted to see you here! You've saved face for me tonight by giving me at least *one* national to present to His Majesty. My American colleague, Mr. Washburne, has twenty-eight!"

Lord Lyons, who forty years earlier had been a midshipman in H.M.S. *Blonde* and still retained some of the gusto of the Navy, smilingly pointed out the plight of the American Minister, who was the centre of an agitated group. Restrained by Congress from appearing in knee breeches, Elihu B. Washburne looked anything but happy as the heavy trains and back draperies of his fair countrywomen swished about his respectable republican legs.

"Do Your Excellencies keep a score in such matters?" asked James with a smile.

"We do indeed, and Washburne is well ahead tonight!" said Lord Lyons. Their conversation was cut short by the sound of a bugle, and the groups round each of the foreign envoys quickly moved out to form two half circles, of men and women, as eight

Swiss Guards in red baldrics filed into the room and struck their staves in unison upon the floor as the Emperor and Empress of the French came in.

Although James held no particular brief for the policies of Napoleon III he was impressed by the mystery and power surrounding the lumpish man with the huge waxed moustache and the great scarlet plaque of the Legion of Honour on his white shirt front. The Empress, that night, was a little less lovely than James remembered her from El Kantara. The new sheath dresses were not so becoming to her as the crinoline. She was still slender, but with just the thickening of middle age at waist and shoulder which made the skin-tight gown a little difficult for her to wear. Even her beautiful bosom seemed to be broadened by the wide purple ribbon of the Spanish Order of Maria Luisa.

When James had seen the Empress at Port Said and El Kantara, Madeleine d'Arbonne had been so near her that he instinctively expected the maid of honour to follow the imperial couple into the Salle du Premier Consul. It was for her that he squared his shoulders, watched the doorway in which Their Majesties stood bowing to their guests. But no lady or gentleman of the court was in attendance. It was their thirteen-year-old son, the Child of France, who followed his parents into the room.

Eugène Louis Jean Joseph Napoléon, the Prince Imperial, was the only child whom Eugénie, after two miscarriages, had brought to birth. He was the innocent cause of the long disharmony between his father and mother, for Dubois, her accoucheur, had allowed her to suffer so long at his birth and had damaged her body so completely that she had never dared to risk another pregnancy. The Prince Imperial was a short stocky boy with his father's inelegant figure and only a trace of his mother's delicacy of feature, but he and the Empress made an appealing couple as she took him by the hand and led him round the half-circle of curtsying ladies.

Slowly the Emperor worked his way round the semi-circle of gentlemen. At last the moment came when Lord Lyons was heard to say very distinctly, as James bowed low,

"Mr. James Bruce of Sauchentree."

The heavy lids flew up, some trace of animation came into the ashen face and the Emperor said in his husky voice.

"Ah! the hero of El Kantara! It is a pleasure to know you, sir." And with a look over his shoulder he summoned his consort. "Ugénie! Here is someone you have met before!"

She came across the gleaming floor at once, and against all protocol gave James her hand to kiss.

"The Emperor has heard the whole story of your generous and skilful act, monsieur."

"Your Imperial Majesty honours me by the recollection. It was a very little thing."

"It was a great occasion for us, monsieur. Thanks to you, I can look back on the seventeenth of November as one of the happiest days of my life."

James bowed again in silence. The Emperor, who had been smiling and tugging at his moustache, continued round the room. When the presentations were completed the Imperial Family passed into the Salle des Maréchaux, and the cheering of six hundred guests echoed through the walls of the Tuileries.

There was a gallery in the ballroom, in which James took his place just as Herr Waldteufel led the orchestra into the opening bars of the imperial anthem. From where he stood he could look over a solid field of French uniforms, Chasseurs, Voltigeurs, Eclaireurs, Zouaves; the pale blue, the green facings, the gold; the red tunics and kilts of Highland officers; the robes of North African caids; the white satin breeches and the black; the beautiful dresses and jewels of the women, set against a background of scarlet draperies fringed with bullion, palms and camellias prodigally supplied by the official florists at La Muette and the twelve life-size oil paintings of the great Napoleon's marshals from which the ballroom took its name.

The imperial couple stood side by side in front of thrones placed on a dais between two marble caryatides supporting a velvet canopy. The Prince Imperial, and Monsieur Ollivier with the members of the future government, stood on the Emperor's left; the princesses and the twelve Ladies of the Palace were grouped at Eugénie's right. James, for all his long sight, could see no one who looked like Madeleine, and for the first time his confidence faltered. Was it possible that she might not be present at the ball? What to do then? Inquire for her through some of the servants? Pay his respects to the Comtesse d'Arbonne, or—

Herr Waldteufel lifted his baton, and the orchestra crashed into *Partant Pour la Syrie*. They did so by a strong effort of musicianship, for there was nothing martial or inspiring about the song which for twenty years had taken the place of the glorious *Marseillaise*. It was a feeble, rambling, mock-medieval ballad written long ago by Hortense de Beauharnais and set to music by one of her many lovers, which ever since the coup d'état had been the official salute to her son the Emperor.

> *For Syria departing, the handsome young Dunois*
> *Begged Mary at her altar to bless all his exploits,*
> *'Grant, Mary Queen of Heaven!'—such was his last appeal—*
> *'That my love be the fairest, myself first in the field.'*

"Tak' a look at Napoleon," said a voice in Bruce's ear. "That's a sang he's more than sick of, but he has to thole it for his mother's sake!"

Dr. Munro had arrived in the gallery, and was peering over his classmate's shoulder. He had prepared for the ball by exchanging his black neckcloth for a white cravat, and leaving the trumpet stethoscope at home.

"You're there, are you?" said James ill-naturedly, as they took their seats, and the honour quadrille began on the floor below.

"There they go!" said Dr. Munro. "Off to anither evenin's jollification. Man, isn't it not an awful-like and solemn thing for two auld Scots bachelors like me and you to be sittin' here on this volcano they call the court o' France, not sure but what it'll erupt at any minute? Look at the Emp'ror—drugged to the eyes to get through the night—I've seen a better colour on a cadaver new fished from the Seine! Hematorrhea, and cystitis, that's his trouble. Aye! And the wee touch o' Venus, ye ken, that doesna help an auld man to heal! Look at Prince Napoleon, that would cut the Emp'ror's throat tonight, and the little lad's too, if he thocht he had a chance to wear the crown! Look at his poor wee

64

wife, Princess Clotilde, that they mairriet off to him as part o' the Italian deal when she was a lassie just fifteen: wouldn't she not willingly play the Borgia, and slip poison in Prince Napoleon's cup if she got the chance? Did ye ever hear o' Prince Pierre Bonaparte, old Lucien's son, that they ca' the Wild Boar o' Corsica? Murder is *his* line. He began wi' killin' a poor Italian gamekeeper, and then a papal guard at Rome, when he was only a laddie; and now he's banned from court, the most blackguardly pistoller in France. Still and on," as James showed signs of protest, "it's out o' such folk that honest men can make good pickings," said the prudent doctor. "If I can struggle through this coming year, I'll not be the first practitioner that has feathered a cosy nest in Paris in troubled times! D'ye see yon wee fat man standin' near the thrones, on the Emp'ror's side, not far from Mr. Ollivier?"

"A man with muttonchop whiskers? Yes, I do."

"That's Tom Evans from Philadelphia, Surgeon-Dentist to the court. He had the wit to set up in practice here, in the days when if ye had a sair tooth ye went off to the Palais Royal and got a man in a red jacket to yark it out on the pavement, wi' a laddie beatin' a drum to drown yer howls. When Napoleon came to the Elysée, Tommy was there to draw his fangs, verra canny and gentle, and always ready to spend an evenin' wi' him and Miss Howard over the cards an' the wine. By the time old Nap got mairriet and the Howard woman was pensioned off Evans was indispensable, and gettin' good tips on the property zoned for development. They say he bought half of what's now the avenue de l'Impératrice for little mair than a song."

"The porter at the British Embassy must be a mine of information," said Bruce. "Excuse me, Munro, will you?" He had seen Madeleine d'Arbonne walk out to join the second figure of the honour quadrille.

She was dressed in plain white satin, with a spray of golden laurel bound into the thick upswept hair that mailed her head in living gold. Her hand was placed lightly on the arm of a tall young man in the palace uniform of the Imperial Guard. Unhampered by the long court train hanging from the shoulders, which as an unmarried woman she was not entitled to wear, her movements were very free and graceful. But her jewels were not a young girl's ornaments, and even Princess Metternich and Princess Rimsky-Korsakov, who were blazing, it was the fashion to say, "like mines of uncut diamonds," wore stones no more perfectly matched than those which Michel Bertaux had hung round the neck of Madeleine d'Arbonne.

Her partner, swinging the dolman upon his shoulder, led her up to the steps of the dais, and Madeleine sank down in the sweeping court curtsy, head erect, hands touching the ground. The pallid Emperor leaned forward to scan her with the leaden eye of an old voyeur, and Eugénie gave her sweetest smile to the graceful girl at her feet. The velvet draperies stirred very softly between the great marble caryatides. There was nothing to remind the sovereigns, or Madeleine, that there were words still scrawled beneath the purple curtains—words which all the scrubbings and scourings of twenty years back had not erased when the new tenants came in to the Tuileries, and which still, though very faintly, read:

> Long live the Republic!
> Long live Liberty!
> For the THIRD time reconquered,
> February 22, 23, 24—
> Eighteen Hundred and Forty Eight!

*   *   *

James had her out on the floor and they were dancing. He had taken her away from her partner at the end of the quadrille, and led her back to the parquet with her gloved hand clasped firmly in his own. Now he was waltzing with Madeleine d'Arbonne, and the great crystal chandeliers, the white fiddle bows, the gleaming caryatides were spinning about them as they revolved.

It was years since James Bruce had attended a ball. At the last, given by one of the London City Companies, the ladies wore crinolines and wreaths of flowers and the ballroom resounded to the clash of steel as their "cages" collided and sometimes even capsized.

He looked down at Madeleine's breast, and the folds of satin above which the pendants of her diamond necklace glittered, and wondered how he had dared to hope that his modest rosebuds might be fastened there. He realized that with the old barrier of the crinoline removed there was a new temptation for a man in love—to press a woman's body, so frankly moulded by its close soft draperies, nearer and nearer to his own.

Was he in love with her? What did she feel for him? That look she gave him when she saw him standing there, that graceful readiness to dance; this soft, pliant swaying in his arms—did it mean that she, too, had thought about Ismailia? Madeleine's face told him nothing. Under the thousand candles, the twelve hundred eyes of the Tuileries she wore her court mask, faintly smiling, deliberately sweet. Only the quickened breathing, the faintest pressure of the hand he held, encouraged him to guide her, when the music stopped, from the dancing floor to one of the great doors leading to the Galérie de la Paix.

The first movement toward the supper rooms had begun, and the long gallery was crowded with the Emperor's guests. James handed Madeleine to a small velvet sofa near the top of the grand staircase, and took his place, standing, by her side.

"Mademoiselle d'Arbonne"—even in his own ears the formal address sounded stiff—"we meet in a crowd again, where it's hardly possible to talk freely. There is so much I want to say to you—and to hear!"

She hardly looked at him. Her blue eyes were scanning the moving throng, and more than once she recognized a friend with a graceful little bend of the head. But she had been listening to him, for she said,

"I thought we had a charming little conversation, before the band struck up the waltz?"

"Yes indeed," said James. "We discussed your good health, my good health, your mother's poor health, the criminal carelessness of the Egyptians in a matter of fireworks and the de Lesseps wedding. That's not what I came to the Tuileries to hear! Is there no place where we can talk alone? Or better still, may I be permitted to call upon you in your own home, at leisure?"

Now she looked at him, half laughing, half surprised.

"But *have* you leisure for paying calls when you come to Paris? Aren't you always—what did you tell Her Majesty—'in transit'?"

James took it in deadly earnest.

"I'm in transit now," he said. "I leave for Marseilles tomorrow; on Monday we start the first inspection before re-engining the fleet. But I can spend a little time in Paris on my way back to London. I shall come to Paris at any time, now or later, when there is the slightest hope of seeing you."

She looked up at him, where he stood beside her, and saw in his firm mouth and faintly frowning brow that he meant exactly what he said. She felt a little flutter of mingled fear and pleasure at the admission of feeling made by such a man, whom it was impossible to measure by the yardstick of the court. Everything that was teasing and capricious in her bubbled up in the determination to test him, as in one way or another, through the years, she had tested all her suitors and found them wanting.

"Come," she said, getting up and shaking out her satin train, "if you find this part of the Tuileries so crowded I will show you another, where our friends may always call on us when we are in waiting. Unless my mother's health improves we shall not receive at home this winter."

She led the way across the Galérie to the big double doors opposite the ballroom, which a lackey flung open at her approach. James followed her into a small anteroom, empty except for two pages talking quietly on an oak settle near the fire, who got up and bowed to Madeleine.

"This is the ushers' room," said Madeleine. "Monsieur Bignet and the men on duty must be in Her Majesty's private apartments. We may go where we please in the public rooms."

The three salons on the garden side of the Tuileries were especially dear to the Empress Eugénie. The great rooms on the Carrousel side were heavy with the history of France and with the hopes and fears of her own life as Empress: she was always consciously regal when she looked out on the balcony where she had greeted her husband's subjects as a bride, or recalled the last departure from the Tuileries of her guillotined predecessor, Queen Marie Antoinette. But into the garden salons, always bright and warm in the afternoon sun, she had poured her own intense femininity, and nowhere in all the royal residences were there apartments which more clearly reflected the personal tastes of the Empress. The three salons had been enlarged and modernized on the Emperor's marriage in a style considered very advanced at a time when interior decorators were just introducing "all-to-match" colour schemes to Paris. In the Green Salon, which James and Madeleine entered first, the greenery was relieved by paintings of tropical birds above the doors and windows, and the room itself was so constantly used by the twelve Ladies and the maids of honour that its magnificence had a certain domestic charm.

There were nearly a score of people in the Green Salon, standing near the fire or chatting on green plush S-shaped sofas, called *confidences* if meant for two and *indiscrétions* if for three. To some of them Madeleine informally presented Mr. Bruce, watching quick interest kindle in the appraising eyes of other women.

"So this is where you spend your days?" said James as they moved through the big room, looking at the tables loaded with albums and sheet engravings and at the stands of hothouse plants.

"Here, or in some other room just like it, every alternate week from October until June; and all through the summer with no break at all."

"Always dancing, driving, travelling from place to place? Always 'in transit'?"

Madeleine's blue eyes sparkled appreciatively. Her own small barb had been neatly returned.

"Naturally the court can't remain in Paris all the time," she said. "We go to Fontainebleau for Easter, spend the early summer at St. Cloud, take the waters at Vichy in July, attend the Châlons manoeuvres in August, go on to Biarritz, then back to Paris, out to Compiègne for hunting in November—that's the way it goes. But wherever we happen to be, our distractions are very dull, I assure you! We embroider, read aloud, play charades, listen to talks by college professors. We always have some 'mania' or other in hand. We've had decalcomania, and dubronimania—you know, reducing sun pictures to the size of postage stamps—and now the craze is for potichomania, which is supposed to turn honest jam jars into porcelain—" She indicated a long table covered, like a charity bazaar booth, with various samples of the ladies' industry.

"Are you any good at this sort of thing?" James turned a potichomania vase gingerly in his big hands.

"I? Not at all. Do you know what my uncle says of me? He says"—and here Madeleine's lips and cheeks puffed out, her voice, deepened and hoarse, took on an absurd resemblance to that of Bertaux— " 'I don't know why they keep you on at court, Madeleine! You can't sing, you can't play any musical instrument and you never think before you speak! You're more fit to be a jockey than a maid of honour!' "

She stopped in smiling confusion as James Bruce's hearty laugh rang out in a peal of such genuine and confident amusement as was seldom heard in that palace, and the seated courtiers looked up in amazement from their low-voiced talk. Impulsively she led the way out of the room, and James followed her into the Rose Salon, where Chaplin had painted a Triumph of Flora on the ceiling. The Empress, painted as the goddess of flowers, watched over her son as an infant Cupid, while around them clustered Loves and Graces drawn from the court ladies of ten years before. The walls and furnishings were carried out in matching and slightly insipid pink. In the Blue Salon, Madeleine pointed out a series of medallion paintings of the most beautiful women of the Sixties, grouped as blondes and brunettes round the walls.

Between the Blue room and the Rose was another of the curious anterooms, which all the replanning of the palace had not quite abolished, empty but for one or two pieces of antique furniture and a dying fire in the basket grate. Madeleine, who well knew its function (for here, late at night, when the Empress had a migraine and all were wakeful and ill at ease, she had sometimes come upon the non-committal figures of one or more of Monsieur Maupas' secret police), would have hurried back to the light and warmth of the Rose Salon. But James Bruce had taken her compellingly by the hand, and beneath the white *glacé* glove she felt the heat of his bare palm rekindling that extraordinary community of the flesh which she had first felt at Ismailia. He detained her there, no more than holding her by the hand, while the little sounds began to be heard in the little room —of rats in the wainscot, mice nibbling through discarded velvet and miniver, voices in guardrooms far away but carried through invisible air shafts from one wing of the palace to another. They heard the voice of the Tuileries: the creaking of forbidden doors, the crumble of worm-eaten woods, footsteps on tiptoe. They could smell the Tuileries: the sweat-stained uniforms and the velvet gowns of governesses, steamed and turned by schoolroom fires; rooms with windows that refused to open, windowless passages where oil lamps burned by night and day. Through it all, faint but unmistakable, came the odour of the commodes and *chaises percées* of sanitation dating from the previous century.

"I must return to the ballroom, monsieur. The Emperor had a fainting fit this afternoon, and Their Majesties are sure to retire early. We have to attend them as they walk through the Galérie Diane to their private apartments."

"Yes, of course. But must your evening end with theirs? Mayn't I have the privilege of taking you in to supper, later on?"

She said almost reluctantly, for her hand was still fast in his, "I'm engaged to sup with my partner in the quadrille—the Marquis de Mortain. He was wounded in the Algerian fighting not long ago. Victor would be furious if I broke my promise to him."

"Then may I see you when I come back from Marseilles, a week or ten days from now?" James persisted.

"Very well!" said Madeleine recklessly. "Write to me here— not at home! I'll escape—I'll run away for a few hours. You shall take me out to dinner, somewhere very bright and gay, and we'll pretend we're back in Ismailia again, and the evening has just started."

She stopped, as he lifted her gloved hand to his lips and began to kiss it. His mouth found her wrist, where the little pearl buttons were undone, and her pulse began to beat faster beneath his lips.

"I don't want pretence," he said, and took her in his arms.

In that exquisite moment of yielding, as she gave herself up to the hard embrace she remembered so well, Madeleine's court discipline asserted itself and she drew away from him.

71

"Not here! Not here!"

The sinister little anteroom, haunted by the ghosts of the Tuileries—perhaps even then raked through a knothole by the eyes of a police spy—was no place for the kisses of a man like the Scots engineer. She drew him after her, determinedly, back into the Rose Salon. Someone had opened the curtains and extinguished most of the lights in the gaseliers. Only candles burned now in the wreathed girandoles upon the walls. Outside, the gardens lay empty and bright under the lines of lamps running clear to the gates of the Place de la Concorde. The whole scene was reflected in four tall mirrors set in the rear wall of the salon like an underwater landscape in which the winter branches were the fronds of seaweed, the myriad lights of the Place de la Concorde the twinkling of phosphorescent fish. Far away, under a foam of moonlight, the Arc de Triomphe was mistily outlined like a rosy coral reef.

"Look at Paris in the mirror!" said Madeleine, delighted.

"It's wonderful by moonlight."

"It's always wonderful," said Madeleine. "In the afternoon the Empress loves to sit at her tea table, over there, and watch the people in the glass. Sometimes we invent stories, each lady tells a different part, about the men and women we see passing by."

"In the mirror!" said James, surprised. He looked out at the wintry gardens and back again at their vague and shimmering reflection. "But then—aren't you seeing Paris the wrong way round?"

III

On the third of January, as James Bruce began his inspection tour aboard the S.S. *Malabar* in the P. and O. dock at Marseilles, the new government started to function in Paris under the optimistic title of the Ministry of Honest Men.

In a matter of days, Monsieur Ollivier and his cabinet were at grips with one of the worst scandals of the reign, when the Emperor's cousin, Prince Pierre Bonaparte, shot and killed a journalist in his own house at Auteuil.

The Wild Boar of Corsica, although an outcast from the Imperial Family, had taken it upon himself to resent some particularly scurrilous attack on the Bonapartes in an opposition newspaper, the *Marseillaise*. His victim, a young Jew named Solomon who wrote for the paper under the name of Victor Noir, had called formally on the prince with another second, Ulrich de Fonvielle, to arrange a duel on behalf of their editor, such visits being standard practice during the Second Empire, when duelling was among the occupational hazards of French newspapermen.

When Pierre Bonaparte's blackguardly temper got the better of him, and he fired his pistol at Victor Noir, de Fonvielle fled out of the fatal house and spread the story far and wide. Within an hour Paris rang with it. In the Legislature, Henri de Rochefort, himself the editor of a banned and scurrilous rag called the *Lanterne*, was demanding vengeance for the blood of Victor Noir. The whole Left Wing took up the cry, and as darkness fell angry crowds were gathering in the workers' quarters of Paris. Clandestine arms made their appearance and a few barricades were thrown up in the streets.

The Emperor, spending the day in the country, heard the news of the murder at a Paris railway station, and was helped home to the Tuileries in a state of collapse. The government thereupon took strong measures. While de Rochefort and his friends made plans to hold a huge political funeral for Victor Noir, Monsieur

Ollivier sent police to arrest the Emperor's cousin, and ordered the troops to stand to arms in every barracks in Paris.

"Mademoiselle really ought not to go out into the streets to-day!" said Michel Bertaux' head coachman to Madeleine d'Arbonne as she crossed the courtyard of her uncle's house on the morning after the murder. The man, dressed in his maroon livery and cocked hat, was supervising the stablemen as they drew a great antiquated daumont slowly into the cobbled yard.

"You don't give a rap about me, Emile," said Madeleine good-naturedly. "All you care about is your horseflesh and coachwork! But I don't expect to meet any rioters between here and the Quai Voltaire, and neither will you. Follow me as soon as the horses are put in."

The daumont was going to bring her father home; or back, at least, to his wife and children; the crest on those maroon panels was her father's crest, with the Crusader's cockleshells and the ancient motto *Foy, Roy, Arbonne* emblazoned on the newly painted panels by the courtesy and the cash of Michel Bertaux. And the last, or all but the last, of her father's own retainers opened a small door beside the great gates to let her pass : a scowling old man who was never called anything but "the Old Poisson," and who was now on the payroll of Monsieur Bertaux, whom he despised.

Madeleine had never in her life walked alone in the streets of Paris. Followed now by her maid Marthe, she set out at a swift pace towards the rue Royale, noting that some of the luxury shops in the Faubourg St. Honoré had run down their iron shutters, but too delighted with the fresh air and freedom to let her mind dwell on the danger of a riot. Just as they reached the Place de la Concorde she heard the regular one-two, one-two-three, of the drums announcing that the Emperor was leaving the Tuileries. The garden gates were thrown open, and a group of shabby loungers at once burst into applause. They were members of the claque whom Maupas of the secret police had organized to lead popular demonstrations for Napoleon III. Now there were too few people in the Place to make an enthusiastic crowd; the cries of "*Vive l'Emp'rrreur!*" rang hollow on the air.

The Emperor, impassive as ever, had no escort other than the aide-de-camp in uniform who sat beside him in the phaeton. His silk hat was set jauntily on the back of his head, a cigarette was stuck in the corner of his mouth : the whole calculated effect was that of a healthy man equal to anything the day might bring. From the way he was handling his American trotters, Jersey and Cob, Madeleine judged that he meant to reach St. Cloud, six miles away, in less than his usual twenty minutes. The Champs Elysées, she saw, had been cleared for him, and mounted Municipal Guards were posted in the side streets. "He has to do this !" she thought compassionately. "He *has* to show himself in public this morning, even if up there at the Etoile, when the phaeton slows in the circle, a friend of Victor Noir should be waiting for him with a pistol !"

She crossed the Place de la Concorde pensively, and entered the world, almost unknown to her, of the royalist Faubourg St. Germain, where in their mouldering *hôtels particuliers* and vast chilly apartments, the supporters of the exiled Bourbons nursed their wrath against the Revolution, the Bonapartes, the Bourse profiteers of the Second Empire and in particular against Napoleon III and his empress, Eugénie. No motives of patriotism or even of common politeness could curb the rancour of these French aristocrats against the upstarts who had replaced the old world of Versailles which their grandparents had seen blown to bits around them. St. Germain was pro-Russia when Imperial France was engaged in the Crimean War. St. Germain, for all its blue blood, was as vulgar as de Rochefort in the nicknames it gave the Imperial Family. To the ruined and embittered aristocrats of the *ancien régime* Napoleon III was always "Badinguet"—supposedly the name of the workman who connived at his escape from Ham prison—the Empress was "Madame Badinguet," and "The Bear Garden," or "Badinguet's Travelling Circus" were two of the least offensive names bestowed on the court of the Tuileries.

Madeleine's father, who belonged to the Faubourg St. Germain by birth, had been dropped by royalist society as soon as he married the socially impossible sister of a buccaneer like Michel Bertaux. His wife and daughters were now received only in a gloomy, mice-infested apartment in the rue du Bac where two old d'Arbonne cousins were dragging out an aimless existence, although there had been a time when the rue du Bac and all the streets between the Seine and the Pré aux Clercs had been part of the d'Arbonne estates. The town house of Madeleine's ancestors, still standing on the Quai Voltaire, was now divided into flats and studios and famous only because a great modern artist had painted there.

The d'Arbonnes themselves had been soldiers of France for many generations. A squire of the house had knelt beside St. Louis when the royal Crusader breathed his last in Africa. The Comte Philippe of his day had followed Francis I from the fatal field of Pavia, and one of his descendants had ridden by Marshal Saxe's side to victory at Fontenoy. His successor had gambled away, over the tables at Versailles, the title to his city dwelling; then came the Revolution, when the Comte d'Arbonne of that time had been one of the few aristocrats able to crack a joke at the expense of Sanson, as the executioner strapped him into place beneath the guillotine. Madeleine's father had been born in Belgium, where his parents had fled with the Bourbon princes, but through all the troubles and losses of the Emigration the family had somehow managed to hold on to a small apartment in their former *hôtel*; saved for them, it was said, by the father of the Old Poisson now in the Bertaux service. The Young Poisson, a youth of fifty, shared with his wife the duties of concierge at the old house on the Quai Voltaire.

"Good day, mademoiselle, this is a great honour! Monsieur le comte will be delighted!" Madame Poisson, a plump little woman with snapping dark eyes, rushed out to drop a curtsy as soon as the young lady came into her courtyard. Madeleine made a little amiable conversation about the Poisson boys, Robert and René, who were both serving in Line regiments, one of them in Algeria, before leaving Marthe to announce the imminent arrival of the daumont. Then she began the climb to the fourth floor, where with only an attic, the merest *cagibi*, between him and the old red tiles, her father had gone into seclusion in his ancestral home.

Louis Marie Joseph Dieudonné, seventeenth Comte d'Arbonne,

opened the door to his daughter with a saucepan in his hand, from which arose a savoury smell of beef stew and onion. He had no fixed hours for eating, and though a strip of kitchen had been cut out of the long room, half library and half salon, which looked over the towers of St. Sulpice and the Sorbonne, he preferred to cook over two iron firedogs in the big grate, with the condiments set ready to his hand along the mantel shelf and a round citronwood table pulled up in readiness for his simple meal. He was in his seventieth year, a clean-shaven man of short stature, having bright dark eyes and curly dark hair without much grey in it: d'Arbonne characteristics, handed on in the present generation to Adèle and Louise. Special to the Count was a flyaway manner—a false gaiety which he had assumed in exile and never discarded in prosperity.

He capered round his daughter now with a wealth of small caresses and admiring cries as he drew off her sealskin jacket and settled her in an armchair by the fire.

"Alone, my dear? No pretty Louise today? No handsome escort from the Imperial Guard?"

"My maid is downstairs, father, gossiping her head off, I've no doubt."

"Your maid—of course; but how brave of you both to venture out! The newspapers say the city is in an uproar."

"I saw no sign of it." Madeleine gave a contemptuous glance at the Left Wing papers which her father, like everyone else in the Faubourg St. Germain, bought for their attacks on the Emperor.

"De Rochefort is making the most of yesterday's misfortune," he said gaily. "That was a neat thing he said this morning—how does it go?" he turned one of the papers over. "Yes—here it is—'in the Bonaparte family, ambush and murder are traditional and obligatory. . . .'"

D'Arbonne's voice droned on. Madeleine sat willing herself to silence. "I will not exasperate him," she thought. "I must not." And she set herself to make an inventory of the familiar objects in the room: the stiff eighteenth-century chairs, the daybed with a worn velvet cover, the tall Norman *armoire*, the desk in front of the double windows covered with scattered sheets of a manuscript on the prosody of the *Chanson de Roland*, on which her father had been actively engaged for thirty years. The walls were quite bare except for two portraits of the martyred Louis XVI and Marie Antoinette. Through the open door of her father's bedroom, Madeleine could see across the Seine to one gable of the Tuileries. "What must it be like," she wondered, "to live here with those relics of the past, and look out every day at the hated present? Poor father!" And she said, "Papa, has Madame Poisson been looking after you properly?"

The Count blinked. "Yes, of course! She buys my food, sweeps and dusts, makes my bed—I'm very comfortable here."

"But not so comfortable, surely, as you are at home, with Frédéric to valet you, and a warm, light room to write in?" It was the first argument that occurred to her. The tall old salon was poorly heated by the log fire, and the far wall even showed a patch of damp.

"Here I'm my own master, Madeleine. Besides," the Count's impish grin flashed out, "as your dear mother has been able to explain on all my previous absences, it's so *very* convenient for the library of the Institut de France!"

"Yes, papa. But that explanation is worn threadbare. And this one has been longer—and different from your other absences from home."

The Count spun round upon one heel.

"In what way, my dear?"

"Because now my mother is seriously ill."

"Really? You mean worse than she deserved to be after that crazy journey through the Indian Ocean, which I forgot my lowly place so far as to forbid? Worse than she was when I paid my respects to her in December?"

"Much worse, I'm afraid. She has some wasting sickness which all the doctors in Paris can't diagnose, and she's getting weaker every day. It's—it's very sad at home now, father."

The old man looked at her in silence, his bright eyes veiled.

"She wants—I know you won't believe it—she wants to get

78

away from Paris. She says she would like to see green fields and grass again. She wants you to take her back to Arbonne."

"Oh!" said the Count after a pause. "Green fields and grass— that's unexpected! Pray is your uncle aware of this new whim?"

"Of course."

"Of course he is! I needn't have asked. Why, we couldn't open the gates of Arbonne without his approval, could we?"

"Father, please—we've been through all this so often. I *know* you feel my uncle has too much say in our lives. I *know* he feels that all we have, we owe to him. I think you're both right, and both wrong, and I won't argue it with you. But for ten years—fifteen!—our home has been wretched because he can neither let go his hold, nor you control him: because we've been torn in two between your world and his. Victor has escaped because he's a man. I escaped to serve Their Majesties, whom you choose to insult, and Adèle accepted the first—the first *creature* who proposed to her, to get away from home. But now Louise is ready to go into society; and she's not like me, father! She won't know how to get her own back when people sneer at her grandfather the fisherman, and her mother the artists' model! She needs the protection of your presence as well as your name. You must come home now for Louise's sake!"

She had risen as she spoke and came across the room with her hands outstretched, to catch at his sleeve where he stood shrunken against the threadbare curtains. Suddenly she seemed to have grown taller. It was a trick of carriage, picked up from the Empress, he supposed, which her father had noticed once or twice before when she took the part of some weaker creature: it changed her from a pretty laughing girl into a grand woman, on whose arm the feeble of the world might rest.

He looked at her—he saw her in that light—for a full minute. Then he jerked his head away, blinking and smirking; the whole expression of his worn aristocratic features showing how little fit he had ever been to be the mainstay of his wife and children.

"What do you want of me, Madeleine?" he said peevishly. "First you ask me to come home for your mother's sake, next you say it's for Louise's. You talk as if the issue lay between your uncle and me! As if you—*poor* little you!—and your sister were being squeezed between two millstones. Have you ever considered your mother's share in all this?"

He thought she said, "More often than you think."

He turned back to the window and looked down into the courtyard, pointing across at the studio, two floors high and with a glass north light in the roof, which stood on the site of the old d'Arbonne stables. A white Persian cat lay licking its fur in a patch of winter sunlight before the door.

"That cat's name is Chérie," said the Comte d'Arbonne in his inconsequent way. "She's a pet of mine! . . . That was the studio of Ingres; you know that, of course. It was at a party Ingres gave there that I saw your mother first. That must have been in '42, not long after I came back to Paris. They hadn't begun to call me 'the Crazy Count' in the back streets of our *quartier* then. But to my friends I was 'poor old Louis d'Arbonne,' and no wonder! Do you realize that I've lived through *two* terms of exile, Madeleine? That I was *born* in exile, and had fifteen years of the Ghent cobblestones and the smug Belgian faces before I ever saw my own country? Well, I was too young to have learned a lesson. I was ready to go through it all a second time, at thirty. To follow King Charles to Scotland and waste my best years in the cold empty rooms of Holyrood, all for the sake of the Crusader's crest, and the words *Foy, Roy, Arbonne*! When I made my peace with the Orleans régime and came home, this was my house of refuge. Madeleine, I have been happy here."

"And my mother?" the daughter whispered. "Where was she then?"

"She was living with the painter, Delacroix."

The bright colour ran out of her cheeks and lips as she looked at him.

"I think you guessed it long ago, my child. You know from the pictures in the Louvre how many times he painted her, and how well. I think you guessed it from Eugène Delacroix himself, when he painted you before he died."

Madeleine nodded.

"Well, I took your mother away from him, and she was glad

to come to me. She was past thirty then; a little like that white cat down there, plump and sleek, with sharp claws beneath the fur, but oh! so caressing and kind when she wished to be! It was the heyday of what we called then 'the Bohemian life'—long before Badinguet and his Spaniard taught us vice—and Marie and I could have been as happy here as any other scribbler and his sweetheart if—"

"If Uncle Michel hadn't stepped in to look after the business arrangements?"

"Quite right, my dear. You have a sharp enough mind when you care to use it. Michel looked after everything, including the priest and the wedding ring. Marie Bertaux became the Comtesse d'Arbonne, and our love for each other was turned by her dear brother into something like another of his transactions on the Bourse."

"A profitable one for all concerned!" said Madeleine dryly.

"Highly profitable. You did well to remind me of that. He bought back Arbonne and settled it on your mother. He installed us all in his house on the rue Laffitte, where you were born, in that charming *ménage à trois* which used to be town talk before Badinguet provided Paris with new topics for gossip. He was always there, planning, purchasing, directing; Marie was always singing the praises of her wonderful brother. How he and she walked barefoot from Trouville to make their fortune in Paris! How he held horses' heads outside the Bourse until he picked up a few tips for speculation on the kerb! Poor old Louis d'Arbonne counted for very little in their brilliant lives!"

"I remember the house on the rue Laffitte," said Madeleine. "It was a dark house."

"So is the new house, Madeleine."

"Father, you're needed there."

The Count's face, so unusually grave and earnest as he looked back into the past, creased into its familiar nervous lines.

"I shouldn't have to see too much of Michel?"

"He won't go to Arbonne in winter, you know that."

"Then I'll come with you, Madeleine."

She took quick advantage of her victory. Telling him that his valet, Frédéric, would be sent over later to pack his clothes and papers, she helped her father to make ready for the street in the flowing paletot and wide-brimmed hat which he affected as a man of letters, and found his favourite gold-headed cane. He submitted to these attentions like a child. But as they were about to leave the old apartment, where the noon sunlight now lay in long bars on the dun-coloured carpet, he surprised her by handing her the key of the door.

"Madame Poisson has another key," he said. "She'll come out and in and keep the place in order. But I want you to have this one. I don't think I'll come back to the Quai Voltaire again. And some day even you, Madeleine, may need a house of refuge."

IV

At eight o'clock that night James Bruce was pacing up and down the avenue Gabriel between a coupé which he had hired for the evening from the Petites Voitures and a tall grille behind which gleamed the lights of the Bertaux mansion.

For a man about to meet the lady he admired, James was not in the best of tempers. He had been vexed to find that the rendezvous, appointed by Madeleine herself in the three-cornered note answering his letter from Marseilles, had brought him to what he took to be the back door to her uncle's house. James was not aware that Bertaux, emulating his rivals the Rothschilds, had built his splendid dwelling with its courtyard, or rear, entrance on the Faubourg St. Honoré and its "palace front" turned to the gardens and sunshine of the Champs Elysées. Through the door on the avenue Gabriel the financier's most distinguished guests had come and gone. The Emperor's brilliant, bastard brother, the Duc de Morny, had slipped in by that way to discuss his schemes with Michel Bertaux; the Comte d'Arbonne had used it to take his little girls for rides in the goat-man's carriages beneath the chestnut trees. Probably neither policy nor sentiment would have influenced the engineer, for whom it was still uncompromisingly *the back door*.

Until her gay little letter reached him, James had been thinking in very serious terms of his next meeting with Madeleine. Their visit to the private rooms of the Tuileries had impressed him, as perhaps she had intended, with her position in the inner circle of the court, and James, who cared little for riches, was Tory enough and romantic enough to be struck by the palace atmosphere of high politics and imperial intrigue.

Besides, the formal courtesy—with an intimation of fire beneath the ice—which she had shown him at the ball had exactly balanced the passion of their first meeting. The two qualities made an irresistible appeal to a man who had never contemplated marriage until now.

In a period when middle age began for men at thirty, James thought of himself as still young at forty, encouraged to do so by his driving energy and youthful good looks. In the hurry of business and ambition he had never been inclined to "settle down," or think of himself as a husband, still less a father, and he did not realize that the part he had played in his brothers' lives, as teacher and arbiter of their careers, was an unconscious usurpation of a father's rôle. As the eldest born he had felt *responsible* for all his brothers and sisters—that was the way he put it—morally bound to help them, both with money and advice. Now, for the first time in his life, he was tempted to lay down those family responsibilities. Now might be the moment to think of a new relationship.

Madeleine d'Arbonne was the girl for him, he had begun to believe; but was she the wife for him? Didn't this rendezvous of her own choosing show that she expected him to embark on an affair of clandestine letters and meetings at the servants' entrance? Then if she was ready to be treated with less than due respect, wasn't he free to take what he could get out of their evening together? She had flung herself into his arms on the promenade at Ismailia. What other favours would she grant in a *cabinet particulier*, where the wide velvet divan in the alcove was half hidden by a well-set table and a laden buffet?

The whole feeling of the night and the city increased the fever of desire which the very thought of a yielding Madeleine aroused in James. Paris lay with her lovely breast unveiled to the stars, and from the river and the gardens, the great restaurants and the lighted cabarets came a sensuous appeal which could almost be smelled and tasted : the appeal of femininity, pleasure, sex. It was the time of the evening when the thoughts of every Parisian with money in his pockets turned to enjoyment, when every woman's turned to her lover; when the boulevards glowed with the gas-lamps of a thousand cafés, dance halls, poolrooms and gambling dives. It was the time when no one thought of tomorrow—even of such a tomorrow as de Rochefort and the Reds were presumably preparing for the city. Already, as James could hear from where he stood, the fiddles of the Jardin Mabille were playing the dancing girls into their first performance of the *chahut*, that tumult of frothy petticoats and kicking legs which took Paris by storm several times a night.

Madeleine heard the same music through her bedroom window (raised a little, as the month of January continued to be so mild) and smiled as she slung a black cloak over her severely cut brown dress. An odd little flurry of military fashions had appeared in the midseason collections, and Madeleine's hat, tipped over her eyes in a cascade of bronze cock's feathers, was described by her modiste as a "Windsor helmet." The combination of black, brown and greenish-bronze, possible only for a sophisticated and very fair woman, was infinitely becoming to Madeleine: she was pleased and excited, her troubles of the morning nearly forgotten, as she tiptoed downstairs, through the conservatory, and allowed Marthe to close the garden door behind her.

For her this outing was a gay adventure—a taste of the freedom she perpetually craved, and just the kind of escapade the *coco-dettes* of the court enjoyed sharing with the *cocottes* of the Bois. Any society woman, married or single, wanted the thrill of courting recognition and scandal by entering a public restaurant or theatre with an admirer, and would risk the even greater thrill of dining in a private room; for the Parisiennes the risk was all. There were some, the most degenerate, who looked for sensation at students' balls, or even on the boulevards, and would slip out of their mansions to masquerade as prostitutes, tasting the ultimate thrill of the blows and brutalities which varied the pattern of paid love. These adventures, small and great, were all capable of leading to blackmail, dreadful family quarrels, face-slappings and horsewhippings at the Jockey or the military clubs, and of course to more duels for the hard-writing, hard-shooting columnists of the daily press.

"There you are!"

James had heard a light footfall on a gravel path before the door swung open, and was ready, silk hat in hand, when the enchant-

85

ing figure appeared, framed in a hood of ivy which topped the gate and draped the grillwork on either side.

"Am I terribly late? I didn't mean to be so late!"

"Only ten minutes," said the literal James, and the cabdriver hastily unhooked his horse's nosebag and led horse and vehicle towards them.

"Where are we going? The Maison Dorée? The Grand Véfour?"

"I think not," said James, and as the light from the first gas lamps of the Place de la Concorde shone inside the cab she saw his grave smile. "I would rather take you to Lapérouse, if you like the place, that is. On the Quai des Grands Augustins."

"I know where it is—a long way away, and very quiet. Can't we go to some place where there's music—like a café-concert on the boulevard?"

James shook his head. He was determined to stand no nonsense about the choice of restaurant, at least. Take her to be stared at in a *caf'-conc'*—as well take her to romp with the medical students at the Bal Bullier! As soon as Madeleine appeared, he had fallen under her spell again, that peculiar blend of innocence and audacity which made him ashamed already of his thoughts on the gaslit avenue. No noisy cabaret and no private room either, for the beautiful girl who had granted his wish of seeing her alone! He trusted to the discretion of Lapérouse, and was gratified by their reception there. After he had directed the driver to wait in a side street and handed Madeleine through the tiny vestibule and up a short narrow stair, they were received by a canonical head-waiter with white Dundreary whiskers, who performed a curious evolution at sight of them: a pivot allowing him to turn either way and show them into one of the dining rooms or to a private room above. The slightest motion of Bruce's head, and the experienced waiter was bowing them into the smaller of the two dining rooms.

There were as yet no other guests at any of the four tables, glittering with silver and crystal, on each of which an épergne held feathery gold plumes of mimosa from the Riviera. Madeleine

86

surrendered her cloak and settled herself with a sigh of pleasure. It was a décor which seemed to suit her exactly: luxurious, and brilliant with the light from the fishtail flames of a dozen gas globes reflected on ivory-painted walls picked out in gilt. Yet, and due perhaps to some trick of perspective caused by the unusually low ceiling, the place had all the intimacy of a shadowy room. It was heavy with the secret embraces of the alcoves overhead as if the mists rising from the Seine, on the far side of the deserted quai, were creeping in through balcony and door.

The dinner began with a glass of dry sherry and a tureen of lobster bisque. A *vol au vent* followed, and a duckling with orange sauce came after the *vol au vent*, while a Chambertin of '55 was reverently presented in a wicker cradle. It was the first time these two had shared a meal, but the mood of intimacy which James had hoped to establish in their unexpected solitude did not develop easily, for the waiters hovered, and Madeleine seemed determined to play the grand court lady, and he had some difficulty in following her smart, slangy French. But after the second glass of Chambertin was drunk, and only the subdued hum of voices from the larger diningroom next door indicated that Laperouse had any other guests, her manner softened, and she said to James almost coaxingly:

"Now tell me about your home in Scotland, please. Is it in the Highlands, like the romances of Sir Walter Scott?"

"No Highlands, no romance and no Scott," said James. "Sauchentree's in Buchan, a bare windy place; and my brothers and I were brought up there on porridge and ambition—and on hard work too, my father saw to that. He was a blacksmith, the sole support of his widowed mother and her children, when he was only fourteen years old."

"You're very proud of him."

"Yes, I am."

"You're lucky to have a father you can respect. Is he still a blacksmith?"

"He's been a cripple for over forty years."

"Kicked by a horse?"

"He lost his way one stormy night on the way to see his sweetheart. He fell over the sea cliffs, and was so badly injured they had to take his leg off at the knee next morning."

"You Scotsmen must be very reckless when you fall in love."

The waiter came in with a *soufflé maison*, the wine waiter at his heels. "Bring champagne!" said James, pointing to a number on the thick red-bound wine list. The chain of office round the *sommelier's* neck tinkled very slightly as he closed the door behind him with a firmness which showed how well he understood his business. He knew the "English milord" was in no great hurry to have that bottle of champagne uncorked.

"This room is empty tonight," said Madeleine, but not regretfully. "People must be afraid to come so far from the boulevards. They're afraid of Monsieur de Rochefort and his rabble—how silly!"

It was the first time she had alluded to the murder of Victor Noir. It was typical of James that he had almost forgotten it, although twice during the previous night his train had been stopped by disturbances at Avignon and Lyons. He had seen a good many rioters in his fifteen years of travelling across France, and had always been calmly confident that a Scots engineer, accustomed to handling excitable lascar stokers, could cope with any of them. But now it struck him that he had a lady in his care, and that they were at some distance from her home in a city which however smooth and brilliant on the surface had its own lava boiling darkly underneath. With a word of apology he rose from the table and unlatched the window opening on a little balcony above the quai.

"What's the matter?" asked Madeleine. "Do *you* think you hear de Rochefort and his men?"

James shook his head. All was silent on the Quai des Grands Augustins. But his ears, attuned to the many voices of the engine room, had caught a far distant scurrying and murmuring, like the brush of dead leaves in autumn along the verges of the Seine.

He drew the curtains gently and looked at Madeleine. In her plain dark dress, with her shining hair in a chignon and no ornaments but a pair of diamond earrings, she made as always an irresistible appeal to his senses. But now the first faint warning of a coming danger stirred all his chivalry. "This is the woman I must protect and cherish," he thought, as he looked at that proud head, now drooping a little beneath the bronze cock's feathers of the Windsor helmet, and then, "This is the woman I must marry!"

He was absolutely certain of it now. She was the only possible wife for him. She was the prize he had to win. He moved round the table and sat down beside her, close enough to be aware of some fresh scent like clover, which she wore instead of the fashionable violet or gardenia. For the first time that night he took her hand in his. The long fingers curled gently about his own.

Because he was a tongue-tied northern Scot he hesitated for the right words to say and Madeleine put in, with a smile,

"I've been meaning to ask you—where did you learn to speak such beautiful French?"

"In Scotland!" said James, extremely gratified.

"That accounts for the Scots accent, then," said Madeleine mischievously.

James stared at her. He had long ago discarded the dialect of Aberdeenshire as an outworn communications tool, and no trace of accent remained in his English speech. It was disconcerting to be told that his birth revealed itself when he spoke French.

"Is it very noticeable?" he said rather stiffly. "My teacher was a Frenchman. I daresay I've had too many years of dockyard French at Marseilles and Beirut to keep up to his pronunciation!"

"Did you have a French tutor, then, at Sauchentree?"

She softened the harsh gutturals into So-shan-tri, and Bruce's dark eyes shone.

"It's a pretty name when you say it! No, we had to walk to our French lessons. Four miles to Rosehearty and four miles back, two nights a week, after a long school day and a fair share of the blacksmith work. My brother William and I thought nothing of that when we were—what? Fourteen—fifteen? We used to swing along the coast road with a wind from the North Pole blowing through our jackets, and the alexandrines blowing through our heads and hearts! That was where I learned to speak French and love France—on the shore of the Moray Firth, from a poor devil of an *émigré*, who was glad to earn a few shillings teaching the polka and Racine!"

Madeleine watched him, sitting so near her that only the slightest movement would bring their lips together. She wanted him to kiss her. She wanted that firm, tanned cheek against her own. She wanted to hear him say *aimer, amour,* and mean herself. She was past flirting with him now. She wanted not only to be caressed but to caress. To stroke away the two furrows which emphasis and excitement had drawn between his brows. To smooth the heavy dark hair which grew so thickly over his strong neck—

Then the sense of his last words came through to her, and she asked,

"Did you say an *émigré*? Who had left France—when?"

"With King Charles; that would have been in 1830; but he quarrelled with the exiled king at Edinburgh and came north. Vicomte Ferdinand d'Arblay was his rank and name in France, but the Rosehearty youngsters called him 'Dancey Darbles'."

"Have you any idea what it means to be an exile?" she said angrily. "Do you know that my father was 'a poor devil of an *émigré*' too?"

Against her will the tears she had held back since the morning's painful talk with the old man at the Quai Voltaire came into Madeleine's eyes. She shook them away angrily, but they brimmed again on her gold-brown lashes, and James, appalled at his own gaucherie, took her into his arms and began to kiss her on the mouth.

"Madeleine!"

She caught her breath. She knew by instinct how much it meant to the Scotsman to call her by her Christian name. She let him kiss the tears away, and whisper that he was sorry, had never meant to speak lightly of the exiles of France; and then he told her that her eyes were just the same blue as the band of turquoise light which on clear days would separate the grey skies of Buchan from the grey waters of the firth. He felt her hands on his hair, stroking, forgiving, pressing his head more closely down to hers, and then he covered her throat with kisses and laid one hand on her thigh to strain her more closely to himself.

"James! No! The waiter will come in!"

"To the devil with the waiter!" said James hoarsely. "Do you reject me, Madeleine? You were kind to me at Ismailia, do you repent it here?"

"This is Paris, after all—"

"And I mayn't aspire to make love to a court lady, is that it? To the daughter of an exiled nobleman—"

"The granddaughter of a Norman fisherman."

"It's the great past—the d'Arbonne past—that counts the most."

"I'm sick of the d'Arbonne past!" said Madeleine drawing away. "I heard enough of it, only this morning, to last me for all the rest of my life! I live in the present, and I mean to *enjoy* the present, and nobody, I tell you *nobody*, is going to push me back into the Middle Ages on account of my *name*!"

She shook her head in her vehemence, and sparks of light glinted from the diamonds in her ears. The very air about her seemed charged with electricity.

"By God!" said James Bruce violently, "we'll drink to that, Madeleine! To *our* present—yours and mine! What have they done with that champagne? *Sommelier! Sommelier!*"

There was a sound of hurrying footsteps in the corridor. James got to his feet quickly, to stand between her and the opening door and give her one unsteady moment to look at herself in the mirror behind their table. The wine waiter came in empty-handed, giving James a rare excuse to bluster out,

"Why don't you bring me the champagne I ordered?"

"Your pardon, monsieur"—the man was visibly nervous. "Can't you hear the mob, monsieur? They're rioting, and wrecking property, all along the Boulevard St. Michel!"

Before the waiter could prevent him, James had pulled the curtained window open.

The sound of blown leaves had swelled now into the running of many feet, and the roar of a crowd, shouting "Rochefort! Rochefort to power! Remember Victor Noir!"

Lighted torches came wavering out of the Place St. Michel as Madeleine went to lean with James over the little balcony. She was not in the least afraid, her clasp was firm on his arm, but she tightened it convulsively when two men in the white blouses worn by artisans came running hard along the quai in their direction, one of them bleeding from a shallow cut on the brow.

"The Emperor's White Shirts!" she said beneath her breath. "He sent them to make trouble in the streets! Listen—that's the *rappel!*"

The sound which swept over Paris was the chilling note of the tocsin which again and again had roused the city to massacre or revolution. Through it came the drumbeats, two long and one short in a steady rhythm, calling the National Guard to arms.

V

When they hurried down the steep stair into the street the wounded White Shirt and his mate had disappeared, presumably into one of the dark recesses by the river. A company of the National Guard, in ragged formation, was streaming across the bridge and down the Quai.

Cabdrivers waiting for some of Lapérouse's other guests, caught between the citizen soldiers and the oncoming rush of the rioters, were shouting at each other distractedly. The driver of Bruce's coupé had driven out of the side street and added to the confusion. When his passengers got in he was standing on his box, whirling his whip at the guardsmen and shouting, "We can't get by! We can't get by!"

"Turn about!" cried Madeleine. "Drive up behind the Monnaie and go round by the Institut de France!"

The man pulled his horse frantically round and laid on the whip, the vehicle sped through the quiet district at the back of the Mint.

"That was well done," said James admiringly. "The fool had lost his head, and I had no idea which way to go."

"I only know the main landmarks on the Left Bank," confessed Madeleine, "but I can always find my way back to the Quai Voltaire. Look—that's the old *hôtel* d'Arbonne!"

She was breathing quickly, still not frightened but excited, as the noise of the *rappel* died away behind them, and the cabhorse came to a slow trot on the macadam of the Pont Royal. When James took her in his arms he could feel her trembling, and she met his kisses with a slow, burning response that sent him mad for her. He was hardly able to control his voice when the many lights of the Tuileries shone out on the right, and he knew they were out of danger.

"Madeleine, I'm going to tell this man to drive us straight to your home—to the front door this time!" She looked at him uncomprehendingly. "Then, if you'll allow me, I'll escort you into the house."

"Oh, James!" On her French lips his solemn Scots name turned into "*Zhamms*," and in delight he kissed away the "No!" which followed.

"I must; your family will be worried about you, and I must take the blame for exposing you to danger. Otherwise your father won't allow me to see you again—"

"My—*father*! He'll be asleep by now, and when he reads about the riot tomorrow morning, he'll be delighted to hear of any challenge to the Emperor! Don't you understand yet that my uncle is the master in our house?"

"Then I shall ask for your uncle," said James firmly. "I'll be bound Monsieur Bertaux is quite wide awake at half-past ten o'clock at night. You, driver!" The man opened the little trap-door in the roof and looked down at them. "To the Faubourg St. Honoré!"

After the lighted boulevards, wide and orderly, which Haussmann had designed to be cleared by the Emperor's cavalry in five minutes, the Bonapartist Faubourg was silent and dark behind its stately portals. But inside the courtyard of the Bertaux mansion lights were blazing from lodge and stables and domestic offices. Two gaseliers in the form of torches held by life-size bronze figures of Nubian slaves lighted the marble steps. The great glass doors, protected by wrought bronze grillwork and a fan-shaped glass canopy opened, at a signal from the Old Poisson's lodge, to disclose a major-domo with a chain of office round his neck and two footmen in powder and silk stockings.

"Has Monsieur Bertaux come in yet?" asked Madeleine, as one lackey took her cloak and the other relieved James of his coat and hat.

"Monsieur is in the study, mademoiselle. And, if you please, madame la comtesse has been asking for you."

James produced his cardcase. "Be so good as to take my card to Monsieur Bertaux. Say I desire the favour of a few words with him."

Both footmen withdrew into a rear vestibule, as if to produce

Monsieur Bertaux under escort; the major-domo hurried to open the door of the grand salon. Madeleine and James were left in the wide entrance hall, lavishly decorated with flowers, ferns and statuary, on the left of which rose a broad staircase. On every shallow marble step stood a tub of pink or white azaleas, and over the balustrade of the landing peered a number of statues, life-size figures sculptured in polished pink granite. The whole décor was stunning enough in size, weight, scent and colour to dwarf the human beings it enclosed.

"You are absolutely determined on this interview?" said the girl in a low voice.

"I can't go on in secret, Madeleine. I have to go to London in the morning, and from there to the Clyde; I don't know how soon I can return to France. I must have your—your guardian's permission to write to you, and come to you here when I get back." He added in a voice even lower than her own—somehow in the glaring garish Bertaux hall there was the same feeling as in the dark anterooms of the Tuileries that secret police were listening round the corner—"Ismailia was a wrong beginning; we must start again from tonight."

Without a word she turned and led the way to the drawing room.

Halfway along the hall, where open doors gave glimpses of a small salon, a music room and a library all lit by fires and lamps as if an evening reception had been planned, James was arrested by a life-size painting of Madame d'Arbonne. It was clearly meant to be the focus of the house, for the elaborate gilt frame was lit by gas and flanked by Etruscan vases filled with forced white lilac. The subject of the painting was identified, to prevent any possible mistake, by a gold plaque with the legend, "Marie-Madeleine BERTAUX, Comtesse d'Arbonne."

Devéria had painted Madeleine's mother in a robe of ice-blue satin with enormous puffed sleeves and a sapphire-studded aigrette in her hair. The background of sage-green draperies gave full value to her brilliant colouring. Her expression lacked the bright charm of Madeleine's, and her fair hair was sleeked close to her head with bandoline, but otherwise the woman in pale blue looking down from the canvas bore a marked resemblance to the girl in brown, looking up.

"There are better likenesses of my mother than this," said Madeleine, as James studied the portrait in a sympathetic silence. "If you go to the Louvre you'll see her as *Liberated Greece* and the *Bride of Abydos* in the Delacroix Room. This was commissioned to hang at Arbonne, with all the ancestors. Only when it came to the point my uncle couldn't bear to let it go. He'd *paid* for it, you see."

"Did he never have *you* painted?"

"Oh yes, my portrait is somewhere in the attic—it's never been hung downstairs. Monsieur Delacroix himself painted me in '63, just before he died; but uncle wasn't pleased with the picture. He said it was too revolutionary."

"Revolutionary in art?"

"No, no; revolutionary in politics, but the Emperor, bless him, allowed it to be shown at the Exhibition. The rest of the family portraits are in the drawing room—they're quite conventional."

Certainly there was nothing revolutionary about the landscape above the mantel in the grand salon, where the Comte d'Arbonne pirouetted with his two youngest daughters, a gun dog and a dead hare, against a background of flowering laurel; or the kit-cat of a younger Victor in his first regimentals, or the portentous life-size of Monsieur Bertaux, one gloved hand in the breast of his frock coat, in the style of the great Napoleon.

"Should you go to your mother now, Madeleine?"

The calm suggestion, the first assumption of authority, did not displease her. But she said warningly, "Do be careful what you tell my uncle!"

"I'll say no more than you gave me the right to say—"

There his French and his feelings broke down together. He wanted to use the words "that we care for each other," an impassioned phrase by Buchan standards. But that was a translation he had never learned from Dancey Darbles, and his stiff tongue refused to say "*que nous nous aimons.*" So he said nothing at all, and Madeleine, after a moment of irresolution, left him with a quick touch of the hand. James was free to observe the salon, overstuffed with crinoline chairs and sofas of heavy tufted satin, and the flower-filled conservatory which formed one side of the room.

Either Madame d'Arbonne or her brother had been seized by the "all-to-match" craze, and with less success than the Empress, for the colour selected was dark red, and the crimson flock paper and turkey carpet had the effect of sealing up the unwary guest in a kind of furnace fed by the blazing logs in the great fireplace. The tables were laden with bibelots of onyx and alabaster, while bronze warriors and marble goddesses were grouped about two great breakfront bookcases crammed with uncut classics in gilt-edged morocco. All this expensive vulgarity left James Bruce unmoved. He envied no man's material possessions, and the flaring gaseliers were what interested him most. "What extravagance!" was his eminently practical reaction. "What can their gas bill be?"

While James waited, Michel Bertaux was turning his card over and over in his thick fingers as he stood beside his study fire.

He was already aware of his niece's escapade, thanks to Marthe, who like every servant in that house was venal, and had betrayed her young mistress again and again for a gold napoleon from Monsieur Bertaux. But Marthe had not been able to tell him the name of the man waiting on the avenue Gabriel, and Bertaux learned it now with great surprise. The episode at Ismailia, reported to him in part by both Adèle and Victor, had not particularly impressed him—he knew his Madeleine, excited by new surroundings and champagne—but to have the Scots engineer from Suez reappearing in his house in Paris was more than he had bargained for. It was a new irritation, coming at the end of a day when Madeleine had already annoyed him by bringing her crazy father back into his house. With an oath, Bertaux threw Mr. Bruce's card into the heart of the flames.

Bertaux had dined at the Jockey Club, and afterwards passed an hour at an apartment on the rue de Miromesnil. He had installed Madame Clarisse Delavigne there ten years earlier; their liaison had for long been a mere formality, a bow to the convention which said that a great Bourse operator had to keep a mistress—she had bored him intolerably that evening. He had left her boudoir, which smelt of lapdogs and chypre, and walked the short distance home in the clear January night keyed up to the stimulus of a quarrel with Madeleine. Now, somewhere in his own rich house, between Madeleine and her just punishment stood the figure of the Scots engineer.

Michel Bertaux buttoned his crimson velvet smoking jacket, drew a hand down his pomaded moustache and imperial, and went soft-footed to the drawing room. The door stood open. He could see Mr. Bruce standing with his hands in his pockets, coolly surveying the tropical plants and palms through the glass wall of the conservatory. A jealous pang puckered his face in the familiar tic.

The financier was not in good condition, and he knew it. Tall enough to carry his weight well, he knew that his paunch was increasing, his jowl grown slack. Too much fat living had ruined the fine physique of the fisher boy from Trouville, but he believed that at fifty-five a rich man had a right to the stoutness Napoleon III had made fashionable. Now here was this Scots fellow—no youth—sauntering about his own drawing room with the supple movements and muscular co-ordination of a much younger man. Bertaux caught a breath of rage at the thought that less than an hour earlier his niece's body might have been held—how close?— to those broad shoulders and strong thighs.

"This is an unexpected pleasure, Mr. Bruce."

He walked quietly into the salon and exchanged bows with his uninvited guest, while the footmen who followed close behind him placed gold salvers with brandy decanters and cigars on tables next to the armchairs on either side of the great fireplace.

"I must apologize for calling on you at such a late hour, monsieur," said James, when the servants had left the room. Bertaux, murmuring politely, was sizing him up across the flame of his vesta. The fellow could wear his clothes well, certainly, but his face showed that he had been through the mill in the past few hours. It was strained and yet instinct with feeling, more worn and yet younger than Bertaux remembered it. And like a young man he was determined to rush his fences, for here he was, blurting out,

"Mademoiselle d'Arbonne honoured me with her company at dinner tonight."

"How delightful for you both. Where did you go?"

"To Lapérouse."

"Excellent taste. Did you hear anything of the disturbances on the Left Bank? Before I left the club there was word of rioting in the student quarter, and also near the Montparnasse station."

"You take it coolly, sir!" said James. "Yes, we *did* see the rioters, and heard the National Guard called out, and we saw two of the Emperor's *agents provocateurs*, one with a broken head. We dodged the lot of them, thanks to the quick wits of Mademoiselle d'Arbonne."

"Yes, she's a good girl in an emergency," agreed her uncle. "So the White Shirts were out, were they? I thought they might be. You see, Mr. Bruce, this is the Emperor's technique. With a big row coming up tomorrow, and de Rochefort all ready to lead two hundred thousand marchers straight from Victor Noir's grave to the Tuileries, shouting, 'Down with the Bonaparte usurper!' Napoleon starts the row tonight—there were outbreaks at five other points in the city—and before daybreak all the waverers are convinced that it's no go, the authorities are too strong for them, and they decide to stay at home and keep out of mischief. It's one way to handle trouble, and I think it'll work well enough tomorrow."

"You don't take de Rochefort very seriously, then?"

"Rochefort? A damp squib, a mere front for Assi and Raoul Rigault and the Communist cell which has been giving my friend Schneider so much trouble at Le Creusot. Twenty political funerals, Mr. Bruce, won't do France as much harm as one strike in an arms factory, but the new government isn't smart enough to see it!"

"You're not impressed by the Ministry of Honest Men, monsieur?"

"About as much as I am by your Mr. Gladstone's cabinet. I've seen too many French governments rise and fall since I came to Paris forty years ago to put much faith in Ollivier. After all, how is France governed in the long run? By the Bourse, of course!

By the men who have the nerve to run risks, and are still on their feet on settling day! As opposed to the corpses of the failures, fished from the Seine and laid out to drip on the slabs of the Morgue!"

"You're thinking of the suicides which followed settling day in April '66?"

"Yes," said Bertaux, "and it may happen again in April '70, now that every man, woman and child in Paris is playing the market, and gambling on margin from the Parquet right down to the kerb outside the Café Grétry!"

"That's not the Leadenhall Street forecast, as I see it."

"Indeed," said Bertaux, sipping brandy. He was handling the interview in his own way, as he had handled refractory board meetings for years. Let the man talk, let him show what was in his mind, let him commit himself on general topics before coming to the particular. "And what is the Peninsular and Oriental's forecast for 1870, may I ask?"

Bruce smiled. "We have our own problems, monsieur. I'm sure you as a director of the Messageries Impériales must know that the opening of the Suez Canal has hit us very hard. We are re-engining the whole fleet, and I expect to spend the next three months on the construction of our new four-thousand-tonners, *Australia* and *Indus*."

"*The Times* calls *Australia* the P. and O. ironclad," said Bertaux. "Are you putting your merchant fleet on a war footing, by any chance?"

"Are *you*?"

"Should we?"

"If you think Bismarck wants war—yes."

"So they're discussing that possibility in London." Bertaux sighed. "Your brokers are more enlightened than our headstrong friends at the Tuileries. Too bad you didn't take advantage of your audience at El Kantara to give Her Majesty some realistic counsel, for a change. The court believes that the Spanish Question is settled, and Bismarck's fangs drawn for good and all."

"That's not how Frank Hartzell presented Marseilles opinion to me, when I saw him a couple of days ago."

Bertaux's heavy-lidded blue eyes became alert.

"Ah! your former travelling companion. I didn't realize you had come from Marseilles, Mr. Bruce. So you saw my Mr. Hartzell there?"

"I saw 'your' Mr. Hartzell twice," said James, with the slightest emphasis on the pronoun, and smiled. "He seems to be doing very well for himself—and for the Société Anonyme Bertaux."

The smile, the flash of very white teeth in the brown face, had touched off a new idea in the financier's devious brain. So that's all it was, he thought disgustedly. The Scotsman and Hartzell are operating together—this fellow wants his cut on the wine freightage, probably. I thought better of Frank Hartzell! Madeleine was the pigeon, to bring this man straight here to me. His mind, accustomed always to look for the base motive, ran rapidly down the crooked passages of thought.

James abruptly brought the conversation back to its starting point.

"Monsieur Bertaux, will you permit me to come to the real purpose of my visit?" he said. "As her guardian, I feel sure you must disapprove strongly of my having persuaded Mademoiselle d'Arbonne to dine in public with me tonight—"

Bertaux blinked rapidly, and the tic jumped in his cheek. "I was right the first time," he thought. "Damnation!"

In his mildest manner he said aloud, "It *was* a little unconventional! When you Englishmen come to 'gay Paree,' as you call it, you seem to feel that any man's daughter, or niece, can be treated as you certainly would not treat one of your own young ladies. Then we're blamed for the licentiousness of Paris! . . . I beg your pardon for introducing the word. I'm sure it can't apply to any entertainment *you* may have offered my niece."

An expert in sarcasm himself, James was not deceived by Bertaux' bland manner. "Thank you," he said, ignoring the barb, "that sets my mind at rest! That gives me leave to hope that you will regard me as a fit person to be received in your home from time to time, and to conduct a correspondence with Miss Madeleine."

"Correspondence!" said Bertaux. "I don't know about that.

I don't believe Madeleine does write many letters, although come to think of it I've seen some very terse compositions written to my head groom at Arbonne when one of her horses had an attack of colic. In any case I need not attempt to place sanctions on her correspondence : she is free to receive letters at the Tuileries without any reference to me."

"I am glad you agree that your niece is of an age to make her own decisions, monsieur."

"Are more important decisions to be sought? What is to be the purpose of the letter writing, Mr. Bruce?"

James drew a deep breath.

"The purpose of paying my formal addresses to your niece, sir. Eventually of asking for the honour of her hand in marriage."

Bertaux allowed a silence to fall.

"Forgive me if my enthusiasm seems to be lacking, Mr. Bruce. I supposed that your interest in Madeleine could only be a fatherly one."

"It's not an *avuncular* one, at any rate," said Bruce rashly.

"Shall we forego these amenities, monsieur? They can scarcely help us to a better understanding. You intend me to take this offer of marriage seriously?"

"I address it to you as her guardian, sir. I should have preferred, I tell you frankly, to have made it to the Comte d'Arbonne."

"Her father I think would agree with me," said Bertaux, "that if we wanted to marry Madeleine to a middle-aged professional man—I use the expression because I don't really know your exact position with the P. and O.—we could certainly find a more suitable *parti* in the engineering division of the Messageries Impériales, who would have the added advantage of being of her own faith."

"If you make a point of the disparity in our ages, let me remind you that Monsieur de Lesseps recently married in the face of one very much greater—"

"Yes; and do you know what they say about de Lesseps? *There's no fool like an old fool.*"

"As regards my professional position," said James, refusing to be drawn, "I am the Chief Shore Engineer of the Peninsular and

Oriental Steam Navigation Company, and expect to be made a Manager in the near future."

"I must have half a dozen men with equivalent jobs on my various company payrolls," said Bertaux. "Of course it hasn't escaped your attention that my niece, if she marries with my approval, will be a well-endowed young woman?"

Bruce sprang to his feet. "I'm not a fortune hunter, sir!"

"I'm sure you're not. But have you an *equal* fortune to bring into a marriage settlement?"

James Bruce earned one of the largest salaries paid by his company. His savings were conservatively invested in Consols and in the debenture stock issued by the P. and O. under its Third Charter of 1854. He knew that neither the salary nor the savings would be at all impressive to a man reputedly one of the richest industrialists in France.

"I'll take the lady without a penny, if she'll have me," he said. "But let me point out that no man can propose an *equal* fortune until he knows what figure he must match."

"You must play a good game of poker, Mr. Bruce. Very well, I think I can make a fair guess at your situation. Would your brother be prepared to come down with something handsome, if we came to terms?"

"My *brother*? The minister of a seaboard parish, with a stipend just sufficient for his needs, and his wife's small income for their charities?"

"I mean, of course, your brother Robert. The engineer officer who introduced you to me at Suez. He is said to be one of the richest men on the Hong Kong station."

"*Robert* a wealthy man? You're dreaming, sir! My brother has nothing in the world but his Chief's pay, and lives most frugally! On his last home leave, five years ago, he walked the forty miles from Aberdeen to Sauchentree to save coach fare, as we all did when we were lads—"

"It affects some men that way," said Bertaux. "Personally, I like to keep my money in circulation." He looked round proudly at his crimson salon. "I see you are genuinely surprised, Mr. Bruce. What very secretive brethren you Scotsmen must be! Let me see now. When I first met your brother, he was doing very well for himself in Peking, after the Summer Palace had been looted by the allied volunteers. He then bought out the leakiest, trickiest, least seaworthy line in the Orient, which he runs in the coastal trade under its former name, Bradley's of Foochow. I had some dealings with him in the French Concession in Whampoa in '66—I won't say in what, since the opium traffic is illegal! In Hong Kong he has a clever old Chinese comprador named Ho, who fronts very successfully for that frugal Scot, the Chief of the *Sunda*; most of my recent transactions have been with Mr. Ho. . . . You must get your brother to tell you about them some day. Well now, to the matter in hand. Mr. Robert Bruce is your junior, I believe; he may want to keep his capital for his own marriage settlements. Or do you think you could persuade him to make you a loan, for yours?"

"I wouldn't touch it."

Bertaux passed his handkerchief across his mouth.

"Half a truth, and half a lie, well told," he thought. "The perfect mixture!" He looked contentedly at the man standing as if he faced a firing squad, with his back against one of the breakfronts full of unread books.

"Then, all things considered, you must see that I can hardly entertain the proposal you have done us the honour to make, or consent to letting my niece, accustomed to every luxury and attention, go off to your foggy London and settle down to ordering roast beef and boiled mutton for your midday dinner? What are *her* views on the matter, by the way? Am I to suppose that she encouraged you to seek this interview with me?"

"Quite the reverse."

"Ah! I thought so!"

"But she is aware of my feelings, sir. I hope it's not presumptuous to say that I think she is beginning to return them."

Bertaux pulled the bell rope with such violence that the gilt tassel came off in his hand. "Tell Mademoiselle I want her," he said savagely to the footman who appeared. "Yes—even if she is with madame la comtesse, say I want her here!"

They waited in silence until Madeleine appeared. She was carrying her hat in her hand, as if she had been sitting by her mother's bed and had not yet gone to her own room; her fair hair was a little dishevelled. The diamond earrings swung and winked in the strong gaslight.

"My dear," said Bertaux, with all his usual suavity, "Mr. Bruce has just done your family and yourself the high honour of asking for your hand in marriage."

"Oh!" she said with her hand at her lips. "Oh, why on earth did you do that! Oh, now you've spoiled everything!"

"I thought I had your leave to do so," said James Bruce.

"But we never even *talked* about marriage!" Tears of vexation came into Madeleine's eyes; she jerked viciously at the bronze feathers of her hat. "I don't want to marry you or anyone! I told you I only wanted fun—enjoyment—bright lights and gaiety! It's not the same thing at all!"

Her uncle smiled. But the smile faded as James went up to Madeleine and took her free hand in his. Bertaux felt—even he— the extraordinary pull of the physical attraction between those two, which made Bruce's eyes burn brighter, and put a look on Madeleine's face such as he had never seen there before. The devil! And Bertaux turned away and kicked at one of the cedar logs, so that a shower of sparks flew out upon the hearth.

"I can't be sorry that I went too far," he heard Bruce say. "At least you know explicitly how matters stand with me! Your uncle has called me an elderly fortune hunter, and has told me a few other things I'd rather not have heard, and I can't suppose that he will receive me here again very willingly. But will you promise me this, Madeleine, that you won't forget me; that you'll send for me if you need me—"

"*What* did he tell you that you would rather not have heard?"

"It was something to do with his brother, Madeleine," said Bertaux, facing round. "Not with you."

"Will you promise me this, to send for me at any time if you need me?"

"I promise." She said it magnificently, and let him kiss her hand. But when James had left them, with the briefest possible bow to the master of the house, she turned furiously upon her uncle.

"You dared to say such things to that man? You called *him* a fortune hunter? He doesn't know the meaning of the word!"

"I had to use some means to damp his youthful ardour. Now will you please go back to your mother? You've made trouble enough for one day—you and your idiot father—"

She flung her hat aside and grasped both of his flabby wrists in her hands—those terribly strong hands which could control four plunging horses—and said in a harsh voice, the very echo of his own, "Leave my father out of it! He told me today how you meddled in his life! You be careful how you interfere in mine!"

VI

The Prince Imperial was given a bronze and rosewood velocipede for his fourteenth birthday, which fell in a March so warm that "Badinguet's Travelling Circus" as the Faubourg St. Germain called it, moved out unusually early to Fontainebleau. He swayed up and down the long avenue squealing happily, learning to ride while an equerry ran alongside, and the Empress looked on indulgently from a hammock slung in a sunny place. She felt well and confident as the spring came in. The Victor Noir riots had fizzled out and de Rochefort was behind bars in Sainte Pélagie prison. The Emperor was deep in plans for a May referendum of the French electorate to ratify the new liberal constitution. It was his favourite device : he had fooled the French people twice with his plebiscites, and having every Prefecture in France in his pocket Napoleon III was confident that Gambetta and his Republicans would make no showing against him. Altogether Eugénie felt entitled to a holiday, a time of forest picnics and impromptu dances, and of reading, instead of State papers, her favourite novel, *Lady Isabelle*. Queen Victoria had recommended it to her under its original title, *East Lynne*.

There was only one cloud on the horizon, the Spanish Question, which still dragged on unsolved. The Spanish throne had been vacant since the deposition of Queen Isabella two years earlier: the Spanish Crown had been offered to a relative of the King of Prussia, the Catholic Prince Leopold of Hohenzollern-Sigmaringen. The French objected to a Prussian prince on the throne of Spain, and the result was a prolonged diplomatic stalemate.

To the palace of Fontainebleau there came one fine spring day Monsieur Emile Ollivier, to explain at great length his ideas for the plebiscite vote on the new Constitution.

"Excellent !" said Napoleon III politely, when the prime minister had said his say. "The draft constitution is most impressive;

just make sure you get out enough 'Yes' votes to ratify it, and we shall do !"

"Thank you, Sire," said Ollivier, closing his portfolio with a gratified smile. "I'm confident that on the eighth of May the Liberal Empire will be set on a solid basis of legality—of *democratic* legality," he added emphatically, looking hard into the old dictator's face.

"Quite so." The Emperor lit another of his eternal cigarettes. "What do you make of the news from Prussia?"

"Most reassuring, Sire."

"I suppose so," said the Emperor. "If Benedetti, our trusted ambassador, tells us that the Hohenzollerns have had a family council, and that the King of Prussia and his son the Crown Prince have both advised Prince Leopold to decline the offer of the Spanish Crown, then we must believe him and be thankful for it. I only wish his dispatch had told us more about Bismarck's reactions to the news."

"But, Sire!" protested Ollivier. "What *can* the Chancellor do to put Prince Leopold on the Spanish throne if the Prussian royal family is against it? We know that Queen Augusta hates von Bismarck! We know the Crown Princess is his bitter enemy! Besides, our diplomatic opposition has been too strong for him. France will not suffer a Prussian princeling on the throne of Spain, and Bismarck knows it."

"I hope you're right," said Napoleon. He rose, to indicate that the audience was over, and walked to the window to look down the sunlit avenue. "Still, these conferences keep the Spanish Question open! I wish to God that when the Spaniards deposed Queen Isabella, they had consented to keep that boy of hers, Alfonso, as their king. After all he *is* her son, though God knows who may have been his father."

Ollivier's small eyes glinted. A Liberal statesman was prevented from moving in the Paris circles adorned by the ex-Queen Isabella, but he could follow her adventures in the gutter press. He could lick his lips over the wild doings in the former Basilewski palace on the avenue du Roi de Rome—the Palais de Castille, they called it now—where even the stable straw was dyed in the Spanish colours and the Arms of Spain were emblazoned above the stable drains.

"Don Alfonso is barely seventeen; the Cortes may recall him yet," he said to the bent, rounded shoulders of his sovereign. "The great thing is that we have defeated the Hohenzollern candidacy. Prince Karl Anton will have to rest content with Roumania for his son Carol, and keep young Leopold at home at Sigmaringen."

"I wonder if we've exaggerated the importance of this thing," said the Emperor. He was watching the Prince Imperial on his velocipede. The boy could bicycle very well now; there was no longer any need for Monsieur Filon to keep his hand behind the saddle. "I wonder if by the time we come to look for a bride for Louis, six or seven years hence, there will still be the same anxiety about spheres of influence and the balance of power? Or if we can allow him to marry for love— as I did?"

"Sire?" Ollivier had hardly caught the words spoken in Napoleon's low, hoarse voice. His neat lawyer's mind had readily wandered from the Prince Imperial's future marriage to his great preoccupation, the draft Constitution of 1870.

"Or are we not taking it seriously enough?" cried the Emperor in sudden irritation. "I'll send a dispatch to Benedetti— now—in cipher! I'll ask him to explain, in words suited to the understanding of my ministers, why the Hohenzollerns thought it necessary to have Chancellor von Bismarck—and the War Minister—and the Chief of Staff—all present at their little family council?"

The Travelling Circus left Fontainebleau and went back to the Tuileries at the end of April, ten days before the electors of France were asked to vote "Yes!" for the Emperor and the Liberal Constitution.

On the afternoon of Plebiscite Sunday, the eighth of May, one of the most contented residents in France was being driven through the forest of Fontainebleau to the Château d'Arbonne.

Mr. Frank Hartzell of Philadelphia, in a new suit of pepper-and-salt tweeds made to his measurements by Poole of London, was very much at his ease on the cushions of the open landau which Michel Bertaux had sent to meet him at the railroad station. He was tanned from two weeks of travelling through the vineyards of the Charentais, and his pleasant face had lost the drawn look which had followed the recurrent attacks of China fever. His lack of success at Canton had been forgotten in the manifold interests of his work for Michel Bertaux, and he was exulting in the promotion to a desk in the Paris office which was to follow his engagement to "dine and sleep" at the Château d'Arbonne.

To be twenty-eight, well and strong, making good in a foreign country and with the immediate prospect of spending some time with the most attractive girl he had ever met, were great satisfactions for the young American whose early manhood had been embittered by his experiences in the Civil War. Frank was not, by temperament, capable of being possessed by such a storm of feeling for Louise d'Arbonne as had shaken James Bruce from the moment that he saw her sister Madeleine. The years when as a Princeton undergraduate he should have been enjoying the cotillions and musical soirées of Rittenhouse Square and Germantown had been spent by him in such a fury of haste as the 27th Pennsylvania went into battle, or such a torpor of misery through the years in Libby prison, that he was now content to live his life at an even pace, letting his feeling for Louise ripen slowly, win her gently, if he could. So thought Frank Hartzell, smiling to himself as the landau rolled on beneath the arching beeches, and only restrained by the rigid backs of the coachman and the footman from putting his feet up on the opposite seat.

The place and the time corresponded exactly with his mood. France had never been more lovely or more vulnerable than in the May of 1870, as the late spring shook its promise over the land. The forest of Fontainebleau was decked in living green, every leaf sparkling from an earlier shower of rain, and the cuckoos were calling above the tide of golden broom which had swept across the great crags and outcrops of rock beneath the trees. The fresh scent of damp moss and uncurling ferns came to the American on waves of sweetness only challenged, when the landau swept into the Grand' Rue of Barbizon, by the spring flowers growing round the thatched cottages wreathed in budding wisteria and white pear blossom.

Drowsing in the afternoon sunshine, Barbizon was a hamlet of almost theatrical enchantment. But when the single, grey stone street fell behind them and they swung left on the Arbonne road, Frank found himself in another and more cultivated landscape, cleared from the forest centuries before, where the road was bordered with well-pruned fruit trees and spring work was going forward in the fields. It was an intensely human countryside of neighbouring farms and close-set hamlets where each croft had its own pink apple orchard, each village its ancient church and tower, lying in masses of soft purple beneath the nacreous skies of the Ile de France.

It was the quality of the light, not brilliant but subdued by the gentle movement of the clouds, which gave to that landscape its peculiar charm. Nothing Frank had seen in all his travels was exactly like the effect produced by the thin pencils of sunlight which here and there pierced the clouds to strike a gilt weathercock on a belfry or an implement turning in the rich soil. The pearly colours of the sky then seemed to be reflected in the sheen of the moist earth, and the whole plain to be lying in a lake of light.

The Château d'Arbonne, a composition in perfect drawing, was also the perfect flowering, in terms of stone, of that exquisite countryside. It dated from the beginning of the sixteenth century, when the Comte Louis of his day was prosperous enough to build something more imposing than the old Tour d'Arbonne of his fighting forefathers. A moat surrounded the château itself, built of grey stone picked out with tawny bricks and standing three storeys high, the first and second floors having long windows and the third a row of small round ones, the shapely design being rounded off by a circular tower at each of the two wings. Beyond the moat, and the vast cobbled courtyard with a well in the middle, a curtain wall enclosed the château with the home farm on the left hand and the Cardinal's Stables on the right. The stables, with stalls for three hundred horses, had been added when Arbonne was rented to the great Cardinal Richelieu, to accommodate the relays of mounts required by his couriers on their missions to the king at Fontainebleau. Twin guardhouses above the great folding gates of solid wood set in the exact centre of the curtain wall completed the picture of Arbonne as a place as well equipped for war as peace.

It was a courtyard in which, Frank thought as the landau swept round the well and halted at the footbridge which spanned the moat, mailed warriors might have tramped the cobbles. Instead, he saw the graceful little figure of Louise d'Arbonne emerging from the farmer's house on the left side of the quadrangle, and without waiting for the footman to lower the step he jumped out of the carriage and hurried to greet her.

Louise took a few quick steps to meet him, and then checked herself to a more decorous pace. She was not a schoolgirl now— he saw that at a glance; the dark curls were pinned gracefully high on her bare head, and her muslin dress, still engagingly simple in cut, fell to the toes of her slippers. She had an osier basket on one arm, in which a few pinky-brown eggs, with little feathers clinging to them, were carefully packed in straw. She was even more attractive than Frank Hartzell remembered, and all his intentions of prudence were scattered to the winds at once.

She acknowledged his deep bow with a gracious little bend of the head instead of her old schoolgirl curtsy, and said with much sweetness, "Welcome to Arbonne, Monsieur Hartzell. My uncle has been looking forward to your visit, and my mother regrets so much that she's not well enough to bid you welcome herself."

"How *is* Madame d'Arbonne?" exclaimed Frank with ready sympathy.

"A little better today, I think," her daughter said. "She asked if she might have some eggnog this afternoon. Farmer Blaise helped me to find some new-laid eggs for her. She likes it when I pick them out myself."

She indicated the osier basket, and Frank, looking down at her —the small dark head hardly reached his shoulder—thought that anything might taste better from that kind little hand.

"But—oh dear!" said Louise, suddenly looking beyond him,

"didn't my brother and sister drive out with you? The carriage was sent off early, to meet them at the Paris train."

Here the footman presented a folded paper which Frank had seen tucked behind the cockade in his hat, as a strong voice called from the terrace of the château, "Delighted to see you, Hartzell; your train must have been punctual for once. What have you got there, Louise?"

Michel Bertaux came majestically over the footbridge to greet his guest as Louise stood puckering her brows over the message.

"Uncle, I'm terribly sorry. This is a dispatch from Victor. He and Mado can't leave the Tuileries until later. They're coming down on the evening train with two friends."

"Typical," said Bertaux with a scowl. "No reason given, of course; not a word about how things are going at the Tuileries, or at the polls in Paris. What friends does he say, my dear? I can't read this scrawl."

"The Marquis de Mortain and Colonel Aymé, uncle."

"H'm," said Bertaux, mollified. "That might have been a great deal worse. The Marquis de Mortain, eh? Very good. But that wretched Victor promised faithfully to be here to meet the Daubignys. You'll have to tell your friend Blanche that the Emperor detained him to help count the plebiscite votes, ha! ha! Now give your orders, child, and hurry; there isn't much time before they come."

They entered the château, and stood in a black and white tiled entrance hall, spacious and empty except for a dark oak coffer, where two bronze eagles guarded the french windows opening on another terrace above the formal gardens of the Château d'Arbonne. A butler came to receive Louise's request for two more rooms to be prepared, a luggage cart to go to Fontainebleau with the carriage, supper for four to be ready at eleven o'clock. Frank himself was taken upstairs by a footman to a small, attractive room overlooking the gardens and a pleasure canal. He gave the man his keys and splashed water into a basin hastily. He had seen that what Monsieur Bertaux thought appropriate for country house wear did not tally with the ideas of his own father, a Philadelphia dandy of the Fifties, but his employer's model seemed

113

to be the one to follow; Frank changed as quickly as possible from his travelling clothes to stiff linen and a black frock coat and silk cravat. Stopping only to unlock the morocco case containing his evening studs and cufflinks, for the footman to lay out with his dress suit, he ran downstairs. Louise was already greeting new arrivals in the drawing room.

Monsieur Bertaux was a rather glum and silent host to the three ladies who had driven over for tea from a neighbouring château. The Baronne Daubigny, her daughter Mademoiselle Blanche and her widowed sister Madame Kerhouan, were not difficult guests to entertain, inasmuch as they were delighted with everything (except the sad fact of Madame d'Arbonne's illness), petted "dear Louise," inquired tenderly for "dear Adèle" and took their leave as soon as it was decently possible. Frank, handing teacups and silver cake baskets, was soon aware that if "dearest Victor" had been present the visit would have lasted longer, and that Blanche Daubigny, a gentle young woman with a high country colour, was Michel Bertaux' nominee as Victor's future wife.

When the visitors, gracefully concealing their disappointment, prepared to leave, the financier roused himself to escort them to their carriage, and Louise and Frank were left alone together.

"Shall I show you the rest of the rooms on this floor?" she asked him prettily. She opened a door on the right of the hall and led the way into a suite of apartments which began with a magnificent dining room where the d'Arbonne ancestors looked out of their gilt frames at the antiques Bertaux had bought at Paris auctions to refurnish their old home. Next came a large library and beyond it a small circular bookroom set in the curve of the tower.

"We have a short cut to the parish church from this room," said Louise, indicating a shuttered window. "If we didn't have our own footbridge we'd have quite a long way to walk round the curtain wall. We must show you our church tomorrow; it's small, and very old; there's an effigy of our ancestor the Crusader in the aisle. But I forgot—perhaps you would rather not—"

She paused in distress.

"I'd like to go to church with you, Miss Louise—not as a sight-seer," said Frank gently. "I was baptized a Catholic, but my mother died when I was a small boy, and it was made only too easy for me to fall away."

"How sad!" It was the softest little breath of sympathy.

"Did I tell you, when we met in Egypt, that my mother had some French blood? Her name was Eleanor Durrant, but her grandfather spelt his name Durand. I haven't the least idea where they came from!"

Louise dimpled.

"Do you suppose that's why you're enjoying France so much, as you told us at tea?"

"That's one of the reasons," said Frank, with a long smiling look into her eyes.

"Oh, that's where you are," said Bertaux, appearing in the doorway. "It's chilly in here. Louise, why the devil don't you make them keep the fires going everywhere when you know I'm coming down for the weekend?"

"I'm sorry, uncle."

"You'd better see after that idle butler, before you go up to your mother. He hasn't begun to clear away the tea things yet."

Louise slipped away apologetically, and Bertaux motioned to Frank to follow him into the library, where the furniture was upholstered in his favourite crimson, and large oil lamps with clear globes (the château was not piped for gas) gave a better light than working candles could provide. Bertaux held a vesta to the wick of one of them and ran a disapproving finger round its dusty base.

"Everything is neglected at Arbonne nowadays," he said with a scowl. "Louise has no idea of housekeeping—even the wood-basket's empty! Ring the bell, will you, Frank?"

Frank pulled the bell rope vigorously. He was exasperated on Louise's behalf: poor little darling, how could she be expected to run a great place like this? Why didn't her sister stay at home and help her? While a servant brought logs, and endured his master's scolding, Frank feigned an interest in the pictures on the dark red walls. They were all battle pieces by second-rate artists, showing French troops in a series of contemporary victories. The horses of Bugeaud's cavalry pawed sand reddened by the blood of Arabs; the Chinese yielded the Bridge of Palikao to General Montauban; Canrobert pointed with his sword towards the Malakoff as his men pressed onward almost breast to breast with their Russian foes. It was a charnel house of bursting bombs, bloody scimitars and dilated equine nostrils from which the eye turned with relief to a row of charcoal drawings on white board, hung in narrow black frames above the mantelpiece.

Frank, as he looked closer, saw that these were four unfinished sketches of the same subject: the figure of a woman, whose face was no more than indicated, standing on some sort of eminence, perhaps a hill or battlement, with a crowd of people outlined all about her. In each sketch attention had been given to some detail of the principal figure: in one the right arm flung out above the crowd, in another the muscles of the left arm tensed above her head, in another the thrusting bosom, in the last the modelling of long thighs beneath the wind-blown skirt. These details, carefully worked over, emerged from the shadowy background with a strong effect of assurance and power.

Frank leaned across the brass firescreen which the footman had replaced, to decipher the artist's signature.

"You're looking at my Delacroix drawings," said Bertaux behind him. "These are sketches for a painting I have in my house in Paris. I'll show it to you some day."

"An historical subject, I suppose?" Frank ventured.

"What makes you think so?"

"The—er—lady, sir: might she be leading her troops into battle, or something of that sort?"

" A good guess ! Not quite accurate, but I grant you the figure has a heroic look to it, and the artist gave it a heroic title, too."

"What's the title?"

"*The Spirit of France.*"

VII

When Frank came downstairs for dinner he found Monsieur Bertaux in conversation with the parish priest, Father Gillet, and a rosy little Dr. Bailly from Fleury-en-Bière—attendants respectively on the soul and body of the Comtesse d'Arbonne. Before the introductions were completed Louise came in with her father, and Frank saw with tender amusement that she was much too elaborately dressed for the occasion. Her mother's maid had sent her down complete with fan and gloves, and she wore the pearl necklace given her on her eighteenth birthday with matching seed pearl bracelets at her wrists. Frank was not surprised to learn, when he complimented her on her dress, that it had been worn on her one and only appearance at court, when she was invited to a small dance at Fontainebleau.

She was an inexperienced hostess, and her father was no help, trotting about the room and peering out at the dark garden between the window curtains. Was the old gentleman by any chance not quite right in his head? "I could use a mint julep," thought Frank, furtively running a finger round his stiff high collar. "I'd settle for a bourbon and branch water if this goes on much longer." But just then dinner was announced, and they crossed the black and white vestibule and went to table.

The meal, too copious and too rich, was carelessly served, and Frank suspected that the butler had been sampling the wine before starting on his mission of keeping every glass full to the brim and running over on the damask cloth. Certainly he created a vinous diversion in the middle of dinner by bringing in the stable slate and saying the head groom was waiting for his orders *now*, immediately; Bertaux damned his eyes and threatened to dismiss them both for insolence; there was a great deal of arguing about saddle horses for next morning and the different requirements of Count Victor and Mademoiselle.

It was a relief when the meal was over and the older men went into the drawing room, where tables had been set out for cards. Louise lingered in the hall to give some of her diffident orders about supper for the expected guests. "Oh, I *hope* they won't be late," she said earnestly to Frank. "I know my uncle's so anxious for news of the plebiscite! And then if they *are* late Madeleine may be too sleepy to ride in the morning, and I do want to show you some of the bridle paths in the forest, starting from the Tour d'Arbonne. That's the *old* house; it's rented to some friends of my uncle. Monsieur and Madame Delavigne . . . at least *Madame* Delavigne spends her summers there. Her husband is an army Intendant in Algeria."

Her gentle murmur carried them across the hall, where the doors on the garden side stood open to admit the scent of wild hyacinth and young bracken from the fringes of the forest into the candlelit drawing room. The doctor came downstairs reporting Madame d'Arbonne asleep, and took his place at the card table; the footmen carried in trays of coffee and liqueurs. While Louise poured out, the huge gold coffeepot seeming too heavy for her slender wrist, Frank had a moment to think of himself and her. Unlike James Bruce he was easily impressed by material possessions, and he was well able to assess the riches which surrounded him now. The gold plate, the Sèvres dinner service, the Louis XIII furnishings ("each piece a collector's item," Bertaux said) had added zest to his dinner; he remembered that his father, who had married for love and lived to regret it, had always told him that it was "as easy to fall in love with a rich girl as a poor one"; and the money, of course, was here by the million, out of sight in the banks and the business as well as on view in all those mansions and villas of which the Château d'Arbonne was only the first he had seen. And come to that, would her uncle have invited him to the place at all if he hadn't some idea of bringing the two of them together? It seemed so; but Frank as well as being an impressionable young man was also an extremely conventional one. The faintly raffish air which hung around the château was not altogether reassuring: it reminded him that a Bertaux employee in Marseilles, dismissed for drunkenness, had declared that Bertaux' sister had been celebrated in the Paris of the Forties as

Mimi-la-Joyeuse, a *lorette* of more than ordinary talent. Very likely that was a lie. That the Count was slightly crazy seemed obvious, although he was no crazier than several old gentlemen Frank knew in Philadelphia. Put the two of them in one scale, and weigh them against Louise's dignity and charm, and who won?

"Miss Louise, I hope you're going to let us have some music?"

His voice sounded a little fuzzy in his own ears. That glass of brandy had been a mistake on top of so much wine. She, his sensible little darling, had only touched her lips to the *blanc de blancs* at dinner.

"Shall we disturb you, uncle? Papa dear?"

"By no means, child. We should all like to hear you sing." The cards, shuffled and cut, were dealt fast enough to drown her first uncertain arpeggio.

"I have a book of American songs here," said Louise, "which Madame Charles Moulton gave me. She sings quite beautifully at court concerts. When she sings *Suwanee River* Madeleine says the Emperor *cries*. It reminds him too much of his exile."

"Then let's not have *Suwanee*, Miss Louise. How about *Lorena?* D'you know *Lorena?*"

"It's rather high for me, but I can try."

She struck a few anxious chords.

"No, that's not right —"

Frank had taken up his position in the curve of the grand piano, an Erard, which an excellent ear told him was slightly out of tune. It was the accepted attitude for a gentleman listening to a young lady's songs, and it took him back to musical evenings before the Civil War, before Cross Keys and General Cluseret; long before the years in Libby prison. Louise looked up at him with parted lips. It was the first time in her life that she had entertained a young man, going through her scheduled performance without maman, without Adèle, above all without her brilliant eldest sister to absorb the attention of every male creature near her flame. It was the first time that anyone so handsome had leaned on the gleaming black piano lid, which reflected his own shining shirt front and broad cuffs, so young that the clustered candles overhead picked out the lights in his chestnut hair. Louise recollected herself and began to sing.

> The years creep slowly by, Lorena,
> The snow is on the grass again.
> The sun's low down the sky, Lorena.
> The frost gleams where the flowers have been.

Frank smiled as the lovely plaintive melody flowed out into the room. It was *the* war song of all others that the little French girl was singing, who knew as little of that frost at morning which had blighted his whole generation as she knew, yet, of the slow passage of the years. In her quaintly accented English—he guessed that she had learned the words by heart—she made *Lorena* sound quite different from the song he had heard in camp or on the lips of American girls who had good reason to sing of heartbreak and parting. And that very difference helped to draw some of the old bitterness from his heart as he listened to *Lorena*, after half a dozen years, on the other side of the Atlantic.

There was applause from the card players, and Monsieur d'Arbonne called out a request for a French folk song.

"Oh, papa! Let me sing another American one for Mr. Hartzell." She turned the page to *Jacket of Blue*. Louise sang better than she played, and she had practised the American songs for several days. The English words of the simple, tearful verses were more comprehensible to her than *Lorena*, and she sang them well.

> Weeping, sad and lonely
> Hopes and fears how vain!
> Yet praying
> When this cruel war is over,
> Praying that we meet again.

The tinkling arpeggios swept up the keyboard, and silence fell.

"Beautiful, Miss Louise. You'll make me cry, too, like the Emperor."

She raised her eyes from pensive contemplation of her hands.

"Oh why, monsieur? Because it is a sad song?"

"Because it has sad memories, it was written about the war.

All the songs in Mrs. Moulton's book are wartime songs."

"The war you fought in?"

"Yes, Miss Louise. We used to sing those songs in prison. It's wonderful to hear them again in freedom—sung by you."

"You were a prisoner of war for a long time, weren't you?"

"Nearly three years."

He saw, looking into her shocked eyes, that the word *prison* meant nothing to her, unless it were some house of detention which the Empress went graciously to visit for an hour with Madeleine or Victor in attendance; a sanitary ward with model prisoners scrubbed and spruced up for the occasion, responsive to the Imperial kindness. For a moment the taste of Libby prison ran into his mouth like bile. But before he could speak there came the sound of wheels, growing louder as the footmen threw open the château doors, and they heard young men's laughter, and above all a cry in the unmistakable clear voice of her sister Madeleine:

"Victory! Victory!"

VIII

The cobbled courtyard, bathed in moonlight, awoke to feverish life. From the Cardinal's Stables grooms came running with torches, and house servants flushed with food and drink, their livery coats dragged on and buttoned askew, were taking piles of luggage from the wagonette in which Marthe, the lady's maid, had been riding in solitary state. In front of the carriage Madeleine stood laughing and gesticulating, apparently explaining something to the grinning stableboys, and applauded by the three men in uniform who had accompanied her from Paris.

"What's that you say, Madeleine?" called Bertaux from the terrace in a voice as carrying as her own. "Don't tell me the result is out already!"

"It's as good as out!" cried Madeleine. She came running over the footbridge, gave her hand to Frank and kissed Louise and her uncle in breathless excitement. "The 'Yes' vote was leading by four millions when we left the Tuileries. The Emperor can't fail now!"

"Is that true, Victor?" demanded the financier, as the young men came up to greet him. And Victor confirmed his sister's story: the day had begun badly, with a heavy "No" vote in the capital, and poor results telegraphed from Lyons and Marseilles; then the provinces began to be heard from, and by six o'clock in the evening Gambetta and the Republicans had conceded defeat.

"Then come indoors, all of you, and let's have the details; you kept us waiting for them long enough!" scolded Bertaux. He led the way into the bare lovely hall, where more candles had been lit in sconces round the tall white marble pillars, and for a few moments there was a great deal of noise and confusion as Victor led his friends away to remove the grime of their railway journey, the little doctor and the priest prepared to take their departure, and the Comte d'Arbonne, after perfunctory greetings to the new-comers, ran upstairs with the speed of a startled hare and was lost to sight in the shadows of the landing. Then Madeleine declared that she must just look in to see if mother was awake, and change her dress. "I shan't be long!" she promised them, and went upstairs with her arm round Louise's waist. Bertaux and Frank turned back into the dining room. The other men joined them in a matter of minutes, Victor d'Arbonne upsetting the servants, who were running fecklessly round the table, with orders for a bottle of champagne for himself and his friends. He was very much the young master as he stood on the hearthrug, fair and flushed and self-assured, with his shoulder turned on Frank Hartzell (to whom he had given two fingers and a nod when he came in) and talking to his two companions. The newcomers made well-bred attempts to include Frank in the conversation, and he learned with interest that Colonel Aymé, an artillery officer, was a veteran of the Mexican expedition. The Marquis de Mortain, a tall, attractive fellow of twenty-five or -six, had been on Marshal MacMahon's staff in Algeria until the previous December.

"I haven't kept you waiting, *have* I?" said Madeleine from the doorway.

For a woman of fashion, attended by an expert dresser, she had made a very sketchy toilette. The grey tulle dress looped with dark red silk roses looked as if her impatient hand had pulled it from the very back of her wardrobe, and Frank saw her brother's irritation as he looked at her and then at de Mortain. Madeleine slipped into her mother's place in the middle of the table. She and Michel Bertaux sat facing one another with their guests on either side, to all appearances the master and mistress of the Château d'Arbonne.

The new arrivals started their belated supper, while Bertaux and Frank drank wine and Louise peeled an orange. Victor began to bicker with the argumentative butler on some matter connected with the cellar book, a dispute to which Bertaux contributed nothing but a few noisy laughs, while a little page bringing in a tray of glasses stumbled against a console table and dropped his burden on the floor. This drew a shriek of laughter from Madeleine. She was sitting with her elbows on the table, her cheeks hot, and the two lax curls on her shoulder already spraying out into a mist of warm gold.

"We couldn't possibly leave Paris," Victor was arguing, "when we heard those rascally Chasseurs in the Prince Eugène barracks were ready to mutiny. They were roaring 'No!' as they went to the polls, and the whole district was cheering them on. So the Emperor ordered the Imperial Guard to stand to arms."

"We all stood like statues, waiting for the summons to Mass," interrupted Madeleine, jumping up from the table. "Give me a cigarette, Victor.—But light it, light it, please! Only the Emperor walked up and down, smoking and scowling"—she puffed furiously at the cigarette, her forehead wrinkled and her gait suddenly dragging to the Emperor's invalid pace—"until all of a sudden Prince Napoleon and Princess Mathilde burst into the salon, obviously sure that the Revolution had begun!"

"Where was the Empress all this time?" interrupted Bertaux.

"In her oratory, praying. . . . Well, you should have seen Cousin Mathilde Bonaparte. She stood there with her enormous bosom heaving until her bodice buttons were ready to fly off in all directions, begging the Emperor to remember their glorious Uncle and order a whiff of grapeshot for the rabble. Prince Napoleon had one hand tucked inside his coat—you know how—and with the other he was stroking the Prince Imperial's head. Poor Loulou looked perfectly stunned—well he might! He's quite bright enough to know that Prince Napoleon hates him—the one obstacle between himself and the succession to the throne! You should have heard that fat hypocrite charging Victor and his friends to lay down their lives, if need be, to save the Prince Imperial. I'm not sure if they were to keep their last bullet for him, or if he was to shoot them, or who was to kill whom before de Rochefort could lay his hands on Loulou, but the general effect was absolutely grand!"

Frank, watching, saw her face swell grotesquely into the grimaces of the Emperor's jealous cousins.

"And then the Ladies!" Madeleine rushed on. "Oh, my dears, the Ladies! How to save them from a fate worse than death, the fate they all adore—that was the Princesse d'Essling's chief concern. She called us all by name, right down to Angèle de Larminat and me. She gathered us all round her in the Rose Room. Some Ladies of the Palace who won't see forty again were sobbing as if lewd hands were already tearing the clothes off their backs. . . . Then that sensible little thing, Princess Clotilde, looked out of the window and said there was hardly anyone in the gardens, the sentries had been doubled, and hadn't we better go to Mass as usual?"

"Who officiated? Monseigneur Darboy?" asked Bertaux.

"No! It was Her Majesty's friend from Madrid, the Abbé Bauer," laughed Victor. "Go on, Mado; let's hear the Abbé preaching, that's the girl!"

Louise, flushing deeply, closed her lips on an expostulation.

Madeleine was apparently unwilling to preach a sermon. She came back to the table, stubbed out her cigarette, and stood leaning on her chair. There was a general movement as the young men rose.

"Don't move!" She stopped them with a gesture. "I'll tell you the rest, uncle, as quickly as I can. When we came out of the chapel, the election news was better. By the time luncheon was served it was very good. By three o'clock the 'Yes' majority was clear, the loyal citizens of Paris were streaming into the gardens and the Carousel, and shouting hurrah for the Emperor, the Empress and the Prince Imperial!"

"And that was when Madame Eugénie made her first appearance?" asked Bertaux.

She turned on him, her bright face glowing at the hint of criticism in his voice.

"That was the first time *we* saw her," she retorted. "She was wonderful—she's always wonderful! She went from one side of the palace to the other, bowing from this window, waving from that. 'Good people, dear people, God bless you! Loulou, bow again to the people! Sire, all France is on your side—' "

And Madeleine, with swift turns and sweeping curtsies, with something in the arching of her neck and the stiff flutter of her hands, conveyed to her audience an impression of Spanish pride and etiquette, of a part long meditated by the ambitious and romantic woman whom she served. She moved backward and forward across the room like a swooping bird, tulle skirts dragging and bodice slipping further and further off her shoulders, as she kissed her hand repeatedly to an imaginary crowd.

"Well done, Madeleine," said Bertaux when the laughter and applause had subsided. "I only hope the victory won't go to Madame Eugénie's head."

"I hope so too, uncle," she said as she dropped into the chair held for her by de Mortain. Frank, carefully focussing his eyes on her face, thought that some of her animation had drained away while she presented the operatics of the Tuileries. But all the faces round the table now seemed blurred with fatigue, for it was long past midnight; the footmen still on duty were swaying on their feet, and Victor d'Arbonne, leaning forward to seize a bottle and refill his own glass, seemed to loom gigantically toward him and recede to the size of a mannikin in uniform. Frank observed, with superb detachment, that Victor d'Arbonne was drunk.

The high spirits of the whole company appeared to have run down. Louise was counting the orange pips upon her plate, Bertaux was sipping wine moodily; both of them, it was clear enough, were thinking of the sick woman in her room upstairs. Victor was giving only halfhearted attention to Colonel Aymé's long involved account of the Two-Year-Old Stakes at Deauville, to which Madeleine and the Marquis de Mortain were listening in a silence so complete that it seemed to shut them into a private world of their own. Abstractedly, as Frank watched, Madeleine leaned forward and poured a measure of brandy into her goblet of champagne; abstractedly, without taking his eyes off Colonel Aymé, de Mortain made a bracelet of his fingers round her slim wrist and sketched a long caress down the inside of her arm. Unhurriedly, good-humouredly, she freed her hand, lifted the glass and drank; her eyes meeting de Mortain's in a quizzical gaze. God! what a terrible girl! Was it possible that she too was —tipsy? And Louise, the only completely sober person at table, watching from under her eyelashes every change that passed across the American's expressive face, realized the comforting truth: he was neither bowled over by Madeleine nor charmed by her clowning; he was dismayed!

"Well, Miss Pussycat Louise!" Madeleine's voice cut sharply across the reminiscences of Colonel Aymé, "how have *you* entertained your guest this evening?"

"We—we had some music," stammered Louise, taken unaware.

"Some delightful songs," said Frank his tongue thick in his mouth. "Miss Louise sang some American ballads, favoured by your friend Mrs. Moulsey. Moulton."

"Oh, Madame Moulton!" sparkled Madeleine. "Now where was she today? She was just what we needed to cheer us up this morning."

Snatching at a plate which she held before her like a sheet of music, Madeleine jumped up again, drew a portentous breath, pointed a toe, rolled up her eyes and began to sing.

> *I know a maiden fair to see,*
> > *Take care!*
> *She can both false and friendly be,*
> > *Beware! Beware!*
> > *Trust her not,*
> > *She is fooling thee!*

It was a really comic performance, because while Madeleine was unable to carry a tune she had an acute ear for speech inflections, and reproduced Mrs. Moulton's flat New England accent well enough to make Frank Hartzell laugh, at last, uproariously. Madeleine, who by this time needed little encouragement, went on to imitate Thérésa, the darling of the boulevards, singing *Rien n'est Sacré pour un Sapeur!*

Louise slipped away on the pretext of "going to see maman" when the officers began to shout the outrageous refrain. Frank, who had no such pretext, wondered how best to ask his hostess's permission to retire. To leave the room was always considered embarrassing in Philadelphia, but it had never happened to him in Philadelphia to excuse himself to a hostess in the act of imitating a Jardin Mabille dancer, with a Sèvres fruit plate for a tambourine. He half rose, with an appealing look at Bertaux, and

127

the financier, who was beating time to the song with a fork, gave him an indulgent nod of dismissal. He left the room with as much dignity as he could muster.

Ten minutes later, recrossing the magpie-coloured hall, he noticed that the french windows were ajar. Squares of light from Madame d'Arbonne's windows fell on the terrace, and he saw Louise leaning on the stone railing. After a moment's hesitation he went quietly out to join her.

"Dear Miss Louise, is anything the matter?"

She turned with a gasp, and he saw tears on her cheeks.

"You startled me, monsieur."

"I'm sorry. I'm afraid you'll catch cold out here, without a cloak."

"I'm not cold. My mother is very restless tonight, and Soeur Marie-Antoine wouldn't let me stay. Out here I can feel near her for a little while longer."

They both looked up at the lighted windows. The nun's coif, as she went to and fro in attendance on her patient, threw a shadow like a ship in full sail on the blinds.

"Is the noise disturbing her?" said Frank awkwardly.

"She can't hear it in her room—thank heaven."

There was a faint touch of acrimony in her voice, the first he had ever heard there. "Why, she's not a baby after all!" he thought. "Poor little sweet!" And he urged her again gently,

"Do come indoors, Miss Louise. The night air can be dangerous, you know."

"But it smells divine!" She tilted her head up at him, and over the grave little kitten face there spread, for the first time since the guests from Paris arrived, a happy and alluring smile. In her white draperies, Louise seemed poised to fly away over the dark woods by Barbizon, where the white lilies-of-the-valley and the young bracken fronds were breathing out the delicious scent of youth and spring and innocence. It was as much as Frank could do not to kiss her there and then.

He said huskily, "We'll explore the forest thoroughly tomorrow, won't we?"

"Oh, I hope so!"

"Even if your sister doesn't feel up to riding?"

"Why shouldn't I?" said Madeleine.

She stood in the doorway, surveying them with cool amusement. Madeleine was erect, glowing; poised as if her special mixture of champagne and brandy had been seltzer water. "My God, what a woman," thought poor Frank. "How does she do it? What have I done wrong now?" Madeleine had mercy on him. She did not repeat her question, but said briskly, "Victor has ordered the horses for seven; anyone may come who likes. Bedtime, Louise!"

In the hall Monsieur Bertaux was lighting bedroom candles for his nieces.

"Ah, Frank, there you are." To the American's relief, he spoke as pleasantly as ever. "They want you to join in a game of poker; do you care to play?"

"It'll be a pleasure, sir," said Frank. ("And if I don't separate that Victor from some loose change, then I learned nothing in the 27th Pennsylvania," he added to himself.)

Madeleine took up her silver candlestick, irritatingly composed, the perfect chatelaine, as if the Empress and Mrs. Moulton and Thérésa were so many puppets she had tumbled back in their box after manipulating them to amuse her guests. "Good night, dear uncle!" (A cheek casually presented for his kiss.) "Mr. Frank Hartzell, you don't admire my singing, but I forgive you, and I wish you pleasant dreams. Oh, what a long day, and oh, how tired I am!"

She was already halfway upstairs as she spoke.

"Louise, dear, come along!"

Her left hand held the candle high, her right was flung out impatiently, the whole forward movement of her body brought to Frank's rapidly clearing brain an irresistible recollection. All at once he knew who had posed for the sketches above the library fire place, and for the picture which Eugène Delacroix had named *The Spirit of France.*

IX

The Sunday which brought so much anxiety to the court of France passed very quietly at the court of Prussia.

At Potsdam there was a short, simple Lutheran service in the morning which the old king and queen and all their courtiers attended, followed by a long simple dinner of roast goose and beer which everyone enjoyed. After that those in residence at the palace of Sans Souci might spend the afternoon as they preferred. Queen Augusta read her Bible. The Crown Princess, Queen Victoria's daughter, wrote a long, boastful letter to her mama. Some of the court ladies dozed beneath huge eiderdowns, others walked into Potsdam and had an extra snack of chocolate with cream under the lime trees in the leading pastrycook's garden. It was all "simple," "good," "homely"—favourite words at the Prussian court—and as far removed as life on another planet from the feverish dissipations of the Tuileries.

The old king—he was seventy-three—announced that he would spend the afternoon like a good family man, talking with his eldest son, the Crown Prince Fritz. As the queen dozed off over the New Testament she congratulated herself that Count Otto von Bismarck, who had disturbed the peace of many a Potsdam Sunday, was grappling with a bout of indigestion on his own estate at Varzin. She was not aware that two of the Iron Chancellor's agents were at that moment listening to the band in the palace gardens, and would at the appointed time slip out of the crowd of cheerful Potsdamers and be conducted by devious ways to share the Sabbath conference of her pious husband and her son.

One, whose name was Lothar Buchar, was a nervous, shifty-eyed civilian, known as a fanatical Prussian nationalist. With his companion, Major Versen, he had recently been travelling back across France; both dressed as German tourists in search of *Kultur* and armed with guide-books, vasculums and such souvenirs in the way of wineskins and Toledo paper knives as earnest sightseers bring home from Spain.

They had in fact been at Madrid for a series of secret talks with the Regent of Spain, Serrano, with General Prim and with a member of the Cortes called Salazar who like themselves was on the private payroll of the Count von Bismarck.

The Iron Chancellor had his own plans for the year 1870. Plans which he did not intend to drop because Prince Leopold was too timid to grasp at the offer of the Spanish Crown, or the Prussian royalties too cautious to persuade him into it. In his very careful timetable the audience accorded to his agents at Potsdam was of the first importance. That the old king consented to receive them at all was proof that his resolution to have nothing more to do with the matter was weakening a little : Buchar and Versen did their work well. When they had finished their account of pro-Leopold opinion in Spain, and the advantages that backward country would derive from the rule of a forward-looking, scientifically minded Prussian monarch, they had not quite succeeded in convincing old King Wilhelm. He knew France; as a boy of seventeen he had had his baptism of fire in battle against the great Napoleon, and he was not disposed to risk all he had gained for Prussia in a war with Napoleon the Less. But they had certainly convinced the Crown Prince Fritz. When the big blond man began to talk about Prussia's historic civilizing mission in the world, and about his cousin's Christian duty to carry it into Spain, they knew their mission was accomplished and that they could report to their master at Varzin that the thin edge of the wedge was in.

In Paris they had ceased to worry about the affairs of Spain. Both cabinets, the elected and the Black, were occupied exclusively with the plebiscite results. The new Constitution had been approved by an enormous majority : seven million "Yes" votes to only one and a half million "No." But however much Ollivier might beam, and Léon Gambetta's Republicans scowl in their party headquarters on the rue de la Sourdière, there were disquieting elements in the plebiscite returns.

Since all the troops had been polled by mandate, the total strength of the French Army was now revealed to the world. It did not tally with the figures given in the Army List. Instead of the 415,000 troops to be put in the field at two weeks' notice, the election returns showed only 300,000 service votes.

"Where are my soldiers?" the Emperor asked Ollivier, and the prime minister, reminded him that the government, true to its liberal beliefs, had decided to reduce the army by ten thousand men. But that, of course, affected only the conscripts coming up in the class of 1870.

"Where are my soldiers?" the Emperor asked the War Minister, and Marshal Leboeuf blustered that so many were on furlough, so many trooping to Africa, so many in transit to new depots. He admitted that there might be some gaps in the conscript system. Many draftees had sent money instead of the replacements required if they were unable or unwilling to serve. But still that only accounted for a fraction of the missing men.

"I am not able to make war," said the Emperor to himself. He was alone in his overheated study, white-lipped, his eyelids puffed by a new complication of kidney disease. "If Bismarck attacks us this autumn, how shall I mount a counterattack? I should have stopped him in 1866, when he went to war with Austria. One French division sent into the Rhineland then, and he was finished!"

He stood bending over his desk (sitting for any length of time was painful to him now), his chalk-thickened fingers holding down the map of Europe. It was as familiar to him as the chessboard to an expert player—this board on which he had so long manipulated the kings and pawns. The thought trembled at the back of his fogged mind that all the old system of alliances, all the network woven by the great Napoleon, might come to pieces in the reign of Napoleon the Less. He shied away from that thought in dismay. He turned resolutely to consider the speech prepared for him to deliver to the Legislative Body when the plebiscite results were formally announced in the Pavillon de Flore.

"We can now look forward to the future with less dread than at any previous time in our history . . ."

It read all right.

*   *   *

Imperial Paris danced its way through the cloudless May of 1870 and into the equally perfect June, while the members of the diplomatic corps vied with one another in the splendour of the entertainments offered to the Emperor and Empress, and the court devised new cotillions and costume extravaganzas for the amusement of its guests. The imperial couple drove through the city every day—cheered to the echo—nowhere more loudly cheered than by the Chasseurs of the Prince Eugène barracks, who had recorded a noisy and solid vote against the dynasty. The palace was the focus of all the light and colour in which Paris seemed to bask as the wonderful days went by in a blaze of cream and rose. In the Luxembourg gardens the hawthorns bloomed in thickets of ruby and white; along the Seine and the Champs Elysées the tall chestnuts showered down their petals like confetti; and in the palace Eugénie wore bridal white again, and gathered her smiling ladies round her like a bouquet of exotic flowers.

A young man like Frank Hartzell, rich and well introduced by letters from his father's old friends in Philadelphia, was immediately welcomed to the American colony in Paris. Its leader, Dr. Thomas Evans, the Imperial Surgeon-Dentist, presented his fellow Philadelphian to so many residents that soon Frank had more invitations than he could possibly accept. Bertaux worked him hard. In the Paris office he was employed in bulk buying for the two hotels in which Bertaux S.A. held a controlling interest, the Grand and the Splendide, and had to be at Les Halles, when the market carts came in from all over the Ile de France, very early in the morning.

After Bertaux had installed him in a pleasant room at the Grand Hotel, Frank saw little of his employer. The financier was anxious and preoccupied. As soon as the plebiscite had passed without disturbances in Paris he brought his ailing sister back to the capital to consult an eminent American physician, who had come on a visit to Dr. Evans.

Dr. Marion-Sims had shaken his head as sadly but definitely over the condition of Madame d'Arbonne as her French doctors had done. She was sinking fast, consumed by the wasting disease which no one could diagnose, and the shadow of the approaching

133

end was falling over the great house in the Faubourg. Frank saw Louise only once or twice, when Bertaux included him in formal luncheons for his business friends, and the girl slipped downstairs for a few minutes to talk to him in the conservatory. Through the season when she should have entered society, Louise was spending her days and nights at her mother's bedside. All she knew of the gaieties of the time was the dance music which floated in at night from the Rothschild house next door, or from the British Embassy when Lord Lyons entertained the Imperial Family.

The season was to end at the Tuileries ball planned to celebrate the plebiscite victory, and the ladies of the court were not sorry for it. They had been on the move for weeks. Out to St. Cloud to escape the heat of Paris. Back to the Tuileries for a fancy-dress ball or gala dinner. Madeleine d'Arbonne, resting in her small bed-room at the Tuileries on the afternoon before the Plebiscite Ball, was sick to death of the whole thing.

Although her room was on the Carrousel side, it rang with the sound of carpenters at work, setting up a temporary platform against the garden front of the Tuileries at the level of the grand salons, from which a double flight of stairs was to lead into the gardens. Down those stairs, and along the walks enclosed by flowering orange trees brought specially from the Riviera, the Empress of the French would sweep many times that night to mingle with some of her six thousand guests. Madeleine's ankles ached already as she thought how often she would have to follow up and down behind Eugénie, managing as best she could the very tight skirt and pleated train of her new ball gown from Worth. She felt very tired. The painful sights and sounds of the sickroom frightened her, when she relieved Louise's vigil, nearly as much as her mother's trembling and terrified descent into the shadows where the Comte d'Arbonne's mind seemed already to be wandering. Sitting by the dying woman she had thought much of her neglected childhood, when all the mother's love had been lavished on Victor, and Madeleine was left to the very inferior governesses who would take service in their extraordinary ménage, or to the grooms and gamekeepers at Arbonne. She thought, too, of her brilliant early years at court. If her mother had not been so wildly jealous then of the young beauty which put her own in the shade, of the position near the Empress which she herself could never fill—if there had been loving guidance at that time, how many follies might not Madeleine have avoided! So she thought now, with her twenty-sixth birthday, passed in April, seeming to range her with the few old maids of the court, and the familiar round of Paris to St. Cloud, St. Cloud to Vichy, Vichy to Biarritz, then back to Paris and on to Compiègne, stretching before her in all its futility.

Locked away in the little escritoire beside her bed was a bundle of letters—not more than five or six in all—which had helped to dissatisfy her with the Tuileries life. James Bruce, in his hatred of clandestinity, had addressed each one to her *aux bons soins de Monsieur Michel Bertaux, rue du Faubourg St. Honoré*; Madeleine had brought them, one by one, to the little room in the palace where she could be sure of privacy before she broke the neat circle of red sealing wax stamped with the letter B. They were not love letters. They bore no resemblance to the silly, ill-spelled scrawls, usually ending in *je vous adore!* which sometimes reached her in a bouquet of Parma violets or tucked into a cotillion favour. James, who found endearments so difficult to speak, was quite incapable of putting words of love on paper, but his letters spoke for him better than he knew. His personality, and his daily life in a world so strange to Madeleine, came through to her with the utmost clarity.

"I must be falling in love with him!" she sometimes told herself in bewilderment, "if I can *want* to read about the Bruce Reciprocating Engine, developing forty kilograms of pressure to the square centimetre!"

The firm black copperplate handwriting traced a clear picture of the little inn parlour at Dumbarton where James, after a hard day's work on *Indus*, then on the stocks at Denny's shipyard, sat down to write to her. She could almost see the smoky coal fire, the paraffin lamp and the dark head bent intently over the draughtboard which served him as a writing desk. Sometimes she wished, acutely, to be there beside him.

She had not yet bidden him return to Paris, but because of his

135

letters she had closed one door which might have opened on a different future. The court had been at St. Cloud when Charles de Mortain asked her to marry him, one evening when the ladies and the officers on guard were strolling up and down a rose garden at their favourite game of storytelling: making up, paragraph by paragraph, a mock-medieval romance about the fortress of Mont Valérien, whose casemates stood out in such bold relief against the sunset sky. The Captain-Marquis de Mortain, very handsome, very correct in his plumed helmet and white buckskin breeches, had looked like the hero of one of Eugénie's favourite novels as he drew Madeleine under a trellis of pink roses and laid his hand, heart and considerable estates in Normandy at her feet.

She had refused him—the splendid match, on which as she very well knew her family had staked their last hopes for her. He had not taken his congé quietly. There had been sharp words. "You've been making a fool of me, Madeleine!" And then indignantly, disbelievingly, "Can there be—is there—someone else?"

"Is there somebody else? Is there? Is there?" And Madeleine turned restlessly, crushing her breasts against the hard mattress, while the lawn dressing sacque, a little moist with summer perspiration, pulled taut across her naked back and shoulders. "Oh, James!" Dark eyes, strong hard hands, a mouth that felt square and tender like a boy's mouth when he kissed her on the lips— she wanted James Bruce suddenly and violently, as she knew quite well that he had wanted her.

There was a knock outside.

"Wait a minute." She got off the bed and put on a dark wrapper before opening the door. "What is it, Baptiste?"

The footman, with a bow, told her that a foreign gentleman was waiting in the Salon Vert for mademoiselle.

"His name?" The man regretted; monsieur had not given his name. "Always ask the name." It was said mechanically, she was leaning against the door even while she shut it, her knees suddenly weak and her heart beating with great heavy strokes. A foreign gentleman—it must be! James Bruce here in the Tuileries! She dressed quickly, put on a bonnet and gloves; they could walk by the little pond in the gardens, where there would be no

136

courtiers today, only workmen stringing fairy lamps for the ball. Madeleine hurried downstairs.

But it was not James who stood waiting for her beside one of the long windows looking out on the gardens and the pond. It was Frank Hartzell—the first messenger Bertaux had been able to lay hands on—and as soon as she saw his troubled compassionate face she knew the message he had been sent to bring her.

Three days later she stood by her mother's grave, swathed in a heavy veil, with her little sister's hand in hers, and Victor in civilian clothes by their side. A fresh wind from the English Channel blew across the little cemetery; the fisher folk of Trouville were standing watching behind the cemetery walls. Beyond them, in the lane, a few Norman farmers returning from the village were edging their carrioles round the shining hearse, with nodding black plumes on the back of the black Belgian horses, and the great gold "A" on the purple pall, in which Madame d'Arbonne's coffin had been carried from the station to its last resting place.

Michel Bertaux had performed his supreme act of possession. He had refused to let his sister's body be taken back to the little church outside the Arbonne wall, where the Crusader's effigy lay in the aisle before the altar with the cockleshells carved on his stone bier, and had brought her home instead to the village from which he and she had run away to make their fortune, so many years ago. A little gravestone near the place where they were standing, with the simple inscription "Jules Bertaux, 1843—Marguerite Lachaume, épouse Bertaux, 1845" marked the financier's memorial to his parents; he had derived a great deal of comfort, after they all came back from the funeral Mass at St. Philippe du Roule in Paris, in planning a marble mausoleum on which his sister's rank and virtues were to be extolled. Whether the village of Trouville was touched by his fidelity to the past it was hard to say: the fisher folk's faces were impassive, although the men's heads were bared. There was one group of girls, or young married women, whom Madeleine could distinguish through her crape— girls of the same physical type as herself, tall and blonde and wearing the high Norman *cauchoises*, with superb breasts straining at their blue bodices, who seemed to look with active hostility at the little group of mourners. "My uncle is *too* rich," she thought. "They hate us all!"

Behind her the Demoiselles Elisabeth and Henriette d'Arbonne stirred uneasily, as if they too felt a wave of class hatred coming out to them. The old ladies of the rue du Bac had been living at the Bertaux house since the night of Madame d'Arbonne's death: they had come fluttering over from the Left Bank at once, thankful for a good meal, and determined to follow in the funeral train to Trouville "to represent poor Louis, since he is too ill to go with her, and as a last mark of respect to poor dear Marie." In fact the dead woman had always been carelessly kind to them.

The dead woman's husband was genuinely too unwell to leave Paris. If Victor had dared, he too would have pleaded illness: the set of his jaw as he stood by the grave glaring at the inside of his top hat told his sister that he was only there under the duress of a long obedience to his uncle, for Victor had been vehement about the propriety of burying his mother at Arbonne. He looked relieved when the committal ended, and disgusted when a photographer from Lisieux, whom Bertaux had hired to take pictures of the grave and the immense pile of wreaths on either side, came forward with his apparatus and black cloth. They were all glad to step into the waiting carriage and drive away from the little fishing port across the Touques River into the fashionable new resort of Deauville.

It was years since Bertaux had visited either Trouville or Deauville. His sister had loathed that part of Normandy, for her even more than for him full of terrible memories of their brutalized childhood, and long before his historic quarrel with the Duc de Morny Bertaux had refused to speculate in Morny's development of the long empty beach beyond the Touques. Deauville was one of the few places in France where there was no agency of the Bertaux company, and he had gladly accepted the offer made by his friend Monsieur Boitille to use his villa for rest and refreshment before their special train started the seven hours' run back to Paris.

Louise, gentle and appealing in her mourning dress, took her

138

elderly cousins upstairs after the collation served with suitable decorum by the Boitille servants. Victor, still in a sullen mood, lounged off "to have a look at old Boitille's nags" when Madeleine and her uncle walked out into the garden of the Villa des Flots. It ran through pergolas of pink rambler roses to a tall grille shrouded in privet dividing it from the promenade, near which a stone summerhouse, bright with petunias in troughs, held a rustic table and some roughly constructed chairs. Anyone in the summerhouse could see through the hedge without being seen, and Madeleine looked out wistfully at the passers-by walking in freedom, some in high self-confident British voices discussing their croquet scores or the table d'hôte at their *pensions*. "I have a friend in England," she told herself for reassurance; and turned to regard, across the wooden table, the twitching face of Michel Bertaux.

"Michou!" she said, moved to compassion for him, "no one will miss her as you'll miss her. No one ever loved her better than you did!"

"You're generous, Madeleine," said her uncle with a sigh. "And you were kind to agree with me so readily about bringing her here. I'm sorry Victor and your father felt so bitter about it."

"Oh!" with a shrug. "It was logical to bring her here—it was all of a piece with the way your lives were planned. But you know I don't think mother had any particular feeling, either about being buried at Trouville or beside all our musty old ancestors in the vault at Arbonne. If there were a burying ground in the very heart of Paris, where she could hear carriage wheels and theatre orchestras and think herself still part of the gay life she loved, that would have suited her best of all."

"What a pagan you are, Madeleine!" There was a slight edge to Bertaux' voice.

"You, too! If I were a better educated woman, I daresay I could find books to give me some explanation of why you staged that show at Trouville today, with those hostile faces all around us. I don't think it was a Christian impulse, dear Michou! But it's done now, and can't be undone: we must think of it as belonging to the past."

"I hope that means you're thinking of the future, Madeleine; that's what I want to discuss with you."

"What, here and now? Can't that wait until we're back in Paris?"

"In Paris I'll have business arising from Marie's death to transact with Maître Lachmann, and I want a competent medical opinion on your father, too. You and I had better make our own plans first."

"*Our* plans?" with a delicate lift of the eyebrows.

"Certainly ours; you must see that your mother's death makes a great difference to our domestic life. You'll have to take her place in many ways. And if you always acquit yourself as well as you did three nights ago," said her uncle warmly, "you'll be a great asset to the Société Anonyme Bertaux."

Madeleine remembered the evening of her mother's death, when she had stood by her uncle's side to receive half the business world of Paris—the Saccards, the Rougon-Macquarts and other czars of the Bourse, the banks, the new department stores, who had found it very convenient to offer their condolences to the bereaved family on their way to the Plebiscite Ball. It seemed to her that she had been deprived of the tinsel protection of the court in time to see the society of the Second Empire at its most vulgar that night. The wild parties she had enjoyed with the Murat set had never contained that sinister element common to all the loud raffish men and overdressed women who had trailed their unsuitable ball finery through the gaslit salons, eating and drinking—some of the men even smoking—and scarcely subduing their voices in the house of death.

"What exactly have you in mind, uncle?"

"First of all I want you to spend some time at Arbonne. The town house is closed now, to all intents and purposes, and I shan't reopen it next winter—not until our year of mourning is over. Arbonne is in a dreadful state. Louise has no command at all over those rascally servants; they're picking and stealing everywhere, and neglecting their duties; the place needs *you* to set it right. We'll get the two old ladies to look after your father, so you'll be free to ride and drive and enjoy the country all summer long. By October we shall see if Bismarck means business this year or not, and make new plans accordingly."

"Still harping on a war with Prussia! Why, everyone at the Tuileries says the outlook is better now than it has been for years!"

"The *Emperor* says that, and only in public—I wager Conneau and Thélin could tell a different tale. No, war is always possible, but if it does come it won't be until October," said Bertaux positively, "when the harvest is in, and there's fodder for the horses. And at the first sign of trouble," he concluded, "I'll pack you all off to the villa at Biarritz. You'll be perfectly safe there, and if the worst comes to the worst you can get across the Spanish frontier with no delay at all."

"Does the villa at Biarritz need setting to rights too? I haven't been down there for a couple of years."

"All my houses need an efficient mistress, the kind of mistress your mother was."

"What about your own mistress, *la belle* Delavigne? I'm sure she'd be charmed to be your hostess, uncle dear. Especially as Monsieur Delavigne's duties in the Intendance keep him so closely tied to Algiers."

"That will do, Madeleine."

"Oh nonsense," she said sharply, "you can't shut me up as if I were a child. Suppose I told you that supervising my uncle's domesticities made no appeal to me, and that I decline absolutely to play the hostess to his vulgar friends?"

"Who have paid, some of them through the nose, for the falderals on your back, and the bill from Worth I received yesterday—"

"And the diamonds, don't let's forget the diamonds—necklace, earrings, bracelets—"

"And the diadem I shall slip into your bouquet on your wedding day," said Bertaux between his teeth.

Her light, mocking laugh rang strangely in the summerhouse.

"When will that be?"

"*You* say. You tell *me*, Madeleine. Last year you sent away the Duque de Peñaroya; if you had accepted him you would have your own place in Madrid society now—"

"Or I'd be locked up in a dungeon somewhere in the Asturias," suggested Madeleine, "while that half-Moorish brute thought up some interesting variant of wife beating! You have an odd taste in nephews-in-law, Michou, from the Spanish sadist to the Italian sodomite—"

"*Madeleine!*"

"Don't think I didn't see what was going on at Cairo—Federico with his little boys all around him—"

"Like the Empress with her little girls."

She would have struck him then, fair and full in his twitching face, if he had not caught her upswung arm at the elbow, and held her powerless. She faced him like a spitting cat, quite unafraid, and it was he whose eyes fell before hers, and he who said, "I'm sorry, Madeleine. I know that was a slander. I'm sorry." He let her go. "You really think it's true about di Roccanuova?"

"Ask Adèle."

"Does *she* know?"

"She thinks it will be very convenient once the baby's born, and she's free to do as she likes in Rome."

"Oh God," said Bertaux. "That's bad. I was thinking of sending Louise to her later on—"

"Oh no! Please! You couldn't possibly send the child into that pollution! Oh, believe me, I saw very well what it was, when we met them in Italy on the way to the Suez Canal. I heard the gossip about Rico in Verona, in Venice, everywhere! But Adèle can take care of herself, you know. I've always thought that of the four of us she's the one most like our mother. So pretty and so confident, and so determined to shine in society! Now she's the Principessa di Roccanuova, the mistress of that magnificent house in Rome and the villa at Sorrento; and if her baby is a boy her position will be secure forever. Six months from now she'll take her first lover—what do they call it in Italy? her *cavaliere servente*! and then she'll be delighted to let Federico go his own sweet way. I know already what her salons will be like, and the riffraff she and Rico will have gathered round them by next Christmas. Do you think our Louise, so young and so unspoiled, should be sent into that vile atmosphere?"

"Then come home and take care of her, Madeleine," the man said swiftly. "You're twenty-six, not a girl any more; *you* could take her about in Paris by and by. *You* could, if you wanted, have a married home where she could be with you. What about Charles de Mortain, one of the finest young men at court? You're not going to let him slip through your fingers, as you lost Antoine de Noailles eight years ago, by being too eager—too complaisant—giving him too many of your favours? Eh, Madeleine?"

"I refused Charles de Mortain ten days ago, Michou."

"Then will you please tell me what in God's name you're waiting for? For young Louis Bonaparte to turn eighteen? For the Imperial Crown of France?"

"Something much simpler but nearly as hard to get. I'm waiting for a *man*, that's all; not a nice boy in a blue and silver uniform, and certainly not a prince of the Imperial Family; just a real, generous, brave, daring, truthful *man*."

"You wouldn't by any crazy chance be hankering after that Scots engineer, would you?"

Madeleine laughed delightedly.

"Why? Do you think he fills the bill?"

"All right, Madeleine, I take your point. But I decline to let Mr. Bruce enter my calculations. Here they are now; it's very simple. Either let Monsieur de Mortain know that you've changed your mind, and make your plans for a wedding as soon as we're out of mourning, or else leave court immediately and take your proper place at Arbonne."

"Or—"

"Or I send Louise to spend the winter in Rome with Adèle."

"You don't fight fair, do you?"

"Not when I'm dealing with a woman, my dear."

"But you have to give me time. Why are we quarrelling like two ragpickers on my mother's funeral day? Didn't you do enough for the Bertaux glory when you made her a countess, without turning me into Madame la Marquise? I don't say," said Madeleine rapidly, "that I mayn't do as you suggest about

143

Charles, but give me a few weeks of breathing space! The Empress needs us all on duty until the season ends—"

"Even the Empress could hardly expect you to return to court from your mother's funeral, Mado."

"I *must* go back on Sunday. The court is going out to Compiègne next week: it'll be very quiet, but I know I'm to be needed specially."

"*Compiègne!*" said Bertaux. "Compiègne in June! What in the world should take Eugénie there now instead of in November?"

"She's going to entertain some guests from Belgium," said Madeleine in a burst of inspiration. "And then there's only a little while at St. Cloud before we move to Vichy—I think the change would do me good—"

"We might all go to Vichy in July," mused Bertaux.

"You do love travelling in a caravan, don't you? With Clarisse *chérie* and her Pomeranian doggies bringing up the rear?"

"Is it Clarisse you object to, Madeleine?"

"Not more than anything else," said Madeleine with a sigh.

"Then after Vichy you'll come home to us?"

"After Vichy the Emperor goes to the Châlons manoeuvres. Yes, I'll come home then. But not to you! Remember, not because *you* say so! But because you've made me realize today—as I never did before—how much my little sister needs me."

It was late in the evening when they reached the Faubourg St. Honoré, and all the ladies went straight to their rooms. Madeleine slept heavily for two or three hours, and then, after lying awake for some time, fell into a miserable doze between a sleep and a waking, which brought with it a sequence of feverish dreams. She dreamed she stood with the Empress, dressed in deep mourning, in the summerhouse at Deauville, while a stormy tide rose lashing toward them across the promenade. She dreamed that the Ismailia fireworks were bursting in red rain over Paris, and dragged herself from the dream with her head aching, her throat and lips dry. It was a relief to find herself in her own quiet, richly furnished room, where at seven o'clock no sound was to be heard but the singing of birds in the trees of the avenue

144

Gabriel. But as consciousness returned the ugly truths of the scene with her uncle came back in full force, and the bedroom began to oppress her by its very luxury.

"You'll have to take your mother's place in many ways!"

In what ways, Michou? Say in what ways, she thought.

Her mother, in the days of her opulent beauty and often ribald wit, had been the perfect hostess at the lavish banquets which Bertaux gave to show off his gold plate and his chef's skill, and she had kept enough of her Norman prudence to supervise his houses and servants thriftily and well. But Madeleine knew that Marie d'Arbonne had been most valuable to her brother in the long intimate conversations in which he poured out to her the details of his day: his Bourse transactions, his bargainings, his plans for his hotels. As a child she had sometimes dared to interrupt them—the scene was always the same. Her mother in a negligée, lying relaxed in a chaise longue, listening intently. Michel close by his sister's side, sometimes playing with her fingers, talking—both wrapped in that strange intimacy never broken since they starved together in a Montmartre garret, and laid their plans to conquer Paris.

As a grown woman Madeleine had kept her distance from the boudoir during the twilit period which the servants, sometimes with odd smiles, referred to as *l'heure de monsieur*. Nobody, not even her husband, might approach madame la comtesse during "Monsieur's hour." In future, was his niece to be the sharer of that hour—his other self, intimate companion, partner and confederate?

It was a thought which drove Madeleine to leave her bed and dress. Her uncle breakfasted downstairs and always left his room punctually at eight o'clock. An hour of freedom from him, and from the oppressive feeling of being cornered, slowly imprisoned in a mesh of wealth and family ties, and she would be able to face them all again! She left the house quietly. The stablemen were in the courtyard, polishing the carriage which had brought them back from the Gare St. Lazare. They gave her good morning with eyes lowered in recognition of her bereavement; the Old Poisson's greeting was a hearty scowl. At that early hour the old porter liked to show some of the contempt he felt for Monsieur Bertaux, who paid his wages, by sitting on a stool at the door of his lodge like the concierge of some slum tenement, drinking coffee and smoking a short clay pipe. He wore carpet slippers and a striped flannel nightcap instead of the maroon livery cap he would raise to his employer punctually at nine o'clock. His unshaven face, in which the black eyes were very alert beneath white tufted eyebrows grew taut with suspicion as Madeleine approached. He set his cup on the windowsill behind him with a grumble, and let her out into the Faubourg by the postern door. "Now what's she up to, going off like that the very day after her mother's funeral, without crape to hide her face or a maid to follow her?" he grumbled to his cat. "*She's* no lady—I always said so!" The Old Poisson reserved his admiration for "the real d'Arbonnes," Adèle and Louise, and gave grudging approval to his young master, but his private name for Madeleine was "the fisherman's grandchild."

Madeleine was drawn by instinct towards the Tuileries. But she kept her distance, having no mind to encounter officers going on duty at eight o'clock, answer their condolences and invent some reason for her presence in the rue de Rivoli at such an hour. She turned into a side street where at a decent little dairy she bought a bowl of café au lait and a roll of fresh bread. The dairywoman winked at her husband behind Madeleine's back: she had noted the beautiful black dress and all the perfection of the lady's accessories and concluded that her customer was a married woman who had been spending the night with her lover—a very usual happening in that locality. The lady's request for writing materials was less usual; the good woman shook her head, as she watched two sheets, three, filled and crossed. A woman who poured out her feelings on paper so soon after leaving her lover's arms had either too much "temperament" or was born to be the prey of blackmailers! There was both jealousy and pity in her face as she watched Madeleine walk down to the rue de Rivoli and cross the road to the gardens.

The scaffoldings and orange trees of the Plebiscite Ball had already been removed, and the public part of the Tuileries gardens given back to the people. It was the poor people of Paris whom Madeleine saw now in the chestnut alleys where she so seldom walked. The gardens were full of them, hurrying from their homes on the Left Bank to the shops and offices on the Right: the white-collar clerks, the white-bloused artisans, the pert midinettes in their trim black and white, all hurrying past with scarcely a glance for the young lady in mourning who sat so quietly on a stone bench by the little pond. A single jet of water, only a few feet high, rose and fell softly in the sunshine. Madeleine sat breathing the scent from the box hedges, feeling Paris all around her like a peach about its stone, and a little spring of hope began to rise in her heart as the fountain played. It was twenty-five minutes past eight by the palace clock. "I mustn't stay longer," she thought, "if I'm to walk home by the post office !" She took the letter from her reticule and read it over and over again. Then she folded it very carefully on the last sentence:

"James—I need you—come to me."

X

Mr. James Allan, who thirty-three years earlier had been one of the founders of the great P. and O. Company, hesitated when his confidential clerk told him that Mr. Bruce had returned from the Clyde, and was asking for an interview.

As Chief Shore Engineer, James had the right of access to Mr. Allan at all times. As a candidate for Manager, Mr. Allan was not particularly anxious to see him on that fine June Monday morning. Himself old and tired, having outlived his colleagues Willcox and Anderson, he had been pressing the Court of Directors for weeks to decide on the men who should succeed them in the traditional three-man Management. Now, over the past weekend, several influential Directors had assured him that if James Bruce were promoted along with Thomas Sutherland, at thirty the P. and O.'s prodigy, he—Allan—would not be able to retire until the new team settled down.

"Mr. James is a fighter, you know," one Director had warned, "and Tom Sutherland has been cock of the walk on the Hong Kong station. If they can't run in double harness, it might do a great deal of harm to the Company!"

"Ask Mr. James to wait five minutes," the old gentleman said to his clerk. "I'll ring."

He struck his table bell almost immediately. It had occurred to him that Bruce might have other things on his mind besides the Managership. Only two weeks earlier, while James was at the Denny yard, news had arrived from China that his youngest brother, George, had left the Company to join the Jardine, Matheson trading fleet. "Now we'll have a scene!" thought Mr. Allan forebodingly. "Bruce was quite built up in that young man's career."

But James was smiling so happily when he came in that his brother's defection was clearly not in his mind. Mr. Allan had never seen him so fashionably dressed in the City. He wore a frock coat and trousers of a much lighter grey than he usually affected, and carried a grey top hat in which he laid, as he set it down, an astonishing pair of grey kid gloves. He was obviously fresh from the barber's hands, for the thick dark locks had been clipped closer than usual behind his ears, and his dark eyes were sparkling.

"You're very fine, Mr. James!" said old Allan in jocose surprise. "With a white carnation in your buttonhole you would pass for a bridegroom!"

Bruce's smile widened—Mr. Allan had never known him to smile like that!—and something like a flush darkened the face weatherbeaten by the spring winds of the Clyde. The unbelievable truth dawned on Mr. Allan: James Bruce, at last, was going courting.

He listened without surprise to Bruce's request for leave to go to France on urgent private affairs, and only pointed out that *Travancore* and *Hindostan* had arrived at Southampton over the weekend, and must positively be inspected before his trip began.

"Then I'll go down to Southampton on the noon train, start work tonight and catch the night packet to Le Havre on Wednesday," said James firmly. "It means wasting time on the long route to Paris, but no more than if I came back to London for Dover. Is that agreeable to you, sir?"

Mr. Allan sighed.

"You're determined to go over this weekend?"

"Absolutely, sir. The letter—er—requesting my presence has been lying at my Doughty Street chambers for some days."

"It seems a pity to miss Mr. Bayley's dinner on Saturday. He was counting on getting your views on the Suez situation. You've heard, of course, that we're taking a heavy loss on the farms at Zagazig and Cairo?"

"Ismail Pasha is directly responsible for the Suez situation," said James briskly. "The French cockered him up so high last autumn that he thinks he can do as he likes with *us*. If he carries out his threats to seize for Egypt the lighthouses the P. and O. built and operates, and default on the loan we made him for the railroad, the best way to get our money back might be to send an expeditionary force to Port Said."

"Possibly," said Allan with a thin smile, "but this is 1870, Mr. James. Gladstone's cabinet will not go to war for the P. and O., and your influence with de Lesseps, who has the ear of Ismail Pasha, may prove more useful to the Company than British bayonets."

"The ear of Ismail!" James thought of a certain night in the Khedive's pavilion on the dunes outside Port Said. "I wouldn't build too much on that! De Lesseps has his own troubles with the Khedive—and I've seen nothing of him since last November. He and Madame de Lesseps have been at Ismailia ever since their marriage."

"Then come and talk it over with Mr. Bayley," said Mr. Allan swiftly. "Let Mr. Sutherland, and the other guests, hear your views. You've been on the Clyde and at Southampton for months now, away from the centre of things."

"I'm sorry to be ungracious, sir. But this trip to France means the whole of my future life to me."

"I guessed that," said the old man kindly, "but you have your professional future to secure as well. I would like you to have an opportunity of discussing our problems with some of the Directors, and above all with Mr. Sutherland, over a glass of wine. You know Sutherland in the office and he knows you, but I want him to see you on the very top of your form, as you used to be in the old days, when we all had our legs under Mr. Anderson's mahogany. He knew how to draw you out, and so did Brodie Wilcox, but Mr. Sutherland is a very much younger man, and in view of what may develop in the future I would like him to see more of you in a social relationship."

"I don't know if I understand you, sir," said James stiffly. "Is it a new Company policy that a man must sing songs and tell stories, and get slightly fuddled on his colleagues' port, before he can expect promotion? I stand upon my record as an engineer, sir; young Mr. Sutherland is no doubt familiar with it."

"Now don't fly into a huff, Mr. James! You must allow an old man, who knew you from a boy, to put in a word in season.

Don't despise the social occasions, lad; they might make all the difference to getting away from the draughtboard and sitting here," he pointed to the two vacant chairs at the great conference table, "where my dear old friends used to sit. Maybe," he continued with a twinkle, "if your private affairs in France are so very urgent, you'll be giving us some news of a social nature yourself, before long? Eh? Is there to be a Mrs. Bruce to soften your thrawn temper, and charm us all with her French airs and graces? Well—we'll be delighted to subscribe for a wedding canteen of cutlery, and it's certainly not ahead of time."

James forgot Mr. Allan's good advice the moment he was out in Leadenhall Street. He had been in a continuous state of excitement since reading Madeleine's letter. He had waited and hoped so long for the summons which his stubborn pride forbade him to anticipate that only the long discipline of his profession had kept him from hurrying to Paris on the previous night. Only the congenial prospect of crowding a six days' inspection into two, driving himself until he was fit to drop and those under him until they were ready to mutiny, reconciled him to a delay which meant that he would have to follow Madeleine and the court to Compiègne.

Then, of course, he would make her marry him. Her mother was dead and her father less fit than ever to be her protector; her uncle making grotesque demands upon her to preside over his establishments. If, at last, she had sent for himself it meant that she wanted to escape from Bertaux—the old lecher! James had his private views about Bertaux' feelings for his niece. He was well acquainted with some of the sensational marriages of an earlier generation. He had heard of Sir John Acton, a roué of seventy who scandalously married his niece when she was little more than a child. He knew that Baron James Rothschild had married his own brother's daughter, Betty Rothschild of Vienna, who had borne him three healthy sons and still lived, the respected matriarch of the tribe, in the old Rothschild mansion on the rue Laffitte. James knew Madeleine by instinct and by heart too well to suppose that she would ever play the part of a Baroness

Rothschild or a Lady Acton; and to Bertaux, also, he gave credit for being too circumspect for any conduct which would be frowned on by the society of 1870. No; her uncle probably only wanted to be the dog in the manger, to keep her to be admired with his other possessions—thinking that if *he* couldn't have her, nobody else should!

James had known profound discouragement as the spring passed and Madeleine's few brief letters gave no hint that she was eager to see him again. The delay in his promotion had worried him, too—as a Manager he would command twice his present income, which would be something to throw in the teeth of that infernal Bertaux!—and there had been family worries to add to the burden he carried to each hard day's work. Sometimes he wished with all his heart that he had accepted the light, laughing invitation she had given him at Ismailia:

"Won't you come on with us to the Bitter Lakes?"

It was odd, but of all she had ever said to him that one sentence remained most clearly in his memory! Suppose he *had* gone on to the De Lesseps betrothal party? Just for once, for the very first time, abandoned his rigid schedule and gone all the way to Suez in the *Delta*? Spent days and nights with her, knotting a solid tie between them at the very start?

Well, he was going to her now, at Compiègne.

James turned into a telegraph office, to send a dispatch to Madeleine at the Tuileries announcing his arrival for noon on Friday at the Hotel La Cloche, and went off with the old compulsive sense of hurry to catch the midday train for Southampton.

It left Waterloo at much the same time as Bismarck's Spanish agent, Salazar, left Berlin with an urgent message for General Prim.

The Prussian Crown Prince, Fritz, had been a great asset to Bismarck's plot. He had much influence with the Hohenzollern family at Sigmaringen, not only as the future King of Prussia, but as a personage wholly admirable in himself. He was so tall, so broad, so liberal, so truly pious! With such a noble air, like a *Heldentenor* about to burst into song! He had done far more than the secret agents from Madrid to persuade Prince Leopold that his manifest destiny lay in Spain. The young prince had now not only decided to be a candidate for the Spanish Crown but to let his candidature be announced without delay. The word which Bismarck gave Salazar to carry to Madrid was *"June!"*

October, according to Michel Bertaux the logical month to expect trouble, meant nothing at all in Bismarck's timetable. He had no intention of fighting the war on German soil and therefore had no fear for the German harvest, which women could gather if need be, and his magnificent supply system had made ample provision for horse fodder. If the French reacted as he intended he would fight and win his war *before* October, in the best campaigning season, and hold the victory parade in Berlin before snow began to fly. As James Bruce lit his pipe in the corner of his railway carriage, and tried to concentrate on the shipping news in *The Times* newspaper, Bismarck sat down to luncheon with his old confederates, Generals von Moltke and von Roon. Over steins of beer they went through the timetable again and could find no flaw in it. Together within seven years they had attacked and beaten the Danes, attacked and beaten the Austrians, and now, as Salazar slipped away with the fateful message to Madrid, they were ready to open the last drama of Bismarck's trilogy.

The Château of Compiègne was by tradition the great autumn resort of the imperial court. Through November and early December nearly a thousand people were crowded between its walls, brought by special train from Paris and driven to the château in relays of eight persons in the dark green imperial char-à-bancs followed by baggage carts with enormous mounds of luggage. This took place at least four times in the late autumn. The guests were invited for visits of fourteen days at a time, in series nicknamed by Madeleine and her friends the "Musts," the "Bores," the "Fun People" and the "Brains." There were great ceremonial stag hunts and elaborate forest picnics by day, and at night concerts and charades, romping games of blindman's buff and hunt the slipper, and sometimes very beautiful winter balls.

There was no revival of this gaiety when the imperial party went down to Compiègne in the last week of June. The Emperor, attended by Dr. Conneau, went at once to his rooms. The Empress gave a few perfunctory orders to the groom of the chambers and retired in her turn. The only one in good spirits was the Prince Imperial, who had now mastered the velocipede and given it up in favour of roller skating, which he was delighted to have leave and space to practise on the terrace. He skated noisily until dusk fell, telling Madeleine, who had come out to watch him, that he "wouldn't be satisfied until he could dance the sailor's hornpipe on skates like Professor Fuller," for he had been greatly impressed by his American instructor at the rue Jean Goujon rink in Paris.

Next day the Empress only left her husband's side once, to take a short walk in the long arbour called the Berceau which the first Napoleon had planted for the Empress Marie Louise. Her chosen companion was Madeleine, whose rather subdued mood suited Eugénie's heavy heart. For the "guest from Belgium"—there was only one—was as the inner circle had known for some time a French surgeon travelling by road from Brussels, incognito; and the consultation at Compiègne was a subterfuge characteristic of the Emperor, whose interest lay in keeping his most recent illness a secret from the newspapers as long as possible.

Four Paris doctors, sworn to secrecy, met with Professor Germain Sée when he arrived from Brussels, with the faithful Dr. Conneau added by courtesy to their talk. Their examination of the Emperor lasted for two hours and brought them to the same conclusion as Dr. Larrey, the Surgeon-General, had reached when Napoleon was taken ill on manoeuvres two years before. They told the Empress the truth as gently as possible. Napoleon III was suffering from purulent cystitis and major surgery was now inevitable.

The Empress did not appear that night, and her women sat sewing and whispering fearfully until the earliest permissible moment for retiring. Madeleine, who detested embroidery and often interrupted the others at such work, for once earned the Princesse d'Essling's approval as she sat silent, hands folded in her lap, until the difficult hour was over.

Madeleine's thoughts, in fact, were completely occupied. The Emperor's grave illness, following so soon after her mother's death, seemed to foreshadow many changes in her life: that was much. James Bruce was arriving at Compiègne in the morning: that was a great deal more.

What was she going to say to him? There had been time to think since she scribbled her impulsive summons. She realized now that by sending for him she had given him the right to renew the proposal of marriage which had taken her aback in January. How was she going to answer it in June?

For the first time in her life Madeleine found herself forced to think, to face realities as she had never done in all her blithe career at court. The two natures which made up her own character—the buccaneering vigour of the Bertaux strain and the romantic chivalry of the d'Arbonne—had wrestled powerfully with one another as the girl struggled to see where her allegiance should be given. To the two helpless members of her family—her father and Louise? To the Empress, whom she had devotedly served for years? Or should she throw her cap over the windmill and leave them all for the man who had offered marriage without once saying the words *I love you*?

What would her life be like, if she left Paris to become James Bruce's wife? Would she have to follow him to the smoky inn at Dumbarton or keep house in London, struggling with domestic problems in the language she hardly spoke at all? Would his family disapprove of the French wife, the Papist, as strenuously as Bertaux had disapproved of James? What would they have to say to her at Sauchentree?

That she might be poorer, in material things, as the wife of a Scots engineer than as Mademoiselle d'Arbonne never for a moment entered Madeleine's calculations. There were other differences which she considered, while Madame Carette whispered sibilantly with Angèle de Larminat, and the Grand Mistress turned the pages of a pious book. He and she belonged to different and sometimes opposing countries. They belonged to different and always opposing creeds.

There was everything against their marriage.

There was nothing.

Before she blew out her bedroom candles that night Madeleine faced and accepted the ultimate truths of her own body. She had wanted James Bruce for her lover from the first moment when he kissed her beneath the oleanders at Ismailia. Now some atavistic, arrogant impulse inherited from her mail-clad ancestors said to her, "Take him and make him yours!"

It was another and better impulse, stifled for years, which told her that she wanted this man for her husband and the father of her child.

By next morning the truth about the illness of Napoleon III had been distorted into every form of rumour both above and below stairs at the Château de Compiègne. The Emperor was dying— the Emperor was dead—the Emperor was to undergo the knife that very day—the place was buzzing with bad news. It was almost a relief to Madame Lebreton, the Reader, and her rival, Madame Carette, both usually so jealous of any mark of favour, when a message came from the Empress summoning Mademoiselle d'Arbonne.

The Empress was writing in the library, close to her husband's bedroom. It was a dull morning, and the room looked heavy and sombre with its mahogany and gilt furniture and upholstery of the Bonaparte dark green. The Empress was dressed in black, and her glorious hair, which seemed to have lost some of its lustre, was flattened as if she had been writing with her head supported on her left hand. Her eyes were dim with watching, but her lovely enigmatic smile flashed out in the old way as Madeleine knelt beside her and kissed her hand.

"Madame, how is he? How is His Majesty?"

"He is better now. He had some natural sleep last night. I think his mind is easier now that he knows exactly what lies before him."

"They will operate, Madame?"

"They talk of an *exploratory* operation first. They must use a sound to explore the stone, and then they will crush it by a process called lithotomy—it sounds perfectly horrible." Tears came into Eugénie's eyes.

"And will it be done here, at Compiègne?"

"That's what I wanted, if it must be done at all. It would be so fresh and peaceful here for his convalescence. But the Emperor objects to being so far from the capital while he is recuperating, and so next week the doctors want to move him to St. Cloud. But the reason I sent for you, dear child," Eugénie continued, "was to ask the name of the American doctor who was consulted in your mother's case."

"Dr. Marion-Sims, Madame. He was recommended to my uncle by Dr. Evans."

"Marion-Sims—two words?" asked the Empress, making a note on her page. "With a hyphen—of course. And I can reach him through our dear Evans? I shall write today."

"He was very kind," said Madeleine doubtfully, "but I never heard that he was a specialist in His Majesty's complaint."

"I've explained to Professor Sée," said the Empress earnestly, "that I *insist* on having an American physician's advice *after* the operation. The Americans are far ahead of us in the treatment of wounds, and since His Majesty's doctors say the area to be explored is already terribly infected, there may be great danger of pyemia. I think this American doctor will be able to help us there."

"I'm sure of it, Madame. Oh, if only I could help you in a practical way!"

"My dear," said the Empress, "you help us by being yourself. I do appreciate your faithfulness in remaining with us at such a sad time in your own life. You're very pale, child, and it's no wonder! You must come with me this afternoon when I drive to Pierrefonds, and get some fresh air in the forest!"

"Does Your Majesty drive out this afternoon?" said Madeleine, surprised.

"I must go and compliment Monsieur Viollet-le-Duc on the Pierrefonds restorations, that's my official reason for being here," sighed the Empress. "Come in one of the carriages, or on horseback—we'll start at four; and then this evening you may rest in your own room. I shall dine alone with the Emperor, and only Comtesse Clary will be on duty. Thank you, Madeleine."

"Then, Madame—"

Eugénie frowned. She had given the little nod that meant dismissal, and her mind was already on her private letters: to Dr. Evans, to her mother, to her relatives among the grandees of Spain.

"Madame, may I ask a great favour? If I'm not required to be in attendance this evening, may I leave the château for a few hours?" She saw Eugénie's look of surprise, and plunged. "I expect a visitor from England, whom I would prefer to meet alone—not here. Your Majesty knows him. Mr. Bruce, who cleared the Canal at El Kantara."

"Mr. Bruce!" The Empress rose from her chair, her long fingers feeling nervously for the five rings on her left hand. "The engineer! Coming to Compiègne to see you—by special arrangement?"

A little curtsy sketched Madeleine's assent.

"Is he in love with you, Madeleine?"

"He hasn't said so, *Majesté*!"—demurely.

"But you think he will today, is that it? . . . My grandfather was a Scotsman," said the Empress with some pride. "I understand the Scots; their withdrawals, their reserve that conceals fire! What shall you say to this reticent gentleman when he makes his declaration?"

It was the tone of light mockery which Eugénie kept for all the trivial love affairs of her court. Her favourites knew it well enough, and also how to parry it with light tinkling laughter and gay denials. But Madeleine stood biting her lips, silent.

"You can't have fallen in love with that man?"

"I—don't know."

With a sigh Eugénie drew the girl into her arms and held her in the embrace that was like being pressed to the bosom of a marble statue, as the cold lips and the cold cheek, faintly scented with camellias, touched the warm mouth of the maid of honour. It was the imperial caress, well known: today somehow inhuman.

"Poor child!" said the exquisite voice, as the Empress released the girl and turned away. "I think you must care a little, if you told him where to find you! . . . How far has this gone, between you and Mr. Bruce? Is it possible that you would consider marrying him?"

"It is possible, *Majesté*."

Eugénie sat down again at her desk and covered her eyes with her hand.

"So you want to leave me too, Madeleine!" she said. "Soon everyone who was our true friend will have gone away! Some are dead—the Duc de Morny, Mocquard, Maupas, Saint-Arnaud! My beloved sister, and the dear Duchesse de Bassano! Now the Emperor's very life is in danger, and Louis is only a child. It may be left to me alone, without one faithful friend beside me, to be the leader of France if we decide on war—"

"On *war*, Madame!"

Against all etiquette, Madeleine had impulsively interrupted her sovereign. The beautiful face, unreproving, looked stonily up at her.

"*Italy* must be taught a lesson! The King's attacks upon the Papacy are no longer to be tolerated! Before the Emperor was taken ill I begged him to strike a blow for the spiritual power against the temporal—but he refused."

Madeleine, aghast, drew closer to the desk. Long accustomed to her uncle's predictions of war with Prussia, she had never dreamed that Eugénie's desires for victories to bolster up the dynasty might lead her into some crazy adventure elsewhere in Europe. She well remembered, and had known far more of the facts than she had ever confided to Bertaux, how Eugénie's religious fervour had driven France to install, and for a time to support a Catholic emperor in Mexico; and everyone knew what the Mexican expedition had cost the French in lives and gold. Now she saw that among the letters on the big desk there were some obsolete ordnance maps and bundles of notes on the Italian liberation campaign of 1855.

"Your Majesty is overwrought," she said as naturally as she could. "The Emperor will surely never go to war with Italy, which he freed and unified. And you have many friends, far more powerful though not more devoted than a maid of honour, who will never leave you—"

"But *you* will stay with us?" said Eugénie swiftly.

The girl hesitated. She looked down sorrowfully at the lovely head and the desk laden with threats to the peace of France. Then she felt her wrist taken and held by strong cold fingers, and—

"*Promise me!*" said the Empress of the French.

Very few passengers descended from the train which arrived from Paris shortly before noon that day. The pallid loungers near the Compiègne railroad station, who looked like racetrack touts from Chantilly and were in fact members of the secret police, were able to give James Bruce their full attention as he handed his bag to a porter with a handcart and strode across the bridge over the Oise and into the centre of the town. James was unaware of their scrutiny. As he entered the Hotel La Cloche he was hoping that Madeleine might be waiting in one of the shaded parlours opening off the hall. The innkeeper was all apologies; there was no visitor and no message for monsieur; but James caught a look of complicity from the valet de chambre, and when they were alone the fellow, grinning, showed him a rim of white in the pocket of his wasp-striped waistcoat.

"A groom brought it from the château only an hour ago" he began confidentially; and then, silenced by Bruce's scowl, caught Bruce's five-franc piece with one practised hand while he gave him Madeleine's letter with the other.

Her message was terse and to the point.

"The Empress goes to Pierrefonds this afternoon. She will stop to pray in the church at Vieux-Moulin and permits me to leave her there. I shall be at the Etangs de St. Pierre at five o'clock. —M."

A younger man might have pressed the letter to his lips; James folded it away in his breast pocket with a smile. "The French," he thought indulgently, "bless their melodramatic hearts! How the hell am I to get to Peter's Ponds, wherever that may be?" A map of the forest, framed on the wall just outside his bedroom door, gave him his bearings, and on the back of Madeleine's envelope he quickly drew a little map, beautifully scaled, of the Vieux-Moulin salient. It was the kind of transportation exercise in which he excelled. He ran downstairs whistling like a tone-deaf schoolboy.

The table d'hôte was full of robust farmers and dealers from the market, well into their second bottles of wine and making huge inroads on country cheeses and open tarts, while the servants came and went with fresh supplies of food. Although he had breakfasted lightly in Paris, James found that he had little appetite. His heart was beginning to beat with a young man's excitement, and his hands, when he unfolded his napkin, were not as steady as they might have been. He ordered a slice of country pâté, an herb omelette and a salad, with a pint of Pauillac, and lost himself in a dream of Madeleine.

. . . "So Badinguet is at the château again. What a treat for the Compiègne girls!"

The loud rough words, interrupting his reverie, had been spoken by a fat farmer in corduroys, who was soaking lumps of sugar in marc and tossing them rapidly into his mouth from the back of his hand.

There was a general laugh, but one of the other men looked at Bruce in his corner and muttered something beneath his breath.

"Ah, bah!" said the fat farmer, "that's no police spy. That's an English milord, ha! ha! Notice the nice little thrifty meal! The English have no stomachs for good French cooking. No, Badinguet isn't paying for *that* fellow's lunch." And he snapped up another sugar lump, with finality.

"Things seem pretty quiet at the château compared with the old days," said a man at the foot of the table. "No juicy scandals for a long time; no outings to the pretty little chalets in the woods! Do you remember when Napoleon broke with Madame Marguerite Bellanger, and she came down here and rented that house on the Soissons road and swore she'd set fire to the château if the Emperor didn't take up with her again? Remember after his carriage was seen at the door, how the Empress stormed out of Compiègne and went back to sulk in Paris? My! that's a long time ago!"

"He's past it now," opined the man who had drawn attention to Bruce's presence. "They say he can't mount either a horse or a woman these days."

"My friends," said the man in corduroys, tapping his nose with his right index finger, "a bull like Badinguet is never past it. The only difference is that he no longer goes outside for his fun. Those pretty ladies we see driving with *the Spaniard*—they're the ones who share his pleasures now! They say that every night on the stroke of midnight he meets one or other of the ladies in waiting in the Blue Room at the château, with fifteen thousand francs' worth of jewellery in his pocket to reward the dear creature for her exertions—"

"Fifteen thousand francs!" interrupted a shocked voice. "One hundred and five thousand francs every week?"

"Correct," said the fat man, winking hugely at his audience. There was an outburst of derisive laughter, in the middle of which James Bruce swallowed the last of his wine, flung a few coins on the table and left the room. As he went he heard the same scandalized voice complaining,

"And he has the nerve to tax us to keep up his army!"

It meant nothing at all, of course. Those boors were merely repeating a French version of what people in Britain had been saying for some years past about the Prince of Wales. James Bruce had forgotten his irritation before he reached the livery stable recommended by the innkeeper, where a rakish chestnut, the only animal in the string up to his weight, showed a disposition to rear which gave him a good deal of trouble in mounting and brought the stablemen out to stare and whistle. At last the brute was persuaded into the rue Mounier and under the walls of the château, and the forest took them into its comfortable shade.

With a sigh for the new light grey trousers on which every saddle stain would show, James Bruce crammed his hard hat well back on his head, cut a switch from a convenient bough and sat down to ride. It was years since he had ridden a horse of anything like the chestnut's very limited breeding—probably not since his father had sent him off from the Sauchentree smithy to take the factor's newly shod mare home to Aberdour House—but he felt instinctively the same exhilaration as the squires of the kings of France had felt for a thousand years, following their masters in the stag hunt through the royal forest. He rode through the *carrefours* of the historic names, past the *clairières* where the does and their dappled fawns lay hidden, and as he went he watched the red signposts pointing back toward the château, the white pointing on to Pierrefonds. At length he came out on the slope above a little marshy valley and saw on the far side the Route d'Eugénie which Napoleon III had constructed for his Empress, to bring her smoothly from her château at Compiègne to pray in the church at Vieux-Moulin.

As he checked his horse and looked across the red-tiled cottages in the valley at his feet, he saw a little procession of carriages and riders appear beneath the wooded slope of the Mont St. Marc. It was the Empress, he knew, on her way to Pierrefonds, and he counted three vehicles filled with bobbing parasols before he saw the sun strike on the helmets and breastplates of the Lancer escort. He did not dream, as they passed slowly and easily across his field of vision, strung out along the Route d'Eugénie in a frieze of power and circumstance, that he was looking at one of the last processions of the Second Empire, or that the country children at the cottage doors would one day tell their descendants how they saw the last Empress of the French ride by, on her last visit to the Château de Compiègne. He gave them ample time for the halt at Vieux-Moulin before he cut across their path to Peter's Ponds, a dull and uninviting stretch of water lying in a clearing between verges dusty and withering in the June drought, where a little lodge, a kind of gingerbread chalet, stood quite close to the water with a broad path running round about it.

Long before the Revolution, monks had fished for their Friday fare in St. Peter's ponds. The courtiers of the Second Empire had been more interested, on the Emperor's hunting days, in gathering there to eat great beef pasties and drink good wine, or on less public occasions to embrace frail ladies in velvet habits and feathered riding caps on the deep dusty sofas. Some ghosts from those hours of indulgence must have lurked about the place, for as James rode slowly round the chalet, bending low in the saddle to look inside the windows, it conveyed to him something so furtive and unpleasant that he abruptly turned into the forest track leading to Vieux-Moulin. It was dark and cool there, with great

163

copper beeches arching above his head, and a sweet sappy smell rising from the grass and mosses. It was fifteen minutes past five by the King of Prussia's watch ticking in his pocket, and in Spain Salazar was changing from one diligence to another on his slow devious journey to Madrid.

Madeleine came round a bend in the track with hardly a jingle of bit or stirrup irons, riding so lightly that her black mare, a thoroughbred from the imperial stables, seemed to be guided by a rein of gossamer. She was wearing the dark green habit of the Imperial Hunt, the tunic with its orange facings and silver gilt cuff braid taut above the flowing skirt which revealed only the toe of one beautifully cut boot in the polished stirrup. Her fair hair was tightly braided *en catogan* beneath the dark felt tricorne hat. She looked like a young soldier of the Sun King's wars, with one decoration on her breast: the horn Button, given to so few women members of the Imperial Hunt that it was a real badge of skill and horsemanship. James had no idea of its significance, but the whole of Madeleine, Hunt Button, fringed gloves and supple crop, glowing face above the high hooked collar, was so wonderful in his sight that he was ready to fall on his knees before her, there on the dusty verge of Peter's Ponds.

Madeleine, smiling at him, saw a boy's face looking up at her: ardent, full of naked feeling, the mouth as soft now as the beautiful eyes; the face of a man in love for the first time in his life. Then James put his head down in the folds of her habit, feeling the slim strong leg beneath his lips, reaching up blindly until she put her hands in his and very gently slipped from the saddle into his arms. In that long kiss the forest seemed to rock around them: it was Madeleine who broke from their embrace at last. "The horses! Mind the horses!"

But the horses were well mannered. The chestnut was cropping grass a few paces away, the black had stood like the thoroughbred she was, with her hairy lower lip now and again thrust out to nuzzle at Madeleine's shoulder.

And James and Madeleine stood in the forest clearing in the late afternoon sunshine, talking with the same impetuous community of words as they had talked under the gaslights of Lapérouse, pouring it all out to one another—Madame d'Arbonne's death and the terrible return to Trouville, the long lonely evenings in Scotland, the Emperor's illness and the endless strain of work in the Southampton yards—hands locked, and lips not quite touching, until James said tenderly,

"What now, Madeleine? How long can you spend with me, or how long may I stay here with you?"

"Hours if you like. The Empress has been an angel, James: *she* was the one who planned that I might drop behind when we came out of church—I'm supposed to have had a headache and gone back to the château. Even Princesse d'Essling couldn't say a word when *Her Majesty* ordered me to turn back!" Her face was sparkling with the mischievous look he loved.

"Well then, where are we to go? It's too early for dinner, but by the time we ride back to Compiègne—" He stopped, remembering the ribald farmers at the Cloche; *that* wouldn't do. "Would it be possible, would it be permissible, to dine at Vieux-Moulin? *You* say—I had my way about going to Lapérouse, and look what happened there—riot and civil strife!"

"We do seem to attract disaster, don't we? . . . I think *not* Vieux-Moulin, we should ride straight into the Pierrefonds party coming back. There's a quiet place not far from here, where we can sit and talk in a country garden; would you like that? Then will you put me up?"

Her light foot touched his hands for the fraction of a minute, and then she was in the saddle. He caught the chestnut, inwardly giving thanks that the impulse to rear had been switched out of the brute, and side by side they trotted out of the shelter of the trees and passed by the shrunken waters of the old stewponds into a region of barnyards and tilled fields.

"Isn't it dry!" said Madeleine. "Farmer Blaise at Arbonne is in despair over the hay crop, and look at that!"

She pointed with her whip at a field of grain, the ears prematurely shot above the baking earth.

"A dry summer means a good vintage, doesn't it?" said James.

"The grapes are very well formed; see the clusters on that trellis, James!"

But James was looking at her, and thinking how when she came the world appeared in a clearer light, a deeper dimension. He had seen Paris with new eyes since he first saw her, and now, with her "look!" and her "see!" she was bringing the rural landscape into a sharp focus for him. James had been a hard-worked country boy; he was no admirer of nature for its own sake, and the mid-summer beauty of the Compiègne woods made no particular impression on his senses. But when she was there what was flat before sprang into another dimension, like a picture seen through one of the new stereoscopes: she made France come alive, a country like no other country, with a motion and a spirit all its own. And he surrendered himself to this enchantment, riding away with her between the beech hangars on the one hand and the red roofs of Vieux-Moulin on the other, until they left the road and struck away along a path so narrow that there was scarcely room to ride two abreast, between honeysuckle hedges fringed with the colours of her country, bluebells, white marguerites and the crinkled red of half-opened poppy buds. Then they let the horses walk, and Madeleine shifted her crop to her left hand and gave him her right to hold as they rode deeper into the green twilight of an apple orchard that ended in a cobbled inn close with an old well and a mossy bucket, and she told him with a sigh of happiness, "This is Le Vivier-Frère-Robert."

It was the quietest place in all the world. There were only half a dozen cottages in the hamlet, bowered in trees, and only one or two children, too small to be at work in the fields, who came shyly out under the protection of an old woman to gaze at the newcomers. But the quiet of the drowsy garden they could see across the cobbles was sharply broken when the innkeeper and his wife came hurrying down from the house: they were rustics with a veneer of sleek town manners, overeffusive, overdiscreet as the woman curtsied their guests indoors and the man took charge of the horses. At the back they had a tiny taproom with a sanded floor, very cool and clean; James liked it better than the front parlour to which he and Madeleine were inevitably condemned, which smelled close and musty. He opened the french windows, not without difficulty, while the landlady ushered Madeleine into the next room and went off to fetch warm water. Through the half-open door he could see the corner of a four-poster bed with a patchwork cover, on which she was in the act of laying down her hat. "I think I'll make sure the horses are all right," he said over his shoulder, and walked out into the green garden.

When he came back she was standing beneath one of the apple trees, heavy with unripe fruit. Against the dark green leaves and bright green apples her fair head stood out like a polished coin. She had unhooked the collar of her tunic ("she must be hot in that thing," he thought, "don't women wear a shirt, or some sort of bodice, that would allow them to take it off?") and a little triangle of white skin showed at the base of her neck, even more enticing than the bare shoulders revealed by her evening gowns. Her greeting was deliberately casual.

"The stabling's all right, isn't it? I wager your hack was glad to get his saddle off, I noticed the girth was rather tight. . . . Look, the landlady wants to give us a roast chicken with green peas, new potatoes with parsley butter and a bowl of wild strawberries —she sent the children into the woods to get some. Does that appeal to you?"

"I hope it eats as well as it sounds. How about wine—have they any suggestions about that?"

"That was left to you. But they'll have one or two good bottles 'behind the faggots' for special guests like us."

"You know this place well, then?" asked James casually. "You've been here before?"

"I've been here once or twice. I know it well enough to show you the whole of Le Vivier-Frère-Robert," said Madeleine with a laugh. "Shall we walk?"

There was still no sign of life in the tiny hamlet. The old woman had gone indoors to her cooking pots, the children were gathering the *fraises des bois*, and a tortoiseshell cat, methodically stalking butterflies, was the only active creature in the whole drugged summer landscape. They walked on admiring the little vegetable gardens and the vines round every door which were already heavy with clusters of hard green grapes. The cottages and gardens ended in a grassy marshland, where a tiny rill, shrunk to the merest trickle, meandered between banks where celandines and forget-me-nots were withering in the drought. Its name, said Madeleine, was the Ru de Berne. At some time in the vanished centuries, Frère Robert, perhaps an independent-minded lay brother from the establishment at Peter's Ponds, had set up his own little *vivier* there, and stocked it with carp or some other water fish; but there was no trace of a stewpond to be seen now. Green grasses and sedges had choked the hollow, where the silence was broken only by the tiny silver voice of the Ru de Berne.

James drew Madeleine into a green ride, and put his arms about her.

"Madeleine"—he had never called her "dear" or "darling" yet, his stiff Scots lips refused to shape the words—"do you know, have you any idea, what it means to me to be here at last, with you?"

"Perhaps I have." But she would not let him kiss her; they went slowly on, with his arm about her, until on one of the high banks on either side of the ride she saw a gleam of red and dropped to her knees delightedly.

"Oh look, wild strawberries! The children should have come this way! They're ripe and good—do taste!"

James sat down with more caution. Riding had produced an ache in unexpected sinews. "I shall be as lame as a tree tomorrow," he thought, and pushed the thought away. A lover with lumbago—good God!

"Do you like them?"

"They're a little bitter—it's a special taste."

"She'll serve them with sugar or kirsch, and ruin them. This is the way I like them best."

She was leaning sideways, resting on her elbow, putting the little red berries one by one between her lips, and licking frankly at a trickle of bright juice ready to spill down her chin. Her green habit lay upon the moss in sculptured folds that showed every line of her long thighs, and the strawberry flowers and blossoms of the yellow tormentilla were crushed beneath her knees. As James watched her the centre of gravity shifted in his body. The desire she had kindled in the winter rose in midsummer fire, and

168

all at once he began to cover her face with kisses, tasting the wild flavour of the berries and sweetened by her mouth; calling her *mon amour, ma bien-aimée,* Mado, Manon, Madelon, and then all the tender foolish names he had never called a woman in his life.

"I love you, Madeleine, I adore you ! Promise that you'll be my wife !"

"Oh, James !"

She let her hands, which she had knotted tensely behind his head, drop to the grass, and sighed,

"Isn't love enough? Why do you ask for promises and pledges, when we don't know what the future holds for us?"

"The future will be just what *we* want to make it," said James Bruce.

They dined in the garden, beneath the apple tree. They had seen nobody but the landlord, a gamekeeper, and a few cottagers who had crossed the garden with a word of apology to drink wine in the little taproom at the back. After coffee was put on the table no one came near them.

"How dark it is," said Madeleine, "it must be very late."

"No, it's not ten o'clock yet, but it's a cloudy night. No moon."

"And here comes the rain." One or two drops, heavy as franc pieces, had fallen between the thick leaves of the laden apple tree.

"Let's go indoors, then, I'll carry the candles," said James. "These people seem to have forgotten all about us."

The parlour was no longer musty, for the fragrance of night-scented stock and tobacco flowers had been stealing in through the french doors open on the garden. James heard the patter of rain on the flagstones of the path. "I ought to order the horses round," he thought, "she'll be soaked through if there's a storm." But it was impossible to break the spell of the night. He and Madeleine had stepped out of the world into the utter peace and secrecy of Le-Vivier-Frère Robert: it was a moment and a time and a place for love.

"Isn't love enough?" she had whispered in the forest, but the logical, argumentative Scot who stood so close behind the lover in James Bruce forced him to say now,

"Madeleine, we've got to talk this out. You sent for me to come to France and here I am. I've asked you to be my wife, and you haven't given me a straight answer. What's the reason? I've a right to know."

She answered reluctantly:

"James, I've got to think about Louise's future. I can't leave her alone with poor father and those doddering old cousins, to be bullied by Michel. But if Victor marries Blanche Daubigny this winter the whole situation would be changed. Blanche is a neighbour's daughter, in the country, and very fond of Louise. She'll take her into society, and probably marry her off to some country squire who will appreciate the property she has just inherited—"

"Louise has come into property?"

"Yes, Victor is being rather mean about it. You know Arbonne belonged to my mother really. My uncle bought it back for her when she married, with the reversion to a son and heir—or to an eldest daughter if no son were born," she added. "That would have been me! But maman made a special arrangement a few months ago, Maître Lachmann told us after the funeral, giving Louise the old Tour d'Arbonne, 'in return for her dutiful affection and devoted care.' Wasn't it nicely put?"

"Very. Can this old place be lived in?"

"It's rented to my uncle's mistress." And James, recovering from the slight shock which Madeleine's bluntness always gave him, was rather pleased than otherwise to hear about Bertaux' liaison. That was normal, at any rate! But he changed the subject by saying,

"Young Hartzell has a great admiration for Miss Louise."

"Yes, I know, he's terribly funny about it. I'll never forget the first time I saw them together at Arbonne, making sheep's eyes across the table. Poor Frank took a little too much to drink that night and was terrified of what Uncle Michel or Victor would say next day. I used not to care much for Frank Hartzell, he was so anxious to please, and so ready to agree with uncle about everything, but he was very kind and helpful when my mother died, and I've begun to be quite fond of him."

"Well, then; look at it this way, Louise is an heiress, a pretty girl eighteen years old. She'll probably be married as soon as she's out of mourning, to Mr. Hartzell or another. Will you be satisfied if you stay with her until winter, when your brother's bride takes charge of her? Louise is a sweet child, Madeleine, but don't sacrifice your own life to your family. Some day Louise may disappoint you, and then where will you be?"

It was said with a bitterness which made her look at him intently in the candlelight.

"Have *you* had a disappointment of that sort recently?"

"More than one!" said James. "Or one which you might call an enlightenment, thanks to Monsieur Bertaux!"

"To Michel? Why to him, of all people?"

"Well, first—this has nothing to do with your uncle—I was very vexed when my youngest brother left the P. and O. to join another steamship line. I taught that boy as a child, coached him for his officer's tickets, did all I could for him inside the Company —and then off he went without so much as a 'by your leave' to me. I tell you, it cut me; but it was nothing to what I felt about Robert. He was my pupil too—very bright—I was proud of him. He didn't do much to help the family at Sauchentree, but that didn't matter as long as I was there to look after them. Then that night I went to your uncle's house in Paris he told me that our thrifty, struggling Robert had other irons in the fire. Was in fact a rich man. Who hadn't allowed us to rejoice in his success, or sent a penny home to his old father and the kind old aunt who helped to bring us up—not Robert—"

Madeleine interrupted the rapid, vehement flow of words.

"Are you sure? Sometimes my uncle lies, to suit himself."

"I don't doubt it! But I made sure, Madeleine. Thank God, not all of it was true! My brother's money was made in lawful trading, though under another name. He has not been trafficking in opium, as your uncle implied."

Madeleine gasped.

"Yes!" said James. "It was very bad. But we must forget it, Madeleine; forget all of them, brothers, sisters, everyone except yourself and me! Let me go back to Paris and tell them that it's settled, and you're my promised wife!"

"Oh no! Oh, that's impossible! Not next week, nor for many weeks to come!"

James Bruce's control snapped. The room was so small that two strides brought him to her side. He took her in his arms and kissed her, not with the slow delight which he knew aroused the same response in her, but with a rough determination and a rough command,

"You're mine, Manon! Who else needs you as I need you! Not Louise, not your father! *Show* me that you love me—"

Then her hands came up again, and fastened behind his head, dragging his mouth into hers, and he only left her lips to kiss the white triangle of flesh at her open collar which had kept his senses on the knife edge of anticipation all evening long, and then the hooks of the dark green tunic were pulling apart beneath his hand. And what she wore beneath it was not a shirt, but a thin shift of the finest lawn. And underneath the shift, there was a breast of snow.

The rain came on heavily later in the night. In the deep four-poster, with Madeleine's head upon his arm, James heard through his sleep the gutters filling and spilling round the roof of the silent inn. The green plants of Le Vivier-Frère-Robert drank thirstily, and the dust of June was washed from the orchard trees. Silver threads of water began to meander through the meadow as the Ru de Berne brimmed its banks, and the parched land became a pool.

THREE

THE DISASTER

Summer 1870

I

Two bowls of steaming *café au lait* stood on the table when Madeleine entered the parlour at six o'clock next morning. James had brought the coffee from the kitchen himself after paying his bill and leading the horses from the stable to a hitching post beside the garden gate. He felt sure that Madeleine wanted to see nobody, and intended to keep her away from the prying eyes of the innkeeper and his wife.

"You brought the horses round? How good of you," she said.

"My darling girl, sit down and drink your coffee." But Madeleine remained standing. She lifted the bowl and drank quickly, every tense movement revealing her impatience to be gone.

"I'm on duty at eight o'clock, James. The Empress breakfasts early at Compiègne."

He wanted to say "You're not a soldier", for the words "on duty" had irritated him, but with restraint he said,

"You'll be in time. I'll take you to the palace, ride into the town to shave and change, and come back for you at noon, or earlier if you like."

"Come back—?" Madeleine set down the empty bowl, and James put his arms around her.

"I'm taking you back to Paris in the afternoon."

"Oh, James!"

"I'm your husband now, you know."

Beneath his lips he felt her mouth quiver in what might have been a smile or a sob, but she said nothing, rubbing her soft cheek against his rough one, burying her face in his shoulder, moving her body against his in a way that aroused desire again.

"Are you happy, Madeleine?"

"Oh, very—very happy, but we must go now."

She was out of his arms, putting on her hat, snatching up her gloves and crop, and almost running down the path without a backward look at the inn at Le Vivier-Frère-Robert, where their happiness had flowered. On the bridle paths through the forest she set the pace, riding ahead until they reached Vieux-Moulin and struck into the high road to Compiègne. Then James pulled alongside, and laid one hand on her reins.

"Not so fast, Madeleine. We've got some plans to make."

"Have we?"

"Yes. I want you to tell the Empress, or the Grand Mistress, or whoever is the right person to tell, that you're leaving Compiègne today. Going back to your home in Paris, to get ready for your marriage to me."

"I can't go back and blurt that out—"

"Why not?"

"There's a reason."

"What reason, for God's sake?"

"The reason that brought Their Majesties to Compiègne. The Emperor's health. You must have heard the rumours about his health? Well, nearly all of them are true. He's a very sick man. He came here for a consultation with a famous doctor, who advised major surgery without delay."

"So Hector Munro was right about the Emperor," said James. Madeleine, stiffening a little at his dry tone, continued as she urged the horses forward:

"When I told the Empress about us yesterday, she was very sweet at first, but then she cried, and said all her old friends were dead or had left her, and she had no one left to rely on. She asked me to promise, and I did promise, not to leave the court—leave France, that is, until His Majesty is well again, or until—"

"Until what?"

She spoke so low that he could hardly hear her.

"—until the Regency is well established."

"It's absurd!" said James violently. "She has no right to extort such a promise from you! People at court marry to suit themselves, so far as I ever heard, without waiting for a diseased man to be cured or a woman's ambition satisfied! Madeleine, if you were in earnest when you sent for me, if you mean all you've said to me—you'll put our happiness before the Empress!"

"*But not above my country, James!*"

She went on, ignoring James's brusque movement of impatience.

"When the Emperor's operation is made known, there will be great unrest in France. If he dies, the Reds will try to overthrow the Empress and the boy. If he lives—and he'll have a long convalescence—the cabinet will be hard to handle, and—she's very headstrong, James! She may do something reckless that will lead us into war—"

"Oh come," said James, "that's exaggerated! You've got constitutional government now, and surely the ministers are dead set against war! I read in the Paris papers yesterday that Ollivier himself had made a speech somewhere saying European peace had never seemed more certain than at the present time."

"But in France things change from day to day," said Madeleine. "Ollivier may be out of office himself tomorrow! And my feeling is that I must stand by the Empress while she needs me. I can't do much, but I may just be able to say one word at the right time, or even not speak at all but let her talk it out, which would make all the difference to her strength at a crucial moment. Do you understand at all what I'm trying to say?"

"No, I don't understand," said James roughly. "What the hell has the French Government to do with you and me?"

Madeleine touched her heels to her horse's side. It was her own understanding that had failed now: she could not comprehend the blow given to James's pride by her remaining as determined by morning as at night, to postpone their marriage for any reason, family or political. He rode up fast beside her, arguing that they *must* be married now, so violently that Madeleine's own temper flared up and she said "I won't be treated like a fallen woman, to be offered reparation without delay!" She had not guessed the impression made on the Scotsman by her smuggled message, the ribaldry about court ladies he had listened to in the hotel, and the sinister chalet at Peter's Ponds, and she made matters as bad as possible by the reckless suggestion that their liaison might be continued in secret for a while. They were very near the entrance to the château when she said that, and James grew so pale at the very word *liaison* that Madeleine laughed miserably and called him an English hypocrite. Then his classical French deserted him completely, and he flung out at her in his own language, "D'you want me to treat you like a light o' love?" It was already an old-fashioned expression in 1870, with its overtones of Surrey-side melodrama, and he regretted it as soon as the words were out of his mouth. For whether Madeleine understood it or not, she gave her mare a cut on the flank with her crop that sent the beast towards the gates of the château at a gallop. James Bruce kept pace with her and said "You're not going to leave me like that, Madeleine?"

"I'm not leaving you. I'm only asking you to wait."

"And I say you'll come with me today or say goodbye."

"Goodbye!"

Then she was alone, riding up the empty avenue, and the only sound was the birds singing.

Madeleine reached her own room unseen, and tore off her riding habit. She sat down by the window in her white wrapper, stunned by the emotional conflict through which she and James had passed so rapidly. "How could he leave me now," she thought, "unless he knew, he might have known last night, that I'm not what he thought me, not what he calls good!" She could hear the stablemen whistling in the yard below. The sound roused her more fully to another aspect of her situation – the possibility of discovery. Her early return to the château had attracted no attention, for she often rode in the park at morning; but it was only a matter of time, she knew, before the stable foreman checked the long absence of the black mare from her stall. And then with a word from the maid who had brushed a riding habit with torn hooks, and another from the gamekeeper who had saluted a lady in Hunt livery at Le Vivier-Frère-Robert, there would begin to snowball one of the great court scandals—the sensations which surged up from the domestic offices to be dissected, analysed and laughed at by the ladies in waiting and the equerries until they seeped outside the palace walls into the barrooms and bistros of the towns. Madeleine had smiled at many such a scandal in her time. Now it was highly probable that she was "in for it," and that the precarious reputation of Madeleine d'Arbonne would be ruined once and for all. "If it gets to the papers!" she thought with a shudder. "The columnists! Victor!" For Captain d'Arbonne fancied himself exceedingly as a duellist, and had already been "out" twice in connection with his own affairs. "God!" prayed Madeleine, as the summer morning brightened and a breath of lime blossom drifted up from the park, "let us get away from here before anybody finds out! Let something happen to keep them from talking about *me*!"

Her prayer was summarily answered.

In Spain, the next day, Salazar arrived at Madrid. He left the capital within the hour, grim and anxious after a conference with Zorilla, the President of the Cortes, who broke the news to him that the Deputies had dispersed for the summer and were scattered all over Spain. It was not concern for Prince Leopold, whose future crown was still at stake until the Cortes had endorsed his candidature, that sent Salazar hurrying to the nearest post house for fresh horses and a capable postillion.

"I need the best animals in your stable, *señor*! To take me to La Granja without delay!"

It was fear of Bismarck which drove him on. The agent who had been entrusted with the all-important opening of Phase Two of Bismarck's plan had a fair idea of what vengeance the Iron Chancellor might take for delay. All that day, even after he had found General Prim and persuaded him to summon the Spanish cabinet to La Granja, Salazar wondered how Bismarck was reacting to the telegraphic message he had sent in cipher to Berlin.

Bismarck cursed the Spaniards and their eternal *mañana* for a night and a day. Then fate put a new weapon into his hands. In Britain, the Foreign Secretary died suddenly, and there was a diplomatic pause while his successor, Lord Granville, received the seals of office. In France, the Emperor seized the opportunity to delay his departure for St. Cloud and the arrangements for his operation, halting in Paris on his way from Compiègne to exchange the proper ceremonies and condolences with the British Ambassador. It exactly made up to Bismarck for the delay that Salazar and Prim had cost him. He was almost good-humoured as he put back his zero hour from June to July.

The courtiers of Napoleon III were glad enough to spend a few days in Paris, although it was less comfortable than usual at the Tuileries. The summer cleaning of the palace was already in progress—carpets up, curtains down and crystal chandeliers lowered for the annual washing. All the furniture was in lilac chintz slipcovers. Eugénie's Spanish dresser, Pepa Pollet, and the sewing maids were overhauling the formal robes and dresses which the Empress would not wear until October. The elevator ropes creaked steadily as one elaborate gown after another was hoisted to the upper Garderobes, to be sheeted and hung with bags of orris root or cedar shavings.

"Frank!" said Michel Bertaux, coming abruptly through the wicket of his own front office on the rue d'Antin, "I want to see yesterday's Wall Street reports and the closing prices on Philadelphia 'Change, in my own room, at once."

It was the first of July. Frank quickly unfiled the Hartzell Brothers' cables of June 30, clipped them to the stock market reports given by the *Figaro* and carried them to the financier. Bertaux was seated at his desk, his silk hat on the back of his head, scanning the lines from his runners at the unofficial Black Bourse, which never closed. It was still very early, and trading on the Parquet had not yet opened.

"The market was steady at the close of trading yesterday," volunteered Frank, laying the American cables before his master.

"Yes, I see that." Bertaux drummed with his fingers on the desk. "Frank: is your cousin smart enough to cable *immediately* if any rumour breaks either in Wall Street or Dock Street during the day?"

"We've rubbed it well into him, sir, that that's the sort of service we expect from him." Frank's grin betrayed his pleasure in "rubbing" instructions from the S. A. Bertaux into August Hartzell. "Should we expect something to break over there today?"

Bertaux laughed shortly.

"No—this side. I had a cipher message two hours ago, before I got out of bed, from my man in Madrid. He says the editor of the *Epoca* is spreading the story that the President of the Cortes has been blabbing to him that all the Spanish Deputies are being recalled to Madrid. It's by order of Prim and the cabinet—to accept Prince Leopold as the only candidate for the Crown."

"Good God!" said Frank. "I thought Leopold's refusal was absolutely final!"

"That's what Bismarck meant us to think. Now listen, Frank, we've discussed all the political implications of trouble in Spain often enough; I don't need to repeat where the danger lies. We have to be prepared for anything from now on. First, I trust you absolutely to keep this story to yourself. Not a word in the front office, not a movement in the Coulisses. I shall go on the Parquet as soon as trading opens and take Leroy and Martin with me. You stay here and cable Hartzells to start unloading from this list. Tell them to make all payments to my personal account at the Girard Bank."

He took a folded folio sheet from the inner pocket of his frock coat and passed it across the desk to Frank. The young American studied it in silence, a lock of chestnut hair falling over his worried brow as he did so. It was a list of gilt-edged and common American stocks.

"These are my *personal* holdings in the United States, Frank," said Michel Bertaux, watching him. "Nothing whatever to do with the Société Anonyme Bertaux."

Frank, who had been trying to remember what he knew of the Limited Liability Act of 1856, looked up in relief. He had never attempted to pry too far into the workings of Bertaux as a joint stock company, nor during his short term of employment had he been required to attend a shareholders' meeting. His private opinion was that as far as the direction of the company was concerned, Monsieur Bertaux was his own board of directors and his major stockholder as well.

"You can rely on me, sir," Frank said quietly, and he transferred the list to his own pocket.

"I know that," said Bertaux. "Don't let that paper out of your keeping until you give it back to me! I'll be in touch with you all day. Now, you have plenty of time in hand, Frank. How would it be if you went along to Pereire and told them to hold a first-class cabin for you on every one of their steamers leaving Le Havre for New York from now through the month of August?"

Frank had kept his excitement well under control so far. Now his pleasant face flushed and hardened as he stared at his employer.

"Are you telling me I must go back to the States before September, sir?"

"I'm telling you to make sure of transportation. If war comes, every American tourist in Europe will be screaming for a passage home; I want to be sure that you can get away, if need be. God! why did this have to happen in the very middle of the season, with both our hotels—both the Grand and Splendide booked solid until October!" groaned Bertaux. "Three years ago the municipality ripped up the street in front of the Grand Hotel at the peak of the Exhibition traffic, and now Bismarck is going to get us into war!"

"Never mind about the tourists," said Frank Hartzell. "They're not working for you. I am! Or I thought I was!"

Bertaux glared at him.

"Of course you are, you young fool," he said. "Don't you understand me? I want to be sure of getting you back to America because under war conditions you can be far more useful to me there than here. But bear in mind that it takes two to make a bargain. You seemed to be afraid, just now, that I was going to let you go. Remember that by the terms of our agreement *you* can leave *me*, in the beginning of September. I may lose all the time that's been invested in training you, in introducing you to the wine growers and the wholesalers at Les Halles—and all the confidential information I've passed on to you. Now then! What do you say? Is it go—or stay?"

Frank Hartzell smoothed back his unruly lock, and sighed.

"What can I do in the States that would be more useful than staying here?" he hedged.

"A variant of the work you've been doing since I brought you up to Paris—bulk purchases. If we go to war, as I think we shall, and the war turns out the way it will, France is going to need a big stockpile of provisions of all kinds. But anybody who carries that kind of responsibility has got to be a man with the sort of touch you proved to have at Marseilles, and in your transactions at Bordeaux and Cognac. Not only that, but a man who is a neutral and yet completely devoted to our cause—such as it is!" concluded Bertaux grimly. "I gather from what I've heard you say from time to time that you fight shy of causes—now."

The tall, loose-limbed American flung himself back in his chair, his black cutaway unbuttoned and his hands deep in the pockets of his shepherd's plaid trousers. He did not meet Michel Bertaux' eyes.

"Do you blame me?" he said. "I fought to save the Union, and look what that got me—three years in a war prison, and years of ill health to follow! I kind of made up my mind then, long before I started working for my cousins, that I wouldn't get involved in any more wars. I think we're going ahead too fast, sir, if you don't mind my saying so. Give me leave to put off my visit to Pereire, until things are a lot worse than they seem to be today."

"As you please," said Michael Bertaux with a shrug. He looked at his gold watch and got up with an exclamation. He stopped Frank with a gesture as the American moved to open the closed door.

"There's just one thing I'd like to know about you, Frank," said the great *boursier* slowly. "Why you're doing any of this at all. Not only why you're in France, but why you ever went to work for Hartzell Brothers after the Civil War? You were left no interest in the firm by your father, though he made you a rich man in your own right. Why didn't you develop some of his interests in the Pennsylvania coal mines, or the new smelting processes? What did you find so attractive in the food business, and the wage your cousins paid you?"

Frank looked stubborn.

"What was wrong with going to Hartzells?" he said. "It's the family business, after all! My grandfather, old Franz Hartzell, founded it not long after he arrived in Philadelphia from Hanover, and my father was the junior partner before he sold out. I guess what took me into it—and made me want to try my luck in France after what happened at Canton—was that I wanted to show my cousins August and Hermann that I'm a better man than they are, in spite of the years they said I wasted in the army."

"Quite so," said Bertaux with a sour smile. "Family dissensions can sometimes forge ties as powerful as family love. . . . The brothers Hartzell are not a great deal older than yourself, I think you told me? You got on with them quite well when you were boys?"

"Well enough," said Frank with a shrug. "Their father and mother were very kind to me after my own mother died. It was the war that parted us! Those damned cousins of mine were the worst pair of scrimshankers in Philadelphia. They sat the whole thing out in Nebraska, while my old uncle ran the business, and then came back full of tall tales about the money they'd made trading with the Indians. Indians, good God!" said Frank.

"It was the war that parted you," repeated Bertaux. "Well—we shall be finding out all that for ourselves quite soon now."

That was on Friday morning. On Saturday, the early edition of the *Gazette de France* printed the substance of the story Bertaux had had from Madrid. On Saturday night Monsieur Mercier, the French Ambassador at Madrid, sent an official communiqué to the Emperor. It reached him at St. Cloud, and drove the Empress nearly frantic.

Through the long Sunday which followed, the court stood aghast at the sight of the Emperor, whose health had been the sole concern a week before, dogged by Eugénie's arguments as he limped from room to room.

"Think of Loulou! Save the dynasty! Think of the insult to France! Remember your invincible army!" The passionate head-long phrases were repeated until Dr. Conneau insisted on rest for his patient. There was no question now of an operation on Napoleon III. His place, exulted Eugénie, would soon be at the front, leading his troops to battle!

Around her, at the summer palace, the Empress had as usual gathered a little group of intimates, including her petted young Alba nieces of the florid Spanish titles—Maria Duquesa de Calisteo, Luisa Duquesa de Montoro—with whom she liked to talk the language of her girlhood. That was dropped now, for Eugênie knew the danger of being called "the Spaniard," even in her own court, when a great Spanish crisis was unfolding. The Princesses d'Essling and de la Moskowa, Comtesse Clary, Madame Aguado, were all hanging on the lips of their imperial mistress; but even they, the practised courtiers, grew faint and weary through that interminable Sunday, Monday, Tuesday, as the lights burned through the nights in the gilded salons, and the tide of rant, discussion, cajolery never ceased to flow. But Madeleine d'Arbonne, who had so often waltzed until daybreak in that very palace without tiring, now drew upon her splendid strength to match the passion of her Empress. She was always on duty—always ready to listen—to propose a cup of hot chocolate or bouillon to sustain the woman too nervous, now, to sit through a meal—to chafe, from time to time, the icy hands. So quickly, the call had come to help the Empress through a hard hour—it was as if Madeleine sent her unspoken pleading to James Bruce across the Channel: "You see! I *had* to be here when She needed me!"

But James had seen the flaw in Madeleine's reasoning. Helping the Empress was not automatically the same as helping France, and Madeleine could not follow her mistress into the council chamber. She could only comfort and encourage her on her way.

"How glad the Emperor will be to have you at the cabinet meeting, Madame!" she sa'd when the Empress was ready to attend the council—her first cabinet since January—called for the morning of the sixth of July.

Eugénie drew a deep breath.

"I too am glad to meet the ministers again, dear child." She stood up, and the folds of her black satin polonaise fell into place at her slim back. "It's impossible for her to be ungraceful," thought Madeleine, and as the door closed upon the curtsying ladies she pictured the Empress sailing like a black swan between the bowing ministers to seat herself beside her husband and lay one lovely hand, for an instant, reassuringly upon his.

But to the sick Emperor that hand felt like a dead weight. He knew from the very start that his wife's presence was a strong irritant to the peace party in his cabinet, a gift from heaven to the ministers determined upon war; and he himself, the man who must hold the balance true, was not certain how long his weakened will could prevail against his wife's insistence that a victorious war would save the dynasty. The dynasty! She was furious when Monsieur Plichon, one of the junior ministers, spoke out bluntly. "The King of Prussia can afford to lose several battles, Sire! For you, defeat means revolution!" In his heart the Emperor agreed with Plichon.

Then Marshal Leboeuf, the War Minister, began to bluster that there was no need to expect defeat. "We'll whip the enemy!" he cried. "The army is more than ready; the Chassepôt rifle is vastly superior to the needle gun; and then we have *the secret weapon*!" A murmur ran round the conference table; everyone was impressed, more or less, by the secret weapon which was understood to make France secure against any attack by land or sea.

"*Gentlemen!*" in his softest, most persuasive voice Napoleon gathered their attention to himself.

"Gentlemen, aren't we being a little premature in supposing we *must* go to war with Prusssia over this matter? It seems to me there are other ways of preventing Prince Leopold from becoming King of Spain besides marching across the Rhine, which surely is a step in the wrong direction!"

"Your Majesty doesn't propose to march across the Pyrenees?" cried Leboeuf.

"Not at all," said Napoleon coolly. "But it might be possible to let others do the marching! That wretched country (forgive me,

184

Madame) is so torn by faction that the Spanish exiles would be delighted with an opportunity to fight it out on Spanish soil with Serrano and General Prim. Suppose we were kind enough to open our Pyrenean frontier and supply them with the necessary funds? Eh? Mightn't that be one solution: to bring pressure on the Regent Serrano with the threat of civil war?" He looked round the circle of doubtful faces.

"And then," said the Emperor, "aren't we forgetting that the Sigmaringen family is decidedly vulnerable in other directions? Here's a letter that young Leopold's mother, Princess Josephine, wrote to me in June of '66, thanking us for our kindness to her son—"

"And how Leopold could *dare* to do this to us!" burst out the Empress. "We gave the most beautiful ball for Antonia and him when they came to visit us—"

"We did, my dear; several balls, as I remember," said the Emperor kindly. "But the thanks in this case were for what she calls my 'august protection' in the establishment of her *other* son, Carol, as Prince of Roumania. She says here, 'I beg you to sustain him in the task to which he has given himself with all the ardour of his young heart.' Nicely put, eh?"

Ollivier, the man of peace, relaxed in his chair and began to smile. The old fox! He would turn and twist away from the danger, after all!

"Now," said the Emperor. "Why don't we do a little horse-trading with Prince Karl Anton? Play off one son against the other, and explain that if Leopold goes to Madrid, our august protection will no longer cover Carol in Bucharest? Let Carol prove the ardour of his young heart," said the Emperor benignly, "by fighting to save his principality! The Turks would jump at the chance to dismember Roumania as soon as France's guarantee is removed—and I'm sure we can count on the Sultan's co-operation after Her Majesty's great personal and political success at the Suez Canal!"

A smile crept over the downcast face of the Empress. "By God!" swore Ollivier, watching, "if he can persuade *her*, then he *is* the greatest diplomatist of our time!"

He persuaded them all, before the cabinet meeting ended. "Remember!"—it was his last admonition, spoken in the hoarse voice of utter exhaustion—"the Cortes does not meet until the twentieth of July to ratify Leopold's election to the throne. We still have fourteen days to solve the Spanish Question without bloodshed. Temporize, procrastinate, and we'll outwit Bismarck yet!"

But the Emperor reckoned without the Duc de Gramont.

The duke was a man of whose capacity for stubborn folly Bismarck had the highest hopes. *Das Rindvieh*, as the Chancellor called him, had been a controversial French Ambassador at Rome and Vienna. Now, as Foreign Minister, he completely overrode the cabinet's decision to refuse a parliamentary debate on Spain. When the Legislative Body met that afternoon de Gramont not only made a long inflammatory speech about the relations between France and Spain, but actually mentioned the part played by Prussia in promoting Leopold for King—and threatened Prussia with the wrath of France.

It was the greatest success the Duc de Gramont had ever scored in his noisy and tactless life. He was cheered to the echo by all the Deputies. All the way round from Jérôme David's Right to Léon Gambetta's Left rolled the wild applause of the unleashed House as the President made only a pretence of ringing his bell for order. From the press tribunes, hurrahing newspapermen threw their hats down to the floor, and in the public galleries strangers embraced each other. Michel Bertaux was one of the few not emotionally affected. He said to Frank Hartzell, who sat spellbound by his side,

"That does it, I should think, or all but. Come on back to the office, I want to talk to you about your trip."

The maroon brougham made its way with difficulty across the bridge and the Place de la Concorde. Half Paris seemed to be in the rue Royale, pressing eagerly toward the Legislature, shouting its approval of the lesson de Gramont had just read Prussia. Groups of young men, and girls from the big dressmakers' and department stores, were singing *Mourir pour la Patrie* and a new song beginning

"I think we've heard the last of *Partant Pour la Syrie*," said Bertaux. "In a few days the police will be winking at the *Marseillaise*; probably singing it themselves, in fact. All this, of course, is meat and drink to Bismarck."

In Berlin the Iron Chancellor was indeed rubbing his hands over de Gramont. "The Calf" had bellowed in his own bovine way; he had made France issue the first challenge to Prussia. The other Powers stood back shocked and dismayed. By the ninth of July it was clear that France must wage war, if war came, entirely without allies.

So some days of the fourteen passed. Then the Emperor's astuteness had its reward. The Regent Serrano, unwilling to risk civil war in Spain, dispatched General Dominguez to tell Prince Leopold as tactfully as possible that he might not suit the Spanish people after all. At the same time Prince Karl Anton telegraphed to General Prim that he wished to withdraw his son's candidature for the Crown. He had solved the equation put before him by the Emperor's agents and decided not to trade a positive throne for Carol at Bucharest against an illusory one for Leopold at Madrid.

The Emperor was smoking with his cronies when this news was brought to him. They crowded round him with the old intimacy of their London exile in Carlton Gardens, when they were plotting their way back to France, exclaiming, "You've done it again!" wringing his swollen hands and beaming at each other over his grey head. "By God, you astonishing fellow, you've done it again! Done it with eight days to spare!" And the Emperor with real colour in his face, laconically said, "I hope so!"

"You'll read them the dispatch from Benedetti as soon as the cabinet meets?" hinted Pietri. While the Black Cabinet was in session, the real one could be heard gathering next door.

"Listen to that!" said Napoleon obliquely. There was a scrape of scabbards on the floor of the adjoining room, and even the clink of spurs. "More than the Honest Men are here today. My fire-eating generals are all present! From Marshal Leboeuf to

187

General Bourbaki, who has three times taken off his sword and threatened to leave the army if I don't declare war, they're all ready to shout that they 'know their way back to Jena!' What if the Prussians have another general like Blücher, who knows his way back to Waterloo?"

Thélin and Franceschini Pietri looked at one another. This was the way their master had talked all along, on a note of defeatism very strange to him.

"There are two things to be done, as I see it," began Thélin briskly. "The first is, muzzle de Gramont. See that he never gets a chance to make a fool of himself from the tribune, as he did on the sixth of July. The next is, get Ollivier to mark time somehow until the end of the session, and disperse the Deputies as soon as possible. The mobilization should of course be halted as of today."

"So clearheaded, my dear Charles!" said the Emperor mockingly. "So much too chivalrous to tell me that first of all I must muzzle my own wife. She hasn't de Gramont's opportunities for public speaking, but I assure you she does very well in the cabinet."

"Her Majesty is bound to be calmed by today's good news," said Conneau, the peacemaker.

"You think so? We can always hope; but then, what about Thélin's next proposal? Disperse the Deputies! It could be done, but will you tell me how I am to disperse the people of Paris? The whole city is mad for war! Every time I drive to the Tuileries I hear them shouting 'To Berlin!' from one end of the Champs Elysées to the other! I ordered every newspaper I control to print the pleas for peace which have come in from the Prefects of all the provinces—do you think that made any difference to Paris? The Empress knows the temper of the capital, Conneau—so do the generals!"

He got up stiffly, the little sluggish civilian whose Star had burned above so many battlefields that his old friends hardly recognized him as the champion of peace. But he made an attempt to square his shoulders as he walked into the next room and faced the swooping Empress.

She scarcely gave him time to tell them the good news of Prince Karl Anton's withdrawal of his son's name.

"Who is to believe a word of it? Sire! You surely won't accept *his* assurances unless the King of Prussia confirms them?"

"Give them time, Eugénie," said Napoleon wearily. "King Wilhelm is drinking the waters at Bad Ems—"

"What do we have an ambassador for?" she raged. "Benedetti is there too! Your Majesty must instruct him to get the King's personal guarantee that he associates himself with Prince Leopold's withdrawal—"

"—and will never again sanction a Hohenzollern candidature for the throne of Spain," concluded de Gramont. A deep murmur of approval ran round the council room. Napoleon looked helplessly from one to the other.

"Meantime continuing the mobilization," said the War Minister, Marshal Leboeuf. "The Army of France, as you know, is ready to the last gaiter button, but the Army of Africa will need equipment for a European campaign. We should order embarkation, beginning with the units most distant from Algiers."

"Have you *all* gone mad?" The Emperor found his voice at last. "Don't you know we haven't enough transports in the Mediterranean to bring the African Army home? Do you realize that six thousand Navy men are not only on furlough, but can't be recalled, because like sensible fellows they're fishing with their families off the Dogger Bank? Do you know there isn't a decent set of charts of the North Sea at the Ministry of the Marine, or enough staff maps of eastern France to supply one brigade headquarters in my entire army? These are facts, Madame! This is the truth, Marshal—I've been finding it out in the past few days! We're not in a position to dictate terms to the King of Prussia. We must accept Leopold's withdrawal as a fact and thank God we've got out of this safely! We've got peace with honour—"

With that a storm of derision, which no respect for him could prevent, broke across the council room.

They wore him down in the end. Overnight, and in Ollivier's absence, the Empress and de Gramont persuaded him to telegraph to Benedetti at Bad Ems for the King of Prussia's "'guarantee."

If Bismarck had known the whole story, he might have slapped his thigh and roared out that you could always count on *das Rindvieh*, by God, to put his hoof in the trough. But Bismarck had to sweat through the long hot hours of July 13 until half-past six in the evening, when a telegram from King Wilhelm told him that day's news. Count Benedetti had taken his instructions from Paris extremely literally. Not acute enough to see that the hypocritical old King was actually equivocating when he said in his mildest manner that he had read *in the papers* of Leopold's withdrawal, but had no *official* intimation of it, he returned again and again to the demand for guarantees. At last King Wilhelm, still mildly, declined to discuss the matter further on that day.

When the king's dispatch came in Count von Bismarck was gloomily smoking with his confederates Generals von Roon and von Moltke. Bismarck had exhausted his repertoire of army oaths and Pomeranian stable filth at the expense of Prince Leopold and his father, the cowardly, crawling, Catholic curs who had let him down. Even the tight-lipped, spectacled, taciturn Roon had temporarily lost faith in the personal friendship of the God of Battles.

Then the message arrived. It produced a blast of rage at French insolence in demanding guarantees, which lasted until Bismarck took up his pen. Transposed a clause here, deleted a sentence there until the text and sense of the dispatch were subtly altered. Flung it across the table with a grin,

"How does that read to you now, gentlemen?"

Roon, a killer with the face of a superannuated governess, hitched his spectacles further up on his prim nose, studied the text and answered,

"It reads as if the King had dismissed the French Ambassador. Permanently!"

And that was how it read to the world.

By nine o'clock that night, the Prussian envoys at all foreign capitals had orders to announce that the French Ambassador was *persona non grata* at the court of Prussia. By ten, the printers at Bismarck's own paper, the *North German Gazette*, were ready to set up the edited message from Ems in bold type for a special edition which reached the streets of Berlin before midnight. The timing of Bismarck's Phase Three was perfect. The story broke in Paris on July 14, Bastille Day; the day of all others in the year when Frenchmen were most ready to resent a slur on their national honour. All that day the tension mounted in the Paris streets. The songs, the flag-waving, the *Marseillaise* a thousand times repeated, the cries of *"à Berlin!"* went on without a break until nightfall. Monsieur Ollivier could hear the shouting long after his carriage had taken the road through the warm, still alleys of the Bois to the evening cabinet meeting at St. Cloud.

They argued until half-past eleven; met again at nine next morning. The Empress, beautiful and frantic, repeated one phrase over and over: without revenge for the Prussian insult, she said, "the Empire would fall like a house of cards—a house of cards!" and her sobs echoed through the room. The Emperor, limp in his chair, a hollow man, made one last attempt to procrastinate by suggesting that the whole matter be submitted to an international conference.

"That would be a dastardly thing!" burst out Eugénie. The generals agreed. It went quickly after that. The Legislative Body met in the afternoon. They voted military credits, confirmed the general mobilization and called out the reservists, in scenes of unbridled enthusiasm for the war. Carried away, even Monsieur Ollivier forgot to be prudent. He shouted out, in the end, "the government accepts the challenge of Prussia—*with light hearts* !"

That was how Bismarck brought Phase Three to a satisfactory conclusion, and the Emperor lost his game with five days of the fourteen still to go.

II

The declaration of war delivered Madeleine d'Arbonne from the state of shock in which she had existed since her parting from James at the gates of Compiègne.

None of her companions, preoccupied by the drama unfolding around them, had detected any difference in the maid of honour. By day she had apparently been carried along on the same tide of anger, patriotism and emotional belief in France's invincible army as drove everyone at St. Cloud to rally round the Empress, and the great majority of Parisians to the frantic demonstrations of the streets. It was only by night, when the storms of that wet July dripping from the laurels of St. Cloud reminded her intolerably of the gentle rain of Le Vivier-Frère-Robert, that Madeleine's guard was down. Then, as she lay half dressed and half undressed across her bed, exhausted from her vigils with the Empress, she relived with remorse and humiliation—and finally, to her self-contempt, with desire—every hour she had spent in James Bruce's arms.

At first, secure in her pride and beauty, she had said to herself every day, "He will come back to me!" She could not believe that the man to whom she had made that complete surrender, in that green and drowsy, secret corner of the Compiègne forest, would accept her impulsive decision without appeal. She still believed that decision to be the right one, for Eugénie needed help more than ever—even in the hour when her old ambition was gratified, and she was proclaimed before the whole council as Regent of France while the Emperor was in the field.

The hours which Eugénie spent with her husband and his advisors were fruitless hours, given up to drafting vain appeals. To the Emperor of Austria, reminding him of his recent defeat at the hands of Prussia and urging him to avenge himself by taking the field with France. To King Victor Emmanuel—no question of going to war with him now—reminding him that the Emperor was the liberator of Italy and asking him to come to the Emperor's help. To the Bavarians, and other members of the South German states, asking them to rise against Prussia, as soon as the French Army was across the Rhine. Hours of it, folios full of it—the sterile Spanish statecraft of the woman and the conniving and contriving of the old gambler by her side—while the precious days went by, and reports of great troop movements beyond the German border were treated contemptuously, or ignored. Madeleine, sitting at one of the round tables in the anteroom, clumsily shredding lint into charpie for field dressings, found it dangerously easy to let her mind slip back to that hushed room in the forest with the birds twittering in the early morning, after the rain had stopped.

One day Captain Victor d'Arbonne came riding out to see his sister, to tell her jubilantly that he had been posted to Imperial Headquarters at Metz, and was leaving for the front next week.

"I envy you, Victor!" she said, and she meant it. For La France and L'Armée stood on twin pedestals in Madeleine's simple pantheon: to fight for France seemed a great destiny. After all, in her twenty-six years of life she had never known France other than victorious.

"Yes," said Victor, "we'll make short work of the Prussian swine. Once the Army of the Rhine crosses into Germany, the South Germans will come in on our side, and your little brother will be riding behind the Emperor down Unter den Linden, within a couple of months from now!"

She clapped her hands—they were walking out of doors—and looked at him admiringly. There had never been much sympathy between Madeleine and Victor. Perhaps in a subconscious recoil from the cloying affection between their mother and Michel Bertaux, this brother and sister had bickered in the nursery and disagreed about much that happened in their adult life. Now she respected him. Now he was much more than "poor old Vic"; he was a French officer, going out to fight for the honour of France.

"My uncle wants to know if you'll be at the Tuileries tomorrow," said Victor, after an interval in which he passed judgment, indulgently enough, on the Emperor's four English chargers, which were being walked up and down behind the rails against which they had halted. "My father would like to see you before he goes down to Arbonne."

"Oh—I'm sorry, Victor! I have to go to Cherbourg with Her Majesty in the morning. She's going to lead the Baltic squadron out to sea. Must papa go to the country tomorrow, of all days?"

"Well, you know what Michel is like, when he starts making plans! I think this has something to do with the old ladies. Michel is sick of having them underfoot in the Faubourg, and they've closed that awful apartment in the rue du Bac. So off they all go on the evening train tomorrow."

"I'll write to papa—I'll send him a present," said Madeleine. "Is Louise going along with them?"

"She says she has too much shopping to do," said Victor with a chuckle. "She's going down next week. Louise is getting to know her own mind these days, Mado! Did I tell you what she said when Adèle's invitation came?"

The Princess di Roccanuova, safely delivered of a son and heir at the end of June, had sent an urgent message to Paris when war was declared, begging her father and sisters to come to her at Rome.

"No, what did she say?"

"Well, she drew herself up to her full height," smiled Victor, indicating a point below his shoulder, "and she spoke out like a character in Corneille, 'Tell Adèle my place is at Arbonne in time of war!'"

"That little thing!" said Madeleine tenderly.

"She's a big girl now! But I don't mind; let them all go to Arbonne if they like, the old ladies too," said Victor generously. "Louise will have to turn Madame Clarisse out of the tower, though, if she wants to house them all after Blanche and I are married."

"You're going to go through with that?" said Madeleine with a smile.

"Yes, why not?" said Victor, reddening. "Blanche Daubigny hasn't got your style, Madeleine, but then I never meant to marry a Tuileries *cocodette*! I only regret that that damned Suez Canal trip kept me out of France last autumn. That's when I should have married—before my mother's health broke down; and then I might have gone off to the war knowing that a child of mine would follow me at Arbonne—whatever happened."

He looked away from his sister as he spoke, his jaw stiffening under the chin strap of his plumed helmet, and Madeleine laid her hand impulsively on his arm.

"It'll be all right, Victor—dear Vic!" she whispered. "You'll come back to us in triumph—"

There was a high whinny from far up the exercise ground. The four troopers riding the imperial chargers had wheeled round and begun the gallop back to stable, sabres in their hands. Hero, Bolero, Sultan and Nabob responded nobly to the spur. They came past Victor and Madeleine in a perfectly matched stride, like war horses on an antique frieze.

"What a girl you are, Madeleine!" her brother said. "You never did know which side your bread was buttered, did you? If anything happened to me now, *you* would be the lady of Arbonne; haven't you thought of that?"

She stared at him, the warm affectionate concern draining out of her face.

"No, I never have," she said shortly. "You and your children after you are welcome to Arbonne, for all I care. . . . Let's go indoors, Victor, it's too chilly to stay out here."

Her brother's graceless remark came back to Madeleine many times during next day's long train journey to Cherbourg. It made her realize as nothing else had done since her mother's death how completely she was dependent on her uncle's bounty, how utterly without resources of her own.

She began to think of it on the way across Paris, where she stopped to buy the promised present for her father. On the spur of the moment she got him a bedside clock, for the Comte d'Arbonne, who modelled much of his conduct on King Louis XVI, had cultivated the royal martyr's talent for tinkering with the insides of watches. As a matter of convenience she bought it from the best jeweller in the Place Vendôme. It was a costly trifle, and of course it was Michel Bertaux' money which paid for it. Her uncle gave her a large allowance, in gold, every month of her life.

In the train she reflected on the changed fortunes of her family. Victor, by the terms of his mother's marriage settlement, was now the owner of Arbonne, and his estates would be enlarged by his marriage with Blanche Daubigny. Louise already had her beloved Tour d'Arbonne, and Adèle had received a handsome dowry, including a block of stock in the Société Anonyme Bertaux, on her marriage with the Italian prince. That Madeleine herself would be similarly endowed she had no doubt—it had brought her several proposals from men known to be encumbered by gambling debts. But, unmarried, Madeleine d'Arbonne had no possessions in the world.

There was *one* man—just one—who had cared nothing for that, and James Bruce had gone away.

It was a relief to get out of the train at Cherbourg, and smell the clean smell of the sea. Even the Empress felt it to be a holiday. Eugénie closed her eyes, and apparently her beautiful ears, to many disquieting things that day, in the sense of freedom it gave her to go aboard Vice-Admiral Bouet-Villaumez' flagship and accompany the Baltic squadron for a short distance on its mission to blockade the Prussian Navy in the Bay of Jade. She refused to be upset by Prince Napoleon, although he was there in his most obnoxious mood. The short voyage from Peterhead to Tromsö, from where he was recalled on a trip to Spitzbergen by the dramatic news of war, had made Prince Napoleon an expert on the North Sea as a theatre of operations. He was sulking because he had not been given command of the task force of Marines, and the Marines were sulking because the command had been given to an army officer. The Empress ignored all this. She ignored, as they passed along the docks, the great sections of the prefabricated ironclads, which were to be rail-roaded east for assembly and used to cover the crossing of the Rhine at Maxau, and which had been reported on their way to Strasbourg several days before. Wrapped in a Navy boatcloak, Madeleine stood for an hour behind the Empress on the deck of the flagship, while the fleet of fourteen ironclad frigates bucked their way into the Channel spray. It was a stormy day. Several of the ladies were overtaken by seasickness and went below. Eugénie herself, an excellent sailor with any amount of physical courage, talked and smiled with the Vice-Admiral, while the wind whipped out her bronze-gold hair and stung colour into her cheeks. Once she looked behind, and laughed, and said to Madeleine,

"This isn't much like El Kantara, is it?"

Madeleine smiled and shook her head. Nothing could have been less like the Suez Canal under the brassy light of noon than the grey high-running Channel seas.

"Oh! what wouldn't I give," she thought, "to see James come aboard as he came on board the *Aigle*—into the middle of all this indecision and quarrelling? With that special way of talking with his head high, and that broken cap in his hand, and that you-be-damned way of looking round him that means, 'There's nothing wrong here that a Scots engineer can't set right!'"

Immediately after the return from Cherbourg, Madeleine spent a day in Paris. Victor was about to start for Metz, and every court lady was permitted to leave the Empress to say good-bye to a near relative going to the front—that front where, in the crucial first ten days after the declaration of war, there had been no activity except an occasional raid by Prussian vedettes.

An imperial vehicle deposited Madeleine in front of her uncle's house, and she stood for a moment enjoying the sunshine in the narrow street while the Old Poisson watched her malevolently from his lodge. The great gates were open, and a real lady, he knew, would have had herself driven right up to the porte-cochère —but not, of course, "the fisherman's grandchild"! Look at her — look at the clothes she wore—not a month after her mother was laid to rest! His bow was perfunctory as Madeleine passed him with a smile, in the white dress which she wore by the express orders of the Empress. "No mourning, now!" said Eugénie with a shudder. "Dear child, it's so very bad for the morale of our people!"

The general mobilization had already made gaps in Michel Bertaux' domestic staff. The grooms had reported to their regiments (and in the confusion of the War Minister's arrangements, the depots of the Paris regiments were usually at the other side of France), and the major-domo, an elderly man, received her without his attendant footmen. Victor was already in the hall, looking pensively at their mother's picture.

"Madeleine!" he said, "I'm glad you're here before the others get back. They've gone to the Bon Marché."

"What on earth for?" asked Madeleine. "Is Louise extending her shopping to the department stores?"

"Apparently," said Victor, pulling down his blue and silver tunic. "She suggested to Uncle Michel that the price of household linen would probably rise because of the war, so they went posting off to buy enough for this house and Arbonne too, twice over! But never mind that. What I wanted to tell you was, I've asked Charles de Mortain to come to lunch. He's off tomorrow with du Preuil's Cuirassiers."

"Does Michel know you've invited him?"

"Knows, and thoroughly approves."

"Well, I don't," said Madeleine. She began slowly to lay her hat, gloves and frilly white parasol on a chair near the window. "I thought this was to be just a family gathering, Victor—in your honour."

"Well, if Michel can invite that fellow Hartzell, I don't see why my best friend can't be here, too," said Victor belligerently. "Why Hartzell, I ask you? Why is he constantly asked here now?"

"Don't be jealous, Victor! Michel says Frank Hartzell is the best young businessman in the company and quite indispensable to him. But you won't have to see much more of him—he's sailing for New York at the end of this week."

"Good riddance, then—we don't want any Yankees here."

"Louise doesn't agree with you!"

"Oh, don't be a fool, Madeleine. Louise has her head screwed on the right way—better than you have, apparently! Why did you refuse de Mortain, dear?" he went on in a softer tone. "He's the best of good fellows, and wild about you—"

"I know, Victor."

"And he has a glorious old place down there in Normandy, without even a dowager to bother you. Won't you give him another chance, Madeleine? Just to please me! I'd like to see you settled before I go off to the war."

That brought her straight into his arms, remembering only the years when they had been playmates, racing their ponies round the paddock at Arbonne while the little sisters watched them from the railings. Victor hugged her awkwardly, and they called each other by their nursery names, Totor, Mado; until the present came back with a rush when he asked her:

"You didn't send Charles away because of the Scotsman, did you?"

She kept her head down on his shoulder, and murmured,

"What do you mean?"

"I mean that Scots fellow you met on the Canal. I saw him hanging about you at the Tuileries; and my uncle says you correspond with him—"

She drew away from him, tall and grand as she knew how to be.

"You and Michel are mistaken, Victor. I am not in correspondence with Mr. Bruce."

Before he could say more the sound of wheels was heard in the courtyard, and they moved to the glass door in time to see Bertaux handing his youngest niece from the maroon brougham.

Her deep mourning was becoming to Louise d'Arbonne. Between the black silk of her pelerine and the black lace of a decidedly adult bonnet her little kitten face had a pure, healthy pallor, and her small pink mouth was set in an expression of great gravity.

Madeleine, in her impulsive way, ran down the marble steps to greet her.

"What a darling you looked, perched up there!" she said gaily. "But sweetheart, *not* a bonnet, please! It's far too old for you!"

She started to untie the ribbons which Louise had tied so carefully, like a small cat's bow, beneath her chin. The little sister pushed that loving hand away.

"Don't fidget me, Madeleine—you're not maman!" she said.

"Really, if I were allowed to comment on *your* clothes, I might tell you that you ought not to be wearing white! Do just let me run up to my room—our guests will be here at any minute!"

"The little chatelaine!" said Madeleine as the glass door closed behind her sister. "Was that intended to be a snub?"

"You asked for it, my dear," said Michel Bertaux, an amused spectator of the scene. "Come along indoors, and give me all the latest gossip from St. Cloud."

Between Madeleine and her uncle there now existed a kind of armed neutrality. She presided at his table on her rare visits home, but he no longer demanded her presence there. "Oh, the Empress, poor woman," he had said abstractedly, at their first meeting after the outbreak of war, "of course you can't leave her now, stay with her while you can"; and on social occasions like the present he did not allow her to direct the talk as his hostess. Instead, he himself threw the conversational ball adroitly between young de Mortain, Frank Hartzell and a lively gentleman, the Vicomte d'Hérisson, who had just arrived from the United States.

"What were the American reactions to our declaration of war, monsieur?" he asked the newcomer, almost as soon as they were seated at the table.

"In one important respect," said d'Hérisson with a sardonic smile, "pretty much the same in Washington as in Paris! Your Minister Washburne"—he bowed in Frank's direction—"lost no time in taking the German nationals here under Uncle Sam's protection as soon as he got back from Carlsbad, did he?"

Frank Hartzell's grey eyes clouded. He had had to hear a good deal about the American Minister's gesture in the last few days. He was sharply aware that he was the only neutral at that table—and that he looked it, too, in the dark sack suit which contrasted with the gorgeous uniforms of the two young officers. He wondered if Louise, who was looking at him intently, thought he showed up badly by comparison.

Louise was only thinking his firm clean-shaven mouth very handsome. She was *tired* of those silly moustaches and imperials!

"Mr. Washburne acted according to the usual diplomatic procedure, I believe," said Frank. "There are thirty thousand citizens of the various German States here; someone had to protect their interests. A neutral envoy was the obvious choice."

"Someone should freight the whole lot back to Germany in cattle cars," Victor put in.

"So now, I hear, the Stars and Stripes is flying above the German Embassy in the rue de Lille," said d'Hérisson.

"Washburne was in the devil of a hurry to hoist the flag," Victor grumbled.

"But remember," said d'Hérisson, "Ambassador Washburne is the friend and protégé of Ulysses S. Grant, and President Grant has never forgiven the Emperor for his intervention in Mexico—"

"Ah!" said Bertaux deeply, "what did I always tell them?"

"—and then the German immigrants have kept their national sentiment very much alive through their social *Bunds* and *Turnvereins*. I saw street demonstrations in New York, and my Cunarder was full of German-Americans going home to fight for the Fatherland."

"Let them all come!" said Charles de Mortain cheerfully. "We've got something worth all their *Turnvereins*, whatever that may be. We've got the secret weapon!"

"What exactly *is* the secret weapon?" Monsieur d'Hérisson inquired.

"It's only a secret to the artillery," said Bertaux. "It's been kept so *much* of a secret that very few officers know the parts, or the drill; no doubt they'll open fire on a few of our own regiments before they learn."

"Colonel Aymé knows," said Frank. "He told me all about it at the Jockey Club last Monday. It's a kind of mitrailleuse, monsieur, mounted with twenty-five gun barrels firing in the same direction. We used the Mark I in the Union Army, but it wasn't a great success. This is DeReffye's Mark IV, but I guess it has all the old drawbacks: the field of fire isn't wide enough, and the weapon itself takes up just as much space and horsepower in traction as a field gun."

"You being an authority on field guns, of course," said Victor d'Arbonne.

"I know what I'm talking about," said Frank, in tones so unusually sharp that the sisters looked at him in surprise. "Your mitrailleuse throws a better ball than canister, and your Chassepôt is better than our minié, but what about the Krupp fourteen-inch, firing either shot or shell of one thousand pounds? The American papers say it's in full production now, and has been for months! Now don't take offence, Captain d'Arbonne," he said firmly. "I know you and Captain de Mortain are enlisted in a just cause, but I reckon the Johnny Rebs thought *they* had a just cause, nearly ten years ago, and they had some good men to lead them, but what beat them was Pittsburgh! *Pittsburgh!* The coal and the iron of Pennsylvania, and the factories and mills of New England! What you're up against isn't just the Prussian Army! It's Krupp's—it's Essen—it's the Rühr!"

. . . "I'm very sorry, sir," he apologized, when he was alone with Bertaux in the study after Monsieur d'Hérisson had taken his departure. "Don't know what got into me, to make me talk like that. Count Victor never did like me, but he won't give me the time of day after this."

"No harm done," said Bertaux. "I'm glad these young men heard the truth for once, even though they don't believe it—yet. And I'm glad *you* heard what d'Hérisson had to say about American opinion. He's a pretty shrewd observer, and I asked him here to give you some idea of the state of mind you'll run into when you get home. How it will affect you I don't know—I just *don't know,*" he went on emphatically, as Frank seemed about to interrupt him. "You're sentimental about France, I know that, but at the same time you see where all this flag-flapping and shouting about *La Gloire* is likely to lead us. This isn't your war! You've told me so a score of times in the past six weeks, and I shan't blame you if you want to keep out of it. But I do want to find out how realistic you'll become after six weeks, or two months, in Philadelphia. That's why I'm sending you over now, before any major engagement has taken place—because I don't know how much time we have, and that's the truth."

It was an unusually long speech for the laconic Bertaux, and Frank looked at him uncertainly.

"The job you've given me won't take two months to do, sir."

"Perhaps not, but see you do it well. After that, if you don't want to go on with a French concern under war conditions, I think your cousins will be impressed enough by the experience you've gained here to say no more about Canton, and start again on the old footing when your leave of absence, as you call it, is over in September. If you do want to work in France again—well, I expect still to be in business after the war is over."

It was said with a deliberately chilling effect which Frank as deliberately brushed aside.

"Either way, I can never thank you enough for all you've done for me, Monsieur Bertaux. I think you know there's one reason above all others which will bring me back to France—"

The nervous tic twitched at Bertaux' eyelids as he gruffly said, "Louise?"

"Yes, monsieur. I'm sure you know how I—"

Bertaux jumped up from the armchair and laid his hard hand on the young man's shoulder.

"Don't say it, Frank! I forbid you to say it! When you say good-bye, not a word of it to her! She'll have enough to shoulder in the next few months without weeping and worrying over you. Mind, if you come back to us, I don't say no! But no love-making —no pledges, no farewell vows—remember!"

It was not easy to remember when, after scouting down the long hall, Frank came upon Louise in the library where no one read, and found her with a quill pen in her hand, working over a pile of papers. His step fell noiselessly on the thick carpet, and she did not look up when he stopped in the open doorway to feast his eyes on the small intent figure at the big desk.

She was very young to have the burden of Arbonne laid upon her. But much of the kitten look had gone with the dancing curls, now coiled into a smooth chignon at the nape of her neck, and there was a woman's decision in the small hand casting up the long columns of figures on a list before her.

It struck Frank for the first time that there was a certain likeness between Bertaux and the niece who bore no physical resemblance to him. In the way of sitting at work—he had often noticed how awkwardly the financier squared up to a table desk, his chair set too far back for comfort, and his writing paper at an angle approved by no school of penmanship; and Louise was sitting in just that way. In the habit of drumming with the fingers of his left hand while he thought—as Louise was drumming now,

Tatum. Tatum. Tatumtatumtatum.

"Are you very busy, Miss Louise?"

She started up at once, her face rosy.

"Oh no! I was just making a note of the invoices from this morning. If I don't do it at once I get the books in such a muddle, and then uncle's cashier is so annoyed. I have to count on my fingers, you know—so stupid!"

She moved away to a sofa near the fire which Bertaux liked to have burning even on a warm day, and took up a tambour frame. The silk on which she began to stitch fell across her hands in dainty folds.

"Victor and Monsieur de Mortain were sorry not to see you again," she said to Frank without looking up. "They had to go to the War Ministry, and they took Madeleine back to the Tuileries—she had to get something the Empress wanted from her study. They left you all sorts of *bon voyage* messages."

"I'll bet," said Frank dryly. "Did you have coffee here in the library?"

"Victor and I did," said Louise with a smile. "I don't think Mado and Charles de Mortain drank any coffee. They had a long talk instead, in the conservatory."

"Oh! Am I to congratulate you on the prospect of a brother-in-law?"

"Not judging from appearances."

"Too bad. He's such a nice fellow; and rich, too. What more can she possibly want? H'm? What are you screwing up your little face so wisely for? Tell me!"

"I know what she wants—or whom," said Louise; "and you do too."

"You mean there's someone else? Somebody I know? Colonel Aymé? But he's too old for her—he must be forty if he's a day."

"Try again," said Louise with a little laugh.

A recollection of the night at Ismailia, and the rockets bursting in a trail of fire, came suddenly to Frank.

"You couldn't possibly mean James Bruce?"

"Madeleine doesn't know I've guessed it," said Louise quietly, "but I have. Mr. Bruce was certainly in love with her last winter and I feel, somehow, that she loves him."

Belatedly, Frank remembered Bertaux' orders. This was getting as near "love-making" as any conversation might, without coming from the general to the particular. It was very hard not to come to the particular, as he stood by the mantel with one arm laid along the ball-fringed cover on which a number of Dresden figurines were arranged under small glass bells, and looked down on that equally dainty human figure, with the very white parting in the top of its shining black head. But Frank had a promise to keep, and the bright American dream of success to turn into reality; he contented himself with a few conventional words about being honoured by her confidence, wishing her well at Arbonne and trusting in a speedy victory for France. Then he could not resist taking the tambour frame gently from her cold fingers, and kissing them one after another in farewell.

"You know I'm coming back, Louise?"

"I'll be waiting."

And all the time he was taking his hat from the major-domo, crossing the courtyard, giving a farewell tip to the Old Poisson, it seemed to him that these words had been spoken already by hundreds of thousands of men in armies he had known, the boys in blue and the boys in grey; and that *his* war was slowly merging into *this* war in a long continuity of pain.

The Old Poisson watched him dispassionately as he passed out by the postern gate.

He saw them all come and go.

III

Exactly three weeks after that luncheon in his uncle's house, where he had clinked glasses with de Mortain and drunk the popular toast "To Berlin!" Victor d'Arbonne was one of an army in full retreat across Lorraine. It was called the Army of the Rhine, but it had come nowhere near the Rhine: the prefabricated boats which were to guard its crossing were lying disassembled in Strasbourg, and Strasbourg itself was besieged by the enemy. If the French army drank any toast with feeling on this day, August 16, 1870, it would undoubtedly be "To Paris!"

There were, however, no emergency rations of food or wine to be issued to the cavalry standing on the slopes between Rezonville and Mars-la-Tour, waiting to join a battle which had begun two hours earlier as an artillery duel between elements of the German First Army and Marshal Canrobert's field guns and mitrailleuses. The troops had had their *soupe* at first light, as soon as it became apparent that Marshal Bazaine, the new Commander-in-Chief, had failed in his operation of getting them all out of the fearfully narrow road, little more than an old Roman causeway, which was their only direct way from Metz to Verdun and the railhead to Châlons. Nearly twenty-four hours had passed since the Emperor had given up the supreme command and fled with his son in the open travelling chaise which Victor, on escort duty, had followed through the terrible days at the beginning of August when the Emperor trailed round and round his beaten armies. In those twenty-four hours they had come barely twenty-four kilometres. One hundred and fifty thousand men, with their caissons, limbers, sutler wagons, vivandières pushing little carts of wine; one hundred and fifty thousand men encumbered by all the refugees streaming west out of St Privat, Woippy, Rezonville, Vionville, the villages in the angle of Metz and Mars-la-Tour, and the cattle being driven ahead from the farms with the odd names—Leipzig, Moscow, La Folie—which the Engineer corps was hastily making into strong points: one hundred and fifty thousand men *could not* make better time through the ravines that led to a chance of safety on the Marne.

They had lost their supplies. The extra rations for ten days, which would have put some heart into the waiting cavalry, as well as one million francs' worth of tobacco, had been captured with blankets for the whole army by the commander of the German Second Army, the "Red Prince," Frederick Charles of Prussia, when he cut the railroad between Metz and Nancy. They had very little left except their courage and their gaudy uniforms, for the Army of the Rhine was staging the last pageant of the Second Empire as it wound through Lorraine, down into the poplar ravines and out on the stubble where a miserable harvest had been cut too soon. The infantry were slogging along in the blue, white and red of the national colours, blue cutaway coats and baggy scarlet trousers over the white gaiters which Marshal Leboeuf had insisted were so well provided with buttons. It was just possible that in some remote depot, say Châteauroux, there were millions of gaiter buttons in boxes marked *Infantry, For the Use of*; but they were not in Lorraine—what mattered a great deal more was that the boots beneath the gaiters were already in need of repair and there were no replacements. Above the blue cutaways floated the raspberry cloaks of the Spahis as the African cavalry jogged by, then came all the colours of the rainbow as the Zouaves and Turcos came in sight, followed by the schapskas, dolmans, furred and frogged jackets, gold braid and feathered hats to which Hussars, Lancers and Dragoons had clung by tradition since the wars of the First Empire.

Behind and around them, in the gigantic pincers movement planned by von Moltke at Pont-au-Mousson, only thirty miles away, there closed in a solid wall of Germans: Saxons, Würtemburgers, Hessians, Badeners, Bavarians, Prussians, all incorporated by Bismarck into the Prussian Army, and to be known by the French for ever after simply and collectively as *les Prussiens*. Among them were veterans of Düppel and Sadowa, hardened by six years of conquest, but the green troops had been put through many months of marching and counter-marching: they had muscles of iron, and they pursued the French with the fast relentless rhythm of a metronome. The old King of Prussia was as hardy as the youngest recruit in the Pomeranian Grenadiers. He could sit in the saddle for fifteen hours at a stretch, and at night lie down beside his charger, with his old cloak wrapped around him, and bivouac in the heart of his army.

King Wilhelm was an extra asset to Bismarck, who with von Moltke and Roon had forged this superb war machine, complete to the last cog, complete to its field ambulances, field posts, identity and wound cards, and "special service" supplies of beer and sausages. They were handling men capable of being swayed by a degenerate kind of mass fanaticism, a cult of the superman which they called "devotion to a Leader." Not one of the three was personally capable of inspiring this kind of hysteria. When they went by, a chill fell on the troops as if the fresh-faced, blond boys from Baden and Darmstadt saw three Fates engaged in spinning out the lives of men. But let that hoary old hypocrite the King of Prussia appear on horseback, his white beard blowing and his lips wet with a prayer to the God of Battles, and the troops were ready to fall down and worship him. His son Fritz, the *Heldentenor*, could produce the same effect; only mass emotion could have swayed the Bavarian troops of his Third Army into blind loyalty to their Prussian commander.

The Prussian war machine had already dealt the French shattering blows. Three defeats in three days, at the very beginning of August, had lost France the whole province of Alsace and sent Marshal MacMahon fleeing with the survivors of two army corps through the defiles of the Vosges to Châlons camp. At Wissembourg and at Wörth the Crown Prince Fritz himself led his men to what he joyfully called "bloody victory." The king, his father, telegraphed the good news to the doting mother and wife waiting together at Potsdam. "May God help further!" after Wissembourg—"Thank God for his mercy!" after Wörth. The Crown Prince, plainly, had the most powerful of all Allies.

And the Leader of the French? The Emperor?

"—Charles, it was hell from the first moment to the last," said Victor d'Arbonne.

The day before, when the Emperor turned over the command to Bazaine at Gravelotte, Victor had succeeded in getting himself transferred from the imperial escort to General du Preuil's Cuirassiers, in which de Mortain was serving. He had not come up with his friend until the night bivouac, when both were exhausted; this was the first moment duty had allowed them for any sort of private talk. The troopers round about them were very quiet. MacMahon's Cuirassiers had died to the last man at Reichshoffen, one phase of the terrible defeat at Wörth; the odds were that du Preuil's men would that day pass into legend too. They were still dismounted, and two privates held the great bay chargers of Charles and Victor. The officers had removed their huge helmets, and wore forage caps; the rest of their equipment was monstrously heavy. The Roman breastplates which the Cuirassiers had worn since the seventeenth century as the mounted shock troops of the army weighed enough to make the bay horses, up to the sturdiest work in the cavalry, necessary even for such light riders as Victor and Charles. From above, the sun of noon blazed down on the bare upland. It was drying the ground rapidly—almost the first sunshine of the six weeks which had ruined France, and a little wind was blowing scraps of paper, torn cloth and blood-soaked linen down from the action already joined at Vionville.

"I didn't see the Emperor at Gravelotte," said Charles, "but I heard the troops received him quietly. No cheering, of course, but no booing, either."

"There wasn't very much of that along the roads. Sometimes he got a few catcalls and shouts of 'Sold! Sold!' especially after the news of Wörth got out; but just the sight of him seemed to shock them into silence. He's taken to painting his face, Charles; every morning you could see the rouge sticking out on top of that ghastly yellow colour, and when the pain hit him he'd bite his lips until the saliva ran down his chin on to his uniform—you never saw such a scarecrow."

"How about the Prince Imperial?"

"He's had his baptism of fire, poor little devil, and he stood it well enough. When I saw him on horseback, I thought it was quite a difference from fooling about on his velocipede."

"Did the Emperor ride at all?"

"At first he did. They sent all his English chargers down from St. Cloud, and he tried Hero, Bolero was too much for him, but oh God, Charles, the jolting hit his bladder so that he had to be helped to dismount and get over to the roadside every few miles. Then our heroic duty was to line up and make a screen for him as the troops went by. . . . I didn't join the army to be part of a travelling *pissoir*, I know that!"

Charles shook his head non-committally. He was only a year older than his friend, but he had been in action in the razzias of the desert, and he hoped to God "the youngster" would stand fire well. Victor had been given command of a half-squadron, sixty men, none of whom he had trained or even knew by name. Too much palace duty, too much garrison duty in Paris, too many balls at the Tuileries had produced an officer whose hands, Charles could see, were shaking a little as he drew off and put on his heavy gauntlets and fidgeted with his sabre belt. But Victor *had* had the guts to ask for his transfer, when he might have been at Verdun by this time, entrained with the imperial suite for what they all seemed to think of as the great refuge of Châlons camp.

De Mortain thought their own chances of reaching Verdun were small. Steinmetz' First German Army barred the way at Mars-la-Tour, and the vedettes on reconnaissance had reported the Red Prince coming up fast on the flank; the day might well turn into another Wörth, with the French hopelessly outnumbered and outgunned.

Bazaine had been holding the cavalry in reserve since the first wave had gone down before von Redern's guns at Vionville. So far he had depended on the French riflemen, in whose hands the new Chassepôt breech-loader, opening fire at fifteen hundred paces, was cutting swathes through the German infantry. But the men complained that the weapon dirtied up too fast. They had started spitting on the cartridges as they loaded, and the slowly accumulating delay from fouled barrels was giving Steinmetz just the time he needed to wait for the Red Prince.

The Marshal now saw that he must fight the battle as a Napoleonic set-piece, always distasteful to a commander who preferred the impromptu effects which had brought him earlier victories in Africa and Mexico. He disliked the terrain of Mars-la-Tour, an evil combination of barren uplands and quarries. He disliked exceedingly the mixed advice he was getting from Marshal Canrobert and Prince Joachim Murat (spurring about in a gaudy dolman, trying to repeat his grandfather's bravura of the Bonaparte days), and also from Bourbaki. The half-Greek general was nearly hysterical about the need to defend Metz, Metz-la-Pucelle, the virgin fortress, even if it meant falling back on Gravelotte.

"We are too old to fight a war like this!" General Bourbaki was declaiming at the command post; he meant, of course, that they were too young. Too thoroughly versed in the tactics of the beginning of the century; too confident that courage, confidence and the *furia francese* must triumph over the great guns from Essen, the thousand pounders booming on the ridge above Mars-la-Tour and the little three-hundred pounders lobbing their shells into the valley which the French must cross to regain possession of the road to Verdun. But even Bazaine, when it came to one o'clock in the afternoon, when Murat's Dragoons had broken and fled before the Krupp guns, was forced into the next move in the set-piece: the unleashing of the "French fury" of the cavalry he had been holding back at Rezonville.

"Prepare to mount! Mount!"

The commands were echoing down the lines within a few minutes after Bazaine came spurring up the hill to confer with General du Preuil, waiting anxiously with his staff around him. Victor and Charles stuffed their caps inside their belts, put on their helmets and swung into the saddle. There was just time, before they moved out in front of their men, for Charles to fling at his friend, with a grin,

"Do you suppose the Emperor is holding manoeuvres today at Châlons?"

Victor answered with a laugh that was very nearly a groan. They had all been thinking of that the night before – how the Emperor, punctual to the yearly tryst, was heading for Châlons camp on "St. Napoleon's Day." But this day's work (with the horses nearly unmanageable already with the smell of blood, and

211

the accursed thud and whistle of the shells all about them) would be like no manoeuvres Captain d'Arbonne had ever known. The Commander-in-Chief had passed very close to him, and he had heard what Bazaine was saying to an aide—something about "must sacrifice a regiment—see what the Lancers can do." The trembling which seized him then was so violent that he thought it must be noticed. He clamped his jaws and tightened his knees on the leather till the bay horse reared and plunged.

At heart Victor d'Arbonne was not a bad fellow. He had been spoiled by his adoring mother, and taught to think too well of his future position as the eighteenth Comte d'Arbonne, but it was not snobbery which made him rude and touchy to men like James Bruce and Frank Hartzell. His worst defect was an excessive chauvinism, for Victor was the kind of Frenchman for whom the foreigner is always wrong. But somewhere in him there was a vein of poetry which the meretricious court life of the Second Empire had not entirely quenched. As a child he had often crept into the little parish church at Arbonne to gaze at the effigy of the young squire who died at Carthage, and the tattered banners of his ancestors hanging on the dark walls. With the same awe he now saw the Lancers' guidons disappear downhill into the smoke of battle and the colour bearers of the Cuirassiers move forward with the Eagles raised above the names of their great Napoleonic victories:

Austerlitz 1805
Essling 1809
La Moskowa 1812

Bazaine, through his glass, saw the Lancers break and wheel, and sighed. There went his sacrificial regiment, broken against that terrible German III Corps, all Prussians from the Mark of Brandenburg, whom he guessed that Bismarck would be watching with especial pride. His vedettes had told him that the King of Prussia was watching the battle too. In fact the old man was praising the Frenchmen, "Gallant fellows! Oh, the gallant fellows!" and licking his lips as he saw them fall. Von Moltke stood beside the King and Bismarck, waiting with his watch in hand for the arrival of the Red Prince. The time had come for another French effort and another sacrifice. Bazaine turned to du Preuil.

Achille Bazaine was a soldier's soldier, a man who had come up from private of the Line to Marshal of France, while retaining something of the two-fisted sergeant of the Foreign Legion he once had been. The rough joke and the volley of barrack-room bad language were part of his equipment in steadying troops under fire, he used them now as he rode up and down the Cuirassier lines, reminding them of their prime function to silence batteries, and pointing with his marshal's baton to the Krupp gun emplacements on the far side of Rezonville. Under the steel corselet Victor felt a cold sweat break and pour over his whole body. He took up his reins in his left hand, unsheathed his sabre at the word of command, screamed an order at his half-squadron and dug in his spurs as the bugles began to sound the charge.

"En avant!"

They went headlong down the slope, the Eagles ahead, the song of the bugles behind, for the first five minutes it was glorious, better than any steeplechase, the bay lengthening his stride and the curb bridle gripping him close, left hand low above the pommel and right hand swinging the great sabre aloft. Then the bullets began to sing and whine among them, they were close enough to the Prussian riflemen for the needle gun with its far shorter range to kill at close quarters, and on either side of Victor men were swaying and falling, and riderless horses, with bumping empty saddles, were careering over the battlefield where the wounded Lancers were trying to drag themselves out of the way of the Cuirassier charge.

"The guns! The guns!"

Some fantastically gaudy figure—one of the Murats, of course—was riding neck and neck beside du Preuil in the van, trying to shriek out an order, scarcely heard and impossible to obey. For between the French cavalry and the Krupp guns still rose that impenetrable wall of young men with the drugged dazed faces of fanatics, who as fast as they fell for King and Fatherland were replaced by others, the Brandenburgers of III Corps, whose fire was murderous. Against them the Cuirassiers began at last to swerve to left and right, running out among the potato fields and blood-soaked clover of Lorraine. At once the German cavalry came after them in pursuit, Colonel von Rauch's 1st Hussars, with the death's head grinning above their shakos. The French turned and faced them again in a terrible, earth-shaking melée of hand-to-hand fighting by mounted men such as had not been known, except for the slaughter of Wörth and the Spicheren, for half a century on the continent of Europe. Victor's sabre bit deep into the shoulder of a tall Hussar corporal. The shock of the blow almost unhorsed himself. He dragged the red blade out and struck wildly at the next man, the frantic horses biting and kicking as furiously as their riders swung their sabres, and then the Hussar was off and down, lost in that madness of ironshod hoofs and the heaving limbs of men.

The French were through von Rauch's barrier, but von Bredow's Heavy Brigade was forming to charge, and the covering fire from General Canrobert's rifled ordnance was useless to the Cuirassier stragglers who had run out beyond Rezonville. Victor's half-squadron came up around him, there were twenty-five in the saddle out of the sixty who had started down the hill, and as the bugles began to sing Retreat he knew it was his duty to take them back across that field through which the Heavy Brigade had already begun to gallop. He hesitated for a moment, just as he had hesitated at the cut-and-laid in his first hunting field, and then he heard a voice shouting *"En avant! en avant!"* as Charles de Mortain galloped past him with the remains of his own squadron riding in a beautiful steady formation. Victor, with a cheer, led his stragglers after him.

De Forton and the French Dragoons came roaring downhill to the rescue as Charles, going unerringly for a platoon of von Bredow's which had begun to break and turn, took the Cuirassiers out of the trap and back to their own lines. They were all but out of range when one of the little Krupp guns found the moving target. The shell burst in the middle of them. Victor was blown clean out of the saddle, down on the riddled turf in his encumbering breastplate, as little able to move as a turtle laid upon its carapace. Then for one fearful minute, while the whole world seemed to be full of smoke and shreds of flesh and bloody cloth, he saw his friend still upright in the stirrups, still leading the Frenchmen on, but with a red hole gaping from side to thighs where shell fragments had torn away his stomach and intestines and only his spinal column holding his body together. It lasted only for an instant of mortal pain. Then Charles de Mortain threw up his arms and fell, while his horse, with a last frantic kick, caught Victor on the temple. Blood spurted from the young man's ears and nostrils, while all about him, from the wounded and the dying, the Vintage of 1870 poured and soaked into the soil of France.

IV

After the carnage of Mars-la-Tour, Bazaine fell back on Grave-lotte, and there, two days later, the Red Prince beat him again, in another appalling slaughter. Bazaine was driven back inside Metz, the virgin fortress, with one hundred and seventy thousand men, the survivors of the Army of the Rhine, and General Steinmetz and the Red Prince held him there like two cats at a mousehole. The whole of Alsace and Lorraine were now in German hands; Metz and Strasbourg were besieged, and one hundred thousand Frenchmen had been killed, wounded or taken prisoner within six weeks.

It added up to what was called all over France *La Débâcle*, the disaster. It meant, sooner rather than later, the end of the Second Empire.

The Empress and her court had been at the Tuileries since the red dawn that followed the shattering news of Wörth. They had come up from St. Cloud helter-skelter, after the terrible night hours when Monsieur Filon and two secretaries, on their knees on the floor of the grand salon, decoded the messages coming in from headquarters, and Madeleine d'Arbonne put the pages in order for the Empress. They had been back in Paris in good time for the inevitable panic on the Bourse, the fall of "Lighthearted" Ollivier and his government and for the first demands by the opposition that Napoleon III should abdicate.

But the Imperial Standard still floated over the Tuileries, and in her study the Empress-Regent sat writing, cajoling, browbeating her new prime minister, the aged Count Palikao, and sending directives on tactics and strategy to her beaten corps commanders. She was still very lovely in the dresses she had now adopted as a uniform, of grey silk trimmed with black crape for the fallen, with all her jewels put away except the five gold bands on her wedding finger and the emerald four-leaf clover, which had brought no luck. All day long men came and went between the study and the great salons—still curtainless and dust-sheeted—carrying port-folios and papers tied in bundles, and trying to advise her in her desperate situation. De Lesseps came, sturdy and concerned; he had brought his young wife back to France for the birth of their first child, and was eager to serve his "guardian angel," Eugénie. Dr. Evans, the Imperial Surgeon-Dentist, came, full of the progress which his committee of twenty-five American residents was making with the construction of an emergency hospital near his home. Minister Washburne came, in the congenial role of a Job's comforter, full of sententious comparisons between Wörth and the first battle of Bull Run. But by night the palace was given over to the women and some wounded men from Wörth, nursed in one of the great halls by Sisters of Charity.

Eugénie's ban on mourning had been removed. In black dresses, now, the one-time *cocodettes* of the Tuileries gathered by night in the sinister anterooms between the empty salons, talking in whis-pers, scaring themselves with stories of the Little Red Man who was said to haunt the palace and appear always when there was to be a change of master. Someone would start up with a faint shriek as the door creaked open and a small figure in an old-world wig came bowing in. It was never anyone more alarming than Mon-sieur Bignet, the head usher, summoning one of the ladies to go at once to Her Imperial Majesty.

The Empress was taking chloral every night. It was the same drug as her husband used, and she took it with Dr. Conneau's grudging permission—only a few grains, to be administered always in the presence of another person. The older ladies would weep from pity and weariness as they saw her sink into her drugged rest. Among the juniors, Madame Carette, a great favourite, sometimes sang to her very softly; Madame Lebreton, jealous of her position as the official Reader, would try soothing her to sleep with a few pages of her old favourite, *Lady Isabelle*. But she liked as well as any the ministrations of Mademoiselle d'Arbonne, who neither wept nor (fortunately) sang, but who had a firm way of saying, "This stuff is very bad for you, you know, Madame. You had much better do as I do : try a half-glass of brandy, or a hot rum grog !" which made the Empress laugh forlornly, and feel that Madeleine-dear-child had almost a *man's* approach to suffering.

Madeleine herself was very calm. It was as if the icy self-control she had begun to practise after her parting from James Bruce enabled her not only to get through the days of the Disaster, but to judge and analyse those about her as she had never done before. The first faint cloud appeared on the mirror which Madeleine had held up to the Empress for so long. Now she watched, and saw, as they drove in a closed carriage through the streets to hear Mass at Notre Dame des Victoires, how little Eugénie really cared for the poor people of Paris, all in grief or anxiety for the army's fate, when she was not required by protocol to bestow on them her ceremonial smile. Protected by her veil, she looked out indifferently on the narrow streets where every little shop or booth bore the legend "Closed for Mobilization," and where women and old men were hurrying about the tasks which might mean the preservation of their city. And yet Paris was very beautiful in those days when the famous lights were dimmed, and the capital rose out of her froth of flowerbeds and gaslit cafés, gaunt and towering like a great grey cliff.

The fortifications of the city assumed a new significance. For thirty years they had been the subject of café-concert jokes and music-hall ballads. Now their names became a litany. Every child in Paris could recite, with respect and pride, the roll-call of the Sixteen Forts: La Briche. La Double Couronne du Nord. L'Est. Aubervilliers. Romainville. Noisy. Rosny. Nogent. Vincennes. Charenton. Ivry. Bicêtre. Montrouge. Vanves. Issy. Le Mont Valérien.

The Empress knew nothing of all this, for she had closed her ears to the voice of Paris. Very often now, Paris came and shouted under her windows from the gardens or the Carrousel. The *Marseillaise* was many times repeated every day. Sometimes there were ominous cries of "*Vive la République!*" or, what was still more ominous, "*Vive la Commune!*" and "Set Rochefort free!" Sometimes the cry was for "Abdication!" or "Dethronement!"

"*Dé-ché-ance! Dé-ché-ance! Dé-ché-ance!*"

It had a wonderful rabble-rousing beat.

Then, in the days immediately after Gravelotte, a more carefully organized demonstration exploded round the Tuileries.

As an emergency measure a body of citizen soldiers, the Gardes Mobiles, had been raised all over France. Ten years younger than the National Guard, the draftees had none of the Guard's training in drill and discipline; from the first, they were more of a liability than an asset. A few, like the levy from the Côte d'Or, were well officered; others, like the contingent from Brittany, marched proudly into Paris with their parish priests among them and religious banners floating above their heads. But the Paris Mobiles—*les moblots*, as they were affectionately called in the workers' quarters—had been riotous from the start. Drafted to join the Emperor and MacMahon at Châlons camp, they had come roaring back to the capital, boasting that they had taken the camp apart rather than fight for Badinguet. They had a song, or shout, adapted from the *"Vive l'Emp'rrreur!"* with which the police claque greeted Napoleon. They had shouted it, for the better part of a day, outside his quarters at Châlons, and they were delighted to bawl it beneath the windows of his Empress:

> *Vive l'Emp'rrreur!*
> *Un! Deux! Trois!*
> *Merde!*

The death-roll of Mars-la-Tour was published, and more than one pretty girl at the Tuileries shed tears for Charles de Mortain and other young men who had danced at the Plebiscite Ball less than two months before. The names of those killed at Gravelotte were issued almost immediately, and the private rooms of the palace were invaded by messengers from stricken homes, summoning a daughter or a sister to return to a house of mourning. When a footman brought Madeleine the card of Michel Bertaux, she rose from the sofa in her little sittingroom in alarm, and exclaimed to her friend:

"Oh God, what can have happened now? My uncle hasn't set foot in the Tuileries since the Mexico row!"

"He'll want to talk to you alone, darling, I'll go to my own room," said Angèle compassionately. "Let me know if there's anything I can do."

"Thank you." With a fast-beating heart Madeleine waited for the financier's appearance. He came in short of breath, complaining about the three flights of stairs he had had to climb, and dismissing the little sittingroom, which he had never seen before, with one comprehensive glance at the shabby horsehair furniture.

"You're not looking well, Madeleine," he said.

"Is anyone?"

"I suppose not." But Bertaux himself looked florid and prosperous as ever. He placed his silk hat and gold topped cane on one chair and sat down on another with the skirts of his frock coat carefully disposed. "You need fresh air, my dear. Are you free to take a drive with me this afternoon?"

"A drive, where to?"

Passing his fine silk handkerchief over his face, Bertaux replied obliquely, "Those crazy old d'Arbonnes! As if I hadn't enough on my mind without worrying about *them*!"

"What has poor Papa done now?"

"Your poor Papa couldn't keep his silly cousin Henriette quiet at Arbonne, that's what. She came tottering back to Paris yesterday afternoon."

"To the rue du Bac?"

"Where else? She got nervous about the apartment, and some silver tea and coffee service stamped with your infernal cockleshells, and her Limoges china, and all the rest of the heirlooms. Madame Poisson sent me word this morning."

"Oh, poor old soul! Do you want me to go and see her with you now?"

"We'll have a short drive first, and then the carriage can take you on to the rue du Bac. I've got to be back at the office in less than an hour." He looked at his watch. "Persuade the old fool to go back to the country, if you can. We don't need any useless mouths in Paris now."

Her uncle's suppressed agitation renewed Madeleine's foreboding. She said slowly, "You didn't break your rule about never entering the Tuileries to tell me about Cousin Henriette, did you?"

Bertaux sighed.

"Something far worse has happened, hasn't it?"

"Yes, Madeleine."

"Victor?" She dropped to her knees by her uncle's side and took his hand. "Is he—dead?"

"No, no, my darling, not that, but it's bad enough: he was severely wounded in the battle of Mars-la-Tour."

"Where Charles de Mortain—oh, my God! Wounded—how?"

"A head wound, which is always serious." And Bertaux's heavy hand stroked the bowed fair head at his knee.

"But where is he? Is there nothing we can do for him?"

"We can only hope for the best, Madeleine. He's safe enough for the present—inside Metz, in hospital."

He helped Madeleine to rise, and walked to the window, waiting until the sound of quiet crying behind him stopped, and he heard her say:

"I'll get ready to go out, uncle. It'll do me good to go to Cousin Henriette."

"That's my girl." But he stopped her on her way to the door with the words:

"How's the Empress standing up to it all? Doesn't she want *him* and the boy back in Paris?"

"The boy, yes perhaps; but she keeps on saying the Emperor can only return to Paris at the head of a victorious army."

"Humph!" said Bertaux. "Does she still give her audiences?"

"Yes."

"Did she see General Trochu this morning?? Would you know?"

"I do know. Madame Aguado and I were in attendance when she received him."

"And how did Trochu strike you, Madeleine?"

"I thought he was a strange man. Arrogant and haughty, and so emotional in the way he spoke—" She stopped and looked at Bertaux enquiringly.

"I don't suppose you ever saw him before," said her uncle in his persuasive way.

"No, never."

"He was before your time, of course. They used to call him the Man with a Plan, because he always had some grand project up his sleeve. He wrote a book about the need for a professional army which got him into trouble at the War Ministry, and since then he's been in the wilderness for years."

"He's not in the wilderness now."

"Restored to favour, eh? His audience with the Empress put Trochu back in the limelight, eh? What had she to say to him?"

"You know we're not supposed to repeat what was said in audience."

"Come on now, Madeleine, I've heard you tell tales out of school a hundred times, and this is a matter of life and death. There's a rumour on the Bourse that the Emperor has appointed Trochu Governor of Paris. Is that true?"

"If it's true, it'll be in the *Journal Officiel* tomorrow, won't it?"

"I've got to know today."

"You're good at killing two birds with one stone, aren't you?" Madeleine said with scorn. The tears had dried on her pale cheeks. "Break the bad news about Victor and get the inside story on Trochu, all in one afternoon call—not bad! Yes, it's true. The General presented his credentials, and when Her Majesty was unwilling to accept him as the new Governor of Paris, he swore on his faith as a Catholic that to defend her and the dynasty he would die, if need be, on the steps of the Tuileries."

"Well, that's that," said Bertaux deeply. "Now we know. And if the Empress believes in the faith of Louis Trochu, then her game is really up."

The sick Emperor faced his doom alone. His son, with the assent of the terrified government at Paris, was detached from the army and sent across the frontier into Belgium. His cousin, Prince Napoleon, already a deserter in the Crimean War, had made off to his estates in Italy. Marshal Bazaine was besieged in Metz. From the Empress came more and more hysterical appeals to leave Châlons and fight a pitched battle "to save the dynasty," to offer an immediate challenge to the Crown Prince of Prussia. The latter, whose kindness to the wounded had been so much praised in the London papers, asked for nothing better than to fight a battle on the grand scale, and his Third Army was eager to play the return match for Wörth. He expected the French to force the issue at Verdun, but MacMahon and the Emperor moved north and east towards the Ardennes, as if they were fumbling their way towards the Belgian border. The Crown Prince Fritz put Beaumont and Bazeilles to fire and sword, the Bavarians under his command making merry as they burned aged and infirm French villagers alive inside their cottages, before he came up with his enemies at a dismal little town on the Meuse, where on the last day of August Marshal MacMahon seemed prepared to make a stand. And there, while the rouged and tortured Emperor sought death in vain under the German guns, the Crown Prince "surrounded and enclosed," as his Order of the Day read, seventy-five thousand Frenchmen with one hundred and twenty thousand Germans,

On the first of September, 1870,
At Sedan.

On Friday evening, September 2, a terrible rumour began to fly about the streets of Paris. First a fact, many times repeated, then one detail after another, piling up into horror and disgrace—

The army had been cut to pieces at Sedan—

Marshal MacMahon had been severely wounded—

And General Wimpffen, newly arrived from Algeria, had assumed command only to surrender—

"No, no," said the voices, coming in from Bercy and Vaugirard and the Maison Blanche where the ragpickers of Paris lived in their "Golden City," coming nearer and nearer to the Tuileries —"it wasn't Wimpffen who surrendered, it was the Emperor. . . ."

Ah, ce Badinguet!

Then where *is* the Emperor?

Dead, let us hope.

Vive l'Emp'rrreur!

Un! Deux! Trois!

MERDE !

"It can't be true !" said Madeleine next morning, turning over the papers with a trembling hand. "*Fifteen thousand* of our soldiers killed and wounded! The Emperor riding Hero up and down the battlefield, hoisting a flag of truce 'to save the further slaughter of sixty thousand men'! Angèle," to her weeping friend, "let's hurry to Her Majesty!"

There was already a large crowd in the gardens, staring up at the palace windows. The terrified women in the Green Salon could hear them shouting, "*Vendu! Vendu! Trahi!*" It had a swing to it,

"Sold! Sold! Betrayed!"

The Empress was in her superb mood, declaring that what the papers said, and verified by telegrams from Belgium, was "one more canard of the Reds." She dictated several messages to "Imperial Headquarters, Sedan," demanding authoritative news of any battle that might have taken place. The German corporals who deciphered them shouted with laughter as they read. Sedan had then been in Prussian hands for hours, and Napoleon III had surrendered his sword to King Wilhelm. He was already travelling into Germany under guard, with a suite of officers whose names read like a roll call from his uncle's armies. Murat, Massa, Reille, Ney de la Moskowa, they all followed the Emperor's dark Star to prison.

In the middle of the same afternoon Monsieur Chevreau, Minister of the Interior, came to Monsieur Filon, who had been handling much of the secretarial work at the Tuileries, and asked for an audience with the Regent. Auguste Filon was a level-headed young man. He begged the Minister to wait for five minutes. Then he went to ask Madeleine, the calmest woman in the Green Salon, to come with him and help prepare the Empress.

"She isn't there!" said Madeleine, coming out of the Regent's study with an anxious face.

"Are you sure? Not in the library, either? Ask Madame Pollet if she went to her bedroom."

"Pepa says no. Pepa thought she was writing. Monsieur Filon! Can she possibly have gone down to *his* study?"

Madeleine had guessed right. For the first time in years, Eugénie had descended the secret staircase to her husband's private rooms. She stood in the pink and gold alcove, where Virginie de Castiglione had lain like a beautiful naked goddess in his arms so many times, and before and after the Castiglione a whole procession of the frail laughing ladies of the Second Empire. She went into the study where, under the marble eyes of the great Napoleon and his son, Napoleon the Less had hatched his plots and counterplots. She started to mount the stairs again, numbed and drained of feeling, holding up her heavy skirts with both hands, when she heard the voices of Filon and Madeleine whispering at her private door.

"What are you doing there without my leave!"

She was in the room beside them, the black swan, beating her angry wings.

"Your Majesty, forgive us. Monsieur Chevreau is here—"

"Ah!" With a wild glance, Eugénie caught at Filon's hand. "With news of the Emperor?"

"Yes, Your Majesty."

"Of his surrender?"

"Madame, yes."

The face of the Empress was suffused with blood. "He dares send me that message!" she gasped convulsively. "He ought to have been killed before he sent it! *Why isn't he dead!* Why didn't he die beneath the walls of Sedan!"

"Madame, you must try to be calm! Think of the Minister, the government!" Madeleine, flinging her arms about the straining, sobbing woman, attempted to lead her to a chair. "Get her some sal volatile, monsieur! Get Pepa to come to her!"

"Madeleine." Like a wounded creature Eugénie laid her head down on that slender right arm, which tightened round her as Madeleine with her free hand stroked her hair.

"Monsieur Chevreau *demands* to come in now," said Filon with a ghastly face.

The dispatch Chevreau carried was not a long one. It had been sent by Napoleon on his way to prison at Wilhelmshöhe, and it read:

"The army is defeated and captive. Unable to find death among my soldiers, I have been obliged to surrender to save my troops."

Then the habit of years asserted itself in the Empress. She rose up tall, tragic, but absolutely composed, and spoke the line for which all her attitudes had been the long rehearsal.

"It is over—the dynasty is doomed. Now we must think of France!"

That night Paris was in the streets. It was a warm night of clear moonlight—of torchlight too, for the men and women pouring in from the Bastille slums, and St. Antoine, and Montmartre had brought their own illuminations in the form of sticks with heads of tow, soaked in paraffin or resin and set alight as needed. The silent palace stood out like a dark island in a sea of flame. Two companies of Grenadiers stood to arms in the Carrousel and three of Light Infantry on the garden side. The garden gates were locked at sunset, but the fiery torches burned all round the Tuileries, in the rue de Rivoli and down by the Seine, and the women kneeling behind the shuttered windows could hear the constantly repeated cry:

"Dé-ché-ance! Dethronement! Dé-ché-ance!"

The Regent sent for Count Palikao, but the prime minister was fighting to save the Empire at a night session of the Legislature, where her own message to the Deputies, asking for national unity in the face of the terrible news from Sedan, was read to jeers and catcalls. The flaring torches were leaping round the Palais Bourbon too. Any Deputy who cared to look out at them was sharply reminded that the old days of the packed Chamber, the puppet politicians endorsed by the Emperor, had come to an end. The constituents were demanding to be heard.

Ferdinand de Lesseps was the only important caller at the Tuileries next morning, and he went out again almost at once on an unusual errand—to get change for a five-hundred-franc note which Madame Lebreton unobtrusively handed him. When he returned with the money he was invited to stay for an early luncheon—a meal which the company made only a pretence of eating; through which the Empress, who had not undressed the night before, and who had been up and about since six o'clock in the morning, sat like a beautiful marble statue at the head of the table. Then he went off again in his energetic way to get news of what might happen when the Deputies reassembled at one o'clock.

The Left Wing took the offensive as soon as the Chamber met. The old revolutionaries of 1848 joined hands with Léon Gambetta and the young Republicans of 1870 in demanding that "the dynasty of Louis Napoleon Bonaparte" be outlawed forever from the throne of France. "Down with Badinguet! Down with the Spaniard!" The yells echoed and re-echoed from one end of the semi-circle to the other. Outside, a crowd of sixty thousand men and women had gathered in the Place de la Concorde. Slowly, with determination, they began to push their way across the bridge toward the Palais Bourbon. Half-heartedly the mounted police in their dark blue tunics and braided képis tried to hold them back. Whole-heartedly the people of Paris pressed onward to take possession of the Legislature.

"Dethronement! Dé-ché-ance!"

The roar was clearly heard by the Governor of Paris writing at his desk in the Louvre. About three o'clock Trochu, the Man with a Plan, the man who had sworn to defend the Empress with his dead body, mounted his white horse and started to ride slowly toward the Palais Bourbon. At every step, he was impeded by excited men—men clinging to the railings of the Tuileries, from the branches of the plane trees overhanging the river; at every step he drew nearer to the great noisy shrieking crowd which had roared through the Palais Bourbon and was now moving downriver toward the Hôtel de Ville.

Only his confessor was ever likely to know with what feelings of triumph Trochu watched that approaching crowd. He had always believed in himself as the saviour of France; and here he was, plucked out of obscurity to sit on his charger in the September sunshine opposite the Solferino bridge, with power in his hands to keep his oath to the Empress or hew his own way to fame.

"Mon général"—Jules Favre was nervously holding his bridle —"will you come with us to the Hôtel de Ville, and join us in proclaiming the Republic?"

The arrogant general looked down at the Republican leader.

"In what capacity, monsieur?"

"As Minister of War in the new government."

"Not good enough," said Trochu, and lifted his reins.

"Then name the place you want, *mon général.*"

The rabble was so close about them now that they could hardly hear each other's words.

"I only join you as *President* of the Government, Monsieur Favre!"

The lawyer gave a hopeless shrug of assent. Instantly the general raised his right hand over the mob in a demand for silence. Then with a solemn upward movement of his arms, within sight of the palace which sheltered the sovereign he had betrayed, he shouted to the enraptured crowd,

"Chantons la Marseillaise!"

Ferdinand de Lesseps, pushing his way through the mob on the Quai d'Orsay on his way back to the Tuileries, saw the mob turn on the palace, with the great roar of a beast seeking blood. He let himself be carried along in the crush to the Pont Royal as the quickest way of getting across the Seine. The Light Infantry were already fraternizing with shouting Gardes Mobiles.

With surprising agility the President of the Suez Canal Company heaved his thick old body up and over the railing of the palace gardens and addressed the crowd from behind it.

"What are you doing, friends? Not breaking into the palace, surely?"

"Hurrah for *le père* de Lesseps!" bawled a Mobile with a sprig of red geranium in his hat, and a pretty girl on his arm. "Just stand out of the way, old boy: we're going to the Hôtel de Ville to proclaim the Republic!"

"Through the Tuileries?" repeated de Lesseps. And the crowd roared back,

"People's privilege! People's privilege!"

He understood them now. They wanted to go through the wide archway from the gardens into the Carrousel, and then on to the Hôtel de Ville—it was the symbolism of it, not as yet the violence, which attracted them. But the weapons in their hands, the army-issue Chassepôts, the old snuffbox muskets, the pikes, the iron rails uprooted along the rue de Rivoli, were the instruments which might turn a bloodless revolution into something as horrible as 1793.

He pulled himself higher on the railings. He beckoned to the dubious officers of the infantry, to the watchful sentries, to one or two older and calmer-looking National Guardsmen who stood among the Mobiles.

"Now then, good people!" he shouted to the crowd. "You all know me, and you know the Canal I built."

Loud applause, and roars of "The Suez! The Suez!"

"All right, so canal-building is my job. Now I'm going to make a little one here, and let the stream flow. Gently, gently—no need to burst the banks, that gets us nowhere—"

He formed the men he had summoned into a double line, arms locked, heads down, at the entrance to the Tuileries. The rioters, enchanted with this new game, came on laughing and shouting, channelled through the narrow lane of human bodies which blocked their entrance to the vestibules of the palace. They poured out on the far side into the sunshine of the Place du Carrousel, screaming with mirth and revolutionary high spirits, yelling to their friends to "come on through de Lesseps' canal!" They came on by the thousand: the square, the gardens rocked with shouting and singing, but the rifles remained unfired, the iron railings broke no heads. De Lesseps felt the seams of his coat part as he hung on grimly to the arms of the infantry officers on each side of him. At least a hundred times he had to let go his hold to shake hands with an admirer, each time terrified that his living banks would burst; each time he clawed his way back to his neighbour's arm again. The sweat streamed down his face, his leg and arm muscles were aching with the strain. "Eugénie!"—he let his thoughts fly to her apartments overhead—"Eugénie, my guardian angel! At last I am guarding you!"

The Empress was standing in the middle of the Rose Salon, in a black cashmere dress, with a little pelerine lined with violet silk laid about her shoulders. For all her pallor, her face had lost none of its haunting beauty; only faint smudges beneath her eyes, where her eye-liner had run, told of the tears she had shed. About her stood the whole court; despairing, for the courtiers had at least the merit of loyalty to the woman who had been queen of their revels for seventeen years. Not one member of the last Imperial Government had been able to make his way through the mob from the Palais Bourbon, but men of weight and worth stood by Eugénie's side: General Montebello, Admiral Jurien de la Gravière and even two of the foreign envoys. These two were telling her that she must think, now, of her own safety—must leave the threatened Tuileries—must fly from the country.

"Why does she listen to them!" raged Madeleine d'Arbonne. "She only has to draw those curtains, step out on that balcony and show herself to the people, to be cheered for a brave woman and a fellow sufferer in misfortune. Why doesn't she face it out?"

But the Empress was at her old trick again. She was looking at Paris in the mirror, in that great wall of mirrors at the back of the Rose Salon, which showed an alarming reflection of the great milling crowd in the gardens, the glint of the sun on rifles, pikes and bayonets.

"You don't think," she said uncertainly, "that I might go somewhere in the provinces to raise another army and continue the fight?"

"No, Madame!"

"No, Your Majesty!"

Signor Nigra, the Italian Minister, and Prince Metternich, the Austrian Ambassador, had spoken as one man.

"General de Montebello! Admiral! What is *your* advice?"

The senior officers shook their heads. "Alas, Madame, it isn't possible to raise another fighting force to meet the enemy. All we can do now is sign a dictated peace, and accept the fact that the France we knew is dead."

Then Madeleine d'Arbonne, forgetting everything, cried out impulsively,

"But France will never die!"

The Empress turned towards her.

"Madeleine, my dear, come here to me. Madame Lebreton, come and stand beside me too!"

She took a hand of each, and with all her old winning charm continued, "You hear what these gentlemen have said. With broken heart I now give up the fight, and I ask you both if you will follow me into exile—as my helpers and dear friends?"

"Everywhere and anywhere with Your Majesty," said General Bourbaki's sister.

"Yes," said Madeleine. But she did not look at the Empress as she said it.

"Your Majesty must please make haste!" cried Prince Metternich. "The mob has broken into the palace! You can hear them trampling about downstairs! Madame, you have no time even to go to your rooms!"

But Madeleine rushed upstairs to her own bedroom. A bonnet —a warm pelerine—the money in her desk—those at least she made sure of, while downstairs in the Rose Room Madame Vinot was forcing her own hat on the Empress, and the Empress was crying, "Where, where is my handbag—I *know* I put it on a table—"

With the bag in her hand she grew calmer, so calm that the most agitated were stilled; and although Nigra and Metternich were fuming with impatience she bade farewell to all her court. From the doorway she looked her last on the painted ceiling where her own young likeness as the goddess Flora was surrounded by the Loves and Graces, and into the great mirror where she had seen Paris the wrong way round. Then she stretched out her hand in a gesture of despair, and whispered,

"Oh, the dream—the empty dream!"

V

Dr. Thomas Evans, the dynamic dentist from Philadelphia, had taken advantage of Sunday afternoon to work at ambulance plans in his office on the rue de la Paix, paying no attention to bursts of shouting and singing in the neighbourhood. These ceased after a time; the west end of the city was tranquil and orderly as he drove home, and like most people on the outskirts of the capital that day he had no idea that he was now living under a Republic.

Dr. Evans was the most surprised man in Paris when he walked into his house and found the Empress Eugénie, dressed in a raincoat too large for her and a round hat several sizes too small, sitting in his back drawing room with Madame Lebreton and Madeleine d'Arbonne. They all began to talk at once, and laugh, and cry, so that sal volatile was the first thing the doctor offered them, and then he insisted on ordering food before they held any sort of conference.

"When did you eat last, Madame?"

Eugénie admitted to having eaten nothing at noon—perhaps only coffee and a roll in twenty-four hours.

"What you need is a light lunch right away," decided the doctor. "Boiled eggs and bread and butter, and hot milk with a lump of sugar in it! That's my first prescription, then we'll get you on to something more substantial. I'll order it at once."

"Doctor," interrupted Eugénie, "might we first—could you show us the—"

"Oh, pray excuse me," said Dr. Evans, much embarrassed. "Dear, dear, if only Mrs. Evans were at home! This way, Madame, if you please—"

But Madeleine did not accompany them to his wife's dressing room, and he went alertly back to join her in the salon. Madeleine was a favourite of his, "a girl with gumption"; he knew he would get a coherent story out of her.

"We got out of the palace by the galleries leading into the

Louvre," she told him, "and Monsieur Thélin came after us with the master key, because the main door was locked. Then we hid in a doorway near St. Germain l'Auxerrois—*that* was horrible, because thousands of people with guns came screaming past us shouting, '*à bas Badinguet! à bas l'Espagnole!*' and the tocsin was ringing overhead. Then the ambassadors found a cab for us, and off we came."

"Straight here?"

"No. We drove up the rue de Rivoli—and oh, doctor, there was one awful moment, when we heard the crowd inside the gardens give a great roar like a satisfied animal, and we looked round and saw the Imperial Standard being lowered above the Tuileries. Then we drove on to the Boulevard Haussmann. The Empress thought of going to Monsieur Besson—you know, the Councillor —but his apartment was all shut up. She was exhausted by that time. She sat on the stairs outside his door for ten minutes before she could go on. Next she said she would be safe under the American flag. We set out to go to Mr. Washburne, but we didn't know where to find the American Ministry. The cabdriver didn't know either. So then we came to you."

"Thank God you did!" said Evans. "I'll save Her Majesty, under Providence; but we must get her out of Paris. The revolutionaries will burn this house down round our ears if they discover her here."

"Do you think so?" said Madeleine. "I didn't *see* any revolutionaries as we came down the avenue."

"That means nothing," said Evans impatiently. "Has Her Majesty any idea where she wants to go?"

"To England," said Madeleine. "She means to throw herself on the mercy of her dear friend Queen Victoria. She wants to catch the ten o'clock boat train at the Gare St. Lazare tonight."

"Hey," said the startled doctor, "*that's* out of the question. She daren't risk appearing in a station crowd. And I must tell you that I have half a dozen men coming for an early dinner, not one of whom must suspect that the Empress is here. I'll get them off by nine o'clock, and by that time she'll be rested and better able to make her plans. Ah! here's your little meal."

Madeleine surveyed it without enthusiasm.

"Would you rather have a glass of sherry and a sandwich?"

"May I say what I really *would* like?"

"Please do."

"A brandy and soda."

The doctor rose without comment, opened the door of his study and led Madeleine to the cellaret.

"Say when." The brandy rose in the glass, the seltzer splashed. A little colour came back to Madeleine's white face.

"Thank you, doctor. I needed that," she said.

"Tough sort of a day," said the doctor laconically. "You going with her to England?"

"I said I would."

Dr. Evans was as good as his word. By nine o'clock his dinner guests had left, his associate Dr. Edward Crane had gone into the city to glean the latest news and Evans was in the back drawing room pressing another meal on the ladies. The Empress, however, shuddered at his proposal of "a steak and a glass of wine," nor would she hear of moving to the guest bedrooms. No! No! they would all stay together in this beautiful little suite and use dear Mrs. Evans' apartments; the fewer servants who saw them the better. They would be a tiny household of three; so cosy, so secure!

The Empress had experienced a mercurial change of spirits. She was now almost hysterically gay, and eager to get to England. "I can't rest until I see the Prince Imperial," she said. "My darling boy!"

Madeleine ventured to say,

"Should we try to get a message through to Belgium, Madame?"

"Oh," said Eugénie, too casually, "they have it! Monsieur Filon telegraphed last night to Comte Clary, asking him to bring the Prince across to Hastings!"

Dr. Evans interposed:

"Then the thing is to get Your Majesty to Deauville. My wife, as you know, is on holiday at the Hotel du Casino; she'll be enchanted to have you all as her guests until I can arrange a crossing. There's only one thing that worries me; the passports. The

British can be very rigid about them, and I think it would be wise to get a *laissez-passer* from Lord Lyons. It means wasting half the morning tomorrow instead of starting for Deauville at first light. And frankly I'm going to be nervous until I get you all out of Paris."

"Here is where I can at last do something to help myself," said the Empress with a smile. "Madeleine, please give me my handbag. Look, monsieur, we are well provided for."

From the bag which she had claimed so anxiously at the Tuileries, Eugénie produced a little pile of foreign passports and handed them over to the American.

"Why, here's the very thing!" exulted Evans. "This British one, signed by Lord Lyons, is for a doctor and his lady patient, travelling for health reasons to England—why, that's perfect! Madame, if you'll be Mrs. B., the patient, I'll be Dr. C., the physician—it all fits in. And the others will do for your ladies. I see they're both signed by Prince Metternich—but you won't mind being Austrians for a day or two, I'll bet! Here's one for you, Madame Lebreton; and Mademoiselle d'Arbonne, how would *you* like to be the Gräfin Paula von Cloditz? Just for the journey," he added, rather intimidated by the look in Madeleine's eye.

"May I see these passports?" she said politely.

"Surely."

She turned the pages quickly, gave them back. All three had been issued and stamped three weeks earlier.

Madeleine, who was to spend the night on a sofa in the salon, heard the Empress crying after she went to bed, and then a long monologue interrupted by Madame Lebreton's soothing voice. "We ought to have brought away some chloral," she thought. "*Why* did we leave in such a devil of a hurry?"

She sat looking at the stars coming out above the formal city garden—the Emperor's Star not among them—until she heard voices in the study and knew that Dr. Crane had come back. She listened to the splash of soda water and the creak of armchairs as the two Americans settled down to talk; then she could bear it no longer, and tapped softly on the study door.

"Dr. Evans, may I come in?"

"My dear, you ought to be asleep."

"How can I sleep until I know what Dr. Crane has seen and heard?"

Madeleine looked imploringly from one to the other. Dr. Crane, who had never seen her before that night, thought that the fabulous Madeleine d'Arbonne was an older woman than he had supposed.

"Be calm, mademoiselle," he said professionally. "So far, there is no sign that the Empress is being pursued."

Madeleine's smile was tinged with scorn.

"I didn't expect to hear of a guillotine in the Place de la Concorde. But did you see barricades? Street fighting? Were the police resisting the mob?"

"There were hardly any police to be seen, mademoiselle; I'm told they all put on plain clothes and gave their guns to the revolutionaries. The mob had a few drinks in honour of the Republic and then went off to bed without any fighting at all."

"The Empire is really at an end, then?"

He looked at her. Evans said she had gumption. Dr. Crane gave it to her straight from the shoulder.

"The Third Republic was proclaimed at City Hall just before five o'clock. There was a huge crowd, all cheering like mad. Jules Favre came out on the balcony and presented General Trochu as President of the Provisional Government."

"*Trochu!*"

"Yes, ma'am; he'd taken off his uniform and gotten fixed up with a frock coat. It seems he made a long speech and was cheered to the echo."

"Proclaiming a return to the good old days of liberty, equality, fraternity?" asked Madeleine dryly.

"He's got another pitch—he made the government pledge allegiance to *his* ideal: God, Family, Property!"

"That's a new one," said Dr. Evans.

"I guess so. But while Trochu was orating Gambetta had slipped away. He wanted to be Minister of the Interior and he made sure work of it. He drove up to the Place Beauvau and moved right in."

236

"And Princess Clotilde?" asked Madeleine. "Did you hear what happened to her? She left the Tuileries before we did."

"She's gone to join her husband. But they tell the damnedest story about her," said Crane enthusiastically. "Her servants wanted her to slip out of the Palais Royal by the back way. 'Not I,' says she. 'I'm a Princess of the House of Savoy, and I won't leave Paris in any less state than I entered it!' She went off in an open landau, with a guard of honour, and the people cheered her the whole way across Paris to the station."

An uncomfortable silence fell.

"It was different for the Empress, of course," said Crane awkwardly. He thought quickly of something else to say. "By the way, de Rochefort is out of prison. The crowd set him free from Ste. Pélagie and dragged his carriage through the streets in triumph, shouting, 'Remember Victor Noir!' I guess Rochefort will get a place in the government too."

"That makes it perfect," said Madeleine. "*One* miserable little Red released from Ste. Pélagie—what a poor second act to the storming of the Bastille!"

The two men laughed in spite of themselves. There was little more to be said. Dr. Crane described the quiet aspect of the streets he had followed, the cafés he had entered, and then Madeleine left them with renewed advice from Dr. Evans to "catch some sleep if she could."

There was no hope of rest for Madeleine. Horribly wakeful, she went on tiptoe to Mrs. Evans' dressing room, and moving with caution so as not to arouse the Empress, she soaked in the largest china tub she had ever seen in her life, patted herself dry with the largest towels and stole back in her white frilled petticoat and lawn bodice to the sofa in the window, which had been heaped with satin spreads and comforters. The garden was brilliant now, for the moon was just past its full and swinging high over the roofs of Paris, shedding its light on the bloody field of Sedan where even yet, on the fourth night after the battle, ambulance men and Sisters of Charity were guided in their work by the feeble moans of the just-living lying in the piles of the four days' dead.

Then the numbed brain, recovering from the successive shocks of the day, began to work again. Steadily, Madeleine reviewed their futile flight, pursued by nobody, through the streets of Paris to their present refuge.

"She didn't leave the Tuileries because she was in any danger. If what the American says is true, the mob never did break into the palace—they passed through the arch—their own sentries are posted at the gates tonight. She left because Metternich and Nigra pushed her out; and we let them. We all ran about squawking like a flock of frightened geese."

She shivered as she recalled what had been for her the worst moment of their flight—the terrified halt at the locked gallery of the Louvre before Thélin came up behind them with the key. They had rushed past the entrance to the Delacroix Room, where her mother's face and form, so like her own, had been depicted by the artist many times in the symbolic scarves and draperies of the Romantic Age. She could even see, through the arched entrance, the great canvas called *Liberated Greece*, supposed to be the best of all the paintings for which lovely Marie Bertaux had been the model. It gave her an unearthly feeling of coming face to face with her own ghost.

"But why Metternich and Nigra, when none of the other ambassadors came near us? What was *their* interest in frightening her into running away? Was it because that would end, once for all, the reproaches to Austria and Italy for not coming to our aid? It could be. It could even have been planned beforehand. Those two Austrian passports were prepared and signed by Metternich.

"*She had the passports ready all the time.* They were issued on the thirteenth of August. Three weeks ago, the Empress of the French was prepared to leave her people to their fate. She was rehearsing her fancy-dress character: Madame B.— the invalid Englishwoman.

"Madame Bonaparte. Madame Badinguet !

"If I had known all this before I promised to go away with her ! To England—if we go to England I can go to James. I can tell him he was right, tell him the Empress is a vain and utterly selfish woman, not worth his little finger; that if he wants me such as I am, such as he knows me to be, I'm still his—"

Her face, now wet with tears, lit up for a moment at the thought of her penitence and their reunion. But other thoughts came crowding as the old struggle between her love and her allegiance was engaged again.

"If he should happen to be out of London, what would I do? Follow him to the shipyards, even to Scotland? Humble myself, to be told in the end that he doesn't want me now? He isn't a boy to be swayed by pity for an exile, and that's what I would be. An exile like my father—an *émigrée*. Listening to Eugénie tell the story of her hairbreadth escape from the Tuileries until my hair is white. Curtsying to the Bonapartes when they gather round her to revile the people of Paris, who threw them out—"

The temptation was very strong, for a moment, to dress quietly and slip from the house of Dr. Evans, and lose herself, flying from them all, in the streets of Paris.

"How can I leave my country now—even to go to James? Who cares who rules in France, if France is saved?

"If I wait here, and am patient, will he come back to me in Paris, when the war is over and the Bonapartes forgotten?

"Or am I throwing away my last chance of happiness, if I stay away now from the man I love?"

When sleep overcame her, the struggle was still unresolved. The moonlight fell upon a troubled face and clenched hands, as Madeleine in her white petticoat lay among the cushions, as much a refugee, that night, as any of the thousands then toiling along the eastern roads of France.

The moonlight silvered the quiet streets of a Paris sound asleep, exhausted by the satisfactions of the day. Badinguet dethroned, the Spanish woman gone, the Deputies made to submit to the People, the Senators dismissed, the words *National Property* scrawled all over the outside of the Tuileries and the Tricolore flying from the Clock Pavilion. All done without a single execution, and beautiful weather for it too.

The moonlight shone on the National Guards posted at the gates of the Tuileries and into the empty rooms with the great mirrors, the Salle des Maréchaux with the tall blank-eyed caryatides supporting the vacant thrones. Now was the time for the Little Red Man to emerge from his ghostly hiding place, and, lifting the velvet behind which the chalk of 1848 had never quite been erased, write with invisible hand a new legend in its place,

> Long Live the Republic!
> Long Live Liberty!
> For the FOURTH time reconquered,
> September 4—
> Eighteen Hundred and Seventy!

At five next morning, Dr. Evans brought a tray of coffee and rolls into the salon for his guests. The dentist was fresh and rosy, every hair of his muttonchop whiskers bristling with excitement. He said he had been "on reconnaissance patrol" on his own avenue and the avenue de la Grande Armée for most of the night. "He's loving it," Madeleine realized. "It's a real Wild West adventure to him!"

"Now, when we get up to the barrier at the Porte Maillot, just leave it all to me," instructed the doctor. "Her Majesty must sit in the middle, well hidden between you two ladies; Crane and I will sit with our backs to the horses, and *I'll do the talking.*"

They set out in Dr. Evans' fine carriage, with his trustworthy coachman Célestin on the box, and went rolling down the avenue before anyone was to be seen but a few tradesmen on their rounds. But the drawbridge was up over the moat at the Porte Maillot, and an elderly officer with a brand-new Tricolore scarf over the imperial uniform was standing swollen with authority in front of the guardhouse when Célestin drew his horses to a stop.

"*Pardonnez-moi, je suis Américain!*" roared Dr. Evans, blocking the open window with his head and shoulders.

"*Américain! Très bien,*" said the officer with a laugh. "And where are you bound for this fine morning? Not New York?"

"Ah no"—in the same bantering tone—"not much further than St. Germain. My friends and I mean to spend a long day picnicking in the forest."

"Excellent idea. You have heard about the Revolution?"

"But of course."

"As an American, you approve of it?"

"Naturally!"

"*Allez! Vive la République! Amusez-vous bien!*"

The drawbridge was lowered, the carriage rolled on freely down the magnificent highway constructed at the Emperor's orders, through woods just reddening with the first tints of autumn. Each milestone had some association for Madeleine, but the Empress seemed to notice nothing. She talked—talked incessantly, the same phrases repeated over and over.

"Oh, why wouldn't they let me die before the walls of Paris . . . The French people have so few convictions. They lack steadfastness. They lack purpose. . . . They are versatile, voluble, completely unstable. . . . In France you can be honoured today and banished tomorrow. . . . *Why didn't I die before the walls of Paris?*"

Twelve miles outside Mantes, Dr. Evans decided to stop at a farmhouse where a bush of greenery hung above the door indicated that victuals were for sale. They had been driving for four hours, and the men were hungry; when the Empress, in a fever of impatience, implored them not to stop, Evans assured her it was better to eat here in this lonely spot and then drive straight on through Mantes town. Madeleine was sent indoors with the doctors to find out if the Empress might get out of the coach without fear of being recognized.

The first thing she saw as she walked into the farmhouse kitchen, to which they were welcomed by a merry red-faced old woman, was a large chromo depicting the Empress as the guardian angel of the Suez Canal, uniting under her sceptre the waters of the Red Sea and the Mediterranean. Madeleine had seen it in the Arbonne farms, for thousands of copies had been sold in France since the previous November. It was a gaudy thing, but the likeness was good, and the travellers, in an eloquent exchange of glances, admitted that if Eugénie came into that room she would be instantly recognized.

"We have a sick friend in the carriage, madame," said Madeleine without hesitation to the housewife. "Prostrated with migraine. Her nurse can't leave her, so I wonder if you could let me have some of that tempting new bread for them, and a jug of milk?"

The old woman was desolated to hear of the sick lady and at the same time curious to see her; Madeleine had to insist on being the one to carry the tray outside along with provender for Célestin. The Empress and Madame Lebreton declared that they had no appetite. Madame Lebreton even became reproachful when Madeleine said she would come back as soon as she herself had eaten.

"How you can *think* of food at a time like this!" she complained.

"I'm hungry," said Madeleine shortly, and went back to the two Americans.

The old woman had spread a table for them in a little grape arbour. She set out country sausage, cream cheese in lettuce leaves, the newly baked bread and a brown earthenware pitcher of rough red wine; food good enough to make even Dr. Evans stop moralizing on the extraordinary reversal of fortune which had brought the Empress from the Suez Canal to this *buvette* outside of Mantes. He filled his mouth with bread and butter, and the three of them sat savouring the food in silence, looking at the bees working among the wine-red dahlias nodding at the foot of the garden, beyond which the Seine was flowing out to sea. Suddenly the old woman came out with a long straw broom in her hands, shouting "*Allez, gros matou!*" as a marauding cat disappeared into a lilac bush.

In one of those moments of vision which last for a whole lifetime the scene was etched upon Madeleine's brain. She saw the old woman with her broom heaved up, the velvety glint of black fur as the cat jumped through the sunshine, and as in a stereoscope she saw every spade-shaped dark green lilac leaf carved upon the lucent September air. The tree, the fertile soil below and the brilliant sky above came together in a supreme synthesis with the fields and the river, the taste of bread and wine in her mouth, the purplish brick of the old farmhouse, the smell of ripe pears and the great nodding heads of the dahlias, into a harmony that meant France and only France. In that moment Madeleine knew that she would not go to England with the Empress.

"Oh my God, I'm saved! I'm saved!"

When the Empress stumbled into the Hotel du Casino at Deauville and literally flung herself on the breast of the astounded Mrs. Evans, she was as nauseated, weary and dishevelled a fugitive as any who had ever taken the exile's road from France to England.

After Mantes their journey had ceased to be comfortable. At Limay Dr. Evans' horses could go no further and had to turn back to Paris. A landau was hired to get them on to Pacy, where an old calèche with a dirty blue cloth lining dragged them ten more kilometres to Evreux. At Evreux the news of the Revolution had gone ahead of them, and there was dancing in the streets, and shouting of the *Marseillaise* and "*Vive la République!*" It was there Eugénie seemed to realize for the first time that she was no longer Empress; that her adored Loulou would never be crowned Emperor in Notre Dame.

By ten o'clock at night the ladies were huddled into one bedroom at the Golden Sun at La Rivière, where Madeleine was called "unfeeling" by her companions because she slept a healthy sleep the whole night through. Next day it was raining hard, and after they had ventured to take the train as far as Lisieux, eighteen miles away, they were all drenched while waiting in the street for Dr. Evans to hunt up one more carriage to take them on to Deauville. The Empress had started a head cold and had only one handkerchief—the lace wisp which Pepa had laid on her prayer book before her last Mass at the Tuileries. Mrs. Evans and her maid, a trustworthy elderly person, were as much appalled by the condition of Eugénie when she arrived at Deauville as by the Revolution which had brought her to this pass.

"I'm just so *mad* at Doctor," confided Mrs. Evans to Madeleine, when all the refugees were comfortable, the Empress lying down and the kindly, stout, American lady and the French girl having tea together before the steel-barred grate in Mrs. Evans' sitting room.

"*Why* Doctor didn't think to give you the run of my bureau drawers and wardrobes, I'll never know," the good lady lamented. "The *idea* of you coming off like that, with nothing but the clothes you stood up in! It's so like a man, you can't trust them with housekeeping matters at all! If only I'd been there—"

"Then we shouldn't have had your wonderful welcome at Deauville," said Madeleine, and Mrs. Evans decided that the poor thing really had a beautiful smile.

The doctor burst in, rosy and energetic from his walk in the rising gale.

"It's all fixed!" he exulted. "Ted and I hunted up and down the docks till we found an English yacht—a little forty-two tonner, prettiest thing you ever saw—and we told our story to the owner, Sir John Burgoyne. He hummed and hawed at first. 'Blowing up for a gale, don'tcha know—too risky to put to sea tonight'; but I spoke right up and told him:

"'Sir John,' I said, 'I'm an American. In my country every man will risk his life for a woman, especially a lady whose life is at stake. I left my home in Paris and all it contains without giving a thought to danger or possible loss. Won't *you* risk taking the *Gazelle* across to England before the Empress is discovered and arrested, maybe murdered by those thugs?' Well, my dear, that fetched him. No Britisher can resist a sporting challenge. Mademoiselle, Sir John expects us all on board at midnight. Yes, I'm taking Her Majesty all the way to England! It'll be a tight fit, with four of us, six crewmen and the two Burgoynes in a sixty-foot yacht, but it can be done."

"Without me," said Madeleine.

"Without—are you serious?"

"Perfectly, Dr. Evans. I think you've been wonderful, all of you; and the Empress should be thankful that she found two Americans and an English yachtsman to help her run away from France; but I'm not going any further with her. I shall tell her so as soon as she sends for me."

. . . The Empress was once again in the setting which seemed most natural to her. The curtains of her comfortable bedroom were drawn on the early twilight and the rain. The warmth of a bright fire was enticing the perfume from a huge bouquet of dark red Provence roses, a tribute from Dr. Evans, and the firelight twinkled on an array of small silver, ivory and tortoiseshell knick-knacks on the dressing-table, in front of which sat Eugénie, studying the arrangement of her hair. Mrs. Evans' maid had brushed it for a full half-hour, and the high bright waves piled above the white brow seemed to be crackling with electricity.

At the sound of the closing door the Empress turned round slowly on the dressing stool, and the voluminous satin robe lent by Mrs. Evans slipped back from her shoulders as she held out her hand to the maid of honour.

"Madeleine, come in, dear child! What plans has Dr. Evans made for us?"

Madeleine hesitated. The tableau before her was very familiar—the Empress at ease in a perfumed warm room, with adoring women in attendance—so familiar that only with difficulty could she speak the words which would shatter her old world forever.

"An English couple, Sir John and Lady Burgoyne, will take you to England in their yacht now in Deauville harbour, Madame. Dr. Evans will wait upon you shortly and tell you all his plans."

"How kind they all are," murmured the Empress. "Burgoyne? I don't know the name. How very kind."

"Madame," said Madeleine with en effort, "there is something I must say to you in private, with your permission."

Mrs. Evans' maid, without waiting for dismissal, slid backwards from the room. The Empress looked up at Madeleine with the shadow of a frown.

"I don't think you have anything to say to me which Madame Lebreton can't hear," she said. "In our new life we poor exiles must have no secrets from each other."

"Then, Madame—and I am sorry if I give you pain—I must tell you that I can *not* go into exile. I can't go with you. I can't leave France. I must go back to Paris in the morning."

Madame Lebreton's sharp gesture of anger was checked by the Empress.

"Madeleine, dear child, sit down here by me." But Madeleine remained standing. "You're tired and agitated, and no wonder. Don't you know that you can't go back to Paris—that your life is in actual danger because you came away with me?"

"I don't think so. I can't believe the fact of having spent forty-eight hours longer in your company than the rest of your court will condemn me to death any more than them. And there are no reports of mass executions at the Tuileries."

The sharp voice, the lack of the usual expressions of respect, stung the Empress into rising from her chair. Madame Lebreton rose too. The personalities of the three women clashed across the room.

"I don't understand you," said the Empress in a soft bewildered voice. "I thought you were so devoted to me, Madeleine!"

Silence.

"What can have changed you so? Yesterday so cold and distant; so critical; almost as if you *blamed* me for leaving France! What else can I do, how can I possibly remain, now that the Emperor has been dethroned?"

Still silence.

"Don't you understand that I want to be with my boy again; eventually . . . with my husband?" Engénie's voice broke on a sob.

"I understand that, Madame. But you must pardon me—*my family* is still in France."

Madame Lebreton came up beside the Empress, and with a familiarity never dared before laid her arm round the shaking shoulders.

"Don't you add to her troubles—"

But the Empress was able to speak calmly. "I accept your reproach, Mademoiselle d'Arbonne, although I don't deserve it; from this hour you are free of my service, and I thank you for the fidelity which lasted for so long—at least until it was put to the test!" And turning to Madame Lebreton she added, fatally, "I should have asked dear Madame Carette to come with us instead —she I know would have kept the faith!"

Madeleine's face flamed. Keep faith! *Foy, Roy, Arbonne*—the very motto of her house! Deliberately she opened the little silk reticule hanging at her waist.

"Then this document may turn out to be useful." She held the Austrian passport out to Eugénie.

"Ah!" said the Empress, "so it was the passports! I saw it in your eyes."

"Yes!" said Madeleine. "It *was* the passports—and the date! And the identity of the Gräfin Paula von Cloditz! Which I surrender with great pleasure to Madame Carette!"

Sir John Burgoyne, nervous and exasperated, had hung a lantern at the end of the gangplank to light the way for his unwelcome passengers. All the other shipping in Deauville harbour was darkened to the riding lights, for hatches were battened down and portholes closed against the rising storm. In the Roads outside the breakwater the Channel waves were running mountains high, and the little *Gazelle* was bobbing like a cork at her moorings. Sir John cursed his wife's sentimentality, which had made her add her pleading to the American's "sporting challenge"— neither one of them had any idea of the risks to be run! He cursed the fate which had made him put into Deauville at the very moment when those damned Frogs were at it again, and become involved with their decamping Empress. He could hear a whole company of drunk Mobiles bawling the *Marseillaise* over there in the wineshops of the Place de Morny. At it—they were always *at it*, rain or shine!

He saw lanterns bobbing over the sand dunes. They were coming that way, of course, to avoid running into the Mobiles; the women would wrench their ankles dodging about among the piles of timber at the end of the wharf! Sir John ran down the gangplank to meet them, followed by a stolid British sailor who gave an arm to Madame Lebreton. She went aboard with an amount of tottering and *ah-mon-Dieu*ing that promised ill for the crossing. Dr. Evans followed her. Sir John Burgoyne bowed low to the *ci-devant* Empress of the French.

At the dead of night, on the deserted dock, with the howling of the gale and the singing of her adversaries echoing around her, Eugénie had lost none of her tragic dignity. Madame Rachel would have been proud of her pupil, whose unrehearsed deportment for How To go into exile was quite perfect. She gave her hand and her lovely smile to the Englishman. She gave him a gracious word of thanks. Then she turned from the foot of the gangplank to look again into the dark land she was leaving, and into the faces of a man and a woman who had followed her at a little distance: Dr. Crane and Madeleine.

"Madeleine, at this last moment, I ask you to change your mind."

Sir John saw the girl's eyes fill with tears. She shook her head, and a scarf, or shawl, which she had twisted round her hair, fell back on the wet cloak about her shoulders.

"Madame, adieu!"

Then for the last time in her life Madeleine sank down in the deep court curtsy, head erect, hands touching the wet ground as her skirts trailed in the puddles; the farewell and the refusal were complete.

Sir John escorted the Empress aboard and left her to his wife. He could hear the little Yankee holding forth in the cabin, and women beginning to squawk and sob—what a predicament for a member of the Royal Yacht Squadron! He looked over the rail. That girl was still standing there, looking up at the *Gazelle*—he could see every feature in the lantern light, until the other American took her by the arm and led her away into the darkness beyond the wharf. Sir John drew a deep breath. He was not an imaginative man, nor even a very articulate one. Not even to himself could he express the thought that just for a moment a veil had been lifted for him—when in that girl's face, stern beneath the blowing hair, with tears and rain on her cheeks and her upper lip drawn back a little over her teeth, he had looked into the proud and tortured face of France.

INTERLUDE:

Philadelphia, September 1870

The French themselves called it the Disaster, but the neutral press had taken to calling it "the fall of France." The Philadelphia morning papers used the expression frequently, and Frank Hartzell, reading while a coloured man polished his boots in the shoeshine parlour of the Hotel La Pierre, scowled every time he came across it.

The fall of France seemed to have brought himself down with it, along with the plans he had begun to make for a future with Louise d'Arbonne. It was over a month since he had heard from Michel Bertaux, although he had carried out his instructions to the letter. The bulk purchases of canned beef and condensed milk which Bertaux intended to hold against an expected food shortage were on their way to Marseilles by the middle of August. Desiccated vegetables and flour being stored in a Front Street warehouse at Frank's own expense, but no further orders had been received at Hartzell Brothers since an ominous cable which said "Stop all shipments!" The news of Sedan and the fall of the Empire reached Philadelphia, followed quickly by the declaration that the new Republic intended to continue the struggle against Prussia. But Bertaux did not reply to Frank's own cable, saying "Confident ultimate victory France will gladly join you any time."

His cousins, the Hartzell brothers, had greeted him kindly enough, although Hermann, the younger, had plainly not expected Frank to reappear in Philadelphia. Hermann was engaged

251

to a Miss Clara Diffenderfer and wanted to employ her brother Hermann in Frank's place. But August, the senior partner, overruled him, having been greatly impressed by Frank's accounts of the Bertaux empire. Inviting Frank to dine and sleep at the pretty cottage in the Schuylkill valley where his wife and baby were spending the summer, August hinted broadly that in September, when Frank's leave of absence was over, he would be welcomed to an office of his own at Dock Street and restored to the payroll with an appropriate salary increase as vice-president in charge of the Bertaux account. Frank, thinking of Louise, was non-committal.

Then came the news of Sedan and the fall of the Empire.

At first the partners in Hartzell Brothers, like all the other Philadelphia merchants, were too enthralled by the drama unfolding at the safe distance of three thousand miles to consider how it might affect their firm. The downfall of the Emperor stirred no pity—he had been too unpopular in America; but the flight of the Empress, a beautiful woman in distress saved from the guillotine and the maddened Red hordes seeking her blood in a life-and-death race across France, by a Philadelphia man, whetted chivalry as well as civic pride. The Philadelphia burghers approved of the State Department's instructions to Minister Washburne to recognize the provisional government of General Trochu, and Trochu's slogan, "God, Family, Property," made a very strong appeal. But it took more than the establishment of republican government in France to make Philadelphians approve of that light-minded country, the Magdalene among the nations, and many Quaker families rejoiced that the Society of Friends had gone forth to do relief work on the Prussian side. It was a trying social air for Frank to breathe. Meantime his position at his cousins' office became more difficult daily, as Hartzell Brothers fretted after news of a consignment of "Havana segars" shipped to the Bertaux warehouses early in July, and of a long overdue shipment of his Bordeaux white wines for which their retailers were pressing them.

Frank flung aside the paper and got out of the shoeshine chair

Philadelphia was in the grip of a September heat wave, and the faces of all the men he passed on his way down to Dock Street were tense and irritable as well as glistening with sweat. He had the sensation of having been handed, for the second time in his life, the parts of a puzzle quite beyond his power to solve.

"Why doesn't Bertaux write to me? Why doesn't he cable?"

Old Lochner, the correspondence clerk, looked up with his pen between his lips and mumbled.

"No mail for you, Mr. Frank!"

Then, transferring the pen to the back of his ear, he added,

"Mr. Hartzell wants to see you. He's in the humidor."

Frank looked round and saw Hermann Hartzell studying him thoughtfully through the glass partition which divided the spice-scented front office from the partners' sanctum in the antiquated premises of Hartzell Brothers. Frank himself, when he started in the business after the Civil War, had occupied a kind of no-man's-land between the two, in a room not much bigger than a hutch at the top of the humidor stairs, of which the only merit was that it gave him a good view of the Philadelphia ladies who dropped in from time to time to smoke a fine Havana in the privacy of their husbands' or fathers' personal cigar lockers on the lower floor. There were no ladies in the humidor this morning; August was alone in the long narrow chamber, full of boxes of cigars stacked upside down in cedarwood containers. Beneath the red brick floor flowed the Dock Street creek, which kept the humidor at an even seventy degrees all year round.

"Hullo, August," said Frank. "You're in the right place for a day like this."

"Morning, Frank," said his cousin. "I was just having a look at the new lot of two hundred and fifties. It's not too early for a glass of wine?"

He led the way out of the cigar chamber into another cellar with a low vaulted roof, in which were stored the fine wines and liqueurs which were among his firm's specialties. Frank saw the iron racks of vintages which he had already shipped from the Bertaux vineyards near Bordeaux, next to the great cases of Scotch whisky and the tuns of wine from Spain and Portugal which had made more than one voyage round the Horn. He sat down on the corner of a wooden table, used as a writing desk for sales and stock-taking, and watched August Hartzell steadily pour two brimming glasses of liquid gold from the cask marked *Vino Vilhissimo*.

The eldest of the Hartzells was a tallish man of thirty-five, with sandy hair already receding from a face showing too many traces of good living, and now relaxing into the contentment of an undemanding marriage. He shook his head as Frank lit a cigarette. "You'll ruin your palate, such as it is!" His firm carried pipe tobacco, but had set its face against the newfangled cigarettes.

"Frank, I thought this might be a good time and place to take a look at how we stand," he said, hooking a kitchen chair from one side of the table with his foot, and sitting down opposite Frank. "Always such a hell of a lot of coming and going upstairs. Lochner says there was no foreign mail for you this morning?"

"No mail of any sort."

"You're completely out of touch with Monsieur Bertaux, then?"

"Yes, for the time being."

"Would you say it looks as if he had lost interest?"

"That, or else he can't get a message out of Paris."

August clicked his tongue against the roof of his mouth.

"That cock won't fight! I was on 'Change this morning, and several men I spoke to had had Paris cables. The Bourse is open for business as usual—though we can't say for how long, of course."

"But damn it, man!" Frank burst out. "The circumstances are quite exceptional. They've had a terrible thrashing, followed by a revolution, and now they're getting ready to stand a siege of Paris. You can hardly blame Bertaux if he has other things on his mind besides me!"

"I haven't said I blame him. I *am* beginning to wonder if his interest in employing you, and doing business with us, hasn't petered out since the war went the wrong way for the French. For all I know, he may be realizing all his holdings and getting out of France as fast as he can travel. Maybe he'll want to start in business for himself over here. He'd be smart, at that."

254

"You don't know him," said Frank. "I do. I've heard him criticize pretty nearly every institution in his country, and swear at the lack of foresight and organization which God knows the war showed up; but I don't think he'd ever run out on France. Remember, he came through '48: Bourse suspension, bank panics, railroad nationalization scare and all, and went on to make another fortune; he'll take all this in stride, you'll see."

"You're sold on him, aren't you?" said August. "Well, fine; but there you've put your finger on another thing that worries me: nationalization. Who can possibly tell how this provisional government is going to turn out? Damn it, they've *had* three cabinets in France since the New Year, and a revolution thrown in for good measure; they're unstable, that's what they are! I don't know that I want to do business with concerns which may be bankrupted, or nationalized, or blown sky-high, or liquidated between one month's end and another. Hartzells is an old established American house, and we did very well for ourselves before we got involved with the S.A. Bertaux. My advice to you is, forget about it; France is ruined, whichever way you look at it. If they accept Bismarck's terms, their finances will be in pawn for years until the indemnity is paid; if they go on with the war they're completely sunk."

"I'll still put my money on Michel Bertaux," said Frank.

"Don't misunderstand me, Frank; when I told you to forget about him I didn't mean this would make any difference to your future with us. If you'd been able to bring us the Bertaux account, it would have made a difference to your salary; but nobody can buck a war, I guess. Come on now, boy, what do you say? Are you ready to quit lounging around between Dock and Front and buckle down to some real work again?"

"You want me to decide today?"

"I'd like to have your decision this week. You know Harry Diffenderfer is anxious to join us—has been for a long time. I can't keep him on ice much longer."

"August, tell me something. Why didn't you fire me outright at Canton last year? Send me three months' wages, or six if you wanted to do the handsome, and let me out?"

"Because I wanted to see if you could make good on your own —which you have—and then give you another chance here, if you wanted it. Do you want it? Or are you planning on retiring to the country and living on Uncle Francis's money for the rest of your life?"

"I think you should go ahead and hire Harry Diffenderfer," said Frank. "Talk about accounts—he'll bring you Schuylkill Beer, that'll look great on the letterhead along with *Vino Vilhissimo*."

"Eat dinner with us today and talk it over, will you? Early—say half-past five at Bookbinder's; I don't want to have to spend the night in town. Baby's teething and Millie wants me home."

Frank was too restless to stay in the warehouse. He walked past Lochner's desk, where the old clerk was engaged in filing that morning's correspondence—orders from the White House, from the Pennsylvania Railroad, from the Schuylkill Fishing Company, from the First City Troop—all concerns which August Hartzell would call "stable." He stood at the street door, thinking of the business his grandfather, Franz Hartzell, had built up in this city, and wondering if he dared risk throwing up his place in it. The clerks, watching him covertly, envied Mr. Frank's London clothes and boots and the grey derby from Lock's set at exactly the right angle on his well-brushed chestnut hair. But old Lochner, with the pen between his lips again, mumbled to his neighbour as Frank idled out,

"All dressed up and nowhere to go!"

He walked across the street to the Stock Exchange, with its graceful Greek Revival columns, of which his father and his grandfather before him had both been members. He was prepared to bet that they had gone on 'Change without any of the worry of divided allegiance and frustrated hopes which perplexed him now. He listened to the proceedings for a time and then walked on to the warehouse he had rented on Front Street, tested the locks and had a look at the piles of merchandise waiting for orders from Bertaux. It gave him the feeling, as he checked through the inventory, of being in business again.

Frank moved uptown; it was getting on towards noon. There

were many houses where his father's son would be welcome at the luncheon table, where Negro butlers would bring him a frosted mint julep or a glass of the Hartzell Madeira. There were others where with less ceremony his brother officers and their young wives would be delighted to offer pot luck to Captain Hartzell. He shied away from all of them—it was so damned embarrassing to have no plans, to have to parry the questions about "Are you going back to Paris soon?" and "Shall you be with Hartzells for good now?" and that other puzzler: "Weren't you lucky to get out of France before the revolution!"

Eventually he drank his lunch in a Market Street tavern, where he fell in with an out-of-work teamster who had served in the 27th Pennsylvania and been wounded at Second Bull Run, three months after Frank was taken prisoner. They fought that battle, and the action at Cross Keys, along the beer-stained counter with pretzels and blobs of cheese from the free lunch, while Frank drank bourbon and the veteran drank boilermakers at Frank's expense; and that took up over two hours of the sickening day. A nap in his stifling bedroom at the Pierre accounted for two more.

When he came downstairs the evening papers were in, with a long dispatch from France which caused his hands to tighten on the paper as the news sank in. The Crown Prince of Prussia in Versailles—the palace turned into a barracks for his troops! God! what a damned shame! Those charming villages he had explored in May and June, Bougival and Ville d'Avray and La Celle St. Cloud, all bombarded and destroyed by those barbarians! And then if they were at Versailles mightn't they also be at Arbonne? He went through the cobbled alleys, foul with horse dung and human spittle, under the brassy sky of a Philadelphia September, in a panic of anxiety for Louise.

He picked up his cousins at the warehouse, not too pleased to find that Harry Diffenderfer was to be one of the party. Hermann's future brother-in-law looked like his sister Clara in trousers, with china-blue eyes set in a brick-pink face, the caricature of a Pennsylvania Dutchman. He had spent most of the Civil War in the Dakotas.

August Hartzell had what he liked to call his *Stammtisch* at Bookbinder's, every day at lunch, and he had reserved it also for their early dinner. Bookbinder's was always crowded at noon by merchants and stockbrokers; the dinner trade was not so busy, but the tables were well filled as the Hartzell party went in. With so many wives and children still in the country it was not surprising that many householders were eating an early meal, like August, before going out on the late trains to join them. August had the gratification of bowing to his Germantown pastor, Dr. Spengler, who had recently baptized his child, and to Mrs. Spengler, an enormously fat woman in a bonnet hung round with jet and bugles, who was one of the very few ladies to patronize Bookbinder's that evening. The restaurant which Samuel Bookbinder had made famous in the few years since the Civil War was essentially masculine in the welcome of its dark woodwork and snowy linen. The food was the best in the city, and the portions were enormous.

Harry Diffenderfer was a glutton. He was also a lecher and a potential alchoholic; Frank noted with amusement that the Hartzells, who were very abstemious, had seen that Harry was carrying a fair load already, and that two straight ryes did not improve his condition. Frank wondered if he himself had erred in switching to rye after the lunchtime bourbon.

Mr. Diffenderfer's cronies were accustomed to admire him as "a reg'lar stemwinder!" and it was easy to see why a conservative businessman like August Hartzell had resisted his approaches for so long. But Harry was not in an aggressive mood that night. He was intent on tucking away two dozen oysters, followed by the famous Bookbinder snapper soup, followed by terrapin, roast duckling and half a dozen other good things from the stalls of Market Street and the rolling farmlands of Cumberland County.

Finally he took a deep breath and said,

"Well, I see where that little feller, Favre, was pretty sassy to Bismarck when they met to discuss an armistice yesterday. That won't do your French friends any good, Frank!"

"Monsieur Favre spoke out like a brave man," said Frank. " 'Not *an inch of our soil, not a stone of our fortresses'*—he couldn't say more, or less than that."

"Ya-aah!" said Mr. Diffenderfer comfortably, patting his waistcoat. "Bismarck will take Paris like Grant took Richmond. He told Favre that if the French didn't surrender Metz and Strasbourg, and hand over Alsace and Lorraine as well as the indemnity, he would burn Paris to the ground!"

"Burn down Paris!" repeated Frank. "You're making it up!"

"It was in the last editions, Frank," said August Hartzell quietly.

"*Ja,*" confirmed Harry Diffenderfer, "and Bismarck swore he wouldn't feed the Parisians when hunger drove them to surrender. He sure is tough, that Bismarck!—Hey, waiter, bring me another stein of beer."

Frank pushed away his plate with loathing. In the expression on Harry's porcine face he saw reflected all the sneers at France which had enraged him since his return to the States. All the self-satisfied, holier-than-thou rejoicings at the downfall of the country too proud, too rich, too gay in her enjoyment of the good things of the world.

"I don't believe," he said with rising anger, "that civilized nations will stand by and let Bismarck commit such a crime. He *can't* destroy Paris—it's the most beautiful city in the world."

"Beautiful girls, too, eh, Frank?" said Harry with a wink.

August Hartzell, with the best intentions, tried to bring the talk back to a lighter key.

"We can't interest Cousin Frank in the Philadelphia belles," he said. "Looks like he's lost his heart to some little French lady—"

"I bet she'll soon be in bed with a Prussian officer," said Harry Diffenderfer.

Only Hermann Hartzell laughed. August, with real annoyance, said, "Take it easy, Harry!" and looked round to make sure Mrs. Pastor Spengler had not overheard. But Frank, with an oath, dashed his fist into Harry's grinning face.

It was a clumsy blow, for the table was between them, but Harry, taken by surprise, went over backwards, and the table, capsized by Frank's weight, went over on top of him. Diffenderfer lay sprawling in a pile of duck bones, half-eaten corncobs and mashed potatoes, while the brothers Hartzell, stooping to help him up, began to slip on shards of crockery and broken glass. Diners at the other tables sprang up to see what was happening. Frank, sucking his knuckles, stood waiting to see if the man wanted to carry the matter further, but when Harry, without looking at him, began to wipe the spilled food off his jacket, he turned on his heel and began to make his way to the door. Over part of the distance he was assisted, at an accelerated speed, by the Bookbinder bouncer, who conveyed him into Walnut Street and stood him up forcibly against the side wall of the restaurant.

"Thanks, Tom," said August Hartzell, who had followed them out of the restaurant. "I'll take over now. Thanks."

The passers-by on Walnut Street looked at the cousins curiously.

"Have you gone out of your mind?" asked August furiously. "Do you realize that the *Spenglers* saw all that, and I don't know who else besides? It'll be all over 'Change tomorrow—that the Hartzells were in a brawl as Sam Bookbinder's—"

"Don't you worry," said Frank, pulling his jacket out of his cousin's angry clutch. "Nobody who knows Hermann and you will ever suppose that *you* were fighting—"

"Are you still harping on *that*?" said the man who had sat out the Civil War in Nebraska. "Frank, I'm sick of it, I thought you'd pulled yourself together, now I see you're just the same bum you ever were—you'd been drinking before you came here tonight, I know it, that's what made you pick on Diffenderfer—"

"Hell no," said Frank. "I knew *he* wouldn't fight either, so I took the quickest way I could to shut him up about the French."

"All right, Frank, if you're so crazy about the French, go fight for them. You've always been ready to wave the bloody shirt; now you can keep that for the G.A.R. rallies, it doesn't go with me; and you can keep yourself out of Dick Street for all time to come. I've done the best I could with you, for poor Uncle Francis's sake, but now I'm finished; Mr. Bertaux' account is closed, and so is yours."

"Aw, go hire a hall," said Frank. He walked away up Walnut Street, pulling out his fine silk handkerchief to wrap round his hand. The narrow street was whirling round him. No doubt about it, rye on top of bourbon was a mistake. As he walked away from the waterfront he was strongly tempted to go back to Market Street, and, starting from the tavern where he had met the teamster earlier in the day, make a real night of it. Then some kind of gambler's instinct, rye-engendered, told him to go back to the Pierre for one more try. It was still early in the evening; the underworld of Philadelphia was just beginning to warm up.

The desk clerk at the hotel looked up expectantly as Mr Hartzell came into the lobby : rather pale, with a lock of hair hanging over his forehead, and his cravat awry.

"Glad to see you back, sir," he said pleasantly. "This came as soon as you'd gone out—guess it's the cable you've been lookin' for !"

There were sheets and sheets of it. His trembling hands could hardly put them all in order. It had been dispatched at Tours nearly three days before and routed via Marseilles, Lisbon and London.

"Regret impossible answer yours sooner," it read. "Was called Marseilles tenth settle arson attempt warehouses by your old friend Cluseret stop have now joined government Tours as underminister supply stop ship all purchases new depot three rue Bugeaud Algiers stop delighted have you with me mailing instructions stop meantime certified cheque one hundred thousand francs deposited your credit Girard Bank Philadelphia regards Michel Bertaux."

FOUR

PARIS IN HER PRIDE

Winter 1870–71

I

The gale which lashed all the shores of France on the night the Empress embarked for England was blowing itself out across the roofs of Paris by five o'clock next afternoon, when Madeleine d'Arbonne walked slowly up the grand staircase of her uncle's house. The maids who hurried ahead of her to light the fire and draw the curtains in her boudoir were shocked by her exhaustion. Mademoiselle, so gay and laughing, who could run upstairs more lightly than little M'selle Louise, was leaning on the marble handrail like an old woman.

Her personal maid, Marthe, had left to be married early in July, and Madeleine was glad of it now. The two housemaids were nervous and blundering, but too shy to make any comments as they helped her out of her crumpled black dress and wrap, and unpinned the reefs taken in the voluminous underwear lent by Mrs Evans. Where Marthe would have pried and asked questions, the two girls were silent as they scurried from one room to another with bath sheets and copper cans of hot water, silent as they brought Madeleine a glass of champagne and a few tempting sandwiches on a silver tray. She had eaten nothing since before leaving Deauville early that morning, under the escort of Dr. Crane.

"Is Monsieur Bertaux expected home this evening?" she asked

when she was settled on a comfortable sofa, with a beaded stool beneath her feet, and wearing a loose silk gown.

"At six o'clock, if you please, mademoiselle."

The weary blue eyes looked up at the servant, looked back thoughtfully at the fire. Madeleine made no reply. The maids curtsied themselves out of the room.

Madeleine had returned to the Faubourg St. Honoré by instinct, as if she had nowhere else to go, although she had told the American doctors, by way of excuse for leaving the Empress, that she must return to her father and sister at Arbonne. She had been numb in mind and body when she arrived at the Gare St. Lazare and found herself in a struggling mob of the rich and timid, hurrying to get to England or at least to the Channel resorts before the Prussian Army came any closer to Paris. Now, in the beautiful little room upholstered in oyster satin, her body soothed and refreshed by her favourite clover-scented rub, she was coming alive to the grief and disillusionment of Eugénie's flight. As a girl of fifteen, Madeleine had been close to the Empress for the first time at a great army review celebrating the victories in Italy, held on the "St. Napoleon's Day" of 1859. From the moment she saw the serene and lovely creature enthroned in the Place Vendôme, beneath a canopy sewn with imperial bees, Madeleine had given Eugénie a schoolgirl's admiration, accepted her as a surrogate mother in Marie Bertaux' place. She had criticized the Empress, sometimes imitated her for the amusement of her friends; but she had never imagined that her real devotion would come to such a painful end.

"Madeleine!"

The door opened, letting a blaze of gaslight from the hall into the firelit room.

"Michou—is it you?"

The tall, burly figure silhouetted against the glare lunged forward, and Madeleine was caught up in her uncle's arms.

"My darling, my darling, you've come back to me!"

He almost gasped the words as he kissed her—on both cheeks, on her damp soft hair, full on the lips.

"I thought I'd lost you, Madeleine! They said you'd gone to England with that damned Spaniard—"

She hardly heard what he was saying. She gave herself up to the comfort of feeling a man's arms round her, of laying her tired head on a man's broad shoulder. For a delicious moment she felt as if James Bruce were with her again. Then the illusion was destroyed as her uncle's moustache brushed across her face.

"Sit down beside me, darling, and tell me all about it."

She obeyed him gladly. It was a relief to tell the whole story, concealing nothing, admitting that he had been right and she wrong in estimating Eugénie. It was a relief to lean against him in the half-darkness, as she had leaned against him after some nursery tantrum when he had intervened to protect her from her mother's punishment. The bulky body, the aroma of starched linen and cologne, even the feel of the big silk handkerchief he put into her hand, with its faint smell of his russia leather cigar case, were for a time infinitely comforting to Madeleine. Then, while she was sobbing out her indignation—"it was all fixed; the Empress even had enough money for the journey—de Lesseps went out to get it for her in the morning!"—Madeleine became aware that her uncle's arm held her too closely, that he was setting his lips too often on the scented damp hair curling over her brow. Through two layers of the thinnest silk, she could feel his fingers tightening on her body.

She drew away from him then instinctively. Jumped up, found a taper and lighted the candles on either side of the porphyry mantelpiece. Sat down opposite him, in a high-backed crinoline chair which allowed her pleated, pale blue gown to swirl about her feet with some effect of formality. Dried her eyes, and laid his handkerchief aside.

"So that was how the story ended, Uncle Michel."

The arm which had held her close lay relaxed on the back of the oyster satin sofa. Otherwise Michel Bertaux had not changed his position. His voice was sympathetic but casual.

"The end which Badinguet must have foreseen from the beginning. Did you know, by the way, that poor Dr. Evans' activities were quite unnecessary? The new government kept a special train with steam up at the Gare de l'Est from Sunday afternoon until late last night, to take Eugénie into Belgium. They even prepared a *laissez-passer* for her—in the name of Madame Louis Napoleon Bonaparte."

"I told you she was well provided with passports," said Madeleine.

"You did. Well, let's hope Tom Evans is reimbursed for all his trouble and expense. Your Spanish friend is not restricted to five hundred francs, you know! Badinguet has been sending money out of the country for years—to Switzerland, South America, above all to England. Mocquard told me before he died that a house at Chislehurst, near London, was bought years ago, just in case there was an abrupt end to the great adventure. It was furnished and provided with a tenant to front for them. Badinguet will have a nice home to go to by and by, and if he's lost a throne, he still has a fortune to leave to that boy of his—and 'Ugénie.' "

"You seem to know a lot about the provisional government's plans," said Madeleine. Her uncle's sharp eyes twinkled.

"The Government of National Defence, my dear. They dislike the word provisional, bless their simple hearts! Yes, I've heard a good deal about their plans. You see, they've invited me to join them," said Michel Bertaux.

Madeleine sat forward with a start.

"But you wouldn't do that?"

"Why not? Did *I* swear undying allegiance to Badinguet or the men who were his predecessors on the throne? I'm no d'Arbonne, to ruin myself for a thankless king. I always gave you credit, Madeleine, for having more sense than your father and brother put together. Now you've proved it! Louis went all the way to Edinburgh with King Charles—you had the sense to stop at Deauville, when you set out with Madame Eugénie!"

"That doesn't mean I would join forces with the man who betrayed her," said Madeleine.

"She betrayed herself, you silly girl. You mean Trochu, the Man with a Plan? You'll tell me I'm splitting hairs if I say I'll actually be joining forces with Gambetta, but that's the truth. Gambetta wants to fight the Prussians. He knows, and he's th only one in the whole gang of piddling lawyers who does know, that a successful attack depends upon supplies. That's where I come in. I'm going down to Tours next week, with two old fools who think *they* can run the country—Crémieux and Fourichon—to get the supply lines set for the Auxiliary Army that Gambetta means to raise. He'll stay here to direct the Paris operations, and we'll let Monsieur Trochu make the speeches and sing the *Marseillaise* with his Communist supporters until he and they are black in the face."

Bertaux, his own face suffused with blood and his cheek twitching, had risen to his feet. He towered over Madeleine as he went on:

"Do you know what Trochu is, Madeleine? He's the scum of France! Oh yes, I know what they say in the Faubourg St. Germain—that the real scum is made up of *boursiers* like Bertaux and Saccard, the dirty dogs who'll do anything for profit, the political whores who'll go to bed with any of the temporary masters of France. But we don't measure up to General Trochu! The soldier who doesn't fight, the priest-ridden Rightist who toadies to the Left, the officer who betrays his Empress to make himself, God save us, *President of the Provisional Government!*"

Bertaux was almost spitting in his rage.

"I'll take care of General Trochu, don't you worry! I'll take a leaf out of his own book, and bring him down from within! But the first thing to do is *fight the Prussians*—get Bazaine out of Metz if we can, and even if we can't, fight them with all we've got!"

Madeleine was on her feet in front of him, her blue eyes wide and shining.

"Fight them—and win! You do believe we'll win?"

Her uncle stared at her. Then, as if he could no longer keep his hands off that slim figure, once again quivering with life and hope, he seized her shoulders and shook her gently to and fro.

"No, I don't, my dear. Unless a miracle happens, we can't beat Bismarck's war machine. All we can do now is fight him until we can end this thing with honour. You used to be very great on the honour of France, remember? And then, when it's over, we must count our remaining assets—and go to work again to pay our debts."

"And the Société Anonyme Bertaux will pile up another fortune?"

"I hope so." He released her, consulted his watch by the light of the candles and went on in a more deliberate tone.

"Well, now we can make some sort of plans for the immediate future. My agent at Tours has been told to rent a furnished house for me—one of those pleasant little châteaux on the Loire—"

"Do you mean Amboise or Blois, by any chance?" said Madeleine sarcastically.

"I'm glad you can joke again, my dear! No, something less than a national monument will have to do. It should be fixed up by Monday, and we'll get away in plenty of time before the Paris Gates are closed."

"What about Louise and father? Won't they be in danger at Arbonne?"

"Not at the moment," said Bertaux easily. "They can come to Tours later on, perhaps; but for the present, until I have a working relationship with Crémieux and Fourichon, I think you must be my only hostess. You know just the kind of intimate little dinner party I'll want to give."

"It really is a revolution de luxe, isn't it?" said Madeleine. Her uncle wisely made no direct answer.

"I'm going over the way to the Ministry of the Interior now," he said. "Gambetta expects me for a conference at seven o'clock. Thank God I came here first to get some papers from the study! I'll tell them to give us dinner at nine—that'll give you time for a good rest. But don't trouble to change your gown, my dear. That pale blue was your mother's colour, and it becomes you very well!"

He lifted one of the wide, winged sleeves of her dress appraisingly. He let it fall back, in a little ripple of narrow pleats, round Madeleine's white arm. It was a gesture of possession which startled her even more than the passionate kisses of his first greeting. She stood looking at the door of the boudoir, when he had closed it gently behind him, as if she had come to the edge of a precipice.

For five minutes—even ten—she stood arrested where he had left her. Then the sound of the great front door closing vibrated through the house and sent her headlong into her bedroom to search through the bag she had carried on the flight to Deauville.

Stay with him? Alone in that great house at a tête-à-tête dinner, watching the admiration in his eyes? Alone at Tours, his hostess; night after night listening to the story of his intrigues with Crémieux and Fourichon as her mother might have done—or his mistress! "He is *too fond* of me!" she faced it. "I dare not stay with him!" For the hundredth time since she held in her hands the passports of the Empress, she thought of James Bruce and the life and love he offered, and said to herself, "You fool! You fool!"

She found what she was looking for in her bag—the key of the wall safe in her dressing room. With its chain slipped round her wrist for safety, she pulled open her wardrobe doors, made a quick decision, rang for the startled maids.

"When Monsieur Bertaux comes back, tell him that I've gone to Arbonne," she said imperiously. "If you're quick about it, I can catch the evening train to Fontainebleau. Take the portmanteau in the closet—there's no time to bring a trunk down from the attic. Armande, pack all the warm things you can find in the wardrobe. My heaviest boots too. Augustine, will you lace me, please?"

The maids, exchanging glances, obeyed her promptly. In her white petticoat, Madeleine stood to let the corset be clasped round her; the laces flew. With her garments over her arm, she stepped into the dressing room and bolted the door. Arbonne! She had no intention of going near Arbonne—to play the *demoiselle* from the château, paying visits of condolence to tenants with sons in the army and kneeling at the Crusader's effigy to pray for Victor's safety! She knotted up her hair and put on a dress and a jacket left over from last autumn—it did her good to feel the taut fit at shoulders and waist—still furiously thinking what to do, and where to hide from Michel Bertaux. An hotel? The Grand and the

Splendide belonged to him; besides, no lady stayed at an hotel alone. Some little *pension* on the Left Bank, where she could rent a room for a night's sleep, and get her bearings? The great thing was not to run away from Paris. Cautiously, she opened the door of the wall safe. Her diamonds and other important jewels had been sent to the Banque de France as soon as war was declared, but the cashbox was there, full of the gold napoleons of an allowance she had hardly touched since June. Michel's allowance—*that* she couldn't help! She lifted the box out of the safe. She saw behind it one of the plain grey envelopes from her writing desk, loosely sealed on something hard and heavy. The inscription in her own handwriting recalled an incident forgotten for months and now, in her extremity, remembered thankfully:

"The key to father's apartment on the Quai Voltaire."

With Madeleine to think was always to act. She ordered a cab to take her to the Gare de Lyon, and waited in a fever of impatience while the Old Poisson went grumbling off to fetch it, afraid that Monsieur Gambetta's eloquence would run unexpectedly dry and her uncle come prowling down the Faubourg from the Place Beauvau. But she had not gone very far across the Republican Paris which seemed as yet so little different from Imperial Paris before she remembered the great obstacle to going into hiding at the Quai Voltaire. The Young Poissons, as watchful at the door of the old house as their father by the bronze gates of the new, would get word to the Old Poisson in half a day, by that mysterious family communications system which extended all over France. Then the Quai Voltaire would be treated to the spectacle of Michel Bertaux arriving in a rage to take his niece back under his protection. Never! There was only one more refuge left that she could think of in her need. Putting her head out of the cab window, Madeleine called up to the driver,

"I've changed my mind! Take me to the rue du Bac!"

Mademoiselle Henriette d'Arbonne was still obstinately defending her musty apartment and the family treasures it contained against a possible onslaught by the revolutionaries. When she nervously drew the bolts of the outer door that windy even-

ing, and saw Madeleine by the flickering gaslight on the landing—
tall, strong and looking like a young fighting angel sent by heaven
to protect her—the poor old lady threw her arms round the neck
of the girl whom she had never liked, and burst into grateful tears.

II

The neutral nations stood back and watched as German Great Headquarters directed the formal investment of Paris. The Prussian watch fires crept as close, by night, as the Forest of Bondy, and shells fell near the town of St. Denis while von Moltke's six hundred siege guns were being hauled into place around the capital. The so-called Maas Army, which had led the Prussian advance from the Meuse after Sedan, took up its position to the east of Paris. The Third Army made a flanking movement to reach the west side of the city. It was led by the *Heldentenor* in person. The Crown Prince Fritz, who had bent so respectfully over Eugénie's hand at El Kantara—who had been entertained superbly at the Tuileries, and, incognito, had sometimes shown the *cocottes* of Paris how a Prussian prince made love—was driving joyfully on to the kill.

It was then that the neutrals began at last to feel some sympathy for the French. They were foolhardy, disorganized, perhaps crazy, but of their courage there could be no doubt. What was called *La Débâcle* had nothing to do with "the fall of France." It was simply one more reverse in France's great pageant of triumph and disaster, two thousand years long; they met it with weapons in their hands, and their hearts high.

There were about one hundred thousand regular troops inside the pentagon of ninety-five bastioned fronts which formed the walls of Paris. Among them, naval gunners and Marines were the backbone of the defences of the Sixteen Forts. Far less adequate although twice as numerous was the picturesque rabble of National Guards, Gardes Mobiles, policemen and volunteers who worked and squabbled over the task of making Paris impregnable. A corps of *francs-tireurs*, or sharpshooters, created before the fall of the Empire, was now enlarged to include such colourful units as the Mounted Scouts (the mounts came from the imperial stud), the Newspaper Snipers, the Crimean and Mexican Veterans—even the Amazons of the Seine, a band of lady marksmen in a neat trousered uniform of orange and black. The Crown Prince Fritz promised faithfully that the Germans would shoot down the *francs-tireurs* without mercy, and execute anyone found harbouring them.

The railroad tracks to Calais and Boulogne were blown up by the French, then the western bridges at St. Cloud, Sèvres and Billancourt; the water gates at Bercy and the Point du Jour were blocked by a double boom of gunboats. When Bismarck uttered his threat to burn down the city, Paris stood up with a brand in her hand and kindled her own fires first. All round the city there was now a circle, twenty-five miles wide, of scorched earth. This glacis extended in front of the Sixteen Forts for eighteen hundred feet before widening into a field of fire where homes and harvests, parks and pleasure houses, had all been ruthlessly obliterated to deprive the enemy of cover. Down went the trees of the Bois de Boulogne and the Bois de Vincennes. Up went poles and cables for the new electric light, hitherto used only for illuminations and *fêtes*, now lighting the workmen who by night as well as by day dug trenches, built up scarp and counter-scarp, strengthened the bastions of the Sixteen Forts. Deep fosses were cut on the Martyrs' Hill for the burial of the dead. Women screamed as bones and mouldering corpses were carried out of the cemeteries and burned to make room for those, still living, who were fated to die on the walls of Paris. Two weeks after the September revolution, the Gates of Paris were barred, and the young Republic stood up to face the enemy.

On the seventeenth of September Madeleine was not only still inside the city, but still under her old cousin's roof in the rue du Bac. The old woman, abandoned by her elderly domestic, a refugee fled to a daughter at Granville, was too unwell to be left alone and too feeble to be put on one of the few and overcrowded trains which left, during the last week, for Fontainebleau and the south. Together, Madeleine and the old Demoiselle endured the noisy terrors of the first sorties made by the Paris garrison. They sat praying while the windows of the rue du Bac rattled with the reverberations of the firing at Châtillon, where the Prussians drove the Parisians back under the walls at their first engagement on the nineteenth of September, and laughed and hugged each other when street urchins came by shouting the news of a successful sortie at Villejuif four days later. But these were the great moments of fear and pride for the women of the embattled city. Daily life, for every one of them, brought a round of drudgery and weariness from the moment that the Gates were shut.

Food was already in short supply. The new government had decreed a moratorium on rents, and the landlords of Paris retaliated by cutting off the domestic heating of their tenants. Madeleine, who had never walked in the streets of Paris without a maid in attendance, now trudged for hours alone in search of such things as coffee and vegetables. Rue de Lille. Rue de Verneuil. Rue de Beaune. Rue Jacob. Rue des Saints Pères, where a susceptible dealer in wood and wine could be blandished into delivering a few *stères* of firewood at Mademoiselle Henriette's apartment. Within ten days she knew every pavingstone of the *quartier* as well as she had once known the parquet of the Tuileries.

Madeleine had never cared for an invalid, swept a room, purchased or prepared food in her life. She did these things clumsily and badly, but without any thought of deserting her old kinswoman for the privacy of her father's apartment on the Quai Voltaire. And after the first week she found that in the back streets where her father had been known as "the Crazy Count" there were many people ready to help his daughter.

One day she was accosted, as she passed the corner of the rue de l'Université with her basket, by a stout matronly young woman of about her own age. who was standing in the doorway of baker's shop with her knitting in her hands.

"*Bonjour*, Mademoiselle d'Arbonne !"

Madeleine, smiling and perplexed, came to a stop.

"*Bonjour*, madame ! I wonder how you know my name !"

The woman laughed. She beckoned Madeleine into the bakery

where the shelves were almost empty, and two children in blue gingham pinafores were playing quietly with a toy train.

"Why, everybody in the *quartier* knows *your* name, mademoiselle," she said, 'just as everybody knows mine—the wife of Leblanc the baker, or Madame Alice, whichever you prefer! We all know that you're nursing poor old M'selle Henriette. Her concierge told us all about it. We think it's very chic; but as I said to my husband, it's just what we might expect from M'selle Madeleine!"

"Madame Alice," said Madeleine in smiling confusion, "you are charming, but I still don't know why you should expect anything from me!"

"Because you were so nice to me when we were girls," said the baker's wife, and she threw back her head and laughed heartily, showing very white teeth. "But I see you don't recognize me, and it's no wonder! Seven years have made more difference in me than in a great court lady like yourself—hard work, and these two rascals, and now all this worry about the Prussians have left their mark on me!"

"Are these your children?" said Madeleine gently. The two little pinafored boys left their play and came to stand beside their mother's skirts, looking up at the pretty lady.

"Yes, they're mine," said the woman, stroking their heads. "Their father's on duty at the fortifications today, with the National Guard. Thank God, his trade exempted him from the general mobilization—or I might have been a widow by now, like so many of my neighbours. Ah, mademoiselle, what deaths among the people you remember! Monsieur Ponsin at the livery stable lost two sons at Wissembourg. Maurice from the paintshop has been a prisoner since Gravelotte, and poor Robert, the locksmith's apprentice, was wounded at Sedan—"

"And my brother Victor is wounded and besieged in Metz," said Madeleine.

Madame Alice touched her arm sympathetically.

"Sadness everywhere! But, *chère* Mademoiselle Madeleine, I see you don't remember the people I've been talking about. Have you forgotten how we all posed with you in the picture Monsieur

Delacroix made of you? Have I really changed out of all knowing, in seven years?"

As Madeleine stood silent in surprise, the woman rattled on, "I daresay you've been painted so often, it means very little to *you*! But you see it was a big day for the *quartier* when Monsieur Delacroix came along from the rue de Furstemberg looking for 'types' to put in the picture with Mademoiselle d'Arbonne! Robert and Maurice and I were excited, I can tell you, old M'sieur Ponsin too, and so were the others; and then you were so nice to us when you came to the studio with madame la comtesse, and you made us laugh when Monsieur Delacroix got angry with us, and said we didn't hold the pose! Oh, we were proud of that picture! When it was shown at the Great Exhibition — that was the year I was married — we all clubbed together and hired a wagonette to go and see it again!"

A wave of heat and shame came over Madeleine. It was so long since she had seen the picture Delacroix painted of her as a young girl that she had truly forgotten what any of the other faces on the great crowded canvas looked like. She remembered the sittings chiefly because it was then she had begun to suspect — from some veiled smile, some careless allusion — that Delacroix had been her mother's lover.

She wondered what those simple people would think if they knew the picture they were so proud of had never been hung, but now stood wrapped in sacking in the attic at the Faubourg St. Honoré.

"I wish I had been in that wagonette with you!" she said impulsively. "Forgive me, Madame Alice! I remember you perfectly now. You're the girl standing just below me, looking up at the Tricolore —"

"With a rifle in my hand — that's me!" concluded Madame Alice grimly. "*Hé*, mademoiselle, I may need that rifle again one of these days, if those Prussian devils come much closer!"

This was the first of many meetings between Madeleine and the baker's wife. Madame Alice had always been a leader in the *quartier*; now, as a purveyor of bread, she was far more powerful than any of the new government officials who came round dis tributing notices about identity cards and ration tickets, and who were either laughed at or disregarded by the public.

"I've found a housekeeper for the old Demoiselle, to replace that rat who went to Granville," she announced the second time Madeleine went to her shop for bread. "A decent person and a good nurse, anxious to find work—her husband has been a prisoner since Sedan. She'll do all your errands, M'selle Madeleine, and I'll take care she doesn't cheat you."

"Bless you, Madame Alice," said Madeleine gratefully. "Now I'll be able to start the war work I really want to do."

The plump shopkeeper studied the young lady sitting by her empty counter—it was always empty early in the day now—and leaning a little wearily against the marble slab.

"What sort of war work, m'selle?"

"At one of the ambulance posts, I thought. Up at the forts, if possible."

Madame Alice sighed. There was a sound of firing from the west, where "La Jeanne Marie," heaviest of all the guns defending Paris, was engaging the batteries of the Crown Prince Fritz. Already the Parisians had grown accustomed to this deadly obbligato to all their conversations.

"With all respect, mademoiselle," she said, "there's work nearer to your hand than at the forts! There's Robert the locksmith's mother, who would be very grateful for a word of comfort; Monsieur Ponsin too. Wouldn't you care to go and have a chat with them, you who chat so very nicely to me?"

"But—wouldn't I be intruding?" There was distress, which Madame Alice realized to be genuine, in Madeleine's face and voice. "Wouldn't they resent my coming—someone who was so close to the Empress and those who made the war?"

"They've forgotten the Empress already," said Madame Alice. "The important thing is that you're here with us in Paris!"

Diffidently, anxious to please as she had never been at the Tuileries, Madeleine began to go about the narrow streets of the old *quartier* which had once belonged to the Sieurs d'Arbonne. There were many homes in which "the Crazy Count's" daughter was made welcome, others where she was rebuffed or snubbed.

The seventh *arondissement* of Paris was largely bourgeois in character, hardly tainted by the Communism which was spreading out from the workers' quarters to engulf the Hôtel de Ville and the offices of General Trochu at the Louvre. But often enough Madeleine was accosted by Mobiles coming back drunk and singing for a day's leave from the fortifications, who resented her dress and manner, and would call her *'sale aristo'* or shout *'Regardez la cocodette!'* as they jostled her off the pavement. But Madeleine persevered, and she who had always dreaded the apparent condescension of visiting the peasants at Arbonne drew a quick and tactful sympathy from the poor people of Paris whose privations she had begun to share.

The autumn weather came early in 1870. The rooms where Madeleine sat with her new friends were unheated, warmed only by the bodies of the many refugees who had reached Paris from the eastern provinces. The supplies of fresh meat came to an end, and the money Michel Bertaux had lavished on his niece put food on many a bare table. Of Bertaux himself his niece knew only what she read in the *Figaro*: that he had left Paris hastily for Marseilles, and now installed at Tours. Of others who had been her constant companions she heard, in those days of rumour and silence, even less. It was a time of outward occupation and inward shock, in which the thought of James Bruce receded from her heart like a spent wave.

Or so she thought. She told herself that she had forgotten him in all the new cares and problems of siege life. She knew that she had deceived herself on the very day when she left the *quartier*, crossed the Pont Royal, and passed by the Tuileries for the first time.

Madeleine saw the blank façade of the palace without emotion. The place which had been her second home was home no longer — that was all. The state apartments, she knew, were shut up and the Crown Jewels confiscated for the State Treasury. The Salle des Maréchaux was about to be reopened as a People's Concert Hall, where the latest popular song, *I'm Just a Guttersnipe* would be sung many times by dreary *chanteuses* from the outer boulevards. The whole place was swarming now with clerks and other functionaries handling the immense mass of paper work created by the new republic.

Madeleine was on her way to the ambulance centre set up by Ferdinand de Lesseps. The newspapers said, with truth, that it was the best run in the city, with the possible exception of the American Ambulance for which Dr. Evans was responsible. De Lesseps himself, discussing the situation that day with a group of British doctors, admitted that building the Suez Canal was child's play compared with the attempt to create a central volunteer ambulance association in Paris, where the volunteer groups quarrelled with each other, and the Red Cross Society quarrelled with them all.

De Lesseps looked up in astonishment when Madeleine d'Arbonne's name was brought to him. With a hasty apology to the doctors he joined her in the next room, where she stood looking down through a glass window at what had been a food market and now housed his wagons and mule teams.

"My dear young lady, I had no idea you were still in Paris!"

"You heard I came back from Deauville?" said Madeleine.

De Lesseps bowed. He was thinking of that last luncheon at the Tuileries, when he had seen this girl with her eyes fixed devotedly on Eugénie's tragic face. He said with a touch of coldness,

"I did indeed. But I happened to see Monsieur Bertaux before he left for Tours, and he told me you had gone straight down to Arbonne."

"No. I'm looking after my father's cousin in the rue du Bac. She had a bad attack of bronchitis, but she's better now."

"Very imprudent of you both, if I may say so, not to leave Paris before the Gates were closed."

"The same kind of imprudence *you* have shown, Monsieur de Lesseps!"

The president of the Suez Canal Company relaxed in to a smile. "Well—it isn't quite the same thing, perhaps," he said. "My duty seemed to lie in Paris—"

"And so does mine."

"Are you serious, mademoiselle?"

"Perfectly. I want you to let me drive one of your ambulances, monsieur. I've heard you tell Her Imperial Majesty"—the old title still came naturally to Madeleine's lips—"that there was a great shortage of skilled drivers, as well as dressers, in all the emergency hospitals in Paris. I don't know how to dress wounds, and I'm sure I couldn't learn, for I'm not a good nurse—ask poor Cousin Henriette! but I *am* a good driver—you know that! I could handle one of those mule teams as well as any man."

De Lesseps looked at her in sheer amazement. She was dressed more plainly than he had ever seen her, or any lady of Eugénie's court, in a dark serge dress with a closely fitting, buttoned jacket such as she might have worn to follow the guns at some country house in the Sologne in a happier October. The tops of strong leather boots were revealed by the short skirt, and her hair was pinned into a firm knot beneath a small felt hat. She was trim and workmanlike, but—she was still the Tuileries fashion plate, country style! How could she endure the gruelling work which lay ahead? How would she stand fire?

"I know you're a famous driver," he said kindly, "but my wagons will have rougher roads to travel than the Longchamps race track, as the sorties beyond the walls go on."

"No rougher than the road up to the Cairo Citadel when I beat Prince Tewfik in a four-in-hand race last year."

"But this won't be a race," said Ferdinand de Lesseps, passing his hand wearily over his thick white hair. "This is war! It's a business for men! Can't you find an outlet for your energy and patriotism in one of the ladies' work parties, or helping the Sisters of Charity in a city hospital?"

"Oh, don't condemn me to that!" Impulsively she laid her hand on the solid old arm of de Lesseps. "I don't want to scrape lint and roll bandages and sit gossiping as we did at the Tuileries! I'm not brave enough or patient enough to empty slops for the Sisters at the Hôtel Dieu. There's just this one thing I can do better than most people—driving—please let me try!"

It was hard to resist those blue eyes, and the tears on the gold

280

brown lashes. De Lesseps thought of his own young wife, and hardened his heart.

"I can't allow you—or any young woman—to expose herself needlessly to injury or death," he said.

"But if I don't care, either way?"

Impossible to mistake the sincerity of that appeal. Impossible not to recognize something else in the proud face—a hint of the authority handed down to her by her soldier ancestors, which took no denial and knew no weakening. De Lesseps bowed.

"Very well!" he said. "I believe you're in earnest. Can you be here at five o'clock tomorrow morning?"

"I can."

"We have stable helpers, but the drivers have to supervise the grooming and harnessing of the teams, and the condition of the wagons. With time for a bowl of coffee and a ration of bread, that takes the better part of an hour."

"I understand."

"Now!" said de Lesseps. "One test! Indispensable! I want you to take one of those teams out this very afternoon! Before you go beyond the walls, behind the troops, we must find out how you can drive in the streets of Paris, which present more problems than the park at St. Cloud . . . One moment, if you please."

He opened the door to his private office. The British doctors got to their feet at once. De Lesseps heard one of them whisper,

"I ken that lassie!"

"Mademoiselle d'Arbonne, may I present our Scottish friend Dr. Gordon, who came here as a British Army observer at the outbreak of war, and has generously stayed on as deputy-inspector of all our hospitals? And his fellow countryman, Dr. Innes, who acts with him as medical commissioner? And their assistant, Dr Hector Munro?"

James Bruce's classmate made a clumsy bow. He was attired in the same suit of rusty black and apparently the same crumpled neckcloth as he had worn in January, the trumpet stethoscope stuck defiantly out of his breast pocket. His small, astute grey eyes ranged inquisitively over Madeleine's face.

"Dr. Munro is obliged to go to the Hôtel Dieu this afternoon, mademoiselle. Will you drive him there in one of the ambulances, and come back alone?"

"With pleasure!" said Madeleine. "Which team am I to take? And may I go down on the floor by myself, please? The mules are not accustomed to a woman, and may be restless if several people go up to them at once."

The men watched through the window as she walked briskly over the floor below and spoke to the astonished stablemen. She watched intently as a team of mules was harnessed to a wagon with the Red Cross on its white canvas tilt. She slipped her hand inside the girths, tested the bits and bridles, and when the swing mule, a vicious brute with a yellow eye, tried to nip her shoulder, her clenched fist flew up and struck him on the nose—just once— to show him who was master. Then she mounted to the driver's seat, sorted out the reins and closed her fingers upon them, and nodded coolly up at the men at the window.

"By Gad!" said Dr. Gordon, "I believe she can do it!"

"So do I," agreed de Lesseps. "But, Dr. Munro, I do beg you, keep an eye on her. Make her wait at the Hôtel Dieu and come back with her, if she seems to be in any trouble."

"Trouble!" said the little Scotsman. "I would as soon expeck that lass to get into trouble as I would expeck Gentleman James himsel'!" And before de Lesseps could ask what he meant, Hector Munro had taken leave of them, and was mounting to a seat in the wagon beside Madeleine d'Arbonne.

With characteristic impertinence the doctor alluded to James Bruce almost as soon as they were out of the depot, while Madeleine was holding the team well in hand for the turn into the rue de Rivoli. For army mules they were frisky; they had not been out for two days, and the pull of their iron mouths made them harder to check than the gaited animals she had driven at Longchamps or St. Cloud. She hardly heard what he said the first time, or hardly understood it, for Dr. Munro's French was a long way removed from the classic elegance of James Bruce's speech. It was a mixture of hospital and barracks slang on a basis of the boulevards which Madeleine found as difficult as the broad Scots dialect which the garrulous doctor offered on his second attempt.

"I'm sayin' I've seen ye, mem, afore now. At a grand ball on New Year's Day, at the palace yonder." Jerk of a not overclean thumb at the Tuileries. "I was up in the gallery, an' I watched ye dancin' wi' an auld acquaintance of mine. Mr. James Bruce of Sauchentree."

This time she caught the name. A wave of colour stained her face, and at the pull of the tightened reins her team tossed their heads angrily. Then Madeleine replied, with a cool smile more crushing than any direct snub,

"Mr. Bruce dances very well indeed."

Hector Munro was silenced. The ambulance wagon went on down the rue de Rivoli, across the Seine by the Pont Neuf, and down to the most modern hospital in Paris, the Hôtel Dieu. Madeleine's tension relaxed. She showed increasing skill in manoeuvring the heavy vehicle, although it worried her to be blinded by the tilt to what might be at her back. The streets of Paris, as de Lesseps had known, presented a different problem from the parish roads round Arbonne, where Madeleine first learned to drive four-in-hand; but the traffic was growing less every day as more and more horses were requisitioned and the double-decker *impériales* disappeared from the streets. She drew up at the side door of the hospital with enough of a flourish for Munro to say apologetically, in his worst French,

"That was well done, mademoiselle. I beg your pardon if I offended you by mentioning a last year's ball. Will you accept my escort back to Monsieur de Lesseps?"

Madeleine smiled at him. Her eyes were dancing; the drive had stimulated her, and for the first time for many weeks she felt confident of her own powers.

"No thank you, monsieur. I shall do very well alone."

With the newfangled gesture which the Empress had introduced among women, she shook hands with him. Munro kept the slim hand for an instant in his own bare paw.

"You've spoiled a pair of gloves already, Mademoiselle d'Arbonne."

"I have, I'm afraid—those rope reins do more damage than

leather. I must hunt up a pair of proper driving gloves before tomorrow."

"You'll be eligible for an army issue now," said James Bruce's old acquaintance.

III

"Don't the French know when they're beaten?"

It was the question Bismarck asked von Moltke and von Roon, when the three met at German Great Headquarters in Versailles and watched the shells from La Jeanne Marie lobbing westward from the Mont Valérien. One of those shells had already set fire to the palace of St. Cloud, where German troops were quartered. The great building, where the court of Napoleon III and Eugénie had spent so many brilliant hours, was nothing, now, but a smouldering ruin.

That, Bismarck conceded, was not by itself enough to make the French give in, but when the fall of Metz on October 28 followed the carnage of Sedan, might they not have had the wits to yield? When Marshal Bazaine ignominiously surrendered Metz, the virgin fortress, nearly one hundred and seventy thousand French troops had gone into captivity or given their parole to fight no more. Bismarck now had over three hundred thousand French prisoners of war in Germany, and his troops released from the siege of Metz were overrunning the whole of France. The victory was as good as won—why wouldn't they admit it?

"Don't the French know when they're beaten?"

The exiles were asking it indignantly of one another as they waited for the armistice that would allow them to go home. The Emperor turned the question over in his mind as he played cards with Conneau and Charles Thélin in his state prison at Wilhelmshöhe (it was grander than Ham fortress in the old days) and the Empress wrote endless letters about it from her well-appointed new home at Chislehurst. Up at Brussels, Princess Mathilde Bonaparte squabbled about it with Ambassador Benedetti at the Bellevue Hotel. From his Swiss estate at Prangins—prudently bought before the Disaster—Prince Napoleon watched with savage pleasure the downfall of his protégé, Trochu.

For General Trochu, without having fired a shot in anger, was beaten—that was certain. He had had his parade along the Champs Elysées, indispensable to any would-be dictator of France, and he had truckled to the Reds and the National Guard all through the month of October, but no one paid much attention to him now. He had taken to hearing voices, and claimed to be in touch with St. Geneviève, the patron saint of Paris. When he made one of his regular public appearances, and invited the people to *chanter la Marseillaise*, he was just as likely to hear the mocking strains of:

> *Plan! Plan! Plan! Plan!*
> *I know Trochu's plan.*
> *Plan! Plan! Plan! Plan!*
> *He's got a wonderful plan!*

Ridicule, the killing weapon of the Parisians, was also used freely against "the three old men of Tours." MM. Crémieux, Fourichon and Michel Bertaux were speedily nicknamed "Senility, Debility and Sterility," and when in an attempt to bolster up their authority Gambetta himself left Paris in a balloon and was found by peasants of the Somme hanging head downward with his trousers caught in the branch of a tree, there was even some ridicule for Monsieur Gambetta too. The Parisians, it was clear, would make game of anything and anybody—except themselves.

Once at Tours, Gambetta prosecuted the war with a vigour which won new admiration for the French. An Auxiliary Army, short of officers and poorly equipped, was somehow raised to take the place of the defeated and captive armies of the Emperor. General Bourbaki, who had been so eager to declare war, was almost the last of the Emperor's generals still in the field as a divisional commander. New men—Aurelle de Paladine, Chanzy, Faidherbe—emerged to take their places beside him as the fighting generals of the young Republic. A French victory at Coulmiers on November 9 enraged the Prussians and gave the defenders of Paris new heart. Above all, it was their heart, and their resistance, through ninety days of siege, which finally turned the sympathies of the neutral nations away from the Germans and towards the French.

The world was appalled at the spectacle of one of its great capitals—some said, the greatest—cut off by a ring of fire; slowly starving; silent except for the irregular scraps of news which came out by balloon or carrier pigeon. It was known that the sheep and cattle driven in before the siege began had all been slaughtered, that tame cats and rats from the Seine sewers sold for five dollars apiece, and that food of any sort was scarce. What was not known in detail was how the women suffered—fully as much as the men in the forts and along the bastions. Theirs was the task of finding food—forming a line at eight in the evening to wait outside Felix Potin's groceries for the ration distributions every morning, and combing the shops in the back streets for the last ounce of lard or coffee. Their children died before birth or in the week after birth as anaemia attacked three-quarters of the women of Paris. Old ladies like Mademoiselle Henriette d'Arbonne, too proud to seek public assistance, subsided through attacks of grippe and bronchitis into pneumonia, the friend of the aged, and died quietly in the icy rooms devoid of light or heat. The city hospitals were packed to the doors as sortie after unsuccessful sortie increased the number of wounded and fever-ridden men. Ambulances like Madeleine's lost the fresh whiteness of their canvas tilts and stretchers, which had to be cleaned of blood and pus and all the filth of the battlefield after each groaning cargo was unloaded. The terrible year, 1870, declined to its winter solstice, and the dark night of pain and misery came down on France.

On the evening of the shortest day of the year, the ninety-sixth of the siege of Paris, James Bruce ate an early meal in his London chambers.

He sat working at the table on which his landlady, Mrs. Apthorpe, had replaced a green felt cloth when she removed the dishes, in front of a stack of circulars and correspondence which had overflowed weeks ago from his mahogany writing desk. Neatly tied with red tape, most of the bundles were also neatly docketed. The Clothing Society for French War Prisoners. The British War Relief Fund. The *Daily News* French Peasant Relief

Fund. The Lord Mayor's Fund for French War Victims. James Bruce, who had never put himself forward in public affairs, was now an active promoter of each one.

James Bruce was recognizable—that was all. His brothers might have exclaimed if they had seen the face he bent over his papers in the lamplight: burned out, with hollow cheeks, the firm lips bitten and compressed to a narrow line—the face of a sick man. He had not been ill. He was only worn out by all the arguments, public and private, in which he had engaged on behalf of France; all the meetings in the chalky schoolrooms of North London and the Bayswater drawing rooms at which he had solemnly appealed to the solemn, socially conscious audiences of Victorian England for contributions to one or all of the French charities. James was not an emotional speaker like W. H. Bullock of the *Daily News* fund, who knew how to make even the stolid London audiences writhe with eye-witness accounts of the bayoneted babies and old men burned alive in the cellars of Bazeilles; but there was a suppressed passion in what he said which was very effective in its own way.

And he could hardly have told, as the dreadful year 1870 ebbed at last to its shortest day, whether his efforts were really inspired by sympathy for a brave people fighting with their backs to the wall, or by the girl who had given him her love all through one summer night in the forest of Compiègne. France and Madeleine —Madeleine and France—the two were now indistinguishable in his mind.

He had no news of her.

He had been sure that he had found her again when Eugénie's arrival in England was made known, and the first reports stated that "Her Majesty was accompanied by a lady in waiting," giving no name. James did not wait for the second editions but left in his old impulsive way on the first train to Hastings. It was the manager of the Marine Hotel, impressed by his manner and his card, who told him that the lady's name was Lebreton—not to be seen, of course; closeted with the illustrious refugee—and suggested that Dr. Evans might be available instead. The two men met in a private sitting room, where Evans immediately recalled Bruce's exploit at El Kantara.

"I've thought of that time on the Suez Canal again and again," said Thomas Evans. He was nervous and voluble, still riding high on the wings of his adventure. "If you could have seen Her Majesty, Mr. Bruce, lying helpless with seasickness in that crowded cabin, with the Channel seas washing over the decks of the *Gazelle*, and remembered the day she stepped ashore at Port Said in all her glory, I think you might have shed a tear, sir—I'm not ashamed to say I did."

"And her noble ally, the Khedive Ismail?" said James with a curling lip. "After all the treasure France poured into Egypt for twenty years, has there been no help from the viceroy, or his Turkish master?"

"Not only no help, but—I wish de Lesseps were back in Suez," said the doctor obliquely. "The defeat of the Emperor must be a sore temptation to Ismail to start some mischief on the Canal. What do the P. and O. men in Alexandria think of that situation?"

But James returned to the purpose of his visit—to find out about Madeleine.

"You guessed right up to a point," admitted the American. "She did leave the palace with the Empress, but she refused to cross the water. I had a long talk with her and nothing I could say or suggest would shake her. Back to Paris she went, with Crane as escort, on the very next day. I believe she was worried about her family; she went to join them at Arbonne."

"You're sure of that, sir?"

Dr. Evans, in his soaring mood, was sure of everything. So James went back to London and wrote a series of letters to Madeleine at Arbonne which were as extraordinary a jumble of love, remorse and politics as any man ever penned.

He received no answer.

The only thing he could do—and he did it with his might—was to enlist British sympathies for her countrymen. The Clothing Society for the prisoners of war did best after Marshal Leboeuf, of gaiter-button fame, followed Bazaine out of surrendered Metz.

Many people in Britain were anxious to provide winter overcoats and underwear for the men he had sent into the field in summer uniforms, and blankets to cover them in the stinking *lagers* of Cologne, Mainz, Torgau and Coblenz. Then all the subscription lists burgeoned as Christmas drew near, for Londoners with turkey and roast goose in view were disturbed to know that there would be no such good things in Paris this year. Only the very rich would be able to afford a cut of the camel, nilgai and yak calf which Deboos, the English butcher of the avenue de Friedland, had bought from the Jardin d'Acclimatation for the tables of the saddest Christmas Paris had ever known.

So there in Doughty Street, four days before Christmas, sat James Bruce with his neatly docketed bundles arranged round his ebony ruler and ivory pen: a man doing everything a neutral might to relieve the inhumanity of the conflict raging across the Channel, and thinking of his efforts without pride. A *laggard in love and a dastard in war*—the old verse, learned at school, was what he thought most aptly described him now.

It was at that moment of utter dejection and self-disgust that Mrs. Apthorpe knocked upon his door.

He had not heard a cab drive up, for there had been a heavy snowfall, and besides there was straw on Doughty Street for the sake of an invalid in the next house, but he heard a firm step on the stair and a Yankee drawl he knew as soon as the landlady pushed his door ajar. He was out on the landing before she had time to announce his visitor, and wringing the hand of Frank Hartzell.

"My dear Hartzell—my dear Frank!" he said, when he had got the younger man into the warm room and divested him of his heavy ulster, smelling of fog and Atlantic spray. "Of all people in the world, you're the most welcome! Where did you come from, when did you get here, how long are you staying in town? Mrs. Apthorpe, please let me have a kettle of boiling water—and lemons—and sugar, as quickly as you can. Frank, I'll brew you a toddy every bit as good as we drank at Suez! Pull up your chair man; let me put these papers out of the way—"

Frank, delighted by the warmth of his welcome, watched James as he hurriedly poked the fire to a blaze, adjusted an iron trivet on the grate to hold the kettle, got tumblers and a glass bowl from the sideboard and began arranging them in a cleared space on the table. The American saw that this was the James Bruce of Egypt —no suggestion of slippered ease about him at his own fireside this winter night, no relaxation in a velvet jacket; he was wearing his boots and his dark business suit like a man ready at any moment to start on a journey. The same in his quick, decided movements, in his way of taking charge of a situation; but the human warmth and the expansive greeting added up to something new.

"Jim, it's great to see you," Frank said, taking the brimming glass. "Best of luck. Good God!" he added, "I'd forgotten your brew packed such a punch! How've you been?"

"Pretty fair. You're looking well. America seems to have agreed with you."

"It did after the first month." They settled down with their feet on the fender. "I tangled with the Hartzell boys, and things didn't work out there, so they let me go. Not that it mattered a damn, because Mr. Bertaux put me in charge of all his interests in the U.S. and I moved right out of Philly and up to New York."

He described in some detail the office he had opened for the S.A. Bertaux in West Street, and the plans for future development which he had come to Europe to discuss with his employer. He was, as always, enthusiastic about Bertaux, whom he described as having a rough time at Tours, but he did not mention either of Michel Bertaux' nieces. James listened with strained attention for the name d'Arbonne.

"How are you planning to go to France?" he asked abruptly. "The provisional government has been at Bordeaux for days now —you must have known that before you sailed."

"Yes—that was what finally decided Mr. Bertaux to recall me. He thought I could reach him with less difficulty at a port than when they were at Tours; he says it's almost impossible for even an American citizen to travel cross-country."

"They got out of Tours only just in time. General Chanzy withdrew from the city yesterday; the Germans will march in

291

today. But are the Transatlantique boats going in to Bordeaux yet? I hadn't heard of it."

"No; that's the trouble, or was when I left New York. After Dieppe fell on the ninth, and the battle for Le Havre began, the Pereire company had to organize a new schedule. They're going into Bordeaux after Christmas—always provided the Germans don't get there first."

James sighed, and looked at a mahogany table, set beside his well-filled bookcase, on which was pinned an ordnance map of France with flags and pins showing the opposing armies and the riparian theatres of war extending towards the encircling seas. The Rhine, the Meuse, the Seine; the Loire, the Doubs and the Saône—each waterway showed the German arrows clearly pointing at the Channel, the Atlantic and the Mediterranean.

"I suppose the road to Bordeaux has been open ever since Orléans fell," he said. "Good God, Frank, what a series of defeats —and beyond the battlefield, what suffering! Think of the hostages shot because one so-called German 'tourist' hasn't received the proper civilities from some poor devils of French peasants! Think of the villages razed to the ground and the inhabitants killed or burned alive because *one* household has been discovered sheltering *francs-tireurs*! You Americans must have heard that the Prussians shelled Strasbourg Cathedral and burned down the famous library, but do you know about Ablis and Chérisy and St. Dizier? Did you hear about the 'reprisals' at Beaurepaire and Voucq and Grandes Armoises? Are you just as willing as we are, to stand aside and look on?"

Frank watched James as he talked with that fierce animation which made him look young again in spite of the new grey in his hair, while the dark eyes burned with the passion which, Frank had always known, a noble cause could kindle in them. He was fathoms deep in it, poor devil! Obsessed with it! That map and the papers on the table—all those damning facts and names tripping and stumbling off his tongue! Perhaps now, while James rose to mix a fresh supply of toddy, was the time to say what he had come to say.

"Jim," he began carefully, "do you remember that letter you

wrote me way back there in August, when I was in Philadelphia with Hartzell Brothers? You asked me a question that I couldn't answer, and I let it go, because I didn't know what to say to you at that time."

"A question?" said James Bruce, hedging. "What question, Frank?"

"Don't tell me you can't remember, because I know you do. You asked me if I had any news of the d'Arbonne girls."

"Well?" said James with difficulty. "Here it comes," he thought. "I knew as soon as he came in tonight that he'd something to tell me. Something that will resolve this terrible deadlock. Our meeting at Suez led me to Madeleine, our meeting tonight may lead me back to her."

"Well, I hadn't then, but I have now. I got a letter from Louise two weeks ago, posted in Bordeaux. What she had to tell me was so serious that I decided to travel by London and talk to you about it, before I went to France. I could have written, I suppose, but frankly I didn't know how to put what I wanted to say on paper without making it read as if I were butting in on your private affairs. After all, I had no idea how *you* felt about Madeleine d'Arbonne. It was just an idea Louise had, months ago; but when I found out what was going on I figured that just possibly you might want to know."

Frank paused. It was a bitterly cold night, and James had forgotten to build up the fire, but he was sweating. The man on the other side of the fireplace seemed to have nothing to say.

"Mr. Bertaux didn't send for me just to discuss the American operation, Jim. I could have gone ahead for a while on written instructions. But he thought that if I—being a neutral—came to France, I might be able to help out with the situation at Arbonne."

"What's that?" said James with difficulty.

"They've had Prussians quartered on them since the beginning of December."

"*Oh, my God!*"

"It was the stabling that did it, quite as much as the château. There's space for three hundred horses in the Cardinal's Stables.

Anyway the 1st Kaiser's Uhlans moved out there from Fontaine-bleau three weeks ago."

"And Louise wrote to tell you so?"

"No, no; it was Mr. Bertaux who cabled; *her* letter was dated early in November. God! it drives me crazy to think of Louise there with the Prussians! I do see that Bertaux can't get back: he's a minister, and the Prussians would hold him as a hostage; and of course her father, poor old boy, is no use at all. But where the hell is Victor? He gave his parole to the Prussians and went to Belgium. Why doesn't *he* go home and look after Louise and Miss Elisabeth?"

"Who's Miss Elisabeth?"

"Her father's cousin—the only woman she has with her for company."

"*Then where's Madeleine?*"

"In Paris."

It was told at last. They had both started to their feet. Frank felt his shoulders gripped by Bruce's powerful hands.

"Are you telling me that she *went back* to Paris?"

"She never went to Arbonne. She's been in Paris ever since the revolution. Louise thought she was with Bertaux, and Bertaux thought she was down in the country with Louise."

"But Dr. Evans told me she went to Arbonne after she left the Empress at Deauville."

"Deauville?" Frank shook his head helplessly. "I don't know anything about that. You asked Evans? You were trying to find out where she was? I haven't done wrong in coming to you?"

With a groan, Bruce relaxed his hold on the young American and turned away. He was trembling.

"You didn't do wrong. I'm the one! I left her, and the Empress left her, and now her brother and her uncle have shown how much they care about her. . . . Are you seriously telling me that in 1870 a grown woman can disappear and her family take it for granted that she is safe in one home if not in another—?"

"Steady!" said Frank. "She didn't disappear for long, and they're worried to death about it. She wrote and asked Louise not to tell their uncle that she'd gone to live with old Henriett d'Arbonne; and Louise kept her secret until she got frightened, and told Bertaux the whole story a few weeks ago."

"But Bertaux made no attempt to get her out of Paris?"

"How could he, Jim?"

"I could!" said James. "I will!"

His hands were clenched, his head flung up to meet the challenge.

"Six months ago I asked Madeleine to marry me," he said to Frank Hartzell. "She refused. I was—I was angered by the reasons she gave, and I went away. If I had been half a man I would have gone straight to France after I saw Evans at Hastings, but I was still standing on my damnable weak pride, and I failed her then. Now you've given me another chance. I'll go to look for her! I'll start for Paris tomorrow!"

"But my God!" said Frank, "not even a neutral can get in or out of Paris! Old Washburne, for all his pull with von Bismarck, only got the American residents away in a *group*, and the British have only private citizens to watch out for them since their Ambassador went to Bordeaux! You'd have no status and no protecting power if you were arrested as a Prussian spy—"

"I'll apply to the Consul General of Monaco," said James with the ghost of a smile. "He had the guts to stay on in Paris, with your man Washburne. Besides, I think I know a way of getting in to Paris, and out of it too, without using a balloon. Look here!"

He took up the reading lamp and held it over the side table. Frank saw another chart pinned beside the ordnance map of France. On this, enlarged to scale by the engineer from the war maps in the newspapers, was shown the enceinte and glacis of the Paris fortifications, with every fort clearly marked, and also every abortive sortie which the French had made from the attempt at Châtillon at the very beginning of the siege, through the great battle of Le Bourget in late October, to the desperate attempt at Vincennes early in December which was to have brought the Parisians out to join Gambetta in the forest of Fontainebleau.

"I can see three ways to get into Paris, even now. By the Seine, for wherever there are water gates there's a more vulnerable kind of defence than under the forts. By Versailles, under a flag of truce from German Great Headquarters—very difficult. And somewhere hereabouts—somewhere between Brie and Coulommiers and St. Denis, where all the British and American ambulance units have been operating lately. I'll see Colonel Loyd Lindsay about that first thing tomorrow morning."

Although he knew the man he had to deal with, so much brisk assurance was more than Frank expected. He himself had planned to reach Fontainebleau from Bordeaux, although the Red Prince's Second Army lay across the way. To go from Fontainebleau into Paris was a feat he regarded as impossible.

"I think I can get you a berth on the *Massilia*," said James. "She leaves Southampton tomorrow night for Marseilles and Alexandria, and I've an idea she isn't fully booked. I can bunk for'ard myself, if I have to. Yes; that's the way to do it, start north from Marseilles and go first to Fontainebleau; then you stay with Miss Louise and I'll go to Paris. What's the matter?" he said impatiently. "You think it's a roundabout way home, to go all the way down to the Mediterranean? It'll be the shortest in the long run."

Eleven was chiming from St. Pancras' clock when Frank took his departure, and Bruce insisted on walking down with him to the cab rank at the corner of the Gray's Inn Road. It was not so much solicitude for the American which took him out as his own restlessness. The comfortable parlour, scented with whisky and pipe tobacco and the tasty supper Mrs. Apthorpe had brought in on a tray at ten o'clock, was too small to hold him then. He had to be out of doors, atrociously cold though the night was—when they drew the heavy plush curtains to look out on Doughty Street they saw that a thick coating of frost had formed inside the window of the warm room. There was no one in sight, when they let themselves out quietly, but a constable flashing his bull's eye lantern into the areas. The man gave them good night as they went past, and said the weather was "orful"—there was white rime on his moustache.

"I don't envy him his job tonight," said Frank.

"He has a warm uniform, and a tripe supper waiting when he gets home—and first, a good brew-up of tea in the police station

They were silent, thinking of other men in uniform in the trenches just across the Channel.

"God!" said Frank, as they turned into Theobald's Road. "What an amazing thing to be in London. So near them and yet—it's another world."

"We'll be in their world in a few days."

"You really think we can do it?" asked Frank.

"I know we can," said James. "Here's a growler, by good luck. Hi, cabby! Off you go, Frank; sleep well, and get that letter of recommendation from the American Minister, if it takes you all the morning. I'll join you in the station buffet at Waterloo."

James walked in the same direction as the "growler" for a dozen yards, then saw its flickering tail lamp turn off for Holborn, and himself walked off along the Gray's Inn Road. In that thoroughfare, leading to a railway terminal, the gin palaces and ale bars were still doing a roaring trade, and the eating shops, which remained open until midnight, were busy serving fish suppers and savoury messes of stewed eels and chitterlings. Over the district hung the rich meaty smell of Victorian London, compounded of beer and swipes, beef dripping, horse droppings and the smoke from a million coal fires all pressed down on the city by the iron hand of frost and fog.

"Won't you come on with us to the Bitter Lakes?"

He could almost hear the laughing voice as he walked north with great strides, his feet slipping occasionally on the treacherous coating of frozen mud but his head in the stars. Yes—he was going on with her now! He would deliver her out of the beleaguered city! As he walked home along Guilford Street, through the island capital which could never conceivably be threatened by an enemy, James tried to put out of his mind the threat of the Prussian guns, and to picture Madeleine asleep in some old-fashioned room, warm under many blankets, with her fair hair spilled across the pillow.

But Madeleine was not asleep. She was driving her ambulance back to the Slaughterhouses of La Villette after delivering her tenth load of the day's wounded at the St. Louis Hospital.

She was driving a team of broken-winded hacks from the Petites Voitures along dark streets, lit only at the intersections by the oil *reverbères* of an earlier day, through the dim watery regions where the canals of St. Denis and L'Ourcq meet in a dismal confluence. She had a dresser with her—Monsieur Hippolyte Gontard, an elderly pharmacist, one of her new friends from the rue de Lille—as stunned and silent as herself. In all the weeks they had worked together since the Bagneux sortie in the middle of October, they had seen nothing like that day's slaughter outside the Gate of La Villette.

In the bitter cold of twelve below zero one hundred and forty thousand men had fought all day long over the flat land to the northeast of Paris. Now the Prussian medical corpsmen were working furiously from their headquarters at Le Bourget, the French ambulances were moving in an almost unbroken convoy from La Villette, but both sides knew, by midnight, that many of the wounded were fated to die of exposure before the dawn. The French had planned a sortie on the grand scale to recapture the village of Le Bourget and drive on up the Lille road to effect a junction with Faidherbe and the Army of the North. By the ill luck which dogged so many of their efforts, a pigeon carrying the details of the operation to Gambetta fell into Prussian hands, and the sortie speedily became a massacre. The battle spread out from the Flanders road across the plain of Avron until by noon the whole northern perimeter of Paris was engaged. The Forts were firing from Mont Valérien right round to Nogent. The deadly little Krupp three-hundred-pounders were replying, and the plateau of Avron turned into a vast senseless scene of carnage as terrible as the fields of Sedan or Mars-la-Tour. Darkness alone put an end to the conflict. The remnants of the French Marines, as always the backbone of the assault, marched back into Paris with their heads high. The others trailed back as best they might, and the ambulance wagons crept out to seek the wounded on the frozen plain.

"I see the lights of the Abattoirs," said Gontard, breaking the silence. "Thank God!"

Madeleine's reply was muffled by the heavy scarf she wore over

298

an infantryman's képi, twisted round her head, mouth and nostrils. The red flares which marked the Slaughterhouses in the darkness of La Villette made the place seem like an anteroom of hell. More human blood had run into the drains that day than ever flowed at a peacetime Christmas when the plentiful carcasses of beef and mutton were dressed for Paris tables. The army surgeons were operating all night long, without anaesthetics—the chloroform supplies were finished—and down at the Cattle Market the Sisters of Charity were praying over those who had died on the way back to Paris, *morts pour la France.*

"You boys!" cried Gontard, as they swung into the yard, "help my driver down!"

The half-grown lads who blanketed the animals and scrubbed the wagon between trips ran out to help Madeleine as she slipped stiffly from her seat. She staggered a little as Gontard gave her his arm into the field kitchen, and went to forage for them both.

Madeleine stripped her gloves off painfully, and stuck them inside the front of her sheepskin jacket when Gontard brought her a glass of hot grog. The strong navy rum was something better than she had expected: sometimes there was nothing but *petit noir,* a vile brew of sugar, coffee grounds and the lees of brandy boiled up and sold in a hundred shacks along the line of the fortifications, and brought down in boilers to the field kitchens. After a few swallows she was able to go up to the long table for a piece of bread.

By the petroleum flares Madeleine d'Arbonne, like James Bruce, was still recognizable. She was even beautiful, although no Romantic painter would have chosen her as a model now. Perhaps a Manet could have given full value to the planes of that hollowed face shining with its own inner light.

She had strained her body severely, at first, in lifting and carrying the wounded. Very strong for a woman, she knew exactly where to apply the strength in her hands and knees when riding or driving, but the muscular force required to lift a man half as heavy again as herself was something she had to cultivate, just as she had to practise the broken step of the stretcher bearer. She learned how to fling herself flat on the ground when mortar fire began from some zealous German battery still intent on shelling a battlefield given up to the missions of mercy, and how to subdue her rearing leaders when one of the wheelers collapsed and died between the shafts. *That* cost her a dislocated wrist, jerked into place with the maximum of pain by a young intern at a field hospital where she sometimes stood looking in, with a touching admiration, at the wards where Sisters of Charity and civilian nurses took their healing way from cot to cot.

No soldier ever called Madeleine the Angel of the Battlefield, or kissed her shadow when she went by, as the Crimean wounded did for Florence Nightingale. It was doubtful if any of the men whom she succoured realized that the driver in the shapeless garments, who bent over them where they lay in their blood and excrement was a woman. It was doubtful if she thought of herself as a woman when she raised a wounded man on her right arm, where the muscles now stood out like whipcord and the engorged veins bulged above swollen wrist and blistered hand. But the orderlies and drivers who saw her in the lit *salles de garde* or the field kitchens, when the scarf and képi were off and the lamplight fell on her fair hair, were as much aware of her sex as the men who had danced with her at the Tuileries, and when she laughed, and made a cynical joke or two, she could bring them all around her in the old way.

At the Slaughterhouses of La Villette there was no time for laughing, and very little for food and drink. Madeleine's team was ordered out almost immediately to go after a band of wounded reported stumbling away in the direction of the quarries near Belleville, where the limestone kilns, always burning, held a fatal attraction for freezing men, who had already been found suffocated by their fumes of the kilns as they tried to get some heat into their wretched bodies. Four teams were detached at once to move south by the Pantin Gate to round up the stragglers. Madeleine thanked God that groping round the canals was over for a time. She was hardened to the bitter cold, the spill of blood upon the snow, the smell of gangrened flesh, but all that night she had been terrified of driving out across some broken bridge and straight into the water. It was easier to look for wounded men in the pits they dug out and covered with doors and shutters from the shattered hamlets, for the little fires they kindled in these shelters twinkled further than they knew.

Some of the wounded, unable to find firewood, did little more with their entrenching tools than dig their graves that night. In shallow pits, huddled under sacks and sheepskins, nine hundred men were found frozen to death on the plain outside Paris when morning broke.

Madeleine spent all the hours of darkness looking for survivors, and she was still alive at the end of the shortest day and the longest night of 1870.

IV

James Bruce rose before six o'clock next morning, impatient to
start preparing for his journey to France. The parlour fire, covered
with small pieces of coal and dross, was quickly coaxed into a
blaze, and he sat down in his warm wool dressing gown for an
hour's intensive study of his map of the fortifications of Paris.
When certain details were firmly fixed in his memory he went
into his dressing room, where he could hear Mrs. Apthorpe's
domestic setting down the first of the big copper kettles for his
hip bath, and said to the girl,

"Would you bring me a pot of strong Indian tea, as quickly as
you can? No breakfast this morning; I'm going out of town."

He drank the tea in gulps as he moved about, laying out the
warmest clothing he could find. A brass-bound chest, the old-
fashioned "donkey" which he had taken to sea as a Third Engineer, yielded up the money belt he had worn on the rough
journeys of the late Fifties, in which he could carry two hundred
gold sovereigns round his waist. There was another item, carefully
wrapped, at the foot of the chest, which he took out and weighed
thoughtfully in his hand — the pistol which he had used more
than once in those rough-and-tumble days in the past. He put the
heavy Smith and Wesson back in its place reluctantly: if he were
stopped by the Prussians, or by the *francs-tireurs*, it might be as
damning for a neutral traveller to be found carrying a pistol as a
plan of the Sixteen Forts.

For luggage he selected a light, capacious carpetbag and for
outer wear an Inverness cape with pockets deep enough to hold
shaving tackle and a change of linen. Into one of the pockets he
doubled a deerstalker cap, for ears had to be protected against
the terrible frost, and an old Bruce tartan plaid was folded to
serve as a travelling rug.

By eight o'clock he was ready to start on a round of visits, beginning with breakfast at the home of Colonel Loyd Lindsay and

ending with a long talk with Mr. Bullock at the *Daily News* office. The King of Prussia's watch was taken out of his pocket more often than usual that morning as the old compulsive need for haste drove James on through his vital interviews. At last he had the letters he required, and stopping only at a City grocer's to buy some emergency rations and have his flask filled, he paid a visit to his bank, and just after half-past ten arrived at 122 Leadenhall Street.

James had been working for some time at the London Docks, where the supply ships *Haddington* and *Indus* were being converted from sail to steam. His ear had not been kept to the ground at Leadenhall Street, though he knew that his kind friend Mr. Allan, to whom alone he could have explained his reasons for going to France, was confined to bed with one of the hard chest coughs produced by frost and fog in London. He was told when he asked for an interview that he would have to see the Assistant Manager, who could "perhaps fit him in" between a conference with the President of the Board of Trade and an early luncheon with the Lord Mayor of London at the Mansion House.

"Stately names," said Bruce to the confidential clerk. "Tell him my business is urgent."

He filled in time by getting Frank Hartzell a single-berth cabin, the last accommodation available aboard the *Massilia*.

Thomas Sutherland, the prodigy of the P. and O., gave himself a few minutes for reflection before sending his clerk to bring James Bruce to his private room. He was coming face to face, a little before he had intended, with an unhappy situation. He had tried to keep an open mind about "Mr. James," knowing quite well that Arthur Anderson had always hoped that Bruce, the Scots engineer, and Sutherland, the English administrator, might one day work in double harness, and had listened attentively to all the opinions of Bruce which he could cull from the Court of Directors. These fell into two categories, neither half-hearted: an influential majority which called him "a first-class engineer—striking personality—does the Company credit wherever he goes!" and a vocal minority which called him a bitter-tongued devil and a bully. Bruce had trodden on a good many toes inside the Company, but Mr. Sutherland had trodden on enough toes himself on the way to an Assistant Managership at thirty-five not to be unduly concerned about that. He had honourably put out of his head any prejudice he might have had against the brother of Robert Bruce, the Chief Engineer of the *Sunda*, whose dealings on the side were perfectly well known to the young man who had been the leading and best-informed British resident of Hong Kong; but for the past five or six months he had simply sat back and watched James Bruce behaving "like a fanatic," "like a bull in a china shop"—with the growing conviction that after all the man was not a sound Managerial prospect.

"Go to France on private business!" he repeated incredulously a few minutes later. "Pray has this anything to do with the war charities which take up so much of your time?"

"More or less," said James. The touch of mendacity was disagreeable to him, but he had no intention of trailing his coat in front of "young" Sutherland. "Colonel Loyd Lindsay is concerned in the matter, too."

"Loyd Lindsay—British War Relief, h'm? How many distressed British subjects do you expect to succour at Marseilles, Mr. Bruce?"

"I hope to get Mr. Albert Estrine's help in that, Mr. Sutherland," said James adroitly. "He is the Society's local representative."

"True," agreed Sutherland, slightly mollified by the name of the P. and O. agent. "It *would* be interesting to get his first-hand report of the Communist riots of a few weeks ago, but I don't like to feel you're holding a pistol to my head. You tell me you want to leave in the *Massilia* tonight, whereas if you'd wait until next week we could make arrangements for you to go on to Brindisi— Mr. Hadow and I were talking about that this very morning. Yes!"—with a cold smile for Bruce's look of surprise—"your French friends, by blowing up their own railroads and sabotaging the free run of mail from the Channel to Marseilles, have driven us into making a new postal agreement with the Italian Government. From now on the mail goes overland to Brindisi and transfers to the Alexandria run there. The operation may need a little supervising at first, and as we know you're *persona gratissima* with the Brindisi port authorities we thought it would make a pleasant midwinter break for you."

"How long would you wish me to remain there?"

Behind this stalling query Bruce's mind was working fast. Southern Italy and the drowsy Adriatic shore! Just the place for Madeleine to recuperate from the horrors of the siege—if he could get her out without delay!

"About a month, I should think. Then, I must tell you, we've seriously considered sending you on to Alexandria as general manager. That base will continue to be important for many years to come: it has gained rather than lost by the Canal opening; and we think your long friendship with de Lesseps is a great asset—far more important than that row you had last year with Ismail Pasha. An appropriate residence and entertainment allowance of course go with the post."

Well, that—that might be a wonderful idea! She might like that a great deal better than London! James knew the kind of residence which Sutherland had in mind—one of the big white villas on the sea front near Ras-el-Tin, with tall cool rooms and a garden with palms and tuberoses, and a fountain. Madeleine walking with him there when the evening breeze blew off the Mediterranean!

"This is a generous proposal, Mr. Sutherland. May I ask for a little time to consider it?"

"If I were you I'd close with it at once."

The touch of asperity in the reply roused James's suspicions. Were they trying to move him out of London permanently?

"Is there so much hurry?" he asked. "You know I've had good reason to consider myself a fixture in Head Office."

"Well, Mr. Bruce," said the Assistant Manager, losing patience with him, "an absence from London at this time might be the best possible thing for your future in the Company. Some of the Directors take very strong exception to your stand on the war between France and Prussia. It's not the charity work! no," he said, raising his hand as Bruce was about to interrupt, "we have *all* gladly contributed to the funds to alleviate suffering, whether of the Parisians, or the peasants, or the prisoners. But your public statements have not been confined to charity. Some of them have been reported in the public prints and you have always been identified in the reports as a servant of this Company. I have here"—and he opened a file which his clerk had handed him, just before Bruce's entry—"not only reports of what you have said, but a cutting of your letter to *The Times* newspaper, urging Britain to enter the war on the side of France."

"As has been urged in the House of Commons again and again in recent weeks."

"The P. and O. doesn't pay the salaries of Members of Parliament, Mr. Bruce."

"And because it pays mine am I to be silent on one of the vital issues of our time? I wrote that letter, sir, after deep reflection. After the Russians made a deal with Bismarck to denounce their Crimean treaty obligations to ourselves! After the German armies reached the shores of the English Channel! After General von Alvensleben ordered IV Corps to face towards England and give three cheers for King and Fatherland, whereupon they ran into the sea like the Gadarene swine, ready to gobble *us* up when Paris falls! . . . I know our little army, barely ninety thousand strong, is not capable of giving the French the full support they need. But we could create a diversion by landing troops across the Channel, and clear ourselves of the suspicion of being the lackey of Prussia!"

"Now, Bruce, there's absolutely no reason to send a British Expeditionary Force to France. Let the French settle their own quarrels before they involve us—and what quarrels! First the Emperor against the Republicans, now the Provisional Government against the Reds—what the *devil* has any of that to do with us? It's even doubtful if they're waging war whole-heartedly! I read 'Labby's' diary in the *Daily News*—according to him the National Guards and the Mobiles inside Paris are drunk most of the time—"

"But not so drunk," said James wickedly, "as the German Third Army, which General Philip Sheridan, U.S.A., saw laying an almost continuous line of empty bottles from Sedan to Paris! Not so drunk as the German troops in Vandenheim whom his country-woman Miss Clara Barton found more given to rape and murder than all the soldiers of the Civil War put together! Eh, Mr. Sutherland? These are statements by neutrals which pro-Germans don't care to have quoted—"

"And neither do I," said Thomas Sutherland. "Not because I'm pro-German, as you call it, but because I simply do not see what all this has to do with our country or the Company. I consider your incitement to enter the war a public disservice, Mr. Bruce! Surely the one thing that can be said for this unhappy conflict is that it has *not* become a European war. The Parisians have only to surrender, and accept Bismarck's peace terms, for France to have a chance to redeem herself—"

"*Redeem* herself!" said Bruce with a snarl. "Who are we—the Pharisees?"

In the end, of course, he left for France in the *Massilia*. It would have been hard for Sutherland to refuse any employee of Bruce's seniority the right to take a leave for "urgent private affairs"; he granted it with the condition that the engineer should express no political opinions in public while in France. Bruce was just in time to meet Frank Hartzell and catch the boat train at Waterloo.

They had a stormy passage through the Bay of Biscay. James spent most of his time in the engine room, thereby causing a mild panic among the younger officers waiting for promotion, and Frank, who was prostrate with seasickness, saw little of him until they berthed in the Bassin de la Joliette. The American would gladly have spent a night at the Hotel de Noailles to get his land legs back, but Bruce was "in transit" now, with a vengeance, and could think only of moving north at speed. It was a relief to Frank to learn at the Gare St. Charles that the only train north left at five in the afternoon, a delay which at least gave him time to call at the Bertaux offices. If there was communication with Bordeaux, he could send Bertaux a message just before the train left—"*proceeding Arbonne direct*" would be disarming, in case his master should think he ought to have gone to Bordeaux first.

He found Mr. Estrine, the P. and O. agent, at the station with James when he returned, in great excitement, shortly before five o'clock.

"Say, do you know who's going to Lyons on this train?" Frank burst out. "Do you know who's been stirring up *more* trouble in Marseilles, so that Bertaux has a double guard all round his warehouses? Cluseret!"

"Oh, my God," said James, staring. "Cross Keys—I didn't think of it."

"I've been telling Mr. Bruce about this man Cluseret," said Estrine. He had known and liked Frank Hartzell earlier in the year—now he was beginning to think, from the samples before him, that the men coming in from "outside" were at least as crazy as the war-distracted people of France. "Monsieur Bertaux' warehouses are not the only Marseilles establishments to be guarded against Red looting, incited and even led by Cluseret in person. I'm delighted to know he's leaving town."

"Frank, it won't help our mission to get mixed up in any argument with General Cluseret," Bruce warned. "Come on and let's take our places. Mr. Estrine has very kindly prepared a dinner basket for us; we shan't starve yet awhile."

In the unaccustomed rôle of peacemaker, Bruce persuaded the American to get on board the train. The corner seats in their coupé had been taken by four sullen, silent French businessmen, each with his eyes already closed and his travelling rug pulled high round his waist—each a separate island of anxiety, suspicion of his neighbour and resentment of the foreigners. They made way ungraciously for James and Frank in the middle of the carriage.

Mr. Estrine had warned them to talk as little as possible, either in English or in French. The spy mania was as rabid in the south as in Paris, and anyone suspected of being one of Bismarck's "German tourists" might easily be dragged off a train and summarily dealt with; the League of the South held the Rhône valley in a grip of terror, and even an American citizen and a representative of British war charities might not escape from a drumhead court-martial. They took his advice and assumed attitudes as reserved as their neighbours', with the Bruce tartan plaid spread out between them.

The carriage was unheated, but the small oil lamp swinging in the ceiling and the breath of six human beings produced in time a kind of animal warmth. After they had eaten, James fell into a waking doze. He had slept very little on the voyage and was more tired than he realized. His head jerked forward from time to time and then his eyes opened: whenever this happened he saw Frank sitting in the same attitude, with his arms folded and a hard expression on his face.

"What a good fellow he is!" thought James between his waking dreams. "Here with me instead of with Bertaux at Bordeaux, and keeping his mouth shut about Cluseret and Cross Keys! We must not get mixed up in politics—Sutherland was right, more right than he knew, if all Estrine says is true." Furtively he eyed the men around them. They didn't *look* like Reds, or Southern Leaguers—or fighting men of any sort, for that matter. Silk merchants from Lyons, perhaps, cursing Gambetta for continuing the war. Estrine had said it was very unpoplar in the provinces. James dozed again.

He dreamed of Alexandria, and a white house beside the sea, and a girl like an empress standing by his side when they received de Lesseps (but in the dream de Lesseps had his father's face) or sailing with him down-Canal to Ismailia. She walked on the promenade in her violet gandoura, just a little bit ahead of him always; beckoning. "*Won't you come on with us to the Bitter Lakes?*" . . .

"You were talking in your sleep, James," said Frank, touching him on the knee. "Let's have some wine."

To James the night seemed long. He tried to concentrate—to recreate and mentally enlarge the details of the map he had memorized, which was to show him the way into Paris. For the first time his confidence faltered as the chill of midnight invaded the train and cramped the wakeful mind as well as the limbs. It was almost a relief when three of their fellow passengers roused them by getting out at Avignon. The fourth kept them company all the way to Lyons. As soon as he had gone Frank sprang to the window.

"Let's see if we can see him!"

A procession of men carrying the Tricolore crossed with the Red Flag were marching up the platform, chanting some sort of anthem—not the *Marseillaise*—which made most of the travellers scowl and move away as quickly as they could.

"There he is!"

A tall, theatrically handsome man of about fifty, with a cavalry swagger, was striding down the platform bestowing handshakes and waves of the hand on the reception committee. He was followed by a man whom Frank identified as George Train, the American Communist, and another whom both recognized from his many photographs as Mikhail Bakunin, a leading Russian anarchist.

"So that's Cluseret."

"That's Cluseret. The man who makes trouble everywhere he goes. An American citizen by Act of Congress, who disobeyed Frémont's orders and got the 27th Pennsylvania cut to pieces at Cross Keys. Who turned Red in New York! Whom Washburne wouldn't lift a finger to help, citizen or no citizen, when the Imperial Government deported him from France as a dangerous agitator! He and Comrade Train are certainly doing the Union proud."

Frank sat down dispiritedly as a vendor with a pushcart came up to the window, and James bought bread and vile coffee, a variant of the *petit noir* of the Paris fortifications, without the lees of brandy and with watered milk added instead. "Now Cluseret is supposed to be fighting the Prussians alongside his old friend Garibaldi, with a little sabotage thrown in on the side. I don't like it, Jim. I don't like it at all! You saw that demonstration on the platform! Is that man for or against the government? Can Gambetta really win a war on two fronts, if he has to fight the Reds as well as the Prussians? Does Cluseret *want* him to win?"

"I'd be sorry to think my friend Sutherland was right about the Reds," said James glumly. But Frank did not inquire who Mr Sutherland might be. Instead, he stood up and stretched, touching the ceiling with his doubled fists. The oil in the lamp was used up, and in the grey twilight under the station roof they could hardly see each other's faces. Frank said,

"There were quite a few soldiers of fortune in the Union Army, you know. Cluseret for one, and the Orléans princes on Mc-Clellan's staff—those I knew personally, and there were others. Now this French war is getting to be another free-for-all. They've got Cluseret back again, and Garibaldi, and I heard in Marseilles that they've organized an American Brigade—mostly Irishmen! I don't know—"

"You don't know what?" asked Bruce.

"I'm beginning to wonder if they'd like to have me too."

From London to Lyons their journey, while slow, had at least been uninterrupted. But now even this fortune deserted them. Their train was still standing in Lyons station at the hour when —said James, fuming—the prewar midnight train from Marseilles would have arrived in Paris. Their carriage slowly filled up with passengers; other passengers got in and out of the train and raged at the railroad officials, all with no result. In the afternoon, when they had eaten the last crumbs from Mr. Estrine's dinner basket (the station restaurants were closed and locked), a rumour began to spread that they had been waiting for a supply of coal, which had now arrived. Shortly after, they started out very slowly for Chalon-sur-Saône.

Beyond Chalon train travel was impossible. The Red Prince had cut the rails and blown up the viaducts as he went west in his flanking move on Orléans, and they had to bargain for seats in the antiquated diligences which were the only public transport available from one town to another. Between post stations the clumsy vehicles moved with incredible slowness. There were long waits for fresh horses, nearly all the livestock in the Department of the Yonne having been commandeered. There were two over-night stops at inns already plundered by the Prussians, and there were many plunging walks up the long hills between Chalon-sur-Saône and Saulieu. During those anxious days Frank's admiration and affection for James Bruce enormously increased. He was gentle

311

and sympathetic to the dazed country people who travelled with them from one village to another. He could walk for miles behind the diligence, with his head bent into the wind and snow and his tartan plaid round his shoulders, and then at the next *relais* set about instilling fresh energy into drivers and postboys, helping them to harness the wretched teams and urging them forward, always forward, until after two days' travel through the silent land they came to the last halt of the coach service at Fontainebleau.

Beyond Fontainebleau, to Paris and on to the Channel, the country was completely overrun by German troops. The diligence was directed into the yard behind the empty railroad station, and as the passengers descended one by one they were challenged by Prussian sentries and made to pass through a guardroom which had been set up in the freight offices beside the tracks.

"Your papers, please. Your name and occupation? Your business in Fontainebleau? Your address here?—" The interrogation was not brutal, but it was complete, conducted by a town major whose badges announced him to be one of "Prince Louis of Hesse's Own Royal Loyals"—for Queen Victoria's second son-in-law was also in the field and had been doing great things in the way of terrifying countryfolk and pillaging country homes.

The British and the American passports were laid silently in front of the town major.

"James Bruce, engineer. And Francis Durrant Hartzell, businessman." The officer looked up at both of them with narrowed eyes. "What brings *you* to Fontainebleau, gentlemen?"

"Pleasure," said James.

The Hessian looked out of the freight office window, at the bleak empty yard where snow was falling on the railroad sheds, and pursed his lips.

"Where have you come from?"

"Marseilles."

"You reside there?"

"Our addresses are on our papers."

"Do you speak German?"

"Enough," said James in that language. "I picked up a smattering on a job for the Prussian Government at Stettin."

"Very good! And you, Mr. Hartzell—*sprechen Sie Deutsch?*"

"Pennsylvania Dutch," said Frank.

"H'm! I ask, because while I can read English I cannot speak it well, and my French is—just sufficient for the present need. So you have come here for pleasure, sir?"

"He says he reads English," said James to Frank. "Show him that letter from your Minister in London."

There was silence in the guardroom, where they were the only two remaining travellers, while the major spelled out Minister Adams's stately phrases To Whom it Might Concern, begging extra special treatment for Mr. F. D. Hartzell of Philadelphia.

"Adams. Do you know Minister Washburne, sir?" he asked in his halting French.

"He's a personal friend of mine," said Frank.

"Well"—doubtfully—"we are always anxious to accommodate our American friends, and Mr. Washburne has rendered us very great services. . . . But I think I must ask you to give me a more precise reason than pleasure for your presence in Fontainebleau."

"I am on my way to visit a sick friend, sir—M. le Comte d'Arbonne, at his own home."

The major's face cleared as if by magic. He even smiled.

"Arbonne! Sergeant Teitelbaum, isn't that where Captain von Eckhardstein is commandant?"

The desk sergeant's dark, attentive, aquiline face flamed with intelligence.

"Yes, sir! With the 1st Kaiser's Uhlans, sir! Billeted there three weeks ago!"

"Why then," said the town major ironically, "I see no reason to impede your journey in any way. You will be going a few miles further forward than regulations permit, but I know you will be very, *very* well taken care of by the Graf von Eckhardstein!"

"So far so good!" said James as they drove out of Fontainebleau. "Smart fellow that Teitelbaum."

The swarthy sergeant had at once produced an elderly hackney driver with a horse and trap for hire, who was willing for an extortionate fare to drive them out to the château.

"I've run into the sergeant often," said Frank. "Backbone of any army." He looked curiously at his companion. "So far so good!" Had the Scotsman any idea of what lay ahead of him? As neutral travellers, well provided with money, their journey north had been merely slow and uncomfortable. What would it be like to go on through the whole Prussian Army and under the guns of Paris? Bruce's face showed no sign of doubt or weakening as he listened to the French driver's tale of woe. The oppressive measures of the Prussian troops and the high price of fodder and the risks he would run in going back alone through the forest after dark—the string of complaints droned on. As the last light of the last day of 1870 faded from the sky, and only the candles in the side lamps threw a faint glow on the snowy banks on either side of the road, Frank realized that the trees beneath which the Bertaux landau had bowled so smoothly in May had been cut down—whether for firewood or as road blocks against the relentless German advance he could not tell. The snow had stopped, and the first stars were shining. They had been travelling ten days to reach Arbonne, and now he was only a mile or two away from Louise.

"Here's a village," he heard James say. It was only a hamlet— a few cottages on each side of the highway, with all the wooden shutters closed and bolted, and just one lantern swinging over a door to show that human beings were still living there.

"It must be Barbizon," said Frank.

"*Oui, oui, c'est Barbizon*," said the driver, catching at the name. All the gentleness and security of Barbizon turned into this dumb, withdrawn, lockfast place! "The left-hand turning to Arbonne," said Frank with an aching throat. "We're nearly there."

Now the plain to cross, and the moon, four days past its full beginning to rise behind the dark mass of the forest, showing the little villages of Macherin, St. Martin, Arbonne itself and at last the curtain wall of the château. No darkness there! The guard houses on each side of the gate were full of soldiers. Lights were shining through all the slits of windows; lights could be seen over the wall in the upper floors of the château.

"Halt! Who goes there!"

"Friends," said James.

"Advance, friends, and give the countersign."

"Sorry," said James. "Don't know it! Call your sergeant, my man, and tell him there are visitors for Captain von Eckhardstein."

The sentries closed round them. There were four, the men at the corners of the wall having come up in response to a whistle from the men at the gate, all armed with rifles and bayonets and well protected from the cold by long grey overcoats, knitted balaclavas beneath their helmets and high boots with heavy leather soles. Their faces, young and blond and not at all unfriendly, looked up at James and Frank on the high seat of the broken-down trap.

James's authoritative manner, deplored by some Directors of the P. and O., was just the thing for the Prussians. Their sergeant, when he arrived, was almost obsequious. The bags were lifted out of the trap and carried into the guardhouse, and hands were extended to help travellers so numb with cold from their drive through the forest that their feet slipped on the high iron step as they got down. When the man was paid, and had whipped up his horse to make off back to Fontainebleau as fast as he could, and Frank and James were conducted through the gates which the men on guard dragged open, they heard heavy wooden bars fall into place behind them, and massive bolts shot home at the top and bottom. Frank had heard a prison gate close behind him with a very similar sound.

The sergeant, with a detail from the guardhouse, took them across the great courtyard to the château. Instinctively Frank and James fell into the same pace—Left! Right! Left! Right! their boots rang on the cobbles carefully brushed clear of snow. In the Cardinal's Stables troopers could be seen moving about by lantern light: on the left side of the courtyard the home farm was wrapped in the same darkness as Barbizon and the other villages of the war zone. Nearly every window of the château was brilliantly illuminated, not with the soft candlelight which Frank remembered from the summer, but with oil lamps of the Prussians' own installing. Left, Right. The sentries on the terrace wheeled at a shouted order from the sergeant to open the great door. James and Frank, with their escort, arrived in the black and white tiled hall. A Prussian flag had been pushed into the beak of one of the great bronze eagles, a Uhlan helmet was cocked drunkenly on the head of the other. Prussian officers looked down at them curiously from the gallery above. Then the drawing-room door opened, and there advanced to meet them the new master of the Château d'Arbonne, Hans Heinrich, Count von Eckhardstein.

"Oh, Frank! Oh, Frank!"

Before the Prussian commandant could speak, or the newcomers explain their presence, Louise d'Arbonne ran into the lamplit hall and straight into the arms of Frank Hartzell.

V

"Will you try to put yourself in my place, Mr. Bruce?"

James and Captain von Eckhardstein were alone in the dining room, from which Louise—with incredulous joy, as she told them —had watched them walk across the courtyard. The entire suite of rooms on the right of the hall, the dining room, library and small bookroom in the tower, had been given up to the d'Arbonne family, as the Prussian was careful to point out to James. His great desire, he said, was to be "correct." The dining table and chairs had been removed, of course, but no further than the back drawing room, now the officers' mess; the Aubusson carpet—well, he wasn't quite sure what had happened to that, but it couldn't be very far away, and he absolutely agreed with James that it was too bad the painted eyes of all the d'Arbonne ancestors had been drilled out during a little indoor pistol practice. They were standing now beside the buffet, on which a bottle of champagne had been placed by a Prussian orderly, and the commandant was alternating gulps with puffs at one of Bertaux' fine cigars.

"I *might* just have believed your story, fantastic though it is, if you hadn't brought Mr. Hartzell along with you. One has only to look at your worthy Scots face—if you'll permit a personal remark —to believe in *you* as some kind of dominie: a welfare worker, or the agent of some charitable concern. But what am I to think of Mr. Hartzell, with whom my charming little hostess appears to be on very good terms, and who almost in his first words informs me proudly that he is the trusted representative of her uncle—a minister in Monsieur Trochu's cabinet! I noticed you didn't care for his explanation very much."

He stopped, and quizzically regarded the ash forming on his cigar. It was a studied gesture, as much part of the accepted "style" of the Prussian officer of 1870 as the Heidelberg duelling scars and the monocle swinging at the neck of his mess jacket. Eckhardstein was a handsome man of about thirty-five who could

317

be pleasant when he was enjoying himself, and at the moment he was enjoying himself very much indeed. James, who had left his champagne untouched, now lifted the glass to his dry mouth and drank.

"So when you tell me that you're here on a mission to the neutral ambulance corps, and that you want to be sent on your way to their base at Brie-Comte-Robert, I must reply with great regret that if the ambulance men really want you they must come here and fetch you. I can't and won't supply you with transport of any sort to get yourself into the combat zone at Brie."

"Then will you send me back to Fontainebleau in the morning, captain? I believe the town major may prove more co-operative than yourself."

"I doubt it. But in any case tomorrow is New Year's Day, and we Prussians have so much to celebrate that I certainly won't detail any of my men to escort you to Fontainebleau. I don't know if you're aware that King Wilhelm is shortly to assume the title of German Emperor, in a ceremony planned to take place at Versailles about the middle of the month?"

"Exquisite taste," said James with a slight bow.

"We hope the French will think so. After all they do consider themselves the arbiters of taste and elegance in Europe, don't they? Perhaps we can persuade them to surrender before the event takes place. However, that's beside the point, which is that I'm afraid you and that charming American gentleman must reconcile yourselves to being our guests for at least the next few days. The bedrooms upstairs are all in use, but I shall have your bags and a couple of folding cots carried in here, and I'm sure you'll be quite comfortable. There's a dressing room behind the library, I believe."

"I should hesitate to trespass on the privacy of the ladies, sir."

"Isn't it rather late to think of that? Uninvited guests can hardly be choosers, you know, and frankly I shall be happier if I know you're getting a good night's rest in a place where I can keep a sentry on the door. . . . We shall be having some music later, to celebrate the Sylvesterabend. Would you and Mr. Harzell care to join us?"

318

"You must excuse us," said James briefly. "We've come a long way, and shall retire early."

"Tomorrow then? New Year's Day? You mustn't be too exclusive, Mr. Bruce. Give us the pleasure of knowing you a little better."

The library was almost in darkness. The big desk and oil lamps had been removed, and by the light of a pair of candles Mademoiselle Elisabeth kept her vigil beside the old Comte d'Arbonne. He lay, wrapped in a warm robe, on a kind of day-bed, already fallen into the light sleep of reaction from the bewildered excitement with which he had greeted the new arrivals. An arrangement of screens, at the end of the large room, hid the cots on which the old lady and Louise were accustomed to rest. James stood by the small wood fire and talked gently to the old Demoiselle, hearing about her anxiety over her sister in Paris, and the wonderful way dear Louise looked after everything, and how dreadful it was to have no news of Madeleine and Victor, while Louise and Frank talked in the little turret room. They had spent an hour together and looked relaxed and happy when James went in: the girl in one of the big chairs beside the fire, with Frank on a broad stool by her side, holding her hands in his. Happy enough, and secure enough, with the enemies of France all around them, to strike James Bruce with one of his rare pangs of envy.

"No luck!" he said, when Frank jumped up and asked a question. "He means to keep us here, some days."

"Mr. Bruce, Frank has been telling me that you want to go to Madeleine—I think it's wonderful, but oh! do you think you can? The farm people say the Prussians are everywhere between here and Paris, and all *round* Paris we know only too well—"

"The first thing is for me to get out of here."

He sat down, and made her talk to him quietly, telling all she knew about Madeleine's decision to remain in Paris; she showed him the only letter which had reached them, before the city gates were closed. September—and this was New Year's Eve! Exactly a year ago he had been on his way to Paris, to dance with her at the Tuileries ball! For a moment James's iron control deserted him, so that he put his hand over his eyes with a sound between a sigh and a sob. Louise made a tiny movement with her head to Frank, who slipped into the library and left them alone together.

"Mr. Bruce"—she had sunk to her knees on the floor beside him now—"you love my sister, don't you?"

"Yes, Louise. With all my heart."

"She loves you too, I think."

He took her small square hands in his. "Do you think so, my dear? Do you believe she'll be glad to see me, when I get to Paris?"

"How can you doubt it? But to get into Paris, even with the ambulances, as Frank says you mean to do, that will be terrible—and then, can you ever get her out?"

"Louise, I have to try."

She looked searchingly into his face: at the burning eyes, reddened by fatigue and winter weather, at the compressed lips and the firm, cleft chin. With a little sigh she acquiesced.

"I see you must. Then we have to get you away from here tonight, while they're all drinking and singing at their horrible party—but every night, to them, is an excuse for a party—"

"My dear child! Are you never afraid of them at such times?"

Louise shook her head proudly, and James looked at her with a new respect. The schoolroom miss he had met at Suez was woman now, and unmistakably a Frenchwoman, with the same implacable, stubborn look in her face which he had seen on other faces in the war zone—a look of bitterness and hating which had hollowed the cheeks and hardened the mouths of her whole generation.

"I was very frightened when they came here first," she told him. "Poor papa was terrified when they rode into the courtyard. He thought they were revolutionaries coming to take him away from me and send him back into exile; and Cousin Elisabeth had hysterics; but our farmer came and stood beside me on the terrace and I—I *talked* to them! I made them show me the requisitioning order, and I told them what rooms they must leave to us, and about the food and fuel we should need; and then, of course, the

320

stripped us of all the rest. But Monsieur von Eckhardstein prides himself on being 'correct,' " said Louise, and her lip curled. "I'm not afraid of *him* !"

"If I thought you were in any real danger," said James slowly, "I would stay with you, for a few days at least—"

"Don't you think they'll be in danger if we go away?" It was Frank who spoke from the open door. "If we do make a run for it, will that brute with the eyeglass go in for some sort of reprisals?"

James was silent. The whole tragic panorama of the German reprisals unrolled before him : hostages shot, dwellings burned to the ground or systematically looted—dare he risk bringing that upon Arbonne?

"I don't see why," he said. "I'm not an escaping prisoner of war, or even a combatant. I'm a neutral detained against my will and protected by the Geneva Convention."

"Eckhardstein doesn't strike me as a character likely to be impressed by the Geneva Convention."

"Well, that's up to you, Frank. If he starts anything after I've gone, wave the Star-Spangled Banner—tell him Adams and Washburne will both raise hell with his government if anything happens to ladies under American protection."

"I'm coming with you."

"You are not."

"Oh, Frank, no ! Not yet ! Not when you've only just come back to me !"

"Jim, listen. You've heard all Louise can tell us : the woods are alive with Prussians, and the *francs-tireurs* are out sniping for spies; you haven't a hope in hell of getting through on foot. What are you going to do—take one of the Uhlan mounts from the Cardinal's Stables?"

"My first problem is to get across the Seine, if I have to swim," said James. "Once through Melun I can strike the back roads for Brie, where there's a British war correspondent, a man called Forbes, with the Saxon Corps—and I've a letter to him from his editor. Then in by St. Denis, where the Prussians allow neutral ambulances to operate—and we'll get out, God willing, in the same way. Now, my dear Miss Louise, you must try to help me. You say there are servants in the kitchen who bring your meals and firewood and so on—how do they come in here? By a back stair? Prussian sentries there too? Of course. Any way out by a window—a garden way?"

"Yes!" said Louise. "There is a way out, unguarded! And a mount you can borrow, only a mile from here!"

She was not at once able to explain further, for the sound of footsteps was heard on the stair leading up from the kitchen premises, and a maid came in carrying a tray of food. A Prussian orderly followed with a bottle of Bertaux' best burgundy—"With Captain von Eckhardstein's compliments"—and other Prussians were heard in the empty dining room, arranging the baggage and the beds.

"They'll wake papa!"

Louise was here, there and everywhere, competent, watchful, icily sharp with the orderlies, calm and soothing when she passed through the library. Frank and James fell on the food, the first they had had for many hours. A tureen of leek and potato soup, a dish of mashed turnips, another of stewed apples—Louise apologized for the slender fare. "I've had to put the servants and ourselves on a daily ration," she explained. "Luckily we had a good store of vegetables. The Prussians cleaned the place out in three weeks. They even have to bring in grain for their horses from Fontainebleau now—our granaries are empty."

"If only you could all have gone to Monsieur Bertaux in Tour before things got so bad!" said Frank.

"We weren't invited!" said Louise, with a sharp little note in her voice. "And if we had been, what about Arbonne? We can't all go gallivanting off and leave the place to look after itself! If I hadn't been here to argue over every item with Captain von Eckhardstein, there wouldn't be so much as a copper saucepan left in the kitchen. Everything would be on its way to Germany. The troops the Daubignys have quartered on them brought the rinderpest among their cattle—I've had to fight to keep it from spreading to the few cows they've left us here, and what I'm to do about seeds for next year I don't know—they've stolen the ot! And then to make matters worse there's that horrible woman t the Tour d'Arbonne—uncle's tenant, or rather mine, although 'm not supposed to have any authority over the lease until I ome of age. She invites the Prussian officers for meals—entertains hem, gives them details about the people on the estate—it's disgraceful! I know one thing, the moment I see my uncle I'm going o ask him to put Madame Clarisse Delavigne off my property, nd then I'll have it thoroughly disinfected!"

She sat very straight in her chair, two red spots in her cheeks, nd her soft mouth set in a bad-tempered line. It occurred to rank, with amusement mixed with dismay, that he wasn't the rst man who had fallen in love with a little darling, and brought little tartar home. Louise saw the deprecating look he shot at ames and stopped short in the middle of her tirade. She told hem how, with one chance in ten of success, James might get at ast as far as Melun. If they waited until the Prussians had runk themselves into a New Year's Eve stupor, they could cross he bridge over the moat which led directly from the french indow of the bookroom to the side door of the village church— lways open—where she had noticed the Prussians never placed a ntry; and so out beyond the curtain wall to the road leading St. Martin-en-Bière and Forges. It was to Forges—so-called ecause the parish blacksmith had his workshop there—that her wn mare, Queen Mab, had been taken for shoeing two days before. Presumably on account of the heavy snowfall, she had not et been returned to the château.

"They let you keep your own mount, then?"

"Yes, all the others were requisitioned by the French Army st July, but not mine."

"But my dear child," said James, "I ride over thirteen stone; our little mare would founder beneath me."

"I think she'll get you to Melun," said Louise with quivering ps.

When the dishes were cleared away she insisted that they all y to rest for a few hours. It was going on for nine o'clock, and e Prussians across the hall had apparently finished dinner, for e sound of piano playing began to be heard, and there were bursts of singing; James in the dining room, stuffing the pockets of his Inverness cape with necessaries from his carpetbag, heard *Gloria Viktoria* many times repeated, and once, to his annoyance, the strains of *Auld Lang Syne*. He sat with Miss Elisabeth for half an hour, while Frank and Louise murmured in the next room. Then Louise came to take her place beside her father, and James and Frank settled in the chairs by the bookroom fire. It was not easy to compose themselves for sleep, but they dozed off at last. They were both sleeping when Louise came in on tiptoe at two o'clock in the morning, with a dark lantern in her hand. The little room had grown intensely cold, for most of the fuel was saved for the library, and Frank had dragged a rug across his knees. James was wrapped in his plaid. Frank's young face was relaxed and vulnerable; Bruce's, even in sleep, was set in the expression of strained resolve it had worn for days. "Oh, Madeleine, poor reckless darling!" said Louise's heart. "I knew he loved you— I know why you love him—so like yourself, so much the other half of you!"

She roused them softly. The walls of Arbonne were four foot thick, and there was little danger that their voices would be heard, but they spoke in whispers, listening for the footfalls of the sentries posted at the front and back of the château. The man on the terrace was the one they had to fear. If he continued his walk to their side of the moat he might hear them, or see them moving on the narrow humpbacked bridge. With infinite caution James opened the inner shutters and unlocked the glass door. The moon was down; the snow was falling heavily. "Thank God," breathed Frank, "it will cover up our tracks in half an hour."

Louise crossed over first. They could just see her, treading steadily on the snowy bridge, with no handrail, above the frozen moat. Bruce went next, and then, after a long wait while the sentry's footfalls approached and receded, Frank joined them in the darker shadow of the old church door. In another moment they were inside.

"I daren't open the lantern," whispered Louise. "If they saw even a flicker of light through the church windows—" James heard the rustle of her dress and knew that she had knelt to the

324

altar they could not see. They all stood still in the darkness. An indefinable odour rose about them, of stale incense and wax, and the bones of all the dead and gone d'Arbonnes who had worshipped there and gone to their last rest in the vaults beneath the worn oak flooring. A board creaked, and James, with a start of horror, felt something cold, with a human shape, beneath his hand. He had touched the sculptured foot of the d'Arbonne Crusader.

"We'll move on to the other door now," he heard Louise murmur. "Outside we turn directly to the left for Forges."

James had told her earlier that she ought not to come with him. She had argued, reasonably, that the blacksmith would never give up the horse without her order. So now, in silence, they emerged on the highway, and struck off towards the smithy, walking in single file along the frozen verge, Frank in the lead and Louise between the two men. Frank's eyes soon became accustomed to the darkness, and the scene of utter desolation all about him. "*The years roll slowly by, Lorena, the snow is on the grass again!*" There had been snow like this in the Valley, in the winter of '62! Now the whole thing had caught up with him again! He had to fight, no doubt about it; see her safe, and let the hue and cry after that determined devil Bruce die down, and then make off himself—to the Army of the North, or the American Brigade, or wherever he could volunteer. To save the Union—to save France —however much you tried to keep out, there was always some damned cause that sucked you into it—that you couldn't resist and live with yourself at all.

> *Weeping, sad and lonely,*
> *Hopes and fears how vain!*
> *Yet praying*
> *When this cruel war is over,*
> *Praying that we meet again.*

"But—m'selle Louise! m'selle Louise!"
They were in the kitchen of the blacksmith's house at Forges, and the blacksmith's wife, with a shawl thrown over her bodice and petticoats, was weeping and wringing her hands.

"To think they never told you! The devils! Oh, the Prussian devils! I sent a message to the château two nights ago!"

"Madame Léquipe, you know I'd have come at once if I'd only known!"

Over the heads of the women, James Bruce and Frank looked in dismay at one another. The blacksmith of Forges had been kicked in the knee by one of the Uhlan chargers, and was now lying helpless in the next room. The young smith, his only son, was a prisoner of war in Germany.

"Let me see him, if he's awake, poor man!" Louise commanded in her new tone of authority, and the woman, with her apron to her eyes, led the way out of the kitchen.

"Here's a setout!" said James between his teeth.

"Too bad he didn't shoe the mare first," said Frank.

James looked round the kitchen. It was plainly but comfortably furnished, with a big wall-bed, from which three dark-haired little girls looked out timidly at the strange men, a Sacred Heart picture above the fireplace and a lithograph of the Empress Eugénie in diadem and crinoline.

"*Ma petite fille,*" said James to the child on the outside of the bed, "does one of these doors lead to the smithy?"

A frightened squeak and a pointing hand.

Queen Mab was standing in a stall well heaped with straw. She was warmly blanketed, with a feed in her manger; the blacksmith's wife, in the middle of her troubles, had looked after her with care.

"Noo, lassie," said James gently. "Haud ower a bit. Lat me see yer feeties. Wo, beastie! Stan'!"

The old accent, and the old words, came back in the old setting so familiar to him once; and the pretty black mare trembled and whickered softly as his caressing hand ran down her legs.

"Only one shoe off!" said James, straightening in relief. "Two I was done for; but for one there's time."

"What are you talking about?" said Frank, who had been leaning against the stall in utter weariness and discouragement.

James actually laughed. "Horseshoeing, of course, the first trade I ever learned! Now, Frank, I've a job for you—bring a shovel o hot coals from the kitchen and let's get the fire started. You keep the bellows going and I'll do the rest."

Louise came quietly into the smithy and sat down on a bench beside the water trough. It was a curious scene to her eyes: primitive, masculine. Frank was intent on his task of blowing the fire red-hot. James had the little mare's hoof caught between his knees and was examining it with care. He had the hoof clippers in his hand and was wondering, after so many years of lack of practice, if he ought to use it on a hoof grown a little spongy through neglect. Then he let the mare stand free with a gentle pat on her hindquarters, turned round to cut a length off the mould and thrust iron and tongs deep into the heart of the coals.

At that moment he was a more virile figure than Louise had ever seen in her life. Frank, younger and handsomer in his own way, stood in the shadows; it was on James that the light of the forge fire glowed as he stood before it in his shirt and trousers with the smith's heavy leather apron hung round his neck and tied very firmly round his waist. There was soot on his face where he had brushed the back of his hand across his brow; soot on his well-kept, large-wristed hands—the blacksmith's hands he had inherited from his father—streaks of soot on his heavily muscled forearms. It was the classic figure of a craftsman which she saw in the smithy at Forges, and once again even Louise's smaller and more conventional perception saw what it was that had first attracted Madeleine at El Kantara.

> "Adown the firth and away we go,
> With a sweet and pleasant gale!
> And fare you well to bonny Montrose
> And the girl I love so well!"

James was humming his old song, for he was nearly happy for the first time in many weeks. Once more he was in his element: the engineer with a job to do, and in fancy he was back in the smithy at Sauchentree, William Bruce's boy with a hard task-master to satisfy. He began to hammer the iron and after a moment caught the rhythm—three blows on the study, as he had been taught to call the anvil, one on the shoe taking shape beneath the hammer head. Clink-clink-clink-*Clank*. Clink-clink-clink-*Clank*. He had it!

But at the first attempt the shoe was a poor fit, and Queen Mab moved restlessly as he grasped her hoof. Frank sprang to her halter and held her steady. James tried again; he was sweating now and thankful for the jug of wine and water Madame Léquipe brought in. He complimented the woman on the precision of her husband's tools—hammer, rasp, sole iron, hardy—all had been laid in the order proper to his hand. He tried again. Frank blew the fire, the metal glowed white, the new shoe was dipped in the water with a sizzle and a cloud of steam. This time the fit was right, and with a smell of scorching that made Louise gasp he nailed it to the little mare's hoof. The clip and the calker were well in place—he didn't know if the performance would pass muster with his father, but at least it wasn't the sort of 'botched job' the old man despised. The blanket off, a saddle which the blacksmith's son had used pulled from the rafters and fastened on. "Pretty Mab!" said Louise with her cheek against the mare's. "Take him safely to Melun!"

"What time is it, Jim?"

"Nearly four. I must be off."

He checked himself with his gold watch in his hand. It had been so much a part of him for ten years that he had almost forgotten its origin. Now the inscription beginning "*Wilhelm I, Koenig von Preussen*" stared out at him in the light from the dying fire.

"Here!" he said. "I shan't want that again!" and he pressed it into the hands of Madame Léquipe.

"*Non—non, monsieur—*"

"Yes!" said James. "Explain to her, Louise, that she can have the writing erased, or buffed off, by and by. The watch is worth something, I believe. Tell her it's for the use of her husband's forge."

He led the little mare out to the highway and threw the tartan plaid about his shoulders. "To Chailly first, and then down to the river—is that right?"

328

"Oh James," said Louise, reaching up to put her arms about his neck, "God bless you, and take you safe to her!"

"God bless *you*, child. Frank, take care of her."

"Good luck, Jim."

The little mare and her tall rider moved off down the Chailly road, the hoofbeats quickly muffled in the falling snow.

"Louise, are you too tired to go back to the château? Should you wait until daylight with Madame Léquipe, where it's warm?"

"I must go back, Frank—I'm not tired, really. Think of papa and Elisabeth, if I weren't there in the morning! Besides, the longer we can keep the Prussians from knowing James has gone, the further he may get on his way."

They started to retrace their steps. The snow fell on Louise's hood and enveloping cape, and on Frank's ulster, with a thousand cold wet touches like the licking tongue of winter. But Louise's face was warm when Frank took it between his cold hands and covered it with kisses, and asked her between the kisses, "When the war—when this cruel war is over—will you marry me?"

VI

Archibald Forbes, war correspondent of the London *Daily News* accredited to the XII (Royal Saxon) Corps of the Prussian Army and favoured with the personal friendship of Prince George of Saxony, sat in his billet at Le Tremblay on the Paris-Metz road, and listened with a splitting head to the salvos being fired by the batteries on the northeastern perimeter of Paris. He could identify them all, from the bark of the outworks at St. Denis, two miles away, to the voices of seven of the Sixteen Forts: La Briche, La Double Couronne, L'Est, Aubervilliers, Noisy, Rosny, Nogent. The two last were exactly opposite XII Corps HQ., which had been set up just out of range of the French naval guns. When Rosny and Nogent spoke Mr. Forbes' windows rattled, shreds of plaster fell from the ceiling on his table and cot and his head ached exceedingly.

Mr. Forbes was a minister's son, a graduate of Aberdeen University and a former cavalryman—qualifications which had given him one of the strongest heads for liquor in the entire press corps with the German armies. New Year's Day had been celebrated with great enthusiasm by the Saxons, who held a candlelight Lutheran service, it being Sunday, to thank God for the mercies vouchsafed to the German arms. They went on to a party at the Pontoneer Company Headquarters at Vaires, where there was a distribution of Iron Crosses for valour on the field; continued at the 103rd Saxon Regiment's mess, where Major von Schomberg had just received two barrels of Bavarian beer from his wife, and exploded in a burst of intoxication and *gemütlichkeit* in an exchange of visits with the Prussian Guards and Alvensleben's IV Corps. Mr. Forbes, on the afternoon of the third of January, was still feeling some after-effects. He was a tall, strongly built Scotsman of thirty-two, nearly ten years younger than James Bruce but representative, as Bruce had been in engineering, of a new type of Scots career man—the aggressive, progressive journalist.

His critics called Forbes the shooting star of the War of 1870, but there was nothing transient about his talent. Already he had out-paced all his rivals but one, the greatest of them all—the veteran William Howard Russell of the London *Times*, who was at Versailles with the King of Prussia. Russell used only the most distinguished news sources, namely the King, Bismarck, von Moltke, von Roon and the Crown Prince. To Russell fell the private conferences, the great dinners at the Hotel des Reservoirs, with news literally laid on his platter by the German leaders; to Archibald Forbes the long nights of frost and snow on the Plateau d'Avron, visiting the German outposts, dodging the French shells! He wondered, as he began to consider his next dispatch to London, if a story would ever land on his own doorstep without his going out to look for it.

The end of the year had seen another desperate attempt by the besieged Paris garrison to break out and reach the Army of the North. Up at Bapaume, one hundred miles away, General Faidherbe had been fighting for three days to get to Paris, and Captain Payen had handled his Marines so well that the French XXIII Corps had beaten the Prussians in a pitched battle on the last day of the old year. Down in Paris they tried in vain to recapture Le Bourget on Christmas Eve and came out to another awful massacre when the Germans counter-attacked on the plain of Avron on the twenty-eighth and twenty-ninth. Forbes, whose only fault as a war correspondent was a certain lack of objectivity, had identified himself very closely with the German side, and he reflected that the guns "we" were now bringing up, with a long enough range to bombard the heart of the city as well as the forts, would probably finish off Paris within a couple of weeks.

But where was the story—his "lead" for the day? If he were at Versailles, he could easily dig a human story, the kind Billy Russell would be too grand to write, out of Prince Leopold of Hohenzollern, for the man whose acceptance of the Spanish Crown had started the whole war off was now dangling around Prussian headquarters in the gorgeous uniform of the White Hussars. What had *he* felt like—Forbes would ask him—when he heard, just as the terrible year was nearly over and his substitute,

Prince Amadeus of Savoy, ready to sail from Spezzia for Spain, that Prim, the king-maker, had been assassinated in Madrid? Wasn't there something rather ominous in that—showing the undertow of human resentment running under the high triumphant wave of Bismarck's victories? It was the sort of thing that made the French peasants scrawl upon their hovels the sinister slogan:

Prussians from hell, you will never see your wives again!

Archibald Forbes took up his pen. There never had been a day since the war began when he had been so completely without a good lead. He looked out again. Nothing to be seen across the sodden fields, where the snow was beginning to melt in patches, but the distant puffs of smoke from Rosny and Nogent. Nothing to be seen on the highway except the unbroken line of German supply wagons, endlessly rolling along with the matériel which von Moltke had been storing up for years for the subjugation of France.

Hallo! There *was* a break in the procession: a French vehicle. The peasants did that as often as they dared—get a cart into the convoy and then contrive to have a broken axle, or upset a load of potatoes under the noses of a German team. This one was the ordinary tumbril, an open vehicle with two shelves along the sides, and a plough horse stumbling between the shafts. What made it extraordinary was the attire of the passenger sitting hunched up behind the driver. With an exclamation, the man whose father was minister of an Aberdeenshire parish reached out for the field glasses lying on his cot. Right! he hadn't been deceived by that brilliant flash of scarlet. Sitting in the tumbril, on the top of a load of rotten turnips, was a tall man wrapped in a Scots tartan plaid.

Snatching up his overcoat and dashing out of his billet, Archibald Forbes realized that a story had landed on his own doorstep at last.

"My God, that tastes good!" said James Bruce. He was sitting on Forbes' cot, drinking neat whisky out of a horn tumbler, while he war correspondent, over a spirit lamp, stirred up a mess of beans and German sausage for his guest. "Finding you here as soon as I reached Le Tremblay was my first piece of luck for three days."

Between them on the table lay the letters from Colonel Loyd Lindsay and Mr. Bullock, in which Bruce's work for the war charities was fully described. Forbes had been employed as a regular correspondent of the *Daily News* for only a few months, but he knew how much promotion the paper was giving to its Relief Fund for the French peasants, and that a friend and associate of Mr. Bullock required his very best treatment. But even without his recommendation, the man's experience was so remarkable that Forbes would have cherished him; the man's project opened up such a vista of news beats as he could hardly bear to contemplate.

"Begin at the beginning and tell me exactly how you came," he said, and took up his pen.

"Well—I told you I left Arbonne on horseback. I got along to Chailly-en-Bière without any trouble, and then I lost my way in the snow and fumbled about for a bit until I could find a readable signpost, and got down to the Seine. It was nearly daylight by that time and I could see that the bridge was down. I rode up to a cottage where some sort of official lived—a water bailiff, I think—and after a lot of argument he took me along to a ford about two miles downstream and I got across all right, though the water was pretty high. Could I have some of that food now, please?"

"Sorry. Did you get the water bailiff's name?"

"Lagnier."

"L-a-g-n-i-e-r?"

"Yes. After I left him the going was pretty rough. Monsieur Lagnier warned me to keep clear of Melun, where he said the town major was the devil in spurs, and I spent most of the morning dodging German patrols in the forest paths."

"Who occupies Melun?"

"Elements of XI Corps."

"Grand Duchy of Hesse—right."

333

"The mare I was riding was pretty badly blown by that time—a lady's pet, you know—and I finally decided to leave her at a farmhouse where the people seemed reliable. I hope to God they take good care of her and get her back to her mistress one of these days."

"And then?"

"I walked," said James simply. "I walked due north through the woods and fetched up in a hamlet called Guignes, where I fell in with a band of *francs-tireurs* who let me sleep in their post in a woodcutter's hut."

"You know, round here we think the *francs-tireurs* are a pretty bad joke. They can't shoot worth a damn, and they trample about in the woods like a herd of buffalo."

"I suppose that's why the Crown Prince of Prussia gave orders to shoot them down without mercy? Pretty severe punishment for a bad joke."

James pushed away his plate and felt for his pipe and his last shreds of tobacco. He had no intention of describing what he had seen at Guignes: the *francs-tireurs* in their white coats made out of meal sacks, indistinguishable against the snow-laden bushes, and then the two quick spurts of flame as a belated German supply wagon rumbled past, the quick efficient unloading of the food which meant life to the free corps, the quick disposal of the two bodies. Prussians from hell, you will never see your wives again!

"Next morning I was in serious trouble," he said. "The *francs-tireurs* put me on the road to Brie-Comte-Robert, which used to be the ambulance staging point. I didn't know you'd all gone forward! Instead of finding you, Forbes, as Mr. Bullock assured me I should, I walked right into the arms of the Prussians."

"What exactly do you mean by Prussians?"

"The 34th Regiment of Prussian Guards. They kept me under interrogation at their command post, all day long. Very thorough, these gentry! No respect, to speak of, for the Geneva Convention! Lucky for me I can speak the dockyard German I picked up at Settin—that impressed them, the swine!"

"They can be very rough," said Forbes. "You'll like the Saxon officers here, though—charming fellows!"

"Then why the hell don't they stay at home in Saxony?" said Bruce with a scowl. "I've seen the uniforms of all Germany in France, since I set out from Marseilles!"

"Anyway, the Prussians accepted your story in the end?"

"They did. They even fixed me up with a billet of sorts at a market gardener's. The people had plenty of sacks in the barns, and I rolled up in them in front of the kitchen fire."

"The French were still there? Really they're incredible. They come right out under our batteries and gather their frosted cabbages and rotten potatoes in the very line of fire. I tell you on the perimeter near Argenteuil, Potin has them picking stuff for his grocery stores on a regular shift system. Then one of them gets his head blown off, probably by a French shell, and a howl goes up in the press about German inhumanity to civilians."

"Well, I'm very glad to have seen it for myself," said James. "When I get back to London, I'll have plenty to tell *the proprietors of your paper*, sir, about the gallantry and perseverance of the peasants on the outskirts of Paris, and the valuable work the News fund will do in helping them to get on their feet again. That was one of them, by the by, who brought me to Le Tremblay—I'm grateful to you for seeing that he got good food and drink, as well as me."

Forbes scratched the tip of his nose with his pen. Bruce's allusion to his employers had not been lost on him, and he decided not to invite any more pro-French comment from this very unusual charity worker. Now that his countryman had taken off that extraordinary rig of the plaid and the deerstalker cap, and got some hot food and whisky inside him, he struck the war correspondent as an impressive figure—not, as he had thought when the whole project was told to him at the beginning, one of the inoffensive madmen of whom the French war seemed to have loosed an asylumful on Europe. Those memorable eyes, looking steadily at him over the bowl of the pipe held between clenched teeth, were not the eyes of a crazy man.

"You tell your story very prosaically, Mr. Bruce—as an engineer should. I think I'll head it 'Devotion'—it will give the News pride and pleasure to let its readers know how thoroughly the Fund is being administered."

He rose, and lit the lamp. Dusk was falling over the sodden fields, and as he drew the torn blind Bruce cast one look—eager, painful, instantly averted—at the far-distant line of fortifications, where flame as well as smoke was now visible. He had been aware of the rumble of the guns for days, but that smoke and flame meant *Paris*, behind those walls was *Madeleine*.

"Now about those ambulances," he began.

"You're really serious about attempting to get into Paris? Don't you think if it were possible I would have tried it myself long ago?"

"Not necessarily," said Bruce. "You'd get what you fellows call a 'story' by going in, but suppose you were hindered from getting out, then what? Vacancy for a war correspondent on the *News*! And would your colleague Labouchère exactly welcome you inside Paris? He has the monopoly at present, with his 'Besieged Resident' stuff—would he want your competition?"

Forbes grinned. "You must have worked in Fleet Street yourself at some time or other, Mr. Bruce."

But Bruce remained solemn. "What time do the ambulances come in here?" he persisted.

"They don't come this far every day. But there's a good chance one will come through tomorrow, because Dr. Cormac of the British Ambulance has been attending a field hospital full of erysipelas cases and gangrenes down the road at Le Vert Galant. Like all Miss Nightingale's pupils, he wants the windows kept open. The German doctors want the windows shut. Cormac keeps an eye on them fairly regularly. You have a Red Cross brassard, I suppose? Good. Now tell me this: how long do you plan to stay in Paris?"

"Until I can persuade a certain lady to leave the city under my protection," said James.

"Oh! Indeed! A French lady, may I ask?"

"Yes."

"Then, I'm afraid, you'll require something more than ambulance accreditations—not so much to get her out of Paris as to

et her through the German lines. You'll have to have a safe-
onduct both for yourself and her. Now that's where I can help
ou. I can talk to Prince George of Saxony tonight, and take you
o see him in the morning: he's a good fellow, and I think I can
ersuade him to write some sort of *laissez-passer* for you and—er
—Madame—?"

"Mrs. Bruce," said James. "I hope to marry the lady, before we
eave Paris!"

Forbes bowed. "I take it you'll make for the Belgian frontier
nce you're across the firing line? It's your best chance, you know
—if you can get clear up into the Aisne you'll dodge both Faid-
erbe and Manteuffel and get across the border without too much
rouble at Hirson. It's an easy post to pass, my colleagues and I
se it often. There I can help you in another way."

"It's really damned good of you to help me at all."

"Pleasure—we're both north-country Scots, and both Aberdeen
Jniversity men; but I shall want my *quid pro quo*! What I can
et you is transportation halfway to the Belgian border. Keep this
o yourself—don't mention it to Labby, or any other journalist in
aris; but I happen to know the Germans have repaired a lot of
rack the French tore up when the Maas Army was advancing.
hey're able to run a supply train every night from here to Laon.
ll get you two places on it in exchange for your story of Besieged
aris. No, no!"—as Bruce protested—"I don't mean you to *write*
story. I'll do that. *I'll* put in the human touches and the local
olour. You bring the facts; You've got an eye for facts, I realize
hat, and you remember what you see. I want your eyewitness
tory of Paris on the eve of the foundation of the German Empire.
n the eve of her surrender! I want to teach Billy Russell a lesson
e won't forget, and show Labouchère there're other ways of
ransmitting from Paris besides carrier pigeon! If you do this for
1e, I'll send you and the lady up to Laon in the supply train with
our safe-conduct from Prince George of Saxony. Is it agreed?"

"Agreed!" said James, and held out his hand. Forbes shook it.
Mr. Bruce," he said enthusiastically, "from my point of view
ou're a whole lot better value than the last humanitarian from
ondon who turned up at Le Tremblay."

"What was he doing?"
"Distributing tracts for the Bible Society."

Shortly after noon on the next day, after a long argument, James Bruce took his place with Dr. Cormac in the wagon, which flew a Red Cross flag on a short staff. Forbes, who had an eye for the dramatic, suggested swathing James in sheets and bandages and taking him in as a wounded man "discovered" in a shack near the firing line; this was declined both by the doctor and the putative patient. Finally Cormac reluctantly agreed that James was to pose, if necessary, as a Scots physician who had come up from the South of France to offer his services to the Paris hospitals. Privately, Archibald Forbes thought the tartan plaid would do the trick.

The ambulance wagon, having called at the German field hospital on its neutral errand of mercy, stopped at a French hut about half a mile from St. Denis and took on four stretcher cases —amputees wounded in the fighting of December 29 and only now able to be moved into the town for hospitalization. Dr. Cormac remained under the canvas hood with his patients, and James moved up to sit beside the French driver, a surly uncommunicative man in thin corduroys and a thick worsted muffler, thankful to escape from the smell of soaked dressings and of wounded men who had lain in the remnants of their uniforms for several days. Dr. Cormac had told him that five thousand wounded Frenchmen had been cared for by the ambulance teams in the last week's fighting on the Plain of Avron.

As they went they could hear heavy firing on the south. Rosny and Nogent were silent; the Prussian attack was mounted that day against Charenton and Ivry and from there westward round the perimeter to the flank of Paris which had a natural defence in the looping of the Seine.

There was no firing from St. Denis. A few potato parties were working out in front of the glacis, wrapped in the sheepskin coats which Bruce observed to be the popular wear, and the long shadow of the chimney stalks of the modern industrial town fell across the bastions in the first watery sunlight for many days. The Abbey of St. Denis was visible from the plain—that abbey in which the kings of France had been buried for a thousand years, from which the oriflamme had been carried out before the armies of France to the shout of *"Montjoie St. Denis!"*—it was piled high with sandbags. The commandant of St. Denis was a naval officer, Admiral La Roncière: his Marines and Marines artillerymen had defended the town valiantly for four months, but the end was now in sight. Pasteur Saglier, a Protestant clergyman who had taken the lead in organizing the defences of St. Denis, had already asked the Provisional Government for help in evacuating women and children from the doomed city into the capital.

Dr. Cormac's wagon came slowly up to the Fort du Nord. The glacis before it was a mere series of shell pits. One of the two drawbridges had been completely destroyed by Prussian shells, the machinery of the other so much damaged that it could not be raised. Over this bridge the wagon rolled without any challenge from the elderly National Guardsmen who were acting as sentries, and one of whom was actually singing, as he lounged up and down in front of the gate:

"Vive la guerre, piff, paff! Vive la guerre, piff, paff!"

The ambulance stopped at the end of the street leading from the Fort du Nord to the Caserne de St. Denis, and Dr. Cormac irritably indicated that James was now free to go where he pleased. With what assurance he could muster James walked through a great hall, where he passed unnoticed among the crowd watching an exchange of French and Prussian prisoners. One door opened on a terrace below which, in a large courtyard, the international and military ambulance wagons were drawn up. James, exhausted by sheer nervous tension, leaned against the stone balustrade and found himself looking straight down the avenue de Paris to the butte Montmartre.

As in the first sunset of the fatal year he had seen Paris in her splendour, so he now saw Paris in her pride: a great luscious honeycomb of all the soft golds and pearl greys on an artist's palette. The diffused sunlight struck downwards through a dull brown pall of smoke from the Forts to pick out here the Arc de Triomphe, there the towers of Notre Dame, while all round the white smoke of the bombardment curled and licked at the walls of the embattled city. In her beauty Paris had thrilled him; in her pain and defiance James did homage to the queen of the world.

He felt a hand on his arm. He swung round to look into the astounded face of Hector Munro.

"Almichty God!" The man from Strathbogie was the first of the two to speak. "Gentleman James, as I'm a leevin' man! What are *you* doin' here?" And he stared at the Red Cross brassard on James Bruce's arm.

"Munro, for God's sake, speak low," said James, looking round the terrace anxiously. "I'm on my way to Paris—I came in with Cormac's wagon—don't let any of them know I'm not a regular—"

"Ye've come to look for Madeleine."

The conviction, the familiarity of the words took Bruce's breath away. "What do you mean, sir?"

"Awa', man, dinna put on your airs and graces here. I jalouse ye've come to look for the lassie, and if I ca'd her oot o' her name it's because Madem'iselle d'Arbonne and me is auld campaigners—auld sodgers ye micht say—we've been thro' some gey nichts o' shot and shell thegither; and many's the time I've wished ye could see us, dancin' a livelier measure than the Tuilerie polka, wi' the German bullets dirlin' roond aboot us. Jeems!" he went on, "it's true, isn't it? Ye cam' thro' the lines to look for her? . . . Aye, nod yer heid, bend yer stiff neck; I ken ye canna speak. She's nae here, James, it's her day for the Slaughterhouses ye see I ken Madeleine's schedule as well as I ken ma own. Didn' ye not know she was drivin' an ambulance wagon for de Lesseps?"

The sweat was standing upon James's forehead.

"*Madeleine's* an ambulance driver? Like that fellow of Cormac's, who brought me here?"

"But a damned sicht better a whip," said Dr. Munro.

"I was told—her sister thought she was living with an old lady—she didn't tell them she was doing anything else—"

"Ye surely kent her better than think she would sit on her

backside doin' naething through the Siege o' Paris! James, I tell you, she's a lass in ten thousand—a proper heroine, unhonour'd and unsung, as the poet says; and if ye've been man enough to come seekin' her where none cam' before unless he cairried a flag o' truce, ye'll gae doon on yer knees when ye see her and kiss the hand that's been strong enough to raise many a poor devil from what they ca' the field o' honour and help him back to life!"

"Hector," said Bruce, "I've been on my knees before her since the day I saw her first, and I'll put my neck beneath her foot if she requires it—but take me to her, help me to reach her now!"

The doctor glanced at his watch. "I canna tak' you across the river—I'm expected at the Hôtel Dieu, to gie a hand w' the surgery at six o'clock; but I'll do better. I'll tak' ye to Unthank's, and mak' ye free o' ma washstand, for ye're sore needin' a clean-up and a closer shave, and a decenter hat than that deer-stalker arrangement. . . . Faith if the lassie saw ye noo she would tak' ye for the ghost o' an auld Hieland gamekeeper I used to ken at Huntly. Come awa'!"

Once again, and very conscious of his Red Cross brassard, James walked past the National Guardsmen and began to help load eight stretcher cases into a British ambulance.

"Hardly worth takin' in," said Dr. Munro. "They've the fever on them already, from whatever pit or lime kiln they'll have been lyin' in, and God knows it's ragin' in Paris now. We had four thousand deaths from the hospital fever alone last week. It's the amputations, ye see—our doctors havena time for conservative surgery, we just wheep off the airms and legs and leave the lads in unventilated hospitals, and then the gangrene sets in.—What ails ye?" he said, as James with a ghastly face leaned up against the canvas hood of the wagon. "I forgot ye were a green hand at this game. Here, tak' a sup of whisky oot o' my flask, and let's awa' to Paris."

For Bruce the last lap of his journey was in some ways the worst. He had never been seasick in a P. and O. engine room, in the worst gale that ever blew in the Bay of Biscay; but his stomach heaved and churned as the wagon swayed down the venue de Paris with the stench of gangrene and foul gases coming out under the canvas, and the odour of fear and starvation coming up from the milling crowds pushing their beds and tables in handcarts before them as they struggled forward towards the capital.

"There's naething like the Mountain Dew," said Munro, taking another pull at his whisky flask. "The days that food's been in short supply at Unthank's, we've all done fine with a good dram and a bowl o' oatmeal and bilin' water—and whiles a turnip to make it into a dish o' neep brose. But I'll tell ye this and I'll tell you nae mair, I've conceived a great respect for the Paris folk. Lichtsome they may be, and freevolous beyond all tellin', but they've fairly buckled down to see this thing through. I've even got some idea o' hospital rationing knockit into their heads, just by dint of limiting one thing to one place—macaroni to Madame Adam's post at the Music Conservatory, kidney beans for the Comédie Française wards, oil for the Masons, sassidges for Sarah Bernhardt and her actress nurses at the Odéon. (Oh, my, you should see the girrls there, James! Naething like that when I was walkin' the hospitals at Aberdeen!) Then oor ain folk—eicht hundred destitute Britishers fed on naething but rice and Liebig's meat extract—they would ha' starved to death if it hadna been for the British War Relief Fund and the generosity o' men like Richard Wallace and Auberon Herbert. I've been givin' them a hand wi' the rationin' too."

"Haven't the Embassy officials taken charge of that?" James roused himself to ask, for this was one of the questions which Archibald Forbes had underlined.

Munro shrugged. "The Ambassador thinks his place is at Bordeaux, and all the dancin' attachés are there wi' him. If ye look in about at the Embassy, ye'll find that Her Britannic Majesty's representatives are now strictly limited to Colonel Claremont, the military attaché, a French doorkeeper and three sheep in th' cellar. Great, isn't it?"

"Is it true what we read in the London papers, that the rich can buy any comforts they require? Has—has Madeleine had every thing she needed?"

Dr. Munro glanced sideways at him and laughed.

"Ye mean in the way o' food?" he said. "Maybe. I think she's a lot better lookit after now that the poor old lady's dead, and he's back round the corner in the Quai Voltaire. Oh! ye didna know, of course—old Miss Henrietta slippit' awa', about a month go, and nae great loss. That Madame Poisson, the concierge, ak's good care o' the lassie. The Poissons are doin' all right out o' the war—except that one of their lads was killed at the picheren. They're breedin' rabbits in a studio that belonged to ngres, and sellin' them for a king's ransom."

For a long time, while Hector Munro gave James as many details as he could remember about Madeleine's work with the de esseps group, the British ambulance had remained stationary at a point about a mile outside the Porte de la Chapelle. The draw-ridge was up—the word came back among the crowd—and the uard was checking the refugees from St. Denis with especial care. he lieutenant on duty was in the grip of spy fever, and the lovely National Guards had been replaced by a brisk platoon rom a Line regiment.

"Be canny, now, James," said Munro in an undertone, as the ngineer looked at him apprehensively. "They change the guard very two hours, so none o' this lot knows if ye went out wi' me r not. The driver? Promise him a sovereign when we get to the otel and he'll keep his mouth shut."

But the sergeant who lifted his lantern to look inside the mbulance was thorough.

"Who are you, monsieur, and where do you come from?"

"From the naval hospital at St. Denis." The prepared answer vas given by James.

"Your name and identification, monsieur?"

"Bruce, monsieur, Dr. James Bruce, attached to the medical ommissioner's staff."

"*Un brave Ecossais!*" said the officer admiringly, with a glance t the bright tartan.

"Aye, a Scotsman," put in Dr. Munro. "We went through the ollege at the same time."

"Your papers, if you please."

343

It was the crucial moment. James's passport, of course, described him as an engineer. Once again he produced Colonel Loyd Lindsay's letter, somewhat the worse for wear, and spread it on his knee in the lantern light. The man studied the engraved Red Cross on the letterhead, and the printed names of men well known as friends of France.

"At which hospital are you to serve in Paris, doctor?"

One of the names which Munro had mentioned came back when it was needed, to Bruce's mind. "At Madame Adam's post at the Conservatoire, monsieur."

"Aha! Madame Juliette Adam—a good republican! It is well! Proceed!"

"You did fine, James," said Hector Munro, as they turned down the first of the long northern streets of Paris.

"You did, you mean," said James. His head was splitting, not only from the accumulated strains and tensions of his adventure but with the shocks of self-disgust and humiliation. "Good God!" he thought, "I was ashamed to walk into the Tuileries beside him only a year ago; and now I'm proud and thankful for his protection! How small his work for France makes mine appear—my speeches, and my letters written in a comfortable room in London!"

He could scarcely realize that he was inside Paris. The last stage of his journey, forward from Le Tremblay, had been so completely unlike his imaginings as to seem like a dream. There had been no danger, no anxiety even, except during his interrogation at the gate; no shots fired, no shells bursting round his head. Instead there had been this monochrome of despair and near defeat, those tattered and starving figures all about him, this rubbing shoulders with disease and death more fearsome to him than any quick hot action. "And this is what Madeleine has been living through," he thought. "Not protected, not cared for any longer, but going out there upon the battlefield, perhaps at the risk of her own life, while I sat at home! Madeleine! The girl I left because I couldn't make her do everything I wanted, because I wasn't her first lover—how can I face her now?"

He looked about him at the empty streets of her city, and found no answer there.

Although the lanterns were already lit at the city gates, there was still a little light in the long grey avenues down which they drove to the hospital near the Place St. Augustin where their stretcher cases were received: enough to show, as they turned into the more familiar boulevards and made for the rue St. Honoré, the butcher shops with a little horsemeat and a few skinned cats in the windows and the public soup kitchens with long lines of women waiting in front of them. Most of the billboards had been torn down for firewood, but on some of them were still to be seen official proclamations, on which the "We, General Trochu, President of the Government of National Defence . . ." had been altered by some waggish hand to "President of the Government of General Offence," and Trochu's slogan, "God, Family, Property," had been changed again and again to the old "Liberty, Equality, Fraternity!" Sometimes a realist had scrawled underneath:

INFANTRY !   CAVALRY !   ARTILLERY !
                  OR DEATH !

Darkness had fallen upon the city when James escaped at last from the group of eager men at Unthank's, who had bombarded him with questions about the outside world. "Is Princess Louise married? Is Mr. Gladstone still Prime Minister?"—the things they wanted to know had remarkably little to do with the war between France and Prussia. He walked rapidly through the murky streets of what had been the City of Light to the river and the Quai Voltaire. How well he remembered that night, just short of a year ago, when he had held her in his arms all the way from Lapérouse, and she had laughed, and said, "I can always find my way back to the Quai Voltaire!" Now he had found his way there too; and dark though the night was he had no difficulty in finding the old *hôtel* d'Arbonne, not far from the corner of the rue de Beaune. The porte-cochère was locked, of course, but his ring was answered immediately, and he was admitted to Madame Boisson's lodge.

The snapping black eyes of the concierge were swollen an
dimmed these days, for not only had her boy René fallen early i
the war but Robert had been taken prisoner after Metz surren
dered; his mother had no news of him. But they kindled whe
Bruce showed her his name in Madeleine's own handwriting -
he had kept the letter summoning him to France in June, fo
months past – and her sympathy was assured when he slipped
sovereign into her apron pocket. But she would only tell him tha
"Mademoiselle was on duty"; not for love nor money would sh
admit him to mademoiselle's apartment.

"No, of course not," said James, "I wouldn't dream of it, bu
tell me, what time does she come off duty?"

"She should be here by seven o'clock this evening."

"Not long to wait, then."

"And tonight she'll have a good supper," said Madame Poisso
"I made some of my rabbit stew for a sick woman in the rue d
Saints Pères and put a bowl of it in Mademoiselle d'Arbonne
kitchen; she only has to warm it up." She hesitated. "If you're
friend of our young lady, monsieur, will you please make her tal
care of herself and do less for others? I don't speak only of th
driving, though God knows it's no work for a woman, but she
been so good to all our poor people in the *quartier*, you can't ha
any idea! Living all alone upstairs, with only her father's cat f
company, and hardly ever with enough to eat—"

"You don't mean she's actually gone hungry?"

The woman pursed her lips, and nodded. "Monsieur Bertau
had hoarded food, over at the big house. She won't touch tha
she gives it all away; the only thing she takes for herself is a goo
glass of wine. We've been looking after the house; we've broug
her wine and blankets, even flowers from the conservatory, b
monsieur, there's no more food left to bring."

"Then for heaven's sake," said James, putting gold in her han
"buy anything she needs! Run out before the shops shut and g
anything you think would tempt her; I'm told there are still go
things to be had at a price. You take this for your trouble, a
I'll wait here."

"Monsieur is generous." Madame Poisson wrapped herself in

346

eavy shawl, locked her *loge*, and hurried across the dark courtyard.

Since he gave away the King of Prussia's watch, James had only relative idea of the time of day. But a church clock somewhere in the neighbourhood—it might have been either St. Germain des Prés, or St. Thomas d'Aquin—was striking the half-hour after six as he climbed four flights covered with cat-smelling carpet, feeling his way with one hand on the surface of the yellow marbled wallpaper, the other on the greasy rail, until he came out on the top landing of the ancient house. There were two doors: one very narrow, which he rightly took to open on a storeroom stair, and one, broad and made of black oak, beneath which he could see a faint glow of firelight. He knocked impulsively. She might have come back unexpectedly while the concierge was out on one of her errands; she might be there already, resting beside the fire. There was no answer to his gentle tapping, except a mew so close that he looked down expecting to see a cat at his feet. There was no light where he stood, but an oil lamp on the landing below threw a faint glow up the well of the stairs and let him make out the position of a window from which he could look out across the darkened city. He saw the great black mass of the Tuileries, and a lamp on the Pont Royal reflected in pallid gold on the frozen Seine. The church clock struck the quarter before, and the hour, and the quarter past, while he stood there leaning against the window ledge, a beggar at a bolted door. Slowly his ears caught faint sounds of life inside the building—a footfall on rotten flooring—the clink of plates or glasses—the creaks and little whispers of oak beams and ancient stairways which had known three hundred years of life and death. At last, far down in the courtyard, he heard a door close. Madame Poisson returning from the rue des Saints Pères? The sound of footsteps was heard on the staircase, passing the lodge. He waited, breathless, hearing the blood pounding in his ears. The steps came on. He went to the head of the stairs and looked down. He saw a woman in a sheepskin coat, bowed and weary, clambering up with one hand on the rail, halting beneath the little lamp to pull off a soldier's képi and an enveloping scarf. The light fell upon the hair he knew, and the

347

face he knew was lifted pale and wondering but never afraid, a
he took a step towards her.

"Who's there?"

"Madeleine! Madeleine!"

He went down the narrow stairs in two strides. He had her i
his arms, gripping her body beneath the matted sheepskin, and sh
gave him her lips as generously and as truly as if there had neve
been between them that cruel parting at the gates of Compiègn

"Oh, James! Oh, James! I knew you would come back to me!

She opened the door, and took his hand, and led him in to th
old, old apartment which had been her father's house of refuge.
was warm there, though the fire which Madame Poisson tende
was burning low, and by the light of a single candle he cou
see Madeleine, when she tossed her sheepskin jacket and heav
shawls aside, standing before him thin and taut with her uncurl
hair falling about her shoulders. Her feet were in shapeless boot
the lacings crisscrossed round her ankles, her hands in gauntle
reaching almost to her elbows, and when James began gently
pull at the stiff leather she stopped him and drew the gloves
herself, cautiously. James caught his breath at the sight of th
dreadful hands. Palms swollen, cracked open by chilblains, nai
broken and bloodless, one wrist thickened and slightly twisted o
of shape —

"Oh, Madeleine, your beautiful hands! They're bleeding!"

"It's the driving, James — the reins, and the weather — I drive a
ambulance, up at the Forts —"

"I know you do — I know it's killing work! My lovely Mad
leine, you might have been killed, yourself!"

"It was the only thing I could do well."

At that humble answer he went down on his knees before he
as he had vowed to do, and pressed his lips to the hem of h
frayed skirt. And Madeleine dropped to the floor beside hi
taking his head upon her breast, whispering the *je vous aime* sl
had never said before — not even at Le Vivier-Frère-Robert — whi
told him that out of all his boyhood's dreams of greatness or
the best, had been fulfilled: the love of a great woman was his
last.

It was only when her weight grew heavier in his arms that James realized that Madeleine was nearly fainting. He rose and lifted her into a chair beside the fire, chafing her hands very gently and cursing himself for the shock he had given her, until her heavy eyelids opened and she smiled at him.

"Is it really you, James? I'm not dreaming?"

"No, you're not dreaming."

"But how did you get in to Paris?"

"I came up from Marseilles and through the siege lines at Saint Denis."

"Only you could have done it. Only you."

"I was at Arbonne a few days ago. They're all well," he said quickly, it was no time to tell her of the Prussian occupation of the Château.

"Victor?"

"They heard from him a while ago. He's making a good recovery from his wound. What's this?"

It was a little white cat, thrusting herself jealously between them to climb into Madeleine's lap.

"This is Chérie, my father's pet. And I hear Madame Poisson coming; will you let her in, please, while I change my clothes? I'm filthy."

She slipped into what had been her father's bedroom while James opened the door to the concierge. Madame Poisson's face cleared at the sight of him.

"Mademoiselle let you in, then? I've some money to give you back, monsieur; our *quartier* is bare of food tonight, but I got fresh bread from Madame Alice, and four eggs from 'behind the faggots' in the rue de Verneuil. And there's wine—"

She bustled into the tiny kitchen. Little comfort there: a cold-water tap above a stone sink, and an iron stove burning briquettes of small-coal mixed with sawdust. But it was warm, and James, who was not fond of cats, was pleased to see Chérie firmly put into basket near the stove.

"Mademoiselle d'Arbonne is dressing," he volunteered. "Shall I make up the fire and light more candles?"

"Yes, but be very careful, monsieur. A family in the rue de

349

Lille were taken off to the police station last week, accused of signalling to the enemy, just because someone left a candle burning in the kitchen when the blind was up!"

"I'll be careful, madame." James held the door open for the good woman ceremoniously: he wanted to be rid of her, although she obviously had more to say about warming up the rabbit stew. When he was alone he made sure the shabby velvet curtains were tightly drawn across the windows, put two logs on the fire, and with a spill of paper lighted at the flames he lit the candles on the walls. Now he could see the room better, with the flowers Madame Poisson had said came from the Bertaux conservatory, and a daybed with a velvet spread and cushions. A round table of citronwood stood between the daybed and the fire, and on it Madame Poisson had set a bottle of wine and two glasses, the new bread, and on a plate triumphantly in the middle, the great trophy of the four fresh eggs.

Madeleine stood smiling in the doorway. She had washed her face and hands and combed her tangled hair, and put on a black dress with some thin material at the cuffs which fell almost to her knuckles. James went to her and kissed them.

"There's some food, Madeleine, are you hungry?" He was obsessed by the idea that she had gone hungry through the siege.

"Not a bit. I had some hot food at noon at the ambulance depot. But you?"

"Let's have a glass of wine." He poured the fine Romanée Conti carefully, while Madeleine cut the crusty loaf. They ate and drank standing. It was a token feast rather than a meal, and when the glasses were empty James drew Madeleine down on the daybed.

He had her in his arms at last. He held her close in the warm hollow among the pillows, feeling her long limbs moulded to his own. Night and winter and the Sixteen Forts enclosed them in a solitude even more complete than they had known at Le Vivier Frère-Robert. This time they had not come together in darkness, for light from the candles in the glass girandoles fell on the white fur rug before the fire, and on Madeleine's hair, loosened and trailing over a white velvet cushion, and on the white china pots of flowers arranged along the mantelpiece. The great stiff snowy petals of cyclamen were poised like butterflies above their rings of dark green leaves.

James did not look into the shadowy corners of the room, at the stain of damp spreading down the far wall or the melancholy portraits of the departed Bourbons. His life and his love had narrowed down to this white, lit circle where she lay with her lips against his bared throat, with her thin starving body beginning to tense and arch against his own.

"I asked you once to marry me, Madeleine. Now I'm asking you again.

"James, look at me!"

The eyes that met his had looked far beyond his own experience —through the smoke of the battlefield, at the convulsed faces of men ripped by the bayonet, the calm and almost smiling features of men killed by musket ball. It was a stern look she gave him, softened in a moment by her smile; for in the dark eyes bent pleadingly on hers Madeleine saw all she had desired in this man: a passion and a steadfastness of purpose to match her own.

"James, when you went away from Compiègne that day, I nearly died. Or, no—not quite then, but after the Revolution ... when I had nobody left, nobody, to believe in. . . . And then, on some of *those* nights—outside the walls of Paris, I began to think that you might understand me better now, and come back to me again some day; and now you've come. If I say Yes now, my darling, Yes, without conditions, will you stay with me, never leave me, all the rest of the way?"

"Never again, Madeleine. If you can forgive me, if you can take me back, and love me, we'll never part again."

"Then it's yes, James. Yes. Yes."

Her roughened fingertips moved across his naked breast.

"Without conditions—Madeleine?"

Her dress was flung on the white rug. The hampering layers of cloth and linen were discarded in a frantic silence. Then with eyes and mouth and hands, with his whole body, James Bruce took Madeleine to himself, until the white limbs and the white flowers and the white candles seemed to come together beneath him in a coruscating ring, an incandescence of heat and light, and through the old room on the Quai Voltaire there rang her cry of love triumphant.

VII

There had been no fighting outside the walls of Paris since the end of the year, and by special order of de Lesseps Madeleine had been replaced by a relief driver for the routine trips to Bercy on the day after James came to the Quai Voltaire. It was a great piece of good fortune. For all his anxiety to reach the British Embassy and make arrangements for their marriage, James yielded to the temptation of remaining by the fireside with Madeleine in his arms, Madeleine dreaming in the delicious lassitude of satisfied love, while the snow piled up softly on the windowsills. They had food and wine and fuel, and Madame Poisson did not come upstairs to disturb them until the next morning.

"It's so unbelievable to think you've seen Arbonne," said Madeleine.

She was lying on the couch in a pale blue wrapper with a shawl protecting her shoulders from the penetrating draughts of the old apartment. "Tell me again about Louise and poor father—imagine that sweet little creature facing up to the Prussians, and struggling with rationing and things like that!"

She spoke with the gentle concern which had struck him when he told her about the state of affairs at Arbonne—almost as if she were discussing life on another planet. In his very brief experience of siege life James had already observed that there were those who wanted to hear about the outside world and those who did not. All the men he met at the Hotel St. Honoré had wanted details of what had been going on while they were shut up in Paris; Madeleine and Dr Munro were among those for whom the world began and ended at the Sixteen Forts. She spoke of going to Alexandria with him "some day," in precisely the same tone of detachment as she talked about Arbonne. The one place was as real as the other to a Parisian while the Prussians were at the city gates.

She seemed to take it for granted that Frank Hartzell would remain at Arbonne indefinitely, just as she and James were to remain indefinitely at the Quai Voltaire. She did not dwell on the details of the journey the two men had made from Marseilles to Fontainebleau; what held her, and what she breathlessly asked to hear again and again, was the narrative of her lover's journey through the war zone proper.

"It wasn't so bad!" he summed it up. "I just walked in, that was about it!"

"You make it sound like the trips the English take to Paris on their Bank Holidays, but I know better," and she kissed him proudly.

It was no shock to her to learn that Victor had not returned to Arbonne.

"I should think he'd be ashamed to look us in the face," she said. "What possessed him to give his parole to the Prussians! The only thing to do when Metz surrendered was to go as a prisoner of war to Germany—either that, or try to escape and join the Auxiliary Army, without parole!"

"I wonder!" said James. "He went into Belgium, that they know for certain. Could he have crossed the frontier back into France and joined a resistance group?"

"You mean the *francs-tireurs*? Why not, if he'd been free to do so? But not after giving his parole! You don't come to terms with the Prussians. You don't give *them* your word of honour—but if you do, you keep it! You know Ducrot, our new commander, broke *his* word—Paris doesn't respect him for it!'

James kissed her. It was not a day for politics. It was a day for fairy tales, as the snow cut them off from the rest of the world and even the firing was stilled. Not one sound of the rumble of ambulance wheels along the Quai Voltaire broke the charmed silence of the hours. It was a day for telling stories of their childhood, as Madeleine lay with her hands in her lover's clasp and watched his mouth and eyes soften over the remembered tales of Scotland. It was a day for love, when the twilight fell so early that the velvet curtains were drawn before three o'clock, for the slow drowsy loving exploration of each other's bodies until healing sleep came to them, and they woke to see through the bedroom door the salon glowing in firelight like the interior of a ros hell. It was late in the evening when James broached his plan of taking her away from Paris before the siege was raised. What she might have said to it the night before remained forever unknown; the girl he held in his arms was too deeply in love, too completely possessed by him, to oppose him very far. He was ready, too, for all her arguments.

"But if I leave Paris now, I'll be running away, just as the Empress did after Sedan!" It was the first time she had spoken Eugénie's name.

"After Sedan and after the New Year are two very different stages in the war, my love. You've been on duty now for over a hundred days. Even a soldier deserves a furlough after three months of fighting!"

"There won't be any furlough for the other people in Paris, James."

"I know, darling, but don't forget I've seen something of the rest of France: Marseilles, and Chalon and other towns where men and women are going about their business without vexing themselves unduly about the Parisians. Why shouldn't you have as much freedom as they?"

"James." She wound herself round him, her arms about his head and shoulders, and his head pressed into the hollow, faintly clover-scented, between her breasts. "Why must we go away at all? Why are we always hurrying on, backwards and forwards across France, always 'in transit'? Why can't we stay here at the Quai Voltaire, where we're so happy—at least until the siege is over?"

"It's *because* of the siege," said James in a muffled voice, "that I want to get you out of Paris. Don't, darling, let me speak! You know if we're to go to Alexandria, we have to go to London first, and I don't dare stay away much longer." It was now two weeks since his last appearance in Leadenhall Street.

Eventually she promised to go away with him as soon as he could arrange it, on condition that she should herself see de Lesseps in the morning. And for an hour after that she was exquisitely loving, moving and caressing in the circle of his arms in much the same way as Chérie, on the white rug, was curling her paws in gratitude for the warmth of the fire. But their supply of wood was burning low and the iron stove in the kitchen had gone out. They sat so long talking about their future that the room was chilled when James rose to extinguish the candles. "You mustn't catch cold, my darling—where is your shawl?" Madeleine said she was quite warm and comfortable—"feel!" It was true that the lips he kissed were hot and dry.

The lovers slept in each other's arms, dreaming of a happy future, while twelve miles away the three Fates who had altered the pattern of their lives again took up the skein of destiny, as Bismarck, von Moltke and von Roon drew their chairs round the table of an extraordinary council of war.

The King of Prussia was there as Commander-in-Chief. So was the Crown Prince, covering his bearded mouth with his hand as he looked from one to the other. In the Prefecture at Versailles that night, the Crown Prince knew, Bismarck meant to force a decision which his sentimental English wife and the queen his mother would most heartily disapprove, but which he himself had always been willing to endorse when the right time came.

Bismarck put his case bluntly. His timetable had been upset long ago by the stubborn resistance of the Parisians. The men who should have had their victory parade down Unter den Linden in October were still in France. They were fighting outside Le Havre, investing Belfort, only just released from the siege of Phalsbourg; fighting General Chanzy, fighting Faidherbe; suffering as severely as the French from trench feet, frostbite and gangrene. In Germany there was now a public clamour, "Bring our boys home!" In the world, where German victories should have commanded love and admiration, there was increasing dislike and fear of Germany.

The only way to end it was to bombard the heart of Paris now. To give up the daily battering at the Sixteen Forts and use the new long range guns which could destroy women and children, hospitals, churches, libraries—the flesh and the spirit of the stiffnecked city. *Paris must die*, said Otto von Bismarck. By midnight he had brought the council of war to agree with him.

The first shells fell inside Paris at eight o'clock on the on-

hundred and eleventh day of the siege, January 5, 1871. The explosions aroused James and Madeleine, and thousands of other persons on the Left Bank who were sleeping late on the dark snowy morning, for the first target was the Latin Quarter, not too far from the Quai Voltaire. The rue Gay-Lussac, near the boulevard St. Michel, was soon a shambles as women and children were carried out of their shattered homes to die on the cobbles and in the gutters; fires were raging near the Pantheon and the Luxembourg. The southern forts at once went into action, Ivry and Bicêtre first and then Montrouge, Vanves and Issy, and the reverberations of the firing were felt in all the old houses on the Left Bank.

"I don't like being indoors!" complained Madeleine, as she drank coffee made of acorn grounds. She had declined bread, although there was enough for both, saying she was "not hungry this morning." James almost wished she would show some other signs of nervousness. He had been growing accustomed to the intermittent firing around the fortifications, but this furious cannonading, so close that they could hear the scream of the shells, was very trying to a man who had not had Madeleine's experience of being under fire. He knew exactly what she meant about being indoors, away from her team and her freedom of movement on the field: apparently other Parisians felt the same way, for as soon as the great artillery duel began to slacken, they were out in the streets, picking up bits of exploded shell, laughing derisively and even singing in the old incorrigible way. James and Madeleine went out on the little balcony above the Quai Voltaire to watch them.

"They won't beat us with heavy guns!" said Madeleine, glowing. "Listen—we've put them out of action already!"

James thought, but did not say, that it was far more likely the new German batteries had been firing off a few rounds to find the range, while the forts had temporarily run out of ammunition. He felt fear—real fear, gnawing at his heart and body—for the first time since he set out for France. If Bismarck meant to carry out his threat of burning Paris to the ground, then the sooner Madeleine was taken to safety the better; any moment now might be too late. He told her so, bluntly, lovingly, and she did not oppose him. He knew better than to ask her if she was afraid to walk across the city, and she showed no sign of fear when she walked across the Pont Royal on his arm, through the strange silence which had fallen after the first salvos from the new Prussian guns. He escorted her to the door of her ambulance depot and left her there, at her own request, before hurrying off to the British Embassy.

At the dark old palace in the Faubourg St. Honoré the Union Jack was still flying and after some parleying with the French doorkeeper James was admitted to the courtyard. He could hear the sheep in the cellar mentioned by Hector Munro, but saw nothing of Colonel Claremont or anyone else in the great empty rooms where Lord Lyons had entertained the Emperor and Empress of the French in June. There was, however, one representative of Her Britannic Majesty on duty: a pallid and unmistakably British youth of about nineteen, sporting a paper shirt front and exaggerated cuffs, who was munching an apple and reading a railway novel in the deserted Chancery.

"Wot can I do for you, sir?" said this very junior clerk, whose accent hesitated somewhere between the frankly Cockney and the insufferably genteel.

"I should like a word with one of your superiors," said James.

"There's nobody only Colonel Claremont," said the pallid youth. "And 'e's gone out to watch the bombardment, bein' the military attaché, see?"

"Very appropriate," said James. "When d'you expect him back?"

"Beg pardon," said the youth, "but are you a Distressed British Subject, sir?"

"Far from it."

"Because if you *was*"—confidentially—"you'd have come to the wrong shop, that's all. Mr. Wallace and Mr. Herbert, they're looking after the DBS now."

"So I'm told," said James. "My business, however, was to inquire about the time required for performing a civil marriage, one of the contracting parties being British."

"We don't do marriages here, you know."

"What *do* you do, if I may ask?"

"Ho!" exclaimed the youth, shutting his railway novel with a bang. "Wot *don't* we do? Why after the ambassador and the rest of 'em went to Tours, the colonel and Mr. Wodehouse 'ad the whole British colony on their shoulders, and they didn't half create! You'd 'ave thought the whole four thousand of 'em was yellin' for safe-conducts to England at the same time! They was wild, you know, because 'is Lordship only put a notice in *Galignani's Messenger* telling them to go 'ome if they wanted—you must 'ave heard about that, sir! One man, 'e said if his head was blown off 'e'd complain in person to Lord Granville. One woman, she objected to Miss Cora Pearl a-flying of the Jack above 'er house in the roo de Chaillot—said 'er country's flag shouldn't protect a notorious prostitute—you never heard such a setout in your life! Where *was* you, that you didn't hear about it? But Mr. Enry Wodehouse, 'e smoothed them all down, and got them out in parties; then 'e went 'ome himself. Oh, we've 'ad our 'ands full I can tell you! But marriages—no; that we don't do: the Consulate's the shop for that."

"Where are the consular offices?"

"Wal-ker!" said the boy with a whistle, "don't you know the Consulate was closed before the siege began? Mr. Falconer-Atlee's up at Dieppe—he was one of the very first to leave!"

Hurrying in the direction of the Hotel St. Honoré, James reflected with pleasure that Dieppe had been in German hands for a month. "Perhaps the Consul got out in time," he thought. "I hope not! That would astonish Atlee's weak nerves, when Alvensleben and his Prussians marched in! Hell take the man, why couldn't he have stayed at his post as the American Consul did?" In fact James had only a hazy idea of the formalities required for a consular marriage; but he did regret that the "Scots marriage," by declaration before two witnesses, was only valid in his own country. To the son of William Bruce, celebrated in his parish as "pillar of the Establishment," the only religious wedding possible was the one covenanted in the Church of Scotland after the

359

proclamation of banns. That there were other ways of being married, even in besieged Paris, did not occur to him.

He found all three doctors—Gordon, Innes and Munro—eating a nondescript meal, which included substantial bowls of porridge, at the Hotel St. Honoré. His former classmate was in a hurry : he was just leaving to "gi'e somebody a hand" at the Hôtel Dieu, where the wards were now so full that cots and pallets had been laid top to bottom along every vestibule and landing. But he was quite definite about the meaning of the bombardment. "This is the feenish, James, nae doubt o' that. Get the lassie oot, for there'll be death and destruction here for the next two-three weeks, while the flour lasts; and then as soon as the bakeries close Trochu and Favre will throw in the sponge—if Cluseret and the Reds dinna tak' over first. I'm going to St. Denis wi' an empty wagon the morn's morning, and I'll pick you up at eicht o'clock at the corner of the Pont Royal."

The invaluable Mr. Unthank had another change of linen ready for James, and a clean shirt for the pockets of the Inverness cape he also produced a silver turnip watch which one of his kitchen staff was prepared to sell. James, in common decency, could no rush out of the place where he had been so well treated, although he was very anxious about Madeleine; the heavy firing had started up again and though it seemed to be etiquette at the Hotel St Honoré to ignore it there was a good deal of movement in th street outside, as if people were beginning to realize that this wa something more than the artillery exchanges of the past hundred days. The two medical commissioners had seen no London paper since the beginning of the siege, and again detained James fo questioning on events in the outer world. The American Ministe was the only man in Paris who, by special favour of Bismarck, re ceived the current newspapers from London, and after he ha shared them with a few friends he sent them down to Presiden Trochu at the Louvre with the articles uncomplimentary t France carefully marked in ink. From Trochu's office they filtere out to the Paris editors, who rewrote the news pages with thei own political slant, so that the critical little company round Un thank's table d'hôte had no longer any idea what to believe. The were fully aware, however, of the anti-British and anti-American feeling accumulating in Paris, and were amused at James's indignation over the departure of the British representatives.

"It comes to the same thing in the end," shrugged Dr. Gordon. "Go to Tours with Gambetta, like Lord Lyons, or stay in Paris and shake Trochu by the hand, like Mr. Washburne, it makes no difference—they'll hate the lot of us either way. Tell 'em Britain has subscribed twenty thousand pounds for their ambulances, and all they'll say is, 'Ah ça, c'est très bien' but what about the cheap army boots with composition soles that British manufacturers sold to the army contractors—no wonder they can subscribe to ambulances out of the profits!' Tell them the New York Charitable Fund is all ready for distribution as soon as the war is over, and they say, 'Damn their charity, our war has been a godsend to the New England gunsmiths—' and they'll quote you several contradictory sets of figures of the carbines and cartridges bought for cash money from the U.S.A.!"

"The French hate the Yankees worse than us, though," chimed in his colleague, Dr. Innes. "They argue that they helped create the United States by fighting on the colonial side in the Revolution, and so American troops should be fighting side by side with them now. I tell you, Mr. Bruce, the Frogs are ill folk to deal with, for *they* must always be right and the other fellow wrong; but there's a something about them that makes me glad I went through this winter by their side."

"You may be proud of yourselves, gentlemen," said James briefly, and rose to shake hands. Dr. Gordon looked up at him thoughtfully.

"Good luck to your expedition," he said. "A word or two of practical advice before you go. Innes and I will keep our mouths shut about your plans, of course. I think Munro will too, if we can keep him off the Mountain Dew, but don't let them be known to all and sundry! Impress that on the lady, she has a host of friends and admirers, and you never know what news may leak out to the guards at the gate, or even as far as St. Denis. I don't want to see you both dragged back again as a pair of Prussian spies!"

"I'll remember that."

"The second thing is, be sure to take some medical supplies along with you. What have you got in those ample pockets—bandages?"

"No—food," said James. "Liebig's meat extract, cocoa, some desiccated eggs. I gave some stuff to the people in my billet at Brie."

"Liebig," said the doctor, with a groan. "I'll never want to taste or prescribe the stuff again, useful as it has been in the siege! You need strappings, gauze, permanganate crystals—come up to my room and I'll put some stuff together for you. You never know what will come in handy. You may not reach the Belgian frontier quite as soon as you would like."

It was only a short distance from the hotel to the converted food market where de Lesseps had his headquarters. Madeleine was sitting in de Lesseps' office; she had told him the whole story, and the President of the Suez Canal Company was all enthusiasm and congratulations. He shook James warmly by the hand and said the story of his journey to Paris reminded him somewhat of the race to El Kantara. James agreed.

"I can't think of any two people who suit each other better," the canal-builder declared. "In energy and in—what shall I call it—executive fortitude, the perfect match! You know, Mr. Bruce, sometimes when I used to watch this girl with her team, down in the hall there or up at the fortifications, I used to wonder where she would ever find a man to equal her—it was foolish of me not to think of you!"

"Then you approve of my taking her away now, sir?"

"Decidedly—oh, decidedly! If it were my own wife, I wouldn't hesitate. Madeleine, my dear, I kiss your hand respectfully, thank you for myself and for our country and I beg you to look on your task here as honourably ended. You've done the work of three men, as I know well; you deserve your freedom and your happiness."

"Thank you, monsieur," said Madeleine. "May I go down on the floor now and say good-by to Gontard?"

"Be careful," said James. "We don't want a lot of people to know that we plan to cross the lines tomorrow."

"Tomorrow," she said, paling. "So soon?"

The crash of a shell beyond the river seemed to answer, *Not a moment too soon.*

"We have a good chance to go in the morning, Madeleine."

"Oh." She considered, with bent head. "But I must just *speak* to Gontard again! I'll tell him I'm going to have a few days' leave."

When she had slipped from the room de Lesseps' smiling face grew grave. He sat down heavily at his desk, his sturdy old body sagging, and shook his head at James. "I envy you! Soon to be in free land with your lady—what wouldn't I give for that? Do you know that I've had no news of Madame de Lesseps and our child for four months? I would know nothing at all about affairs in Egypt but for the courtesy of the American Minister, who sends me newspaper clippings referring to the traffic on the Suez Canal, and the quotations of Canal Company stock on foreign markets. We hold solemn meetings here of the board of directors—better than any farce—we discuss an operation that the whole world rang with, just over a year ago—a front-page story, everywhere; and now *we*, the men who built the Canal, the men who financed it, the men responsible for running it—we occasionally get news of it in a capsule tied round the leg of a carrier pigeon! How much is known in London of the result of our first year in operation?"

"Pretty well the whole thing, sir. You've had a prodigious run of traffic—five hundred vessels to the middle of December, but the tolls haven't met the working expenses; is that right?"

"Quite right. Then the war will push us further down still, next year. The Germans are certainly going to demand an enormous indemnity, and the French investors will put their money in Liberty Loans rather than in Canal stock. We shall be borrowing money soon, like as your friend Ismail Pasha!"

"Do you think it would have helped matters if you had gone back to Egypt after the revolution?"

"Not much; this is a financial problem now, and the answer to it is here in Paris. No, it never occurred to me to go back to Port Said then."

"But if you'll forgive me," James persisted, "I've been wondering why you chose to stay on, after the Empress had gone; I remember how devoted you were to her! Surely it was contrary to all your belief in the Empire—all the Empire did for the Canal—to stay on and work for the Republic?"

De Lesseps smiled. "You must ask Madeleine to tell you the answer to that question, Mr. Bruce. She knows it very well. What she has done here has been done *for France*; not for my poor Eugénie, not for General Trochu, not for abstracts like the Empire or the Republic, but for something greater than the sum of all of them! I'm glad you're going to take her to Alexandria—she'll have a link with home in the French community in Egypt and you must bring her often to us at Ismailia."

"Gladly, sir—Ismailia was where I fell in love with her."

De Lesseps laughed outright at last. "I shall always believe then, that I brought you two together."

"You had more to do with it, Monsieur de Lesseps, than you can possibly realize."

James saw, after he had taken Madeleine away from the ambulance depot, that she was pensive and downcast; her hand, when he drew it through his arm, was icy cold in its loose silk glove.

"My dear," he said cheerfully as they prepared to cross the rue St. Honoré, "we must think of making some preparations for you on our journey. Will you let me buy you a fur tippet, or a pelerine, or whatever you call it, to put over that cloak you're wearing? It'll be very cold, crossing the fields, and I don't suppose there will be any warmers in the train tomorrow night."

Madeleine hesitated. She could see, not far beyond the corner of the rue de Castiglione, the sign of the "Reine d'Angleterre." Behind the shutters of the famous furriers, closed and bolted since the previous July, was stored a real treasure in furs, capes and cloaks in sable, ermine, sealskin and white fox, belonging to her dead mother and to herself.

"James," she replied in a tone as cheerful as his own, "don

you know that every fur shop in Paris has been closed for months?"

"I ought to have thought of that, I suppose. But some warmer wrap for travelling you must and shall have."

Madeleine tightened her clasp on his arm. She had made up her mind to do something unbelievably distasteful to her—to go back, for the first time since her flight, to her uncle's house.

"It would be silly to start buying new clothes at siege prices," she said, with an air of prudence which sat oddly on impulsive Madeleine. "I've been thinking that I really ought to go to our house in the Faubourg and get some things I shall need for the next few days, and especially a heavier cloak."

"Couldn't Madame Poisson do that this afternoon?"

"She wouldn't know what to look for. Come, James—it isn't far; and there's nobody there but ghosts."

It was true that there was no one living in the great house belonging to Michel Bertaux, for the master had put the remaining servants on board wages before he left for Marseilles and Tours; but the Old Poisson was still very much there, sitting in his lair beside the barred gates as he and his ancestors had always sat at the d'Arbonne doorways, grumbling, spying, passionately loyal; riding out the storms of war and revolution with far more ease than their masters. He greeted "the fisherman's grandchild" without enthusiasm. As the last in a long catalogue of her sins he held that she had deceived him by her pretended departure to Arbonne; and he scowled heartily at her reappearance with a strange man in tow. There was so much drifted snow in the courtyard that he had to sweep a path through it for Madeleine, and the bronze Nubian slaves holding the gaseliers on either side of the steps had turned into snowmen. The load of snow on the glass canopy above the door and on the sills and sashes of the tall windows gave an underwater light to the interior of the great hall.

"Did you ever *feel* such cold?" said Madeleine, almost in a whisper. "It's worse than outdoors."

There was a ghastly chill about the rooms where Bertaux had kept up such a rage of fires and lights.

"I won't be long, darling—ten minutes, I promise. Go into the library and wait for me. It's too cold near the big windows."

She was off, running up the familiar staircase, and into the rooms which had been hers. She found a large bag of fine morocco, with gold fittings, picked up some jewelled trifles which had belonged to her mother and then faced the perplexity of bureau drawers full of lingerie as fine as cobwebs, in lawn, batiste, Lyons silk and convent-embroidered linen, all as unsuitable for a winter journey to Belgium and London as they had been for an ambulance driver. She selected a few garments and snapped the bag shut. The cloak she had worn to Lapérouse with James was hanging in the wardrobe—fine black cloth lined and banded with sable; she found in one of a dozen boxes a little sable toque to match. She put them on, and at once in the long pier glass a familiar figure appeared to greet her: Madeleine d'Arbonne, leader of the *coco dettes*, woman of fashion. "Are *you* back again?" she whispered. "Are you still beautiful, as he tells you? You have to be!" She thought of the journey ahead of them. "I'll wear my sheepskin, not this, and be the relief driver," she thought. "It'll be the last time!"

And she remembered, a little resentfully, that de Lesseps had told her at the end that he would get Pierre Farinet, one of the real relief drivers at the depot, to take over her team as soon as she had gone. "How soon I'll be forgotten! No memorial to Driver d'Arbonne—not even a Cross of the Legion of Honour when they're being given away at the end of the war!" Hurriedly she ran downstairs. There was one thing she knew she had to do. In her uncle's study she found a sheet of paper and scribbled hastily:

"Dearest Michou—When you read this I shall be gone from Paris." (And stopped to look incredulously at the words.) "Mr. Bruce came through the siege lines to find me, and so I shall be married at last to the man I love. Thank you for everything you did for me and forgive me if I hurt you by running away. Be kind to Louise and Frank and don't try to part them, because they love each other—Your loving Madeleine."

It said nothing—it said it all! And on an impulse she added one more line:

"If anything happens to me please give my diamonds to Louise."

James was walking up and down the hall, and he came quickly to take her bag and wraps and put them on a table.

"My darling, I wanted to tell you something, but you ran away from me so fast. Something I couldn't tell you in the street, because I wanted to have my arms around you : Madeleine, we can't be married before we leave for Belgium."

Quickly, he described his visit to the Embassy. She listened leaning back on his arm, scanning his earnest face, with a little smile, half loving and half amused, at the corners of her mouth.

"You set so much store on being married, don't you?" she said at the end of his story, rubbing her cheek against his.

"So do you, I hope."

"But I *feel* married now," she assured him, "at least as much as if we had been pronounced man and wife by Mr. Falconer-Atlee, who used to *eat* such a lot when he came to the balls at the Tuileries !"

"Let's hope the Consul at Brussels isn't such a greedy man."

"Let's—oh, James !"

She had seen something, across his shoulder. She left his embrace and went to stand before a great empty space where the Devéria portrait of her mother had hung for so many years.

"I didn't know that had been taken down. Uncle must have really been afraid of looting."

"I noticed it was gone," said James. "It's left a faded place on the wall."

"It's horrible," said Madeleine. "All gone—James, let us go too. This house is as cold as a graveyard—and as sad."

They went in the direction of the Place Beauvau, where cabs were sometimes to be found outside the Ministry of the Interior, and were lucky enough to find one there. So James once again drove across Paris with his bright beauty in his arms, richly dressed as of old, with the perfumes of her wardrobe clinging to the sable-trimmed cloak, and the faint clover smell that he called "Essence of Madeleine" starting his senses on the wild clamour he knew so well how to rouse. And all the rest of that day she was again adorably loving, there under the roof of the *hôtel*

367

d'Arbonne, and even laughing with her old reckless gaiety when the heavy shelling started again in the late afternoon.

There was not much sleep for anyone in Paris that night, for the shell blasts were doing terrible damage in the southern quarters, and all night long the *rappel* was beaten, calling company after company of the National Guard to the work of salvage. Early in the morning Madame Poisson, with red eyes, came to prepare their coffee, and listened to Madeleine's instructions. Her diamonds to Louise, her stray cat to the concierge—Madeleine's affairs were soon disposed of; and she had enough money left to add something to the handsome present James gave to Madame Poisson. The woman made Madeleine's furred cloak and cap into a long roll wrapped in a dark blanket, which could be pushed well down in an ambulance wagon : it was agreed that it would attract far less attention, and even help their escape if she travelled out of Paris in her old dress of an ambulance driver.

Just before eight o'clock Madeleine took up her station at the window to look for Munro coming over the Pont Royal—it was once again nearly freezing, and too cold to wait at the corner of the bridge. James, going to look for her, found her in her day dress and sheepskin jacket, the infantryman's képi lying on the bed. She had the white cat in her arms. She was looking across the Seine at the Louvre, the Tuileries and the bare snowy slope of the Butte Montmartre. From the door he could see that she was shivering violently.

"Are you saying good-bye to Chérie, darling?" he said with a forced laugh. He was intensely nervous, hardly believing yet that he had won her, that she would willingly leave this city, to which he now knew she was bound by every fibre of her being, to go away with him.

She turned and shook her head. "Poor Chérie ! But Madame Poisson will take care of her, and there's always a fire in the lodge." She set the cat gently on the bed. "I was trying to say good-bye to Paris."

"Ah, Madeleine, don't grieve so much ! When the war is over we'll come back again."

She turned to him eagerly. "Do you promise that?"

"Darling, try to stop shivering. Did you catch a chill in that old house yesterday? Of course I promise."

"And come back *here*, James—I know I could arrange it with my father. Here to my own home? to the Quai Voltaire, where you came to find me through the Prussian lines, and we've been so happy?"

"I promise, Madeleine."

The wagon with the Red Cross flag was coming heavily across the Pont Royal, and up in front, beside the driver, sat Hector Munro, with his inquisitive snout, and his sharp eyes, his ugly, utterly dependable Aberdeen face scanning the windows of the Quai Voltaire.

Very nearly forty-eight hours later they arrived at the railroad station at Laon, in the first grey light of Sunday morning, the eighth of January, Madeleine almost too stiff and cramped from her night in the supply train to get out on the platform.

The journey out of Paris, which James hoped to make as easy as possible for her, had been far more difficult than the journey in.

All had gone well enough as far as St. Denis. The guards at the Paris gate had recognized Madeleine sitting beside the driver, and had passed out Dr. Bruce unquestioningly as the colleague of Dr. Munro. But as they made their slow way up the avenue de Paris to St. Denis the same infernal cannonading as yesterday's had begun; all round the capital the forts started firing simultaneously and no vehicles of any sort were allowed to move out of St. Denis to the east. The wait had been hardest of all for Madeleine, who had been compelled for fear of attracting attention to go down into the ambulance yard and busy herself with the team which had brought them out, while James, under the strictest orders from Hector Munro, made himself as inconspicuous as possible in a corner of the dispatchers' hall. By the time darkness fell there was no question of going out of St. Denis that night, and finally they all slept in the wagon, in the courtyard; the driver braced against the tilt in front, Madeleine on a stretcher and James and Munro wrapped in army blankets on the floor. She said with a laugh that she had had many a good night's rest in the

same sort of place before, but when James awoke in the middl
of the night to hear her teeth chattering and felt her hand bur
ing in his own when he reached up to touch it, he had the fir
misgivings of his wisdom in taking her away from Paris.

She had certainly caught a chill, whether in her uncle's hou
or elsewhere did not matter, for her eyes were heavy and moi
next morning although she still protested that she was very war
inside her sheepskin coat. It was an immense relief when the
were allowed to go forward. Hector Munro's stage was now ende
but he sent them on in one of the Anglo-American wagons wi
a merry Irish doctor, little more than a boy, who was call
Charlie Ryan, hailed from Tipperary and had volunteered h
services at the very beginning of the war. Dr. Ryan saw them in
Le Tremblay, where the war correspondent, Archibald Forbes, ha
been keeping a lookout for them, and on Forbes's army co
wrapped in all the coverings they possessed, Madeleine sle
heavily for what remained of Saturday.

"I'm beginning to wish we could keep you here for a bit," sa
Archibald Forbes worriedly, as he and James Bruce conferred
a room elsewhere in the house where Forbes was billeted. '
looked so good on paper when you were here four days ago, b
now the whole line to the north has become so fluid, we ca
tell at Saxon Headquarters where anybody is. And I hate to see
er—the lady run into any kind of danger. Gad, what a story s
has to tell! Flo Nightingale brought up to date, with a mule wh
instead of a lantern! And this stuff of yours about the Embas:
the three sheep in the cellar and the youngster reading the yello
back in the Chancery! Labby never filed a word of that."

"Just don't attribute it to me by name, that's all," said Jam
"I shall have enough explaining to do when I get back to Lead
hall Street without that! Now, my dear fellow, do show me wh
you mean by the fluid line. I don't know the position in t
north at all."

"All right. Here's our railroad, running northeast throu
Soissons to railhead at Laon. At Laon you're less than thirty-f
miles from Hirson, the last town before the Belgian border. O1
across, you take the country roads to Chimay, where there's

comfortable inn, and then at your leisure make for the Charleroi highway, Brussels, Antwerp and home."

"It's all in the 'once across,' isn't it?"

"I believe you! At Laon, you *should* be able to hire a carriage, at least as far as Vervins, where there's another posthouse, but who can tell what General Faidherbe will be doing by the time you get there? He went for Bapaume hammer and tongs on the third—the day you were here—and threw the 65th Prussians out of the town after fearful slaughter. Since then we don't know what he's up to. He's been reported coming south towards Paris by Albert; other reports say he's advancing through St. Quentin. On the Prussian side General Manteuffel has been superseded at last by General von Göben, who has opened his campaign by cutting the bridges across the Somme. In other words, four days ago the line of battle was fifty miles west of the highway to Hirson. Now it's—what? Twenty as the crow flies. Not very pleasant when you're travelling with a lady—and she looks rather poorly to me. Would you like our medical officer to have a look at her? He's very chivalrous, and I'm sure he'd be discreet."

"I think the less she sees of 'your' officers the better," said James bluntly. "I don't think she wants to be beholden to the Germans. I haven't dared mention Prince George's safe-conduct."

Forbes shrugged. "As you please. I think she ought to eat something before she goes, though. Will she take anything that comes from our mess?"

But Madeleine, when James gently roused her, had no appetite. She was greedy for a hot drink made from the Liebig extract and boiling water, but complained that her throat was too sore to swallow solid food. She wanted to have the candle blown out again—to put her head down and lie in the darkness; but when James told her how soon the train would leave she plucked up her courage, asked to be left alone and completed the transformation from ambulance driver to fashionable lady with the speed and skill she had cultivated in dressing at the Tuileries. With a graciousness exactly modelled on Eugénie's, she thanked Forbes for his courtesy—was sorry to have been such a dull guest—and looked as resolutely through the German train personnel as the Empress

might have ignored some peasant who omitted to snatch his ca
off as she went by. Without one word of complaint, her arr
passed firmly through her lover's, she sat side by side with him o
the lumpy mail sacks at the back of the supply train jolting i
way into the Aisne.

As might have been expected, it was not easy to find a drive
to take them anywhere beyond Laon early on a Sunday mornin
when, after several weeks of such bitter frost and cold that catt
had died in the fields and byres as fast as men died in the trenche
a thaw was making the roads almost impassable. The postin
master suggested that they wait at the inn while his nephew wer
to see if Monsieur Armand, the mail carrier, who was of course o
duty that day, would be willing to drive them at least as far ₂
Marle, about twelve miles away.

Twelve miles—say twenty-three more to the frontier. James w₂
perplexed to know what to do. Marle, he found, was quite a sma
village, probably with fewer facilities than Laon, but was it wi
to risk remaining in Laon, where his keen ears could hear ₂
curious mutter and chatter whenever the wind blew from th
north? He did not think Madeleine had heard it, for when I
returned to the inn he found her sitting with her elbows on th
table, her head buried in her hands in an attitude of utter wea₂
ness. The German troops were coming out of their barracks an
billets now and swaggering about the Sunday streets. It struck hi
with painful force that this was the first time she had actual
seen her country's invaders. Apart from the prisoners she mig
have seen at the Paris forts and the officers and trainmen in th
darkness at Le Tremblay, *les Prussiens* had been for six mont
only a hateful name to her. Now she saw them in complete occ
pation of a French town and countryside, and from that sight sh
had turned away her head.

James sat down and put his arm about her. "My precious gi
can you ever forgive me for giving you such a terrible journey ?

She smiled at that. "You couldn't help the delay at St. Den
and that's the only thing we didn't count on. But shall we g
away from here soon, do you think?"

"Monsieur Armand, the local postman, has a vehicle of sor

which he drives wedding parties in when he isn't distributing
mail, it seems. I've sent a boy to fetch him and we'll try to get forward to Vervins, if we can. And then it's only—let's see—about
twenty kilometres to the Belgian border, where we'll find some inn
with good food and fires and you can rest as long as you like before we go on further." "It sounds wonderful," she said.

But the turnout, when it appeared before the inn, was not
encouraging.

"Oh heavens!" said Madeleine, coming to the door on James's
arm. "I hope he doesn't deliver the mail in *that* thing!"

The vehicle was an old broken-down calèche, with hairy rugs
of doubtful cleanliness in the bottom; the screw between the
shafts had galled shoulders, and Armand the postman was a one-
eyed man of very limited intelligence, too old for military service,
and speaking a thick patois which even Madeleine could scarcely
understand. He made it quite clear, however, that he could not
take them direct up the Marle-Vervins road : *les Prussiens* had
blown a bridge about three miles out of Laon, but he thought he
could make a detour on the back road by Crécy, if the lady and
gentleman didn't mind a few bumps.

The lady and gentleman got in, and the calèche started at a
walking pace.

They had not gone very far before the Prussian sentries stopped
them. Laon, as the railhead of their supply line, was well guarded,
and the pickets had been doubled; James felt his mouth go dry
with anxiety as the mounted men surrounded the calèche. He
produced the Saxon prince's safe-conduct and his other papers,
with an anxious glance at Madeleine. After the first start of alarm
she had sat back in the vehicle, staring straight ahead, ignoring
the troopers as she had ignored the Saxons at Le Tremblay.

"A bad time of the year to travel!" said the Prussian sergeant
morosely, signing to the driver to proceed. "*Bon voyage, madame!*"

"I didn't know you could speak German, James!"

"I don't speak it well."

"What was that paper you gave the man?"

"My British passport, dear."

She said no more. She was cold and shivering, for the cloth

373

hood of the calèche was torn in a dozen places along the ribs of its frame. James took his tartan plaid, which Madeleine had been using as a rug round her knees, and made a kind of nest in one corner, drawing it up high behind her head and about her shoulders. It gave some extra protection against the wind blowing across the melting snow, into which the calèche was sinking almost to the hubs.

"You're my bonny Scots lassie now," he said tenderly, as a few strands of her fair hair, escaping beneath the little fur cap, fell across the vermilion, yellow and lime-green of the bright Bruce tartan. She laughed, and settled comfortably in his arm, closing her eyes; they got through the mud patch outside Laon where the German transport had churned up the road, and on more solid ground the postman's horse actually began to trot. The mutter of the distant guns was heard no longer. "We've done it!" James told himself. "Twenty miles to the border, and I'll have her safely out and home with me to love and to cherish for evermore. My beautiful darling!"—and he began to kiss her passionately until she opened her heavy, clouded blue eyes and kissed him back.

"Is it far from here to Deauville?"

In all his love and exultation, he felt a cold touch upon his heart.

"To Belgium, darling. Not very far now."

"How funny—I thought we were going to Deauville with the Empress. . . . It must be the calèche that made me think of it: we hired one like this, somewhere along the road."

The explanation was rational enough to relax his fear. But he looked at her very closely: there were shadows round her mouth and eyes.

"Did you ever hear what happened to her after she went to England, James? For certain, I mean—not the stuff the papers told?"

"She's living at a place called Chislehurst, not very far from London. She has her boy with her there, and several of the family."

374

"Poor Loulou—they won't be able to marry him to the Queen of England's daughter now!"

"Was that the plan? He's to go to Woolwich, I believe. It's the military academy for gunners and Engineers."

"Well," said Madeleine with the shadow of her old laugh, "Louis has had more practical experience than most of the cadets!"

They came within sight of the houses of Crécy. James had hoped to find an inn there, where he could at least prepare a broth of the meat extract and water; but the inhabitants of Crécy had all fled. Only two or three of the houses were still standing, the rest were down in a huddle of stone and burned rafters, showing that von Göben had passed that way.

"Don't look, Madeleine!"

But she would look; she *would* see what the invaders had done to France. And in the next mile there were worse things to see; worse than anything James had seen in his journey up to Paris: dead men and bloated cattle round the farms which Faidherbe's little army had turned into strong points. They were journeying now across the landscape of a nightmare, peopled by the shrouded dead peering from the windows of roofless homes through drifting mists rising from the bloodstained snow, made all the more hideous by the rays of a watery sun.

It was the position of the sun, when he compared it with the time on his new watch, which at last warned James that they were in trouble. They ought by now to have turned east for Marle and the Hirson road; the direction they were following was still north-west.

"I say, driver! Have you any idea where you're going?"

"Don't shout at him, James. You won't get a thing out of him if you do."

"You try him then. I can't understand him anyway."

Monsieur Armand, under gentler persuasion, halted his horse sullenly and admitted that he had lost his way. It was at the Crécy crossroads, he said. Those Prussian animals had shelled the signpost. He had missed the turning on the Marle detour.

"A hell of a postman you are," said James.

"Crécy is three kilometres outside my area."

"Where are we *now*?" interrupted Madeleine. "That's what we want to know."

There, Monsieur Armand said triumphantly, he was certain of his ground. There was only one possible destination on their way: Ribemont.

"Is there an inn at Ribemont?"

"In principle, yes."

Another mile of slow anxiety. There had also been, in principle, an inn at Crécy.

But there were signs of life at Ribemont. Smoke was coming from several chimneys, and the houses seemed more or less intact. The sound of the guns was much closer. It was coming from west of a sluggish waterway, bridged just beyond the village.

"What's the name of that river?" James was trying to remember what he had seen on the war correspondent's map.

"That's not a river, monsieur. That's the Sambre canal."

"And what lies beyond it?"

"The town of St. Quentin."

The new objective of General Faidherbe's army.

"Maybe we can get a change of horses here—"

It might not, after all, be impossible. He saw three animals in good condition, tied to the iron rings outside what appeared to be the inn, and there was gold enough to buy them all in his money belt.

The calèche ground to a halt at the foot of what might once have been the inn garden, and James, jumping down, turned to hand out Madeleine. She was lying back in the enveloping plaid, with her eyes shut in the strange torpor which had overtaken her at Laon.

"Madeleine, darling! Are you all right?"

"I don't feel well." It was dragged out of her at last, the admission on which she had closed her lips for three days.

"Let me lift you—so—like this. Can you walk? We'll get you into the house, and find a doctor. Hey there!" cried James in the direction of the inn. "Are there no women about this place?"

There was one. A thin, frightened slut in a dirty apron, who came running towards them across the snowy yard.

"You can't come in! You can't come in!"

"Have you Prussians here?" said James, with an eye on the horses.

"No—no—no! But the gentlemen have reserved all the rooms!" Then, glancing back at the inn and lowering her voice, she whispered,

"*Les francs-tireurs!*"

"All right," said James, "we'll do them no harm—what do you take us for? Help me with this lady—can't you see she's ill?"

The girl, intimidated, took the bag and wraps. Very slowly, with his arm about her, James began to lead Madeleine towards the inn.

The entrance had boasted in better times a kind of summer-house front, part glass and part vines, in which they could see as they approached the shadow of a skulking figure.

The door flew open and a tall man appeared on the step.

"*You, sir! What are you doing with my sister?*"

They stared at him dumbfounded. It was Victor d'Arbonne, in the rags of a Cuirassier uniform, with an army pistol wavering in his hand.

"My God!" said the apparition, disbelievingly. "It's the Scots engineer from El Kantara!"

VIII

"Victor!"

Madeleine, who had stopped dead in the moment of recognition, went stumbling up the path towards her brother with her hands held out. But James, at her back, exclaimed,

"D'Arbonne! Put down that pistol!"

The young man wavered, the hand holding the pistol fell. Two men, also in ragged uniforms, who had drawn their weapons and followed him outside when they heard shouting, stood back a little sheepishly to let the tall woman in sables enter the inn.

In a dark parlour, where a fire had been newly kindled and a table set for the *francs-tireurs*, Victor, still furiously, repeated his question to James Bruce.

"What are you doing in France, sir? Where are you going with my sister?"

Madeleine, turning upon him as fiercely, cried,

"And what are *you* doing here? Why are you still in uniform? You broke your parole to the enemy, didn't you?"

"Captain d'Arbonne," said James Bruce, and the weight of his personality, as well as of his fifteen years' seniority, silenced both of them for a moment, "I grant your right to question me, but no in public. Surely there's no need for all these people to hear wha we have to say?"

They had already a considerable gallery. The two *francs-tireur* hesitated in the doorway, uncertain whether to go or stay. One o them, who had the appearance and manner of a gentleman, looke supremely uncomfortable. The other, a deserter from Vinoy' corps, was grinning from ear to ear. The sluttish servant was re inforced by an elderly woman with a cooking spoon in her hand and Armand the postman had tethered his fiery steed to th gatepost and come to see the fun.

"I don't give a damn who hears me," said Victor, but he pu his pistol back in its holster, and his comrades did the same. "It oo bad—it's insufferable—that a man fighting for months to save is country should come on his sister travelling with a stranger n the heart of occupied France! What the devil are you doing ere, Madeleine? Why aren't you at Arbonne with my father?"

"I've been in *Paris*, Victor, all through the siege. Father is quite vell, Louise too; Mr. Bruce saw them only a week ago—"

"D'Arbonne, I know you've no idea of all your sister has done n Paris—but this is not the time or place to tell you. Madeleine ill—one of these people must be sent to fetch a doctor—"

"A doctor!" cried Victor. "Look at her!"

She was drawn up to her full height, backed against the wall, nd with her cheeks and eyes shining with the false brilliance of sing fever, looking superbly well.

"Let's have an end of this," she said. "Victor, you get no ex-lanations from me at the pistol's point, and you know it. Let e go on—Mr. Bruce and I are on our way to be married—"

"So you aren't married yet—I thought so!"

"We couldn't be married in Paris, the British Consul had gone way."

"You bitch!" cried Victor. "Any priest would have married ou, and you know it!"

"Hold your tongue, you blackguard!" James flung at him. We'll be married as soon as we reach Brussels—"

"Brussels! Is *that* where you're headed for! Then what the ll are you doing five miles east of St. Quentin?"

"The driver lost his way. Hey, you, monsieur What's-your-me, tell this gentleman how you went in the wrong direction—"

"I don't even deliver *letters* as far north as Crécy," said the jured mailcarrier.

"I don't believe a word of it!" screamed Victor. "You're headed r von Göben's corps! You're going to report on Paris to your asters! Prussian spy! Prussian spy!"

He struck James Bruce hard across the face.

The force of the blow sent James reeling against the mantel. An bsolute silence fell upon the parlour and the corridor as the red ark of fingers sprang out along his jaw and he took out his andkerchief and pressed it to his bleeding mouth.

379

"Will you fight, you coward?"

"That's enough, Victor," said the more prepossessing of the two *francs-tireurs* immediately. "The insult is complete without a charge of cowardice. Well, monsieur?"

The eyes of every man and woman were upon James Bruce. Instinctively he looked at Madeleine. Her face was set, she was staring at him, he saw no compunction for her brother there. Fight him—the little bastard—James asked nothing better; but a fight to him meant, or had meant long ago (in the school playground in Buchan, in the apprentices' yard at Hall and Sons) a fight with bare fists, in which the best man won, not—a duel! He hadn't even been in a fist fight since he was a Third Engineer! He looked at the table. Not a wine bottle on it; at eleven o'clock in the morning it wasn't possible that the little beast was drunk. He looked round them all, and knew that he was among people who judged courage and cowardice by other standards than those of the bourgeois world in which he had lived so long.

"I'll fight you with pleasure," he said. "Here and now."

"By the canal bank then, with sabres!" cried Victor.

James let his eyes travel coolly over the tattered figure before him. "You forget," he said, "you're not wearing a sword. I presume you gave it up, or broke it across your knee at Metz! I don't pretend to be an expert on the duelling code, but I know I've the choice of weapons, and I choose pistols. Unless you brought your derringers along with you by any chance, we'll use your army issue—I know I can safely confide in *your* honour, Captain d'Arbonne!"

At the deadly reminder of his broken parole, Victor cried out again and lunged forward; his arm was caught by the *franc-tireur* who said, "Victor, this gentleman is acting within his rights. I was a witness to the provocation, sir; if you desire my services as a second, they're at your command."

"Oh that!" said James contemptuously. "You insist on going through all that rigmarole? Then I presume your friend will act for Captain d'Arbonne, unless he prefers the postman? Now will you both persuade the other principal to withdraw for the time being? I'll meet you all in fifteen minutes, down by the water here. Now you, madame"—he turned to the innkeeper, after the three *francs-tireurs* had left the room—"bring me a bottle of brandy, will you, and put your largest kettle on the fire."

"What's the kettle for?" asked Madeleine.

"My dear," said James, taking off his cape and beginning to rummage in the pockets, "somebody's going to get hurt. I don't intend it shall be me, but some kind of first aid will certainly be needed, and that means boiling water and plenty of it. I wonder if Dr. Gordon ever imagined anything like this would happen when he gave me these." And he laid out on the clean tablecloth the roll of bandages, the disinfectant and other things he had carried away from the Hotel St. Honoré, placing them side by side in his own methodical way.

Madeleine burst out in hysterical laughter.

"Oh, James! You look exactly as you did when you came on board the *Aigle* at El Kantara!"

He took her in his arms. Rigid, her teeth chattering, she clung to him.

"Remember the rockets that night, when we got down to Ismailia? We didn't see this coming then, did we? Would you have walked out on the promenade with me, if you'd known we'd come on as far as Ribemont?"

"*Yes!*" she said desperately, lifting her face to his kisses, "and further!"

"Then be my brave darling! We'll get back to Ismailia yet!"

"The brandy, monsieur." James looked hard at the woman: quite useless of course, a soft, fat trollop beaten and bewildered by the fighting which had rolled backwards and forwards along the line of the Sambre canal.

"Have you got that kettle going?" he asked sharply. "Is there a doctor anywhere near here?"

"The nearest doctor is at St. Quentin, monsieur."

"Yes, well; we can't get hold of him in a hurry. That will do, madame! Now Madeleine, take a sip of this, and hold on just half an hour; we'll soon be on our way."

"James." She drank the spirit at a gulp. "Victor is a first-class shot."

"So am I."

"With a pistol?"

"With a shotgun."

"Oh, James!" Her control was breaking, there were tears in her eyes at last. "If anything happens to you, what shall I do?"

He put down his brandy glass half empty, and kissed her—only once. Then without another word he left the room. He was afraid to speak, but not from weakening or tenderness; the passionate temper which he had fought through his life had absolutely mastered him now. He had been insulted—bullyragged—struck in front of gentlefolk and servants—forced into this absurd duel—if it hadn't been that the fellow was her brother, he would cheerfully have killed Victor d'Arbonne. "He raised his hand to me!" he said half aloud, as he went down the yard. "I'll make sure he never raises it again!" And he gave no answer to the driver of the ill-omened calèche, who came out with his hat in his hand to say that *just in case* monsieur should be *unlucky*, would he care to pay for the hire of the vehicle now?

The snow was beginning to fall again, in big soft wet flakes, and the mists were rising off the Sambre canal as he went down to the water's edge, where the three scarecrows were waiting. His second came hastily to meet him. "I ought to introduce myself, monsieur. My name is Voiron—Hercule Voiron; I regret that we meet for the first time in such circumstances."

"Yes!" said James. "What fire-eaters you all are! Why can't you confine yourself to killing Prussians?"

Hercule Voiron smiled. He was a large blond young man from French Flanders, not readily upset by the emergencies of life with the *francs-tireurs*.

"Captain d'Arbonne's conduct was inexcusable," he said in an undertone, "but there are certain allowances to be made! He has scarcely recovered from a bad head wound, received when his best friend was killed by his side at Mars-la-Tour—and then, killing Prussian sentries with a knife, and your face blackleaded, is an occupation which has been known to turn more stable heads than his."

"I don't understand you," said James coldly. "Are you my

382

cond, or his? Does Captain d'Arbonne back out of the quarrel, n the grounds that he is *non compos mentis*? Is he prepared to pologize to his sister, and to me? No? Very well, then; let's get n with what we came to do."

"I can only say further, sir, that if this affair turns out badly or you I'll do my best to help the lady. I'll escort her anywhere e may wish to go; surrendering myself to the Prussians if I ust."

"Very thoughtful," said James, "but it won't be necessary! ave you examined the weapons?"

Voiron's pistol, and the pistol of Vinoy's deserter, had been id on a folded jacket, covered from the snow. James examined e locks and priming carefully. While Victor d'Arbonne looked n from a few yards away, he buttoned his dark jacket over his hite shirt front.

"Will you take your places, gentlemen? In this weather it's ot possible to drop a handkerchief. You will fire at Three!"

The seconds paced the distance. Victor had shaved off his moustache and imperial as a symbol of repudiation after "the Dister," and he looked very like his sister as he stood there in the low, with his chin quivering. James, in the exaltation of his ury, traced no sentimental likeness. "He raised his hand to me!" istead of the flat ground by the Sambre he saw the dam at auchentree, and the wild bird rising out of the rushes, heard his ther's voice, lifted his gun—then the picture faded, and he was ick in France in the softly falling snow, listening to Voiron ying,

"Un—*deux*—TROIS!"

They fired together. He felt Victor's bullet scorch his cheek at e same moment as the young man swayed and fell slowly to s knees in the snow. James had placed his bullet exactly where e intended, shattering the shoulderblade of the arm which had een raised to strike.

When Madeleine saw them coming up through the snow from e canal bank, James stalking on ahead and her brother supported by the two *francs-tireurs*, she shrieked and fainted. The spurt of vitality which had carried her through the whole of the encounter with Victor was exhausted, and even when she was carried into a damp cold bedroom and restored to consciousness by the women, she lay on top of the coverings in a state of near collapse. Whatever first aid was administered to Victor, James knew nothing of it; he only left Madeleine for ten minutes, for a whispered conference with Voiron on the landing.

"The ball's lodged in his shoulder," said the *franc-tireur* "We'll have to get him back to our command post as fast as we can."

"Well, you don't want any advice from me, I know," said James, "but if I were you I'd cut along and join up with Faid herbe's army; the general can't be very far away, and presumably he has qualified doctors on his staff."

Voiron shrugged. "I've been thinking for some time that General Faidherbe was the man for my money. I'm not cut out for guerrilla fighting, and this morning's work has about finished me Funny thing—six months ago I was on garrison duty at Valence and complaining about the tedium of life in the Midi. I could do with a little of it now! How is the lady?"

"Pretty bad."

"A piece of advice in return for yours: why don't you take her in to St. Quentin? You'll never get a doctor to come out here to night, across the canals, and you can't stay in this hole. Damn it man, what's the difference—on to St. Quentin or back to Laon The Prussians hold them both."

The landlady was hotly of the same opinion. She was franti to get rid of them all; the very presence of the *francs-tireurs* under her roof could be punished by death if a Prussian patrol came that way, and James she regarded as an almost equally dangerous guest. He went back into the bedroom after the three men had ridden away with Victor's horse on a leading rein and Victor holding on to the pommel with his left hand. For once James was at a loss to know what to do next. The few remedies he knew were all of the rough and ready order. A swig of brandy, a carbol oil bandage for a stokehold burn, or a lump of cobwebs slapped on when an inefficient workman cut himself with an edged tool

—such was the extent of his robust pharmacopoeia. He stood looking down in absolute helplessness at the girl he worshipped, still lying fully dressed on the dingy bed.

But the brave blue eyes opened when he took her hand in his. "Is Victor all right? Did he ask for me?"

"They've taken him to a doctor, dear. He'll be all right—it was just a scratch."

"You're wonderful, James." She sighed and moved her head on the pillow. "This bed smells horrible."

"Could you try just one thing more? Could you sit in that rattletrap for about five miles, until we get as far as St. Quentin, and find a doctor to help you, and a comfortable inn?"

"Oh, darling, I'm so sorry. I thought we'd be halfway to Belgium by now."

"We'll try again tomorrow," said James with false assurance. He sent the women to her with a cup of boiled milk to which a dash of brandy had been added. It was the only thing he could think of, apart from the eternal Liebig, to give her a little strength to resume the painful journey. Monsieur Armand, too, was restoring himself in the inn kitchen, having at James's expense procured a cut from a hidden flitch of bacon and a bottle of wine; he tripled his price automatically when told he was to go to St. Quentin.

"You're lucky to get anything at all," James told him. "You damned fool, if you hadn't lost the way we might have been at Vervins by this time and all this spared."

James himself was in a suppressed frenzy of anxiety to get away. Not only because of the urgent need to get help for Madeleine, but because now that his rage had cooled he understood that they were in greater danger than at any time since their hazardous journey began. He had seen enough of the *francs-tireurs* at Guignes to know that when one patrol was in the neighbourhood another might not be far away. More men might come to Ibemont, perhaps with the Prussians at their heels, and in that case no safe-conduct, no British passport would prevent himself and Madeleine from being stood up against the wall of the inn with the people of the place, and shot through the head. He had not been afraid when they first arrived, for the quarrel with Victor had excluded every other thought. He knew now that all the time the three *francs-tireurs* had been near them they had been in danger of death.

It was two o'clock before they got away from Ribemont, Madeleine wrapped in the plaid with a reasonably clean quilt bought from the landlady over her knees. Every track and stain of the duel had been blotted out by the snow before they crossed the canal bridge: it was perhaps only then that James fully emerged from the state of shock in which he had fired upon her brother. It was succeeded by a feeling of intense dejection and remorse—not for his punishment of Victor, but for the situation in which he had placed *her*. If that little cad's bullet had come two inches closer—well, she might be on her way back to Laon now, stranded and desperate—

Instead of being on this delightful jaunt to St. Quentin with him.

They passed, as the short day ended, into a region as desolate as the one they had come through on the way from Crécy, with no sign of life in the roofless houses with flapping shutters which they passed along the way. It was a watery region, lying between the two canals of the Sambre and St. Quentin, from which the mists had given Louis Napoleon Bonaparte a special susceptibility to pain when he watched them rise from his cell in Ham prison long ago. Between the two canals flowed the river Somme. From the calèche the whole landscape seemed to be flooded: river and waterways, hollows full of melted snow, fresh-falling snow forming new pools and rivulets. It was a lake, not solid ground, across which they were travelling into St. Quentin.

"*Won't you come on with us to the Bitter Lakes?*"

She lay beside him in his tartan plaid, his captured prize, motionless, her cheeks sunken, her breathing harsh and loud.

—Now these are the Bitter Lakes, my Madeleine; these are the lowest of the Low Countries, where all the wars of Europe sooner or later are decided, here between the Somme and the Scheldt—

This is where the bitter cup will be held to our lips too.

Sentries with lanterns swinging halted them on the outskirts of the town. They were Black Brunswickers, not as easily in ressed as von Eckhardstein's Uhlans by Bruce's language and manner, but enough to summon their lieutenant, who humanely allowed Madeleine be taken to the principal inn before James went under guard to the town major's office. The latter was a decent fellow in his way, sick of the war and longing to get back to his comfortable Berlin apartment; he showed James photographs of his wife and three blond infants before they had been talking very long. A neutral traveller, vouched for by Prince George of Saxony, and an invalid lady concerned him only as two more mouths to feed inside St. Quentin—"and General Faidherbe's not very far away," he said significantly. "We may be the be-sieged, one of these days, unless General von Göben can cut his lines in time!

"Please observe the curfew," he added. "No movement in the streets after eight to-night. But I hope your wife will be a great deal better in the morning, Mr. Bruce, and able to go on with you to Belgium. I don't think you can very well get to Hirson from here, but we might be able to pass you through Le Cateau or the frontier post north of Maubeuge."

It was a better reception than James had dared to hope for, and he set out on the quest for a doctor with renewed energy. There was a great deal of sickness in St. Quentin. The little town had been in Prussian hands since the October battle, and the local hospitals, schools and parish rooms were still crowded with gangrene and pyemia cases resulting from infected wounds.

When James made his appeal for a doctor the few physicians were in conference with the parish priests about the space to be requisitioned if, as expected, a pitched battle were fought at St. Quentin in the next few days. The place was a key point on the road to Paris, eighty miles away: if Faidherbe could recapture it he would be only thirteen miles from Ham; twenty-five more would see him in Compiègne, and then the way was clear through the Ile de France to Paris. Gambetta had impressed upon him that he must try to deliver Paris by the nineteenth of January, for by that time the supply of flour would be almost exhausted. So the army of the North, thirty thousand strong, was mustered at Albert; and the people of St. Quentin waited for the day of liberation and prepared to welcome Faidherbe, the best fighting general of the young Republic.

"How is she?" James leaped at the doctor with his query as the little man came wearily downstairs.

"Come in here, Mr. Bruce."

Dr. Roc drew James inside a little private salon, where there was a small fire and a much greater degree of comfort than at Ribemont.

"I didn't realize your wife was a French lady, sir. I thought you'd come here straight from England."

"So?"

"So I have to ask you if she has been doing nursing work, or helping in a hospital recently?"

"Yes, she has. She's been in and out of hospitals, and in close contact with the wounded."

The doctor shook his head sadly. "That's it, then. Her temperature is too high now for me to get a coherent story out of her about the onset of the symptoms, but I fear there's no doubt that she's suffering from what we call the hospital fever."

"Typhoid?"

"A form of typhoid—we treat it much the same way, with the addition of water packs, and it requires very careful nursing."

"Is it dangerous—to the patient, I mean?"

"Very—and highly infectious, I may add. There's no question of moving her—you have to soothe your landlord, and I'll arrange about the nursing. Now come, Mr. Bruce, you must pull yourself together! Your lady has youth on her side—twenty-six, didn't you tell me?—we'll do the best we can for her, that's all."

"Dr. Roc, tell me just one thing—could she have caught the infection while she was travelling with me?"

"How long has your journey lasted, may I ask?"

"Since Friday morning."

"She caught the infection at least ten days ago. The fever slow to incubate, and if she was doing war work she probably thought the headaches and back pains were caused by sheer fatigue."

388

Ten days—and less than a week ago she had come to him bright nd glowing, radiant in the fulfilment of their love!

"My condolences, sir," said Dr. Roc, buttoning his overcoat. 'll call again first thing tomorrow morning. Try to get some rest ourself."

He took up his bag and said as he moved towards the door, "I *wondered* what she'd been doing to her hands!"

Thus began for James Bruce days of agony such as he had never nown, while in Madeleine's room Dr. Roc and the nurses fought save her life. He gave up the salon on the ground floor and oved into a narrow bedroom next to hers, in a corridor hung ith sheets soaked in vinegar and entirely cut off from the rest the hotel. The Prussian officers billeted there had moved out a hurry when they heard of the dreaded hospital fever, and so mes earned more black looks from the landlord, who had been aking a good thing out of his unwelcome guests and had to be ribed into giving James and the nurses proper attention. James as only permitted to look through her half-opened doorway vice a day. It was always the same thing he saw and heard—a tient in a white hospital bedgown tied at the neck and wrists ith tape, throwing herself restlessly from one side of the bed to e other, endlessly talking in a high hoarse voice. He knew that ven these moments were carefully selected, that there were hours every day when the invalid could be seen by nobody but her urses, as the fever took its dreadful way. There were prolonged tacks of vomiting, rending purges and bloody fluxions which ained her, every day, of more of her failing strength, and for hich Dr. Roc, it seemed could prescribe no remedy. "It must run s course, sir, it must run its course," was his dreary little chant ch evening. So, as the resistance of Paris weakened under the peated blows of Bismarck's heavy guns, the flame of life began to nk in the body of Madeleine d'Arbonne.

She had two nurses, a Franciscan nun who came at night, ex- austed by a spell of duty in the city hospital, but with her face ear and luminous like a washed-out shell as she repeated the ayers for the Sick at Madeleine's bedside, and a little woman

389

whom Dr. Roc had produced for day duty—a bit of human wreckage who, like themselves, had been cast up in St. Quentin by the tide of war. Madame Henri was, or had been, a vivandière attached to one of the French regiments cut to pieces by Manteuffel on his victorious way to Amiens in the precious December. She had somehow found her way east to St. Quentin, still wearing her képi cocked on one side of her head, her red and black spencer with its gilt epaulettes and her stout morocco gaiters, but having been relieved by a band of thirsty Prussians of the little wine barrel she had carried on her hip. She was a battered little woman of forty or more, loyal and willing, and strong enough to help the nun lift their patient into a deep tub of water twice a day. James, standing helpless on the landing, sometimes heard Madeleine cry out that they were drowning her.

The people of St. Quentin got to know James Bruce very well by sight that week. He had a routine to make the time pass, by which they said, you could set your watch. In the mornings he walked up and down the cobbled streets, always following the same pattern. He bought the newspaper, which was full of valiant falsehoods about the situation in Paris. He drew his daily ration of tobacco. He reported, by order, to the town major. Some of the more suspicious townsfolk who followed him at a little distance reported that when they accosted him he was very civil, asked no questions, and did not appear to be a stool pigeon of the Prussians. They wondered a little at his interest in ruined houses, for he spent a couple of hours, every afternoon, wandering among the debris of the October fighting.

James, in fact, was envying the men and women who were gathering the rubble into baskets and starting to rebuild their shattered homes. They, at least, had a job to do, and more than once he was tempted to take off the Inverness cape, now very much the worse for wear, and pitch in to help them. For the first time in his whole over-driven life he was unemployed, with nothing in the world to do but wait; and as he wandered in the streets of St. Quentin it was inevitable that his thoughts should sometimes turn to London, and the situation he had prepared for himself at the P. and O.

He had lost the Managership, of course; that was certain. Quite likely he had lost the post at Alexandria too. Young Sutherland was in the saddle now and hardly likely to promote any man who would disappear into France for a month at a stretch. Not that any of that mattered compared with Madeleine.

He never went far away from the inn. He liked best to be in his own room, where they could call him at once; where he could intercept little bearded Dr. Roc on his hasty visits, if only to hear the doctor repeat in the same hopeless whine, "It must run its course, monsieur, it must run its course!" Long before the curfew rang at eight he had eaten his supper of bread, soup and the eternal stewed apples, and was quite alone, with a few logs to keep his fire alive through the night, and his pipe and his thoughts for company.

Sometimes, with his head between his clenched hands, he tried to pray. "God—help her! God—spare her to me!" He got no further than that, for James, who could still recite the whole of the Shorter Catechism, had never been able to "wrestle in prayer" with the splendid eloquence which he knew his father was pouring out, in that same evening hour, over his diminished household at Lauchentree. Only, his whole being went into the halting words.

The nursing Sister had brought a priest to Madeleine, he knew. No priest could help the stern Calvinist who was Madeleine's lover. He stood arraigned at the bar of his own conscience, and found James Bruce guilty on all counts.

It was the "If" in every case that tormented him.

If anything happened to her family because of him, how could he face Madeleine when she recovered?

It made him wince to think that the only shot he had fired in France had been in a duel with her brother. If the *francs-tireurs* were unable to care for Victor's wound and the fellow died of an infection, what then?

If Frank Hartzell had left Arbonne to join the Auxiliary Army, and Louise and the old people had nobody left to protect them, then were they still safe from Prussian reprisals, or were they bearing the consequences of his own stubborn recklessness?

He knew that he had brought them all into danger. Even, an above all, Madeleine.

If he hadn't been in such a devil of a hurry to get her out Paris. If she had been lying in her own bed at the Quai Voltai now, with Madame Poisson to nurse her, and British doctors, wi the latest medicines, to make her well!

If he had never ridden away in that burst of nervous ang from the château gates at Compiègne. If he had treated her lo like the priceless gift it was, and gone to work to win her awa slowly and gently, from her life at court!

If he had crossed to France as soon as Dr. Evans told him s had refused to go to England with the Empress. If he had go straight from Hastings to the nearest Channel port and hurri to Paris, with a week in hand before the Gates were closed, inste of writing his futile letters to Arbonne!

This was the hardest *If* to contemplate because it carried wi it such a fearful sense of failure. To have had it in his power Hastings that September night *to make sure*; and then to ha gone tamely back to London, leaving her to whatever fate await her in France! To have been alert and ready all his life, graspi the nettle, taking those swift cool decisions, hammering and bar ing away, lavishing sarcasms on those who failed to come to his own standard—and then, when the great test of speed a resolution came, to have failed, himself!

There was something else he had to contemplate, in those hou of self-examination. James knew now that by taking Madelei away from Paris he had brought her into more immediate dang than any she might have run during the bombardment. Gene Faidherbe was advancing on St. Quentin and the Prussians we preparing to defend the town street by street, and house by hou The French general—so town rumour ran—was preparing to ma two flank attacks, at Querrieux and Castel Bellicourt, with a vi to drawing off the enemy to these villages and saving St. Quen intact if he could. But his strategy might not succeed, and th what would be the fate of the townspeople? Would they be caug in the cross-fire, as the townsfolk of Sedan had been, and die the ruins of their city?

James had been glad, once or twice in his journey, and especially when he was searched at the Prussian command post at
Brie, that he had carried no weapon with him. Now the palm of
his hand itched for the feel of the old Smith and Wesson, lying
at the bottom of his sea-chest in London, or any gun or pistol,
so that in the last agony of St. Quentin he could fight for France
and Madeleine.

January dawn creeping round the blind, and the sound of a
soft footstep in the passage.

"How is your patient this morning, *ma soeur*?"

"Monsieur, she is much about the same."

IX

There came a morning, about eight days after they left Ribemon
when the word, miraculously, was "Better!" and James wa
allowed to sit by Madeleine's bedside for a quarter of an hou
worshipping her as she lay smiling at him on her fresh pillow
while they listened to the music of Faidherbe's advance.

For a week James had been shaved and dressed for the day b
six in the morning in the hope that she might know him and b
able to speak to him. Now, when the great moment came and th
Franciscan nun came smiling to fetch him to her room, he had t
present himself with a hastily tied scarf and an unshaven chin
and blessed the circumstance, listening to her first laughter as sh
passed her hot thin fingers over the dark stubble and the unkem
locks of hair. James had been up all night, like everybody else i
St. Quentin, listening to the firing, as Faidherbe's artillery fo
lowed up Colonel Isnard's flying column, which had driven t
Prussians out of Castel Bellicourt before darkness fell. Now t
Brunswickers were in full retreat. The French XXII and XX
Corps were marching into the town, fifes and bugles shrillin
drums beating; and the church bells were ringing for the liberatio
of St. Quentin.

"Do you think all that bell-ringing will bother her?" was h
first query, when Dr. Roc came in pale but exulting to tell h
that their first talk had lasted long enough.

"I think she's very happy to know of a French victory," said t
little doctor. "She'll drop off to sleep now, and sleep most of t
day. Well, Mr. Bruce, I congratulate you; it's been a close ca
If we can get her through the next week without inflammati
or hæmorrhaging, she'll do very well, and she has youth on h
side, as I told you from the start. I wish I could say as much! D
you know that I operated from six last night until three o'clo
this morning, from the moment the Castel Bellicourt wound
started coming in? I must get back to the hospital now—w

on't you walk along with me? Come out and see St. Quentin *en
ête* for once!"

St. Quentin had gone mad with joy. Its heroic Prefect, Anatole
e la Forge, who had been severely wounded while leading the
esistance to the Mecklenburg troops in the previous October, had
rganized a welcome to General Faidherbe which Trochu might
vell have envied—such as even the Emperor in his heyday had
never known. James and Dr. Roc were soon separated by the
ownspeople swarming to the market place, where the Tricolore
vas hanging from every window, and James, never willing to go
oo far from the inn, gave up the attempt to see the victorious
eneral. He posted himself at a street corner to watch the troops
o by instead, waving and shouting to the townspeople, snatching
isses from pretty girls and children. They passed—on horseback,
n foot, on limbers, in sutler wagons, a conquering French
army at last.

James Bruce, taller than most of the men around him, was ex-
ellently placed to see another tall man, leading a company of
nfantry down the cobbled street.

"Frank!"

The shout that Frank Hartzell gave him in reply sounded, for
Union Army veteran, uncommonly like a rebel yell, They kept
ep with each other, grinning and waving, through the uproarious
treets of St. Quentin, until Frank's company received the order
o fall out and stack their rifles, and he was free to shake James
ruce, long and vigorously, by both hands.

Frank was magnificent. They had been able to outfit him in a
niform which the previous owner had had no time to wear out
he powder burn was almost completely hidden by the belt), and
e looked superb in the blue cutaway and red baggy trousers of
French infantryman. The white gaiters alone were missing (that
pply of buttons had never come to light), and the British-made
oots were not high enough, and certainly far from solid enough,
 make up the deficiency.

In the excitement of liberating St. Quentin, he hardly ques-
oned the presence there of the man he had supposed to be now
 London, if not within the walls of Paris. But in a very few

395

moments after his exuberant greeting, Frank's cheerful face fell
James began to tell him about Madeleine's illness, and the mise
able sequence of events which had brought them there.

"Oh, my God, Jim, that's bad!" he said blankly. "Hospit
fever! I saw too much of that in Libby. But she's getting better
you're sure she's taken the turn?"

It was an immense relief to tell Frank all about it, sitting on h
own bed with the door shut on the passage hung with sheets ke
soaked in vinegar. To tell the story to a man, and that man th
one who somehow or other had been with him all the way, fro
that first morning when he saw Madeleine in her reckless beaut
outside the hotel in Cairo, until now. To tell it in English, for th
French taught by Dancey Darbles had not included medic
terms, and James had often been at sea in his discussions wi
Dr. Roc. Best of all, to tell it to someone in high spirits, ready
look on the bright side; who insisted on going down to the tab
d'hôte for the first meal James had eaten outside his own roo
for more than a week.

The dining room was crowded with Faidherbe's officers,
lighted civilians and a large party of officials, headed by Monsie
de la Forge, who were toasting Liberation Day at the pitch of the
lungs. Frank had a pint of whisky in his knapsack, and they dran
it neat while food was got ready for them. James felt his spir
rising by the minute—she was getting better, he was out of h
miserable room and back among men, and Frank was there!

"Now tell me how you came here," he commanded. "Beg
with what happened on New Year's Day at Arbonne."

"That certainly was a day I won't forget," said Frank. "T
Prussians were out like lights till about noon, and then they g
going again. Eckhardstein invited you and me to join them for
drink. We figured you'd had about eight hours' start by that tin
so Louise spoke up very frankly and told him you had to get on
the ambulances and so you had just quietly gone out the back w
and made off to Fontainebleau."

Frank stopped to laugh and slap his knee.

"I've found out this about the Prussians, they believe anythi
you tell them. We said you'd gone to Fontainebleau, so Fontain

leau it was! Off went a patrol of Uhlans, plunging through the
now, searching every house in Barbizon for you—"

"No harm done, I hope?"

"None to speak of—and right into Fontainebleau they went,
where our friend the town major was grilled, I imagine. Back at
Arbonne, Eckhardstein was threatening us with reprisals, hos-
ages, shooting and God knows what, but Louise—say, Jim, that
girl can twist 'em round her little finger! She pleaded, and turned
on the waterworks, and appealed to his *chivalry* as a *Prussian
officer* (can you picture it?) and so he didn't burn down the
château *that* time, after all."

"Then?"

"Then it was my turn and I did just what you said—waved the
Star-Spangled Banner, and pulled out all the tremolo stops about
what Uncle Sam would do if ladies under his protection (meaning
mine) were molested in any way, and finally it worked. I got to
know quite a lot about Hans while we thrashed it all out—"

"Who's Hans?"

"Von Eckhardstein—that's his name, Hans; it seems he's a
younger son with no better prospects than hanging round some
old *Schloss* in Silesia shooting wild boar once the war is over. And
he has a fancy to visit the United States. So, I did a deal with him.
'Be nice to the people at Arbonne,' I said, 'and I'll lay on all sorts
of openings for you in Philadelphia'—"

"Such as—"

"Well, a strong recommendation, by a letter I wrote there and
then, to Hartzell Brothers. I thought he might be just the smart,
soldierly salesman the boys are looking for to push their new line
of peppers. And I also gave him a letter to a fellow called Harry
Diffenderfer, who I told him would do anything for me. Well,
after that, old Hans couldn't do enough to show his gratitude. If
he could have brought back the Arbonne gold plate, and the
Sèvres china, and the carpets and clocks, and all the stuff that's in
Germany by this time, he would have done it laughing. Looks like
Philadelphia will be enriched by a wonderful new citizen, one of
these days."

The waiter put before them an omelette made from the desic‑
cated eggs in Frank's knapsack.

"So after I'd softened up the commandant, I got him to return
me to Fontainebleau in a wagon going in for rations, with hi‑
blessing, and everything fine. I'd always had Sergeant Teitelbaum
in mind. I felt pretty sure he'd have his nest well feathered down
there in Fontainebleau. Remember how fast he produced tha‑
transport for us, on New Year's Eve? Right. He certainly had
beautiful operation going in that town—supplies, transpor‑
clothes, false papers, false noses too I shouldn't wonder, and for
round sum in U.S. dollars Mister Teitelbaum got me a ride on
German supply train that runs right round Paris to the commun‑
cations zone headquarters at Pont St. Maxence. The next la‑
took a bit of organizing, but I came up with French XXII Cor‑
at Peronne, on the tenth I guess it was, and here I am. Easy, whe‑
you know how."

"Frank," said James with deep respect, "I used to think I kne‑
a few things about laying on transport, and getting from place ‑
place in a hurry, but you make me feel like a real beginner. Whe‑
I think how I fouled up our journey to the Belgian border—an‑
Madeleine was so game through it all! If you knew what I p‑
her through—sleeping in that damned wagon the first night ‑
St. Denis, the next night jolting in the train to Laon, then on he‑
—and the fever on her all the time. But never a word of complain‑
not one. Except—d'you know what was the first thing, or almo‑
the first, she said to me this morning? She said, 'Now can we ‑
back to the Quai Voltaire?' Like a poor child that's been punish‑
unfairly, and thinks the punishment has lasted long enough!"

"You thought you were acting for the best," said Frank co‑
solingly. "You got her to a decent inn, and a good doctor—is‑
this fellow Roc all right?"

"Frank, I just don't know. I'm so completely in the dark abo‑
it all. Look, would you talk to him when he comes to see her t‑
afternoon? You could tell him how they treated hospital fever ‑
Libby."

"Libby wasn't a model infirmary," said Frank. "But I'll talk ‑
him!"

Dr. Roc encountered them both in an expansive mood. He had lunched well with the Prefect and Faidherbe's Chief of Staff. He found Madeleine's improvement maintained, and said that "*le capitaine* 'Artzell" might even see her for a few minutes.

The vivandière went to prepare Madeleine, and Frank waited nervously outside her door. He had no idea what he was going to see; visions of the fever lines of Libby rose before him, complicated by recollections of his Aunt Hartzell's crowded cluttered sickroom in Germantown. But the room he was ushered into was bare and sparsely furnished, the curtains and the hangings taken down, the carpet up; the little vivandière with a big white apron tied round her military jacket stood with arms folded by the fire.

Madeleine was lying with her eyes closed, and he saw at once what James had not perceived, how the d'Arbonne outline had appeared beneath the face they knew. The fresh, fair Norman colouring had gone long ago, but now that the pure oval of her cheeks had been wasted by the fever, it was very clear that the bones beneath were those which had been handed down in her father's line for generations—the triangular-shaped brow and the pointed chin of the feline d'Arbonne mask. Lying there, with her hair smooth and darkened by the wet compresses they had put upon her brow, she might have been the d'Arbonne Crusader, who laid his bones beside St. Louis in the sands of Carthage.

Then the eyes opened, and she knew Frank, and the old smile made her into Madeleine again.

"Frank! someone told me you were here—was it yesterday?"

"I was here yesterday," said Frank, with a warning glance at the vivandière.

She focused her eyes on the blue cutaway, the scarlet trousers, the képi in his hand.

"You're fighting for France?"

"Yes."

"Louise knows?"

"Yes, dear."

"Dear Frank! *dear brother!*" she called him then; and he forgot all about the danger of infection and knelt down beside her to kiss that bare left hand on which neither James nor Madeleine, in their ruthless honesty, had ever thought to place a makeshift wedding ring.

"You're going on to Paris?" whispered Madeleine.

"With General Faidherbe—as fast as we can go."

"Then Paris will be saved."

She was silent for a few minutes, and then in something like her old voice said,

"I'm so glad you've come, Frank, because there's something want you to tell James. The Empress was here a little while ago and I asked her too, but I'm afraid she might forget. . . . You know how she forgets! . . . Tell him this; that I love him with all my heart and soul *and strength*."

The feeble fingers scarcely moved in his.

"He knows it, Madeleine; he knows it already."

Her head turned restlessly on the pillows.

"Yes, but I don't mean *already*, I don't mean *now*. I mean *later*. If the wheels go round too often, or the water rises too high . . ."

"Hush, Madeleine, try to rest now; James will come and s beside you soon."

"Frank, if I die—remember this! Don't take me to Trouville Nor back to Arbonne! Let me stay here! With the people wh fought—"

"You mustn't talk about dying, dear. You're going to get we fast, and be a happy girl. Louise will come to you just as soon as she's allowed to travel."

He kissed her hand again and rose quickly to his feet, making a sign to the vivandière to follow him. At the door he looked back. Madeleine was watching him and smiling.

"Give my love to Paris," he heard her say.

"I will!"

Outside, in the passage, he spoke urgently to Madame Henri

"Look here!" he said in a whisper. "Has Dr. Roc told you wh you must watch for specially, in a case like this? You've got keep taking her pulse, at least once every half-hour. You've got keep her warm! Get extra blankets and put them on her bed *now*! If the pulse races ahead, or if she has a sudden chill, send f he doctor without an instant's delay! Give her any stimulant you've got, but don't waste any time, do you understand?"

The woman looked scared.

"Don't you think madame is getting better, *mon capitaine*? If you'd seen her only a couple of days ago—"

"I think she's still seriously ill," said Frank Hartzell.

She became so ill, in the small hours of next morning, that the nun on night duty sent for Madame Henri from the lair in the kitchen premises where the little vivandière spent her nights, and James sat until dawn beside the bed where fever and delirium once more had Madeleine in their grip.

Sometimes, when one of the women bent over her, she would say "maman!" and more than once, in a clear, happy voice, "*Majesté!*" But when her lover tried to hold the fluttering hands, which in fancy she was again knotting round the rope reins of her team, she turned away from him and screamed that the waters were rising above her head.

Once more, for Madeleine, the Channel waves beat against the harbour wall. The desert lake lapped golden in the rocket's light, the Seine twined and looped endlessly through her delirium. Hoarsely, she named the great Canal and the lesser: Suez, Sambre, Somme, St. Quentin. She drove her wagon across the broken bridges over L'Ourcq, St. Denis, La Villette. She saw the fountains of the Place de la Concorde reflected in a great mirror at the far end of a rosy room. She saw a single little plume of water playing in a stone basin in the gardens of the Tuileries, up and down, up and down. She sank with it into the pool and was borne up again on the dancing drops towards the rainy skies of Paris.

Then the wheels began to turn once more for Madeleine. Sometimes she was sitting above the wheels, and that was good, because then she drove Prince Tewfik's Arabs and the wounded men rose from their stretchers and stood beside her laughing and clapping their hands as they all drove hale and well towards the Citadel. But most often she was one of the spokes of the wheel, turning dizzily, never stopping, over the endless roads of France. She named the halts until her throat was raw. Paris—Porte Maillot—St. Germain—Mantes (and the black cat leaped for the lilac bush, the old woman brandished her broom), Pacey, Evreux, La Rivière, Lisieux, and then Deauville! Deauville! *Deauville!* That was the halt above all others which sent her frantic, twisting and thrashing until James had to exert all his strength to hold her still. Then she embarked upon another journey, and the tortured spoke turned painfully along the snowy roads. Paris, St. Denis, Le Tremblay, Laon, Crécy, Ribemont; and back again to the streets of Paris, where the wagonloads of wounded rolled down from Le Bourget to the Hôtel Dieu, went the labouring wheels.

The drums began to beat in the market square at half past five that January morning, and almost at once the hotel was full of the sound of voices and hurried footsteps as Faidherbe's officers retrieved their arms and equipment out of the confusion of Liberation Day. Frank Hartzell, whose billet was in the next street, found the hall crowded with men struggling into their overcoats and knapsacks when he sent a waiter running upstairs to summon James Bruce.

The words on Frank's lips were too urgent to be checked by the shocking sight of his friend's face, the dark eyes set and staring the lips white.

"Jim, we're on the march. The news is bad. Our vedettes report von Moltke himself has taken over from von Göben. He's sending a big Prussian reinforcement, maybe the whole 16th Brigade, up the repaired railroad track from Compiègne. He means to stop our advance to Ham and any hope we have of joining up with General Chanzy. If he succeeds, it's good-bye to Paris."

There was no sign in the haggard face of James that he had understood a word of it. He only put a hand on Frank's arm to steady himself, as if he could no longer stand upright.

"Good God, man! Is Madeleine—"

"Frank, she's worse. Much worse—"

Madame Henri came running downstairs with her hand at her mouth.

"*Mon capitaine*, it happened—the sudden chill and rigor. Her pulse is twice as fast—"

"Send somebody for Dr. Roc! James! Come quick!"

The Franciscan was praying on her knees beside the bed. Madame Henri, bending over the pillow, moistened Madeleine's lips with brandy. And between them the descendant of the 'Arbonne Crusader fought for breath, while the pulse raced faster till, and the water turned the wheels for the last time.

"James, she's coming round. She knows us."

She knew them very well. She had eyes for only one of them, nd for him only a smile. For Madeleine met death as she had aced war, with a soldier's heart, without a tear or a harrowing vord. She only let fall, gently, the crucifix on which the nun tried o close her fingers, and, lost in her private and heroic dream, lutched with her broken hand the tarnished French bullion on he vivandière's shoulder.

James brushed them all aside and took her in his arms.

"Madeleine, my love, my darling, speak to me!"

She gave him her last look and her last sigh and her last word. or all the years remaining to him her lover liked to think that was "James!"

EPILOGUE:

The Spirit of France: Paris, March 1871

Ten days after the body of Madeleine d'Arbonne was buried in the new, raw, hastily constructed military graveyard at St. Quentin while von Göben's artillery fought a duel with Faidherbe's on the outskirts of the town, Paris surrendered. On the one hundred and thirty-first day of the siege the Prussian bombardment ceased, and the guns of the Sixteen Forts fired their last defiance.

The terms of peace imposed by the conquerors demanded the surrender of Alsace and Lorraine and an indemnity of five milliard francs, the German occupation of certain Departments to continue until the final instalment of the enormous sum was paid. Paris was to pay a special fine of two hundred million francs, for having had the impudence to resist Bismarck for so long.

There was one other humiliation which Paris might have avoided—on Bismarck's terms. In all Alsace and Lorraine one fortress alone had resisted the Germans through the whole of the war. The Tricolore still flew over Belfort, where General Denfert-Rochereau's maiden sword was still unsurrendered to Belfort's besiegers. It was to keep Belfort French that Paris, the proud city, agreed to a victory parade and a three-day occupation by the Prussian Army.

The newly created German Emperor and his son decided wisely against entering the city. They held a review, on the Longchamps racetrack, of the thirty thousand men whom Bismarck, von Moltke and von Roon had chosen to represent the final triumph of their plans, and watched them march off across the devastated Bois and up to the Arc de Triomphe.

Les Prussiens were inside Paris at last. They marched down the Champs Elysées, chests swollen with pride and sprigs of laurel in their helmets. They were all there, Badeners, Prussians, Würtembergers, Hessians, Saxons—all the victors. The Bavarians who murdered the civilians of Bazeilles had the honour of taking the lead. The boys of III Corps were there, who broke the French cavalry at Mars-la-Tour; the Kaiser's Uhlans; the Brunswickers of St. Quentin. All singing, all looking joyfully about them, all amazed that an earnest attempt to blow a great city off the face of the earth should not entitle them to the affection of its citizens. They were disappointed in the famous Champs Elysées, as they goose-stepped down to their bivouac in the gardens of the Tuileries. Not a single human being was to be seen on the pavements or at the windows of the two great grey stone rows of houses. Knots of crape were tied to many doors, and only black flags flew.

Les Prussiens were compelled by formal agreement to keep within strict limits during their three days' occupation of Paris. They had hoped to stroll along the rue Royale and the rue de Rivoli, and buy souvenirs of Paris to add to the pianos, watches and china vases they had been looting on their way across France, but this was forbidden by order. No shops were open anywhere in Paris. Every shop and restaurant from the Arc de Triomphe to the boulevard du Temple had run down its iron shutters, except for two cafés on the Champs Elysées requisitioned to serve the troops wine and beer. The Bourse was closed and so was every place of business. Ammunition wagons had been used to close off the Seine bridges and the side streets were barred to *les Prussiens* by troops of the Line.

On the morning of the third of March, when the token occupation ended, there was a little more movement in the city. Some shutters were flung open and heads appeared as the Prussian bayonets, laurel-adorned, flashed for the last time in the sunshine and the band of the Leib Regiment struck up *Die Wacht am Rhein*. A few stragglers came to the corners of the barred street

nd stared blankly, over the shoulders of the French troops, at the
eparture of the conquerors.

Frank Hartzell stood for a little while in one such group at the
orner of the rue Boissy d'Anglas, before turning on his heel in
isgust and making for the great house of Michel Bertaux.

The indestructible Old Poisson admitted him to the familiar
ourtyard where the Nubian slaves held up their lightless torches,
nd he passed into the hall where Monsieur Bertaux' valet was
cting as major-domo. There was already a definite warmth
rough the whole house, where some of the carpets had been
laid at Louise's orders, and every time Frank went there from
is room at the Grand Hotel he found new evidence of returning
omfort. "She's a wonder!" he thought, not for the first time.
Here only a couple of weeks, and the place feels like a home
lready!"

They were waiting for him in the study, Louise sewing beside
small fire and Bertaux writing at his desk. Five harrowing
onths spent in battling the lawyers and poets of the new Repub-
c had bent the broad shoulders of Michel Bertaux; it was the loss
f Madeleine which had whitened his hair and dimmed his eyes.

Frank kissed Louise gently and drew a chair up to the fire. For a
w minutes no one spoke. Then the girl said, almost impatiently,

"Well, Frank? Have they gone?"

"I think so. The last contingent was crossing the Place de la
oncorde as I came by. May I open a window a little? I don't
ink you can hear their confounded music now."

A breath of spring air came into the room. It brought with it
othing but the twittering of birds.

"Gone!" said Louise, with a deep sigh. "Now we can really start
work! Frank, will you take me out into the garden, dear? I've
een cooped up in this house for three days."

He made a little, loving gesture that meant "Wait!" and turned
spectfully to the silent man at the desk.

"How are *you*, sir? Not too tired, after that hard trip?"

"I'm all right, Frank. The trains were slow, but that's to be
xpected. It was seeing that—that place where she's lying—it was

too much for me. You didn't tell me it was—nothing but a field with soldiers' bodies tumbled into a common grave. With he grave marked only by two bits of wood, and nothing but the letter burned on—'M.d'A., 1871.' "

"It was absolutely what she wanted, sir."

"I know—I know; you told me," said Bertaux. "But I was plan ning, coming back yesterday, to get those marble workers dow to Trouville as soon as possible. I thought a whole wall of he mother's mausoleum might be dedicated to Madeleine. With he name in full: Marie-Madeleine Charlotte Laure, *morte pour l France* . . . it would look even better in Latin."

He mused.

"And then a large carving—something symbolic—the figure o Peace, with an olive branch, perhaps."

Frank and Louise exchanged glances.

"But there at St. Quentin, uncle dear," said the girl gently "don't you think the date will tell its own story? Among th fallen—M. d'A., 1871—everyone will know what that means."

"But not for long, Louise; don't delude yourself. Do you thin the war dead will be long remembered? Why, they were a thrown away," said Bertaux with agitation, "from the Cuirassie of Reichshoffen to our poor girl—for what? for nothing! T satisfy Eugénie's vanity and Bismarck's cunning and a renega general spouting about *La Gloire*? To give your brother Victor chance to stump the country with his arm in a black silk slin demanding another war—for revenge? To let Cluseret and t Communists come to power in Paris?"

Louise folded her sewing and came to pat her uncle's shoulde

"Dear Uncle Michel, don't be so bitter! Remember all t people left who love you! Blanche is so sweet; you'll be glad whe she and Victor marry, and Adèle will soon be here to show yc her little baby. And Frank and I will be with you a great deal."

"You're right," said Bertaux. He rose heavily and took up h favourite place in front of the fire. "I've always made the plan haven't I—now it seems that you're the one to look ahead, Louis What did you and Frank decide, while I was at St. Quentin?"

He looked inquiringly at the American.

"I'd like us to be married right away," Frank told him, "but Louise wants to wait until the autumn. She wants to move her father and Miss Elisabeth to the Tour d'Arbonne and see them comfortably settled, while I go back to America and get the new operation running there. And then in October we'll get Father Gillet to marry us, in our own little church at Arbonne—"

He paused, and looked down at the neat black head nestled so confidingly against his shoulders. Louise went on for him,

"—after the harvest is safely in. That's the *first* thing I must do, Uncle Michel," she said. "I don't know nearly enough about our farms, but Farmer Blaise taught me a lot while we had the Prussians at Arbonne, and I can learn! All our tenants need help; they'll be shorthanded until the prisoners come back from Germany, and the Prussians stripped them of nearly all their implements and cattle. I'll get seeds from England—I'll see that every field on Arbonne is planted up to the hedges this spring, while Victor and you quarrel over politics, here in Paris!"

Suddenly she was in tears, and Frank took her in his arms to stifle the noisy, childish sobs against his coat.

"All right," said Bertaux, relapsing heavily into an armchair. "If that's the way you feel. It isn't easy for me to understand the sort of woman you're going to be, Louise—you're not like Madeleine. Go and get your wraps, child, and let Frank take you out in the garden. I want to talk to him for a few minutes—about business."

"What do you say, my sweet?" said Frank coaxingly, as Louise tried to smile and took out a wisp of handkerchief. "Go dry your eyes and put your bonnet on! You've been indoors too long."

"You'll be a wonderful husband to her, Frank."

"I'll try to be, sir."

When Louise had left them, the short train of her black mourning dress rustling over the crimson carpet, Bertaux turned his avid face to Frank.

"I want you to take her back to Arbonne tomorrow and stay with them there for the next few weeks," he said. "Change your sailing date to the middle of April. Our troubles aren't over yet, unless I'm far mistaken."

"The Communards?"

"The Communards against Thiers. They're all ready for rio and civil strife in Paris."

"I hope you're wrong, sir."

"I know I'm right," said Michel Bertaux. He rose stiffly and made a pretence of looking for his cigars. With his back turned to Frank he said,

"Did any news come of—that man—while I was gone?"

"Yes," said Frank reluctantly. "A letter came from his brother William, the minister, James can't write much yet. The wound he got at Valenciennes, just before we surrendered, began to fester while he was at Antwerp, waiting for a boat. He's been ill for weeks, but they've taken good care of him at Sauchentree."

Bertaux grunted.

"His brother, eh? No message to you—from Bruce himself?"

"None," said Frank steadily. He would never show Bertaux the Reverend William Bruce's letter, with one line of writing in a hand he knew scrawled at the foot of the sheet:

"Would God I had died at St. Quentin!"

"He fought for France, sir, at the last. We were comrades in arms." How could he explain to the financier what *that* meant: that, while he lived, he would see Bruce in the trenches of the last stand against the Prussians, his bleeding cheek laid to the old snuffbox musket, and those tragic eyes, dark with the hope of death, steady on the advancing enemy?

"I could have liked that man," said Bertaux with a sigh. "Until I stood beside *her* grave yesterday, I hated him. Now I see that Eugénie's war destroyed his life as well as Madeleine's."

Frank walked out of that room, where Madeleine's uncle stood by the dying fire, in the grip of black depression. Even the future so full of promise for himself, was less bright under the shadow of the past. It all seemed so useless—the war which had cost so much, the heroic lives thrown away—*was* it for nothing? Wasn't there, anywhere in this workaday France now fiercely vowed to paying the Prussian indemnity, planting the fields up to the hedges, winning back the lost provinces, any feeling for an ideal

410

or the kind of ideal which in other days had sent boys like him-
elf out to fight to save the Union, and damn the consequences?

Louise came back, with her black satin strings tied in the neatest
f bows beneath her pointed chin.

"Are you my pretty girl?"

"Am I?"

"Very pretty—very clever—very sweet." So she was, when he
ok her in his arms; not quite as thin as she had been, with pink
heeks and shining dark eyes; she would be wonderful in her
hite veil and myrtle wreath!

"We're going to be tremendously happy, you know, Louise—
en't we?"

"Of course we are." There was a kind of reassurance in her kiss.
Let's go out the other way, Frank. I want to show you something.
ncle Michel had workmen here this morning. They brought
wn Madeleine's picture from the attic."

"I've always wanted to see it, ever since I saw the sketches at
rbonne. I guess your uncle wants it where he can look at it every
y."

"Yes," said Louise with a wry smile, "and not only to remind
im of Madeleine, but because of the subject. Under the Empire
e thought it too revolutionary, but now it's just right for the
epublic!"

Again the little sharp note in her voice! Again, the reminder of
ertaux' calculations!

"Where is it," he said, "in the salon?"

"They hung it in the hall just here, where maman's used to be."

Frank drew a long breath.

"*Madeleine!*" he said.

For there she stood.

There she stood in her young beauty, the dress of a woman of
e people blown by the wind against breast and thigh, the cap
 liberty perched on her flowing hair, and in her left hand, held
oft, the Tricolore.

Delacroix, when he painted her as *The Spirit of France*, had
one back in his old age to the classic theme of the Revolution,
d had imagined that Spirit as a beautiful woman standing on

411

the barricades of Paris, a leader and an inspiration to the men and women at her feet. They were all about her: Madame Alice as sturdy girl with a rifle in her hand, Maurice from the paintshop not a prisoner, and the locksmith's Robert, not yet wounded—faces and bodies crowded on the canvas, some noble, some avid and grasping, some famished and wild, the poor people of Paris above whom her beautiful right arm was extended in a divine gesture of pity and protection. There was nothing transcendental about the picture; this was no Angel hovering above the smoke and flame which rolled about the embattled Parisians; the Spirit of France was revealed as a lovely, faulty, human woman with dust and blood on the feet firmly planted on the stones and rubble of the barricades. The bold proud face was lifted towards no invisible goal, but bent anxiously, compassionately on those who fought in the Spirit's light; yet its every line, and the speaking eyes, expressed a supreme nobility, a belief in the ideals by which men live and die.

Frank felt tears come into his own eyes, and unconsciously he pressed Louise closer to his side. There it was—the something big—bigger than all the balance sheets and calculations in the world.

"Uncle plans to leave it to the Louvre." murmured Louise.

"Good!" said Frank. "I'm glad of that." For this, he thought, will be Madeleine's memorial, far more enduring than all the poor old fellow's Latin inscriptions and marble leaves of olive. She'll be there forever; our children will see her as she was, and so will Victor and Adèle's; they'll know what she was like—Madeleine!

There was only daylight in the hall where they stood, and the great canvas was not lit artificially; yet it glowed and burned with the blue, white and red of the Tricolore and with the light in the beautiful pictured face. For the great artist who had once loved her mother had known how to interpret the soul of Madeleine. Radiant, triumphant, made immortal, she proclaimed to the world the splendid affirmation for which her life had been given

"*France will never die!*"

They went on with clasped hands, and slowly, through the

412

shrouded salon, reached the stone terrace above the garden and stood listening. To the first stunned silence which had followed the departure of the Germans, there had succeeded a faint hum, the rumour of a city moving its paralysed limbs and stretching; Paris was coming to life again. They went out at the gate by which James Bruce had once waited for Madeleine, and crossed the open space where the chestnut alleys had been cut down for firewood and barricades. Here and there, underneath the neglected, frost-blackened geraniums and salvias of the previous summer, clumps of snowdrops had come into flower, and the tips of glossy dark green hyacinths were pushing their way strongly through the earth.

"You were right, Louise," said Frank tenderly, "it's time to think about spring planting!"

They went to the edge of the pavement and stood looking up and down the Champs Elysées. With the trees gone there was a clear view all the way, from the Arc de Triomphe down through the great square to the open gates of the Tuileries gardens, swinging loosely on their hinges; and beyond. At first sight it appeared to be an expanse utterly deserted, spiritually and physically void—a great wide hopeless street of humiliation and defeat. But already, a second glance showed, some signs of life had begun to appear at the upper end of the avenue. Iron shutters were run up above shops and cafés, men and women came out with brooms to sweep the sidewalks clean. A water cart began sprinkling the middle of the street, fouled by the feet and horses of the Prussians.

"Oh look!" said Louise. Her ear had been caught by a tiny sound, clearly audible in the stillness; it was the patter of the hoofs of two goats, the last remaining of the goat-man's flock. He came up the street from the river driving both of them ahead and himself pulling one solitary carriage—getting ready to open for business in the old alley where the chestnut trees had stood.

The spring sun shone over reviving Paris. Across the Seine the dome of the Invalides swam like a great golden bubble in the clear air. The black flags were lowered, the knots of crape removed. As Louise and Frank looked on entranced there was a new movement in the square in front of the gardens where the great stone basin had been dry and choked with leaves. Plumes of water leaped up tossing and sparking gaily; bright sunlit drops were flung recklessly against the sky. The fountains of the Place de la Concorde had begun to play.

The Fortress

This is the true story of a war the historians have almost
forgotten—one in which the hero was the Royal Navy; the
unwilling captive, Finland; and the villain of the piece,
Imperial Russia.

The Baltic—1854. While the Crimean war was
smouldering at the far side of Europe, Britain and Russia
were locked in a furious struggle at sea off the coast of
Finland with, as prize, the impregnable citadel of Sveaborg
—the fortress of the title.

Among those deeply involved were Brand Endicott, a
tough young gunner in the Royal Navy, and the Finnish
girl he loved, Alexandra Gyllenlöve. As the panorama of
mid-19th-century life is majestically unfolded—the social
brilliance of St. Petersburg and Paris contrasting with the
infamous convict hulks and the lawless London underworld
—these two share the excitement of their struggle for
freedom at every turn: in prison and on the high seas, in
war and in peace.

'It would be quite possible to get into the habit of learning
history simply by reading Catherine Gavin's engrossing
novels'—*The Bookman*

'Her writing cuts across life and death, love and war,
debauchery and devotion, with the boldness and not a little
of the grasp of a Tolstoy.'—*Los Angeles Mirror-News*

OTHER TITLES BY CATHERINE GAVIN

All these books are available at your bookshop or new
agent, or can be ordered direct from the publisher. Just ti
the titles you want and fill in the form below.

....

CORONET BOOKS, P.O. Box 11, Falmouth, Cornwall.

Please send cheque or postal order. No currency, and all
the following for postage and packing:

1 book – 7p per copy, 2–4 books – 5p per copy, 5–8 boc
– 4p per copy, 9–15 books – 2½p per copy, 16–30 book:
2p per copy in U.K., 7p per copy overseas.

Name...

Address...

....